SOUTHERN TIDES

BOOK TWO

GARY E. PARKER

Our purpose at Howard Publishing is to:

- *Increase faith* in the hearts of growing Christians
- *Inspire holiness* in the lives of believers
- *Instill hope* in the hearts of struggling people everywhere

Because He's coming again!

Published by Howard Publishing Co., Inc.
3117 North 7th Street, West Monroe, Louisiana 71291-2227
www.howardpublishing.com

Published in association with the literary agency of Alive Communications, Inc. 7680 Goddard Street, Suite 200, Colorado Springs, CO 80920

05 06 07 08 09 10 11 12 13 14 10 9 8 7 6 5 4 3 2 1

Edited by Ramona Cramer Tucker
Cover design by Kirk DouPonce, www.DogEaredDesign.com
Cover photo of couple by Stephen Gardner, www.PixelWorksStudio.com

Library of Congress Cataloging-in-Publication Data

Parker, Gary E.
Fateful journeys / Gary E. Parker.
p. cm. — (Southern tides ; bk. 2)
ISBN 1-58229-431-3
1. South Carolina—History—Civil War, 1861-1865—Fiction. I. Title.

PS3566.A6784F37 2005
813'.54—dc22

2005040220

Scripture quotations are taken from *The Holy Bible*, Authorized King James Version, public domain.

This novel is a work of fiction. Names, characters, places, and incidents either are the product of the author's imagination or are used fictitiously. Any resemblance to actual events, locales, organizations, or persons, living or dead, is entirely coincidental and beyond the intent of either the author or publisher.

Dedication

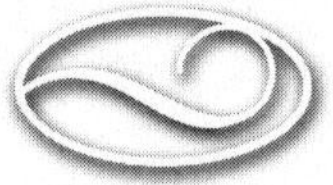

A long time ago, when I was a history major at Furman University in South Carolina, my dad told me, "Son, you can't make a living with a history major."

Well, to some extent, he was right. Yet if I hadn't majored in history, I don't think I ever could have written a story like the one you'll find here. Being a history major gave me an interest in the large canvas of the human story, and that interest in the human story keeps me ever curious. It seems to me that without that curiosity, life gets pretty dull. With it, however, life takes on rich meaning.

So I dedicate this series to all the history majors out there. Maybe you can't make a living with it, but perhaps you can make your life and the lives of those around you a little bit fuller, more colorful, more worth living.

Acknowledgments

Although this is a work of fiction, the social culture of the South Carolina lowland rice plantations just before, during, and after the Civil War certainly wasn't fictitious. The men and women—both black and white—of this time and place lived the lifestyle reflected in the pages of the Southern Tides trilogy. Books such as *South Carolina: A History* by Walter B. Edgar, *Mary's World* by Richard N. Cote, *An Antebellum Plantation Household* by Anne Sinkler LeClercq, *The History of Beaufort County* by Lawrence S. Rowland, Alexander Moore, and George Rogers Jr., *Roll Jordan Roll: The World the Slaves Made* by Eugene Genovese, *Within the Plantation Household: Black and White Women of the Old South* by Elizabeth Fox-Genovese, *Them Dark Days: Slavery in the American Rice Swamps* by William Dusinberre, A *Diary from Dixie* by Mary Boykin Chestnut, *Richmond Burning* by Nelson Lankford, *The Civil War in the Carolinas* by Dan L. Morrill, *Gentleman and Soldier* by Edward G. Longacre, and *The Life of Johnny Reb* by Belle Irvin Wiley gave me both information and context for the telling of these stories. Any historical inaccuracies in these pages reflect on my failings, not those of these eminent researchers and writers.

In addition to the books that gave me confidence I was telling the story correctly, I also need to acknowledge the men and women at Howard Publishing for their enthusiasm for this project, especially Philis Boultinghouse. Ramona Tucker, editor, also deserves appreciation for her diligent approach and eager attention to detail and schedule. Her sharp eye made this work better.

Finally, as always, I express gratitude to my wife, Melody. She keeps the world around me humming so I can have the time to do fun things—like sit down to read, research, and then write the stories of the people you'll find in these pages.

Note to the Reader

The Civil War years were tumultuous ones for the South, years that changed life for everyone, slave and plantation owner alike. Old institutions crumbled, and the system that had kept everyone—socialite, poor white, and servant—in their places disappeared.

In the effort to accurately reflect the time frame in which this historical fiction is set, I have used certain terms that are offensive to me, personally, and that aren't reflective of modern speech and attitudes. Particularly is this true in reference to the men and women held in slavery on the plantations depicted in this novel. Please know that when terms like *darky*, *blackey*, *coloreds*, and *Negro* are used, they are reflective of this time period and not meant as any offense to today's African-American community. Other terms that referred to the slaves, among them the most offensive, are not used in spite of their common uses in the years written about in this project.

Thankfully for all of us, the evil of slavery in our country disappeared as a result of the Civil War, and many of the unfortunate racial terms and attitudes associated with it began to disappear from the American scene. There is no way to estimate—or apologize for—the physical, emotional, and spiritual damage inflicted upon generations of African-Americans through the travesty of slavery. The truths of God teach us that all people are equal, regardless of racial status. May the day hasten to come when we all fulfill God's will in this crucial arena of human relationship.

GARY E. PARKER

Part One

Does the road wind uphill all the way?

Yes, to the very end.

Will the day's journey take the whole long day?

From morn to night, my friend.

—CHRISTINA GEORGINA ROSSETTI

Chapter One

The Oak Plantation, May 1861

Dark still blanketed the South Carolina coastland on the morning that Trenton Tessier decided he had no choice but to take his revenge against the man who had stolen the woman he loved. His face soured by hours of drinking and a night without sleep, Trenton now slouched in a black leather chair by the stone fireplace in his second-floor bedroom.

"Josh Cain," he muttered, his tongue thick with the whiskey. "He took Camellia from me. I gave her a proposal of marriage, but she refused. It's Cain's fault. I will have my vengeance."

Trenton's brother, Calvin, younger by five years, sat in a matching chair across from him. "You're in no shape to avenge anything," said Calvin, gesturing toward the wooden peg that started at Trenton's right knee and ran to the floor. "You're barely a month past the day you lost . . . since you were shot."

Trenton took a sip from the silver flask he held and raised up slightly. A man of thin shoulders and short-cropped brown hair, he wore pleated, tan riding pants and a white shirt with a ruffle at the neck. He lifted one of the crutches that lay in his lap and aimed it at a roll-top desk across the room. "Hand me my pistols," he ordered. "Josh Cain stole what belongs to me. My honor is at stake."

"Your honor almost got you killed," Calvin replied.

"Better death than this!" Trenton pointed to his stump. "I'm a laughingstock! The fine Master Trenton Tessier, educated in the best schools the South can offer; heir to The Oak, finest plantation in the lowlands; a man of the highest social station—none of it matters now! Get me the pistols or get out!"

"You're drunk and crazy from not sleeping," argued the freckled Calvin, obviously trying to calm his brother's rage. "Cain is unconscious . . . in no shape to face you."

"I'm not worried about Cain's condition."

"You'd murder him?"

Trenton dropped his eyes, and his head cleared some. Could he go through with this? Had he sunk so low as to harm a man who couldn't defend himself? Part of him knew this was wrong; maybe he should let it pass.

Trenton took another sip of the whiskey and glanced down at his peg leg again. His eyes blazed as his resolve returned. "Cain deserves it, for what he did to me."

Calvin stood, moved over, and put a hand on Trenton's shoulder. "If you want to shoot somebody, it ought to be Hampton York," Calvin claimed. "He's the one who shot you in the leg."

Trenton glared at Calvin, who was the spitting image of their dead father. With his blocky legs and chest, wide hands and feet, thick jowls and thin hair, Calvin wasn't especially handsome. But he was powerful. If it came to a physical battle right now, Calvin could probably best him—a fact Trenton disliked immensely.

Striking like a mad snake, Trenton jerked Calvin's hand from his shoulder and bent his fingers backward. "You plan on challenging me on this?" Trenton growled.

Calvin's mouth twitched in pain. He eyed Trenton as if he wanted to kill him.

Trenton held his brother's fingers for another minute, then let them go. "Just get me the pistols," he said again.

Calvin stretched his fingers as Trenton took another drink from the flask. He wondered how much longer he could keep Calvin under his control. Every younger brother eventually tested the elder. Was this the time for him and Calvin?

Although his eyes stayed angry, Calvin finally eased across to the desk and pulled the pistols from the top drawer. Grunting with effort, Trenton stood, tucked the flask in his coat, arranged the crutches under his arms, and took the pistols. "Now, hand me my coat," he instructed, arranging the pistols in his waistband.

Calvin stepped to a closet, removed a thigh-length black coat, and handed it to Trenton.

Now fully dressed, Trenton stood before the full-length mirror by his bed and stared at his stump. A set of pins held his pants leg in place in a neat fold just above the wooden peg. Underneath the pants the wound oozed a light but steady flow of foul discharge that required constant cleaning. Trenton ground his teeth against the weakness his leg caused him. He was a cripple!

Every night since the duel, he'd prayed, as best as he knew how, that when he woke in the morning, he'd find losing his leg all a terrible nightmare of pain and humiliation, unlike anything a man of his station ought to have to bear. But every morning when he opened his eyes and reached down, he found nothing but air where bone, blood, and skin should have been.

"How do you plan to get to Mr. Cain's house?" asked Calvin. "It's half a mile from the manse."

"I'll walk," said Trenton.

"On crutches?"

"Josh Cain took Camellia from me. How far I have to walk to kill him is of little consequence," Trenton fired back.

When Calvin wiped his palms on his pants, Trenton stared closely at his brother. He saw fear in Calvin's eyes. "You have no part in this, so don't let it rest on your conscience."

"It's not my conscience I fear for . . . it's you."

Trenton patted Calvin's back. "Your concern touches me."

"Captain York will come after you when Cain is dead," Calvin said.

"I expect so."

"You want him to come, don't you?"

"Yes. He, too, owes me a debt that only his death will pay."

"Your duel with York followed the code. You took your shot but missed. Maybe you should accept that and leave things alone."

"York knew I had never dueled," Trenton claimed. "He took advantage of my inexperience."

"He let you have the first shot," argued Calvin.

"OK!" snapped Trenton. "I missed! And I have cursed myself a thousand times for it. Then York shot me in the knee."

"Then you shot Josh Cain," said Calvin, his voice low and quiet, a hint of accusation in it.

"That was an accident, and you know it! You gave me your pistol; I shot at York but hit Cain."

Trenton grabbed his flask and swilled down a full swallow, hoping the liquor would jolt him into action. No matter how much he hated Josh Cain, Trenton Tessier had never killed a man, so it would take some doing to follow through.

He glanced hurriedly around the room. His portrait, painted by one of the finest artists in Charleston, hung over his bed. A hand-woven, multicolored Oriental rug lay at the bed's foot. A basin and pitcher of water sat on a nightstand by the bed. From the ceiling hung a chandelier, its sparkling glass shining from the light of many candles. Would all of this look different when he returned from killing Cain? So what if it did? None of it meant anything anymore. Without Camellia, without his leg, without his honor, who cared what he possessed?

"Mother will not approve of this," said Calvin, interrupting Trenton's thoughts.

Trenton snickered at his brother's efforts to dissuade him. "The great Katherine Tessier!" He chuckled. "For years she paid little attention to me. Left my raising to a darky mammy while she spent her time in Charleston. Mother cared for nothing but her parties, her laudanum, her fine clothes, and fancy furnishings."

His voice dropped, and a hint of sadness edged in. "Only after Father's death, only after I became the heir of The Oak did she bother to get involved in my life. I care nothing about her approval."

"She loves you, Trenton."

Trenton laughed, but it held no joy. "If she loved me, she would never have accepted Hampton York's marriage proposal—forcing me to challenge him to a duel for his insult."

"She had no choice," said Calvin. "He has money she needs to keep The Oak from the hands of the bankers."

"York is the overseer here! She might as well mate with a darky."

"Do you think killing Cain will end plans for the wedding? Is that what's pushing you?"

"It would be a bonus, yes. York stole his money from us."

"He says not."

"It doesn't matter."

"What will happen to The Oak if Mother doesn't marry York?"

"We're going to war, so who knows? Either way I don't need York to save The Oak. If Cain's death causes him to withdraw his proposal, then I'll have killed two birds with one stone." Trenton smiled at the notion and took a drink to celebrate it.

"Are you sure you want to do this?" asked Calvin, his voice halting.

Trenton lifted a crutch, pushed it hard against his brother's chest, and backed him up against the wall. Trenton's eyes narrowed, and a dark stare came into them—cold and unfeeling. "I know what you're doing," he hissed. "All these questions—slowing me down, hoping I'll change my mind. But I *am* the eldest son, cripple or not. *I* decide my destiny. Not you, not Mother. And you best not forget that."

Calvin's eyes met Trenton's for a few seconds, then broke away. "Forgive me," Calvin whispered, his eyes suddenly filled with tears. "But Cain is a helpless man. I see no honor in harming him."

Trenton eased the crutch to Calvin's chin and tipped it up so he could see into his brother's eyes. "I want you to understand," Trenton soothed. "I love Camellia, and I want her as my wife. But she says she loves Josh Cain. Of course she doesn't. How could she? But as long as he's alive, she won't come to me."

"I still think it's wrong."

Trenton lowered his crutch to the floor. "Who's to say what is wrong . . . and what is right? Cain will probably die anyway from the bullet I already put in him. I'm simply speeding up his passage."

Calvin wiped his eyes.

"I'll return soon," said Trenton.

"I wish you wouldn't do this."

Ignoring his brother, Trenton headed to the door. "I should return within the hour. Then it will be over."

"I expect it's just beginning," whispered Calvin.

Trenton took another drink and hobbled out, his chin set. In his heart, though, he figured Calvin had it right: what he did next would determine his fate—and that of everyone around him—for years to come.

Up and out before anyone else as usual, Captain Hampton York stood on the front porch of the shed by The Oak's main barn, pulled out the day's first chew of tobacco, and bit off a plug. Although he looked forward to his marriage to Mrs. Tessier so he could put his belongings in the fancy study with all the bookshelves in the manse, he hadn't done that just yet. No reason to seem too anxious, he figured. Even if he'd dreamed of achieving a station like that all his life, a man ought not to get giddy and lose his dignity.

He chewed hard on the tobacco for a couple of minutes, then spat on the ground. Although his marriage to the widow Katherine Tessier had been postponed for a few weeks due to Josh's unfortunate injury in the duel, they'd now decided to go through with it at the end of the week. A thin smile played on his bearded face. Who would ever have figured on that? Not many folks, that was for sure. Of course, he'd studied on the possibility for a long time, measuring exactly when and how to offer her his proposal.

Pleased with his achievement, York shoved his hands into his pants pockets, a plain pair of wool britches with worn spots on the cuffs. He'd start dressing better real soon, he decided, just as quickly as he could get to Charleston and buy some fresh outfits. The new head of The Oak ought not to look like an overseer, no matter that he'd worked as that for right near to sixteen years.

York heard feet moving. He turned swiftly and saw Ruby, one of the house hands as she stepped to the porch, a tin cup in her hands.

"I got your coffee," said Ruby, handing him the cup like she did every morning.

York took it without speaking.

"Here's a ham biscuit too," said Ruby.

York accepted the biscuit but didn't eat it yet.

"How's Mr. Josh?" asked Ruby. "I had no chance to go see him yesterday."

"About the same," said York.

"We're all mighty worried about him."

York stared at Ruby. Although she'd worked on The Oak for two and a half years and brought him coffee every morning, he didn't really know her. Not that anybody expected an overseer to really know his darkies. But Ruby and his girl, Camellia, had become friends since he'd purchased Ruby for the Tessiers at the Charleston auction in the fall of 1858. Smart as a whip and taught her letters by the daughter of her former master, Ruby had actually helped Camellia learn to read and write. He'd paid eighteen hundred dollars of Mr. Tessier's money for her, the highest price he'd ever spent on a darky.

York rubbed his beard. Mr. Tessier had liked his housemaids handsome, and Ruby was as pretty as any he'd ever seen. She stood tall for a woman and had a curvy figure. Her skin was a light butterscotch, her wavy hair straighter than most of her kind. Although trained for cooking, cleaning, sewing, and tending children, her brown eyes showed smarts far beyond those simple tasks.

"Would you worry about me if I had taken the bullet?" York asked Ruby.

"That's a peculiar question," said Ruby. "You're the overseer here—about to marry up with Mrs. Tessier. You don't need anybody to worry about you."

York looked out at The Oak, the finest rice plantation in the state. Over eighteen hundred of its almost three thousand acres were under planting, and over three hundred blacks labored on it every day. The Oak produced close to fifty thousand bushels of rice a year—over a million pounds. The plantation had its own mill, which brought in fifty to sixty thousand dollars a year. They didn't just grow rice, but corn, oats, beans, and sweet 'taters too. At least 75 cows, about 60 horses, 150 cattle, maybe 70 hogs lived there. He'd run the whole place since 1844, except for the two years when he and Josh Cain had gone off to fight the Mexican War, and now, after his marriage to Mr. Tessier's widow, he'd own it! Maybe Ruby was right—he didn't need anybody to worry about him. Yet right now, for reasons he couldn't explain, he wanted . . . well . . . something he'd rather not admit, not even to himself.

"Things are changin', Ruby."

She looked surprised. "You're not usually such a talker. What's in your head this morning?"

York spat. "Why don't people put the same store in me that they do Josh?"

Ruby chuckled. "You ought not ask a darky such a question."

"No, I mean it. I want an honest answer."

Ruby wiped her hands on her apron. "You know why," she said cautiously. "Mr. Josh treats folks real nice, no matter who they are. You got more hard edges, especially when somebody gets in the way of something you want."

"I ain't arguin' any of that," said York.

"When are you moving into the manse?" asked Ruby, obviously wanting to move away from such intimate talk.

"Not until the nuptials," said York, letting it go. "No reason to act like a hound dog that ain't ever sniffed a live rabbit. A man got his pride; don't want to seem too eager."

Ruby laughed.

York stared toward the manse, a good rock's throw away from the shed. Standing on four-foot-high stone pillars, the stately two-story white house had four columns on the front. Porches wrapped both the front and back of the house. An oak tree, at least a hundred years old and so wide it took several people to wrap their arms around it, stood to the right of the front porch. The plantation had taken its name from the moss-draped oak.

About a half mile to the left of the manse, snaking its way toward the Atlantic Ocean, the slow-moving Conwilla River created the current that made rice growing possible. A gravel drive, bordered on both sides by twenty-five more oaks, connected about a quarter mile away to a wide dirt road that ran from Beaufort to Charleston.

"I ought to be the one that got shot," claimed York. "Josh threw his body between me and that bullet."

"Mr. Josh got a good heart," said Ruby. "Everybody says it."

"The best." York stared down at the dirt, drier than normal in the spring.

"You leaving us after the wedding?" asked Ruby. "Going off to fight?"

"I got no choice," said York. "The Yankees will come after us for sure now that we got the war declared."

"You expect them to get down here?"

"If they can, they will. They'll take our homes, all we own. A man's got to fight to protect what's his."

Ruby raised her eyebrows. York noted her stare and knew what lay behind it. Ruby had run away a few months ago, and he felt sure she'd head off again if she got any whiff—even a little one—that the Yankees were close enough for her to reach them before getting caught.

"I got me a baby up in Virginia," said Ruby, telling him things he already knew. "Theo. You reckon I ought to fight to get him back?"

"Don't ask me that kind of question," York fired back. "I got no control over the ways things are. They was this way before I was born, and they'll be this way when I'm under six feet of dirt."

"Not if the Yankees win."

York glared at her. "You best not forget yourself. No matter that Camellia puts a lot of store in you."

From the look in Ruby's eyes, the message had been clear. She tucked a stray hair behind her ear.

York glanced away. "Guess I'll go see Josh before the day starts."

"You go see him every morning."

"He's a lot different than me, but he's still my brother—half at least."

"Different mamas made you that way, I guess," she commented quietly.

Suddenly York wanted Ruby to understand him. Maybe it was the war; or the fact that Josh had taken a bullet meant for him; or his upcoming marriage to a woman he didn't truly love; or the fact that his daughter, Camellia, had just recently learned he wasn't her real pa. Who knew what it was? But inside he felt a little shaky, like the ground had just squirmed and the movement left him unsteady on his feet. "You think I'm mean, don't you?" he asked Ruby.

When Ruby kept quiet, York understood. A darky didn't talk straight about such a thing to a white boss. "I know I am," he said, taking her off the spot. "And Mr. Cain is kind."

"He's got the Lord in him," said Ruby.

York grunted. "The Lord never did much good for me—you either that I can see."

"I don't put any stock in the Lord myself. Just saying that Mr. Cain does, and he says that's what makes him the man he is."

"I figure we make ourselves what we are," said York. "The Lord's got no part in it."

"You and me agree on that."

York shrugged. "I ain't made much of myself."

"You're doing all right," said Ruby. "You'll own this place soon enough."

"But I've paid a high price for it."

"We do what we have to do to get what we want."

"That's the truth."

Ruby fell quiet again. A few seconds later, York handed his coffee cup to her and left without another word, his long strides moving off the porch and down the path to the house where Josh lived with his two children.

Josh Cain lay on a single bed inside a plain wood house that sat in a group of three others just like it. A single oil lamp sat on a table by his head, its soft glow washing across his face. Josh's beard—unshaven since the shooting—grew out in all directions, and his face seemed shrunken underneath it, the cheeks hollowed out from lack of food. His breath sounded shallow, like he had lungs the size of pecans. His hair, a sandy blond wavy mass, lay out on his pillow, its color darkened by the sweat pouring off his forehead faster than anyone could towel it off. He'd thrown the covers off, revealing a cloth bandage wrapped tightly around his chest. A spot as round as a saucer marked the bandage where the blood from the wound under it still seeped.

An old black woman lay on her side on the floor by his bed, her skinny legs tucked to her chin, her spriggy gray hair jumping out from all angles from under a green bandanna. Her lips were slightly crusty with the remains of the last snuff dip she'd enjoyed before she'd fallen asleep. A bucket of water sat by the woman's head, and a damp white rag hung on a nail in the wall by the bucket.

Outside the window a dog barked. Josh stirred but didn't wake. The woman snored lightly but didn't move. A door squeaked from the rear of the house. Although it was early spring, the air in the bedroom felt moist and warm as the humidity off the nearby ocean seeped through the house.

Josh's chest rose and fell, fast and thin, and he moaned slightly as he shifted in the sweat-soaked sheets. A soft thump sounded from near the back door, but not loud enough for anything but a cat to have noticed it. Another thump creaked through the wooden floors, then another and another. The old woman might as well have been dead.

The door to Josh Cain's bedroom eased open, and Trenton Tessier moved into the darkened room. A pistol hung in the front waistband of his pants, and his shirt gaped open at the neck. Trenton took a long drink from a whiskey bottle, then calmly returned it to his back pocket, eased the pistol out, and aimed it at the man on the bed.

"Wake up, Josh Cain!" Trenton growled.

The black woman woke with a jerk, her thin body jumping up as if stuck with a knife. "Master Tessier!" she stammered. "What you doin' here so early?"

"Stay put, Stella, this is no concern of yours. Where are his brats?" Trenton pointed at Josh Cain.

"They stayin' with Miss Camellia, so's not to bother Mr. Cain with their noise."

Trenton nodded. "Get out of here!" he commanded.

Stella eyed the pistol. "You thinkin' on doin' a bad thing. Best think that over twice."

"Shut your mouth, old woman. I have no patience for any of your uppity ways."

Stella's stooped back straightened as much as possible. "I helped raise you, Master Trenton," she said, her mouth tight. "Now you done gone and got drunk. That surely lead to trouble if you ain't careful."

"I told you to get out of here!"

Stella glanced at Cain, then back at Trenton. "Mr. Josh ain't in no condition to fend for hisself," she said, refusing to give up. "A man of your station don't do harm to somebody that can't stand up in their own defense."

As Trenton adjusted his crutches, he felt Stella studying him.

"You be born to high privilege," she whispered. "Got charm and fine manners, too, when you wants to use them."

"What's that brought me?" hissed Trenton.

"You got to answer that," said Stella.

"Not much!"

"You got anger, that's for sure, like a snake held by the tail by somebody teasin' it."

Trenton lowered the pistol for a second. "You have some nerve."

"I know you," she said calmly. "Since the day your mama give you birth over twenty-one years ago. You was a good boy, laughin' a lot, some meanness, yeah, but boys be that way at times, like growlin' pups that gets too full of themselves. But you ain't a bad man, Master Tessier, least not yet. You don't want to do this—not really—no matter how much you think this man done took from you."

Trenton licked his lips, and his mouth tasted like sour whiskey. The smell of it filled the room.

"You gone end up like your daddy if you ain't careful," she continued. "A mean old drunk man, rich in land and darkies but plumb poor with friends and everythin' that really matters."

"Cain kept me from killing Hampton York. Took Camellia from me too; he owes me."

Stella peered back at Cain.

"He's not going to wake up," said Trenton.

"Maybe not. He's hangin' between life and the grave."

"I wish he was already dead; it'd save me from doing this."

"You already shot him once," Stella said. "Best leave him be now."

"York should have killed me. Better a fate than this." He pointed the pistol at his stump.

"He spared your mama the grief of a dead son," Stella insisted. "Took aim at your knee instead of your head. Reckon you ought to give him some thanks for that."

Trenton eyed her coldly. "York wanted my mother to marry him. That's why he didn't kill me."

"Expect you be right about that," said Stella. "They done worked things out between them, odd as that might seem to us. But either way, you be still breathin'. So best you leave it at that and get on with livin'."

Trenton took a deep breath.

"You still got goodness in you," offered Stella. "Yep, you done some rough things already, but you can't do this to Mr. Cain. No man whose heart ain't gone completely foul could do harm to another man laid out with a bullet in his chest."

Trenton licked his lips, his mind swirling. Stella stayed still. Part of him wanted to shoot Josh Cain, while another half wanted to break down and cry and run from The Oak, never to return. He glanced around the room, and his eyes landed on a picture hanging on the wall by the bedside table. Stella also looked at the picture, and her eyes suddenly widened. Trenton stepped a pace closer and stared at the drawing. It showed a man and a woman walking on the beach, their backs to the viewer, the sun going down behind them. The images were soft, the work of a gentle hand, the forms indistinct yet somehow still real.

"What's this?" asked Trenton.

"That be one of Mr. Cain's pictures," said Stella. "You know he do some hand drawin's."

"It's them!" Trenton snarled. "Cain and Camellia! He drew it before . . . before she ever told me." Rage, more murderous than he'd ever felt, rolled through his body.

"I think it's Mr. Cain and his Mrs. Anna," Stella argued. "Before she ever died."

"That's a lie!" growled Trenton. "It's Cain and Camellia. He set his heart for her even when he knew I planned to wed her."

"You be wrong!"

Trenton raised his pistol at Cain again. "Enough talk! Get out of here."

"I ain't goin'. I done told you that. You thinkin' to do harm to Mr. Cain, you gone have to come through me."

"I'd prefer not," said Trenton. "But I'll do what's necessary to take my revenge."

Stella stepped closer to him, her penny-colored eyes suddenly bright with anger. "I be over seventy years. Got my children grown and moved on. Death don't hold no fright for me, so I ain't scared of you either."

Trenton's face puffed up with fury, and he pointed the pistol at her. "You think I'm going to take this from you?"

Stella grabbed at his crutches, but before she could reach him, he swung his pistol. The barrel smacked across her chin, and she fell to the floor, a stream of blood immediately flowing from the wound. She reached for his good leg, but he jumped away, surprising himself with his quickness.

Stella's eyes scanned the room. Knowing she was looking for a weapon, he clomped over and lifted his crutch like an ax. She grabbed the water bucket from the floor and threw it at his good leg. The bucket cracked into his knee, but he didn't go down. He swung his crutch at her head, but she ducked and rolled away.

"Get out!" yelled Trenton. "Keep to your place!"

Stella rolled under the bed and crawled out the other side. Blood ran down her chin and into the front of her plain brown dress. "You ain't gone kill him!" she shouted. "He's probably gone die anyway, but it ain't gone be at your hand!"

Trenton's eyes blazed. "I'll sell you as soon as this is finished!"

Stella glanced at Mr. Cain. He continued to lie still, totally unaware. Trenton smiled as he saw what Stella had mistakenly done. The bed now lay between them, and she couldn't attack him again. He raised his pistol and aimed it at Cain.

"The law will come for you," Stella threatened as she wiped blood off her chin. "I be the one to tell them what you done."

Trenton set his crutches to free his right hand, reached to the back of his pants, and took out a second pistol. "He shot at me," he said, relaxed now. "Easy enough to make it seem that way. Especially when I leave this weapon, already fired, in the hand of the dead man."

"Why would Mr. Cain shoot at you?"

"Who knows? He's been out of his head. I came by to check on him, good man that I am. He pulled a weapon on me, and I had to defend myself."

"You got it all figured, don't you?"

"It appears so."

"But I will say different."

He laughed harshly.

Stella hung her head. "The sheriff not gone take the word of a darky over yours."

"You're smart," said Trenton. "Nobody ever said otherwise. Now, you can either go or stay—your choice."

As Stella lifted her apron to her bleeding chin, Trenton realized the old woman still hadn't given up. She'd try to figure another way to stop him. He'd have to act fast.

Trenton pulled back the hammer on the pistol. Just then Stella threw herself over the bed. He fired at her, but the shot missed, and she grabbed his left leg. He whacked her again with the pistol, this time behind her right ear. She yanked at his leg, and he fell over. Footsteps sounded loudly from the back of the house.

Who was it? Cain's kids? Trenton hoped not; he didn't want them mixed up in this! He kicked Stella. She dropped to the floor but then crawled at him again. Swinging a crutch, he caught her in the side of the head, and she crumpled over. A voice rang in the room, a full deep sound, and Trenton rolled over.

There, in the doorway, stood Hampton York, a pistol drawn. Trenton's heart jumped, but he kept his head and aimed his gun at York.

"Step away!" York yelled.

Panting, Trenton pulled himself up and stared at York, at his tanned face and thick hands and shoulders.

York walked a couple of steps closer, his gait easy, like a racehorse sliding over the ground. A well-trimmed black beard covered his face, and his black hair fell over the collar of his tan shirt. A determined look filled his eyes.

Trenton's blood ran cold. York had already bested him in one duel. Was he ready for another?

Trenton moved a pace away from the bed, his pistol still ready. "What are you doing here?"

"You know I rise early," said York. "I came to check on Josh like I do every day. I heard a gunshot; that hurried me up some."

"I came to finish what I started." Trenton nodded toward Cain. "He's about dead anyway."

"If he dies, so be it. But you won't have any hand in rushin' that. Now, put down that gun."

"You're a fool!" shouted Trenton, gun still poised. "If he lives, he'll marry your daughter. Is that what you want? He's little more than a pauper, no way to provide her what she deserves."

York nodded. "He ain't rich, that's true. But he's a good man—somethin' I can't say about you . . . me either for that matter. He'll love her pure and strong, there's worthiness in that. Besides, she ain't really my girl. I just got the chance to raise her, that's all."

"But I love her too," argued Trenton. "And he's the only thing standing between us. She can't love him; she's always loved me."

York grunted. "You just want her. Like a man desirin' a fancy horse. She's beautiful but out of your reach, so you go for her even more. That ain't the same as love. It's selfishness, pure and simple."

"So you're the expert on love?"

"I ain't no expert on much of nothin'. But I do know this: you ain't sneakin' in here to kill my brother when he's still down from where you shot him in the first place. I'd say that's lower than a dog, but that's badmouthin' the dog. So put away that pistol and get out of here. I'm weary of this talk."

Trenton wiped sweat off his chin and kept looking harsh, but inside his gut he knew he was whipped. For the time being, he'd have to leave Josh Cain alone.

"Get his guns, Stella," ordered York.

Stella moved to Trenton. He glared at her, but she took the pistols anyway. Mustering up what little dignity he had left, Trenton adjusted his crutches and moved slowly toward the door. "There'll be another day," he said softly.

York jumped at him like a mad bear. Before Trenton could react, York had grabbed him by the throat and held him still. Trenton's face went white as York squeezed his flesh.

"I'm not a man to trifle with!" growled York. "Josh Cain is a far better man than me or you will ever dream of bein'. You and me have had our troubles in the past, and I can see where you might want to try me again. I expect that, figure it will come down to one of us dead one day—I reckon that's best. But you listen to this and get it straight. You try again to do harm to Josh, and I won't let you go. I'll make sure you never see another sun come up. You hear that plain?"

Trenton's eyes bulged with fury, but deciding to bide his time, he banked it down and nodded. York let go of his neck. Trenton brushed down his shirt and gradually caught his breath. But then, instead of slipping meekly away, he drew himself up to full height and eyed York.

"You forget yourself," he whispered. "Until a few weeks ago, you were a hired hand—not much better than the darkies."

"But now your mother is to be my bride," sneered York. "And I'll have more say over what happens here than anyone, even you!"

"You stole from us!"

York raised his pistol to his eye level. "I said get out!"

Trenton bit his lip. "I'm going. But know this. If I can't have Camellia, nobody will."

"I already said I ain't goin' to let you hurt my brother."

"There are other ways to stop their love," Tessier claimed. "I just have to figure them out."

"Get out of here before I shoot out your other knee."

"This isn't finished," said Trenton.

"It is for now."

Trenton clomped out, his crutches heavy since he no longer cared that anyone heard him. One day, he promised himself, one day he'd take care of York and Cain. What a glorious day that would be.

York put his pistol away and faced Stella. "How bad you hurt?"

"Not much," she said, handing him Trenton's pistols, then examining the blood on her apron where she'd wiped her chin. "Bleedin' slowed most to nothin'. A bump or two on the head. But I'm a tough old gal, you know that."

"I'll get a doc to check on you if you need it."

"I reckon I be OK."

York nodded, moved to Josh, and stared down. "He sleep through the night?"

"Tossed and turned a lot."

"When did Camellia leave him?"

"About half through the night."

"She's with Beth and Butler?"

"Yep, but comin' back over later in the day."

"Glad they're all still asleep. No need to mix them up with any of this."

"That be surely best."

"Yep, so keep this quiet, all right? No use worryin' Camellia or the children."

"You be the boss, Captain."

York put Trenton's pistols in the waist of his pants, pulled a cut of tobacco from his pocket, and bit off a chew. "You figure Josh will die?"

Stella dabbed at her chin again. "I ain't sure. But I expect we'll know soon."

York chewed his tobacco thoughtfully. "I don't know how long I can stay here after I marry Mrs. Tessier. Now that South Carolina has gone and fired on Fort Sumter, I got no choice but to head out to fight."

"When you figure to head off?"

"A few days after the nuptials."

"Master Tessier gone stay here when you go?"

"I don't know. He wants to go fight—every man his age does. But somebody has to stay and run The Oak. With his leg freshly cut on and all, he might stay back, least for a while."

"That causes me some worry," said Stella, frowning.

York faced her again. "Me too. If I ain't here, who's goin' to protect Josh the next time Trenton comes after him?"

"It ain't only Josh I fear for," said Stella.

"You think he'd do harm to Camellia?"

"Master Tessier be a rough man. He figures he's lost about everythin' worth havin'. You marryin' his ma and takin' over as head of this place. Miss Camellia turnin' down his proposal and declarin' her love for Mr. Cain. Him a cripple, not able to go off to war and all the glory he figures come with that. Plus, now he be showin' a real likin' for whiskey, just like his dead pa. He gets liquored up, he might think the best way to keep Camellia from Josh Cain or somebody else is to . . . to . . ." She couldn't finish the sentence.

"'If I can't have Camellia, nobody will,'" York claimed. "That's what he said."

Stella nodded. "We got to do somethin' if you gone leave. Somethin' to protect her and Mr. Cain."

York walked to the window. The early morning light had begun to creep over the land. The year's crop already lay planted, the soil covered by the fresh water from the Conwilla River, water pushed up by the ocean tides and dammed or freed by the dikes built by the darkies and managed by him and Josh.

Stella moved to him. "I ain't nothin' but a servant here, but I loves this place like it's my own. All the people on it too . . . except for, I reckon, Trenton and his mama."

York laughed. "You love me, too, Stella?"

Stella put a hand on his shoulder. "You be a troublesome man. Got a lot of barky edges on you. Drink too much, gamble a lot, used to chase after the women, get in more than your share of fights. But you raised Camellia; I got to give you that. And I love her most of all. So, yep, I reckon I got love for you."

York sighed. "Not many would say that."

"Don't need many," said Stella. "Just the right few."

York looked back at Josh.

"What you gone do to protect Camellia, Captain York?" asked Stella.

York rubbed his beard. "I ain't sure. But I will do somethin', I can assure you of that."

Chapter Two

York stewed all morning about his next step. Should he keep Trenton Tessier's effort to kill Josh quiet or seek advice from somebody else about how to keep Trenton from going after Josh again? But who could he tell? Other than Calvin and his son Johnny there weren't any other white men on The Oak. True, he bossed a couple of other white laborers who lived elsewhere and worked for him, but they weren't of high enough rank to talk to about this kind of thing. Josh had always been his ear for matters of a serious nature, and in spite of the fact that they didn't always agree on a course of action after they'd talked, he could always count on Josh to tell it to him straight. One thing about Josh—a compass lived in the man's heart, and that compass always pointed toward the truth, at least as he saw it.

York pondered on what he'd do if Josh died. He'd hurt more than a dog run over by a wagon, that was for sure. But then he'd have to pick up and go on. A man couldn't let heartache keep him down, not even a heartache caused by the death of the only man he'd ever truly trusted, his only true friend in the whole world.

York considered going to Johnny to talk over his problem but decided against it. If Johnny learned of Trenton's ill will toward Josh, he might just go after the young master of the plantation, and York knew his boy wasn't ready for that kind of fight. Besides, that's the last thing York needed—his last living son battling the son of the woman he planned to wed in a week.

About midday York cut off a new chew of tobacco, stuck it in his cheek, and stood up at his tiny desk. Through the window he could see a bank of clouds hanging over The Oak, but even they couldn't cover the beauty of the place. The last of the year's azaleas still bloomed around the porch of the manse. Fresh green leaves blanketed the oak trees. Honeysuckle grew heavy already on the fence that surrounded the main section of the property. With a light breeze blowing through the low clouds, he could almost smell the salty ocean.

York moved to the porch, his mind unsettled. He couldn't leave The Oak until he'd provided protection for Josh and Camellia. But how? What could he do? An idea flooded his head, and he knew then who he could ask. The one person with as practical a nature as his; one who'd do the best thing, even if it wasn't necessarily the right thing.

Katherine Tessier.

York's teeth worked his tobacco hard as he headed to the manse. Telling Lady Tessier about her boy's cowardly act might cause some sparks to fly, but she might as well know it before something worse happened. One thing about Katherine—she kept a level head, never seemed to let something as silly as love or family knock her off the most appropriate course. She'd already shown that when it came to making choices. She always chose the logical thing, the course that made the best sense . . . not the one that made the most people happy.

As always, York took off his hat as he entered the manse. In spite of the fact that he'd live here in a week, the place still awed him some. He peered quickly around the entryway, as if expecting somebody to shoo him back out. He took a deep breath. Although he was soon to become master of The Oak, it didn't seem right. He studied the fancy furnishings. A large table with a tall oblong mirror sat to his left. A staircase with a shiny wood rail hugged the wall to his right, disappearing into the heights of the second floor. A number of smooth rugs—most of them a shade of burgundy or gold—lay on the hardwood floor. The ceiling, cut with a circular pattern in the center, loomed at least sixteen feet overhead. About halfway up the wall to the ceiling hung a mammoth full-length portrait of Mr. Marshall Tessier. He wore a red jacket with a black collar and gold buttons and a laced white shirt, buttoned at the neck. Black pants and boots, clean enough to eat off of, glistened from the painting. A hound dog lay at his feet on a gold rug.

York reverently studied the picture. Mrs. Tessier had promised him that she'd take down her former husband's portrait the morning of their nuptials. Then, as soon as they could get the artist from Charleston to do it, they'd get his portrait painted and hung in its place.

A smile crossed York's face as he momentarily forgot his worry about Josh. He'd always wanted his picture in a house like this, had figured it about as high an honor as a man could get! Well, his day would come real soon!

Hat in hand, York left the entry and found his betrothed bride in the main parlor. Three Negroes stood around her, listening to their orders. Katherine pointed to this and that, her hands busy, her voice firm as she told the darkies what to do to prepare for the wedding guests.

Although still feeling out of place, York cleared his throat to get Mrs. Tessier's attention. She turned to him, her face blank. He studied her features—her skin as white as flour in a skillet. She had brown eyes with thick brows that almost touched in the middle. A light mustache fanned out over her lip, but nobody could see it without looking real close. She was a touch thick at the waist and hips but not overly so. She certainly didn't take his breath away when he saw her, but he'd seen much worse. Truth be told, she was slightly above ordinary—nothing more and nothing less. But he'd loved beautiful women before, and that had gotten him absolutely nothing. Maybe this way was better. Katherine had attractions other than a toss of a pretty head and a figure that made your head hurt. She owned The Oak, and he wanted her because he wanted the plantation. She wanted him for the money he had that would pay The Oak's debt to the bankers in Charleston and keep it out of their hands. Not a bad trade; both got something they needed. So what if they had to marry each other to get it?

"You don't usually visit me so early in the day," said Mrs. Tessier, her tone showing surprise.

"I got things on my mind," he said. "I figure it's best to take them up with you. Alone."

Mrs. Tessier waved her hand, and all of the darkies slipped quietly from the room.

"Not getting scared of marrying me, are you?" asked Mrs. Tessier.

York smiled. "No, I reckon I'll go through with that."

She pointed him to a chair and he took it. Then she perched on a spot across from him. He put his hat on his knee. "I don't rightly know how to tell you this," he started. "But I caught Mr. Trenton down at Josh Cain's at dawn today. He didn't go there to ask about Josh's health."

Mrs. Tessier fluffed the back of her hair. "I don't understand."

"Trenton went there to kill Josh."

"He'd never do something like that. He's got his honor."

York pulled Trenton's pistols from his pants. "You can give these back to him."

Katherine took the guns as if accepting a pair of mad snakes. She held them by the tip of the barrels for a second, then laid them in her lap.

"He smacked Stella around some," York said. "But I stopped him before he could do Josh harm."

"You swore her to quiet?"

"I did."

Mrs. Tessier clenched her hands on her knees. "He must have been liquored."

"He was."

"He gets angry when he drinks, just like his father did."

"That can be a dangerous trait for a man."

Mrs. Tessier stood, put the pistols on the fireplace mantel, then returned to her chair. "What are we going to do?"

"You need to talk to Trenton. Put some sense in his head."

"He barely speaks to me," she said. "He's so set against our marriage."

"Can't blame him for that."

She sighed. "He's not coming to the ceremony. Swore he'd stay in Beaufort until it was over."

"He figures I'm not worthy of you, like most everybody else."

She smiled. "I don't care about everybody else; neither do you. That's at least one thing we have in common."

"Not much else. It *is* a little loco how we came to our plans to marry."

Mrs. Tessier nodded and York rubbed his beard as he recalled the recent past. Less than a month ago he'd been the overseer of The Oak—a fine job but not one of any social standing. But then, lo and behold, he decided to propose to the widow Tessier.

"In normal days you would have fired me from my labors here and sent me on my way for such an uppity notion," he said.

"But since The Oak had fallen on hard times and I needed cash money and you had some, things took a different turn."

York grinned. He'd come by his money in two ways—one Mrs. Tessier knew about, the other she suspected but couldn't prove. First, he'd skimmed off the top of The Oak's earnings for years. Second, he'd taken what he'd skimmed and placed it all on a stout black stallion during the Charleston horse races back in February. To his delight the stallion had won, and York's wealth had swelled like a river after a week of spring rains.

"You took a different look at me when I showed up with twenty-seven thousand dollars," he said. "Enough to keep The Oak out of the hands of the Charleston bankers."

"Twenty-seven thousand was just about right." She smiled in return. "Enough for me to swallow my pride, poke a stick in my own son's eye, and say 'yes' to you."

"We've shocked everybody, but I don't care. We both get what we want. It's a fair deal all the way around."

She waved her hand. "Enough of that for now. What are we to do about Trenton?"

"He's your son. Tell him to leave Josh alone. If he don't, I'll have to kill him this time."

Her face became a grim stare. "I didn't break our betrothal when you shot off his leg. But what kind of mother stays with a man who kills one of her sons?"

"I ain't wantin' to do it, let me make that clear. Just like with the duel. I had no choice in that."

"Now Trenton is a cripple."

"I spared his life once, but I won't let him go after my only kin again." York's voice was hard, determined.

"But what can I do?"

York looked for a spittoon but saw none. "What about makin' Trenton leave The Oak? Send him to Charleston."

"He's not healed enough. Besides, with the war coming and you leaving soon, I'll need him to run this place."

"Can't Calvin do that?"

"If Trenton goes to war, Calvin will insist on going too," she said. "That would leave me with nobody."

"Can you run the place without them?"

"I doubt it. You know I've never done much around here. Don't know that I can start now."

"If this war goes on for long, both Calvin and Trenton will probably leave here. You got to realize that."

"You figure Trenton can receive a commission?" she asked. "Even with his injury?"

"Don't know—but either way, he likely won't stay here unless it ends fast."

"I'll pray for it to end speedily."

He grinned. "I didn't know you was a woman of prayer."

"When a mother is fearful for her children, she will resort to just about anything."

"Then what do we do?" he asked.

"You think Mr. Cain will live? If not, we have nothing to worry about."

"Who knows? But I don't like the notion of leavin' him here with Trenton if he's still alive."

Mrs. Tessier brushed back her hair. "Maybe there's another way."

"I'm all ears for ideas."

"We need to go to Camellia. She's what Trenton wants. And since we don't know if Mr. Cain will live, perhaps we can persuade her to . . . you know . . . go back to Trenton. The two of them might still end up together. They planned that for so many years anyway. We could give her that option again."

"But you fought their notions of marriage," he said bluntly.

"True. But times are different now."

"I don't reckon Camellia will change her mind about Trenton, no matter what. Remember, he shot Josh."

"That was an accident, and she knows it. Trenton is handsome, wealthy, and educated. She'd be fortunate to get him."

"I reckon she'll say no anyway. She's right stubborn once she's made up her mind."

Mrs. Tessier wiped her face with a silk handkerchief. "If she says no, we'll need to try something else."

York rubbed his beard and weighed another idea. "Maybe we could send her off to Richmond. To her ma and pa."

Mrs. Tessier's eyes lit up. "I guess it was a surprise to you to hear from them."

"Yep, Sharpton Hillard, their hired man, brought big news."

"You thought her mother was dead all these years."

He nodded.

"What does Camellia think of this news?"

"I can't tell. We've talked little of it."

"Does she want to meet them?"

"She's not sure. I can see she's got anger at them for not coming to her sooner. And I can understand that."

Mrs. Tessier bit a fingernail. "Getting her to Richmond would solve many problems. Perhaps I can talk to her about it."

"I suspect she won't go anywhere as long as Josh is hangin' between life and death."

"I'll convince her to listen to reason."

"You think you're the one to do that?"

She raised an eyebrow. "You think you're better?"

"Not sayin' that. But . . . well . . . I ain't sure you have her respect."

Katherine's face clouded. "That's unkind."

York rubbed his hands on his pants. "I reckon it's the truth though."

"I'll go to her anyway."

"Do what you want."

"If she won't listen to me, we'll have to take more drastic measures."

"Like what?"

"I'm not sure, but I'll think of something."

York weighed her words, then thought of Stella's fears that Trenton might come after Camellia. "You think Trenton would ever hurt Camellia?" he asked, deciding to put all the cards on the table.

Mrs. Tessier shrugged. "Why would he do that? He says he loves her."

"He said if he couldn't have her, nobody would."

"He was just saving face. He's not mean, not really."

"His pa was pretty mean," York said, choosing to say straight out what he feared. "He might end up like him."

Mrs. Tessier's eyes blazed. "Trenton's not like his pa! Don't ever say that again!"

"No offense meant," he soothed. "Just wanted to say plain what was in my head. No matter that Camellia's not my blood daughter; I won't let anyone do her hurt, not even your son."

"Of course not," said Mrs. Tessier. "I only want what's best for her, I assure you of that."

York almost chuckled but held it back. From what he knew, Katherine Tessier wanted the best for only one person, and that was herself. He'd cast his lot with a spider, he realized, one as deadly as a black widow. He grinned and took her hand. Just the kind of woman he liked. Maybe even the kind he deserved.

Chapter Three

The day turned muggy as it passed. The breeze that had cooled things in the morning dropped away by midafternoon and never returned. By the time the light had started to fade, everything felt soggy, like a blanket soaked in warm water. Sitting by Josh Cain's bed, Camellia touched a wet cloth to his haggard face and hoped he'd live through another night. The way she saw it, every day he survived meant another day for him to get stronger. If he could only put a few more days between him and the morning Trenton shot him, he'd make it. "You best not die on me, Josh Cain," she whispered. "Not before you know I love you."

Josh didn't respond. Camellia smoothed the hair away from his sweaty forehead and studied his face. Even ill and thin, he still looked handsome to her—his well-formed chin and high cheeks still visible, even if a shadow of what they had been. When opened, his blue eyes held a kindly look, as if a pool of gentle water lay behind them. His teeth were white and strong, with no sign of tobacco like most men she knew. And his speech—oh, how she loved to hear his speech. A man whose mama had taught him to read, he sounded so fine when he talked. Not that he put on airs or anything, but he spoke with a natural cleanness to his words, as if he wanted each one to stand out fresh by itself.

She sighed as she thought of all the qualities she loved about him. Nobody had ever made her feel like he did. Maybe best of all, Josh trusted the Lord like she did, read his Bible most every day, and tried to treat folks like he wanted them to treat him. Although she knew he'd argue with her and point out all his faults real fast, she saw him as just about perfect in almost everything a woman could want in a man. True, he had ten years on her in age, but what did that matter?

"It sure is a crazy world," she said softly. "The man I figured on marrying ends up shooting the man I now know I love."

Shaking her head at the irony, Camellia pulled back the sheet that covered Josh and checked his bandages. Although the doctor from Beaufort had dug out the bullet three weeks back, the hole needed lots more healing. Camellia eased the bandage off and examined the damaged skin under it. The wound looked less inflamed today than yesterday. She breathed a prayer of thanksgiving, and her heart raised a little lighter. Maybe Josh would live.

Camellia heard footsteps and turned to see Stella standing behind her. Stella had a swollen lip and a cut on her chin.

"What happened to you?" Camellia asked.

"I be an old woman," said Stella. "Took me a fall earlier today, gouged a good hole in my face."

"You all right?"

"I be tough as a piece of cowhide," said Stella. "No bother about me. How Mr. Cain doin'?"

Satisfied that Stella was OK, Camellia turned back to Josh and dipped her cloth into the water bucket by the bed. "He stays restless. Moaning and tossing."

"He did that last night. You been here the whole afternoon?"

"Yeah, I came midday to relieve Beth."

"That child is growin' into a fine young woman."

Camellia smiled as she thought of Josh's oldest—a girl nearly thirteen years old, with eyes as big and brown as a deer's, hair the color of beach sand, and a body beginning to round out in ways that brought her a lot of attention the few times a year they took the buggy into Beaufort to shop or go to church. The beauty of her dead mama, Anna, showed up in Beth more and more every day. In addition to becoming handsome in body, Beth also showed strong character, taking on most of the care for her pa and brother, Butler. Trying to help, Camellia and Stella stayed with her as much as they could.

"I fear for Beth and Butler if . . ." Camellia couldn't finish her sentence.

Stella put a hand on her shoulder. Camellia's strength suddenly sagged; she felt like she wanted to cry. Worse than fearing for Beth and Butler, she was scared for herself if Josh didn't make it. Although she'd known him for about seven years, she'd only realized in the last few weeks that she loved him. Those weeks had changed her life more than all the rest of her twenty-one years put together. Now, however, she faced the possibility of losing Josh before she could even tell him how she felt.

"Mr. Cain be a strong man," said Stella. "The doctor says maybe the worst already behind him. The bullet be out, the bleedin' be stopped, and most of his fever be gone. Mr. Josh come to any time now—you just watch and see."

Camellia patted Stella's hand. "What would I do without you?"

Stella stroked Camellia's rich brown hair. "No need to worry about that. I ain't goin' nowhere."

Camellia looked into her friend's face. "You been with me as far back as my memory goes. Gave me a piece of peppermint the year I turned four. I never had any candy until then."

"You the best white person I ever knowed," said Stella. "When your ma ran off, your pa pretty much handed you to me, and I took to you real fast. My children were already gone by then, so I needed somebody to tend."

"I was two when we came here," said Camellia. "Almost four when Ma ran off. I don't even remember her."

Josh stirred and Camellia turned back to him. He looked so thin; the weight had dropped off his bones as if peeled away with a knife.

She leaned closer. "Josh," she whispered. "I'm here. Stella too. We're praying for you."

She thought his eyes flickered, but they didn't open.

"He talk any today?" asked Stella.

"No, but I think he's sleeping better. Hope that's a good sign."

"Could be."

Camellia wiped the cloth across Josh's face again, then stood and motioned Stella out of the room and into the kitchen. "I need to get supper on," she said as they reached a small table in the center of the wood-floored room. "Beth and Butler will come in after dark."

"Master York is keepin' them busy."

"In the manse, easy labor most of the time."

"Your pa is a perplexion to me," said Stella. "One time doin' the wrong thing, the next time the right."

Camellia nodded. With Hampton York, a person never could tell. York liked drinking and never met a card game, horse race, or cockfight he didn't like. Plus, he tended to look out for his own interests more than anybody else's. Yet he'd provided for her, even though he wasn't really her pa, a fact she'd only recently found out.

"You know he's not really my pa," Camellia said.

"Everybody's heard that news, child. Darkies talk, just like the white folks. I know that your mama is alive, that your pa ain't the captain. 'Course I figured the last part of it a long time ago."

"You did?"

Stella chuckled. "I knew him and your mama when they first showed up here—remember? Before your ma run off. Though they never said nothin' about when they tied up with one another, I could tell she'd brought you into the bargain when they married."

"You're a smart woman, Stella."

"I ain't dumb, that's for true."

Camellia took a wet cloth and wiped off the table. Stella took a couple of big spoons from a drawer and set them on the table.

"I thought my mama died of the typhus," said Camellia. "Pa thought it too. She'd sent him a letter, told him her days were numbered, even sent him that red dress and navy cape—you've seen me wear it."

"She sent earrings too," agreed Stella. "And a beat-up old Bible."

"Pa said she never read it, guess she figured he might."

"Reckon not," said Stella. "It's yours now."

Camellia rubbed her eyes, still puzzled by all she'd learned over the last few weeks. "The typhus didn't kill my ma after all. She and my real pa are prosperous people."

"Captain York raised you like you was his own after she ran off," marveled Stella. "Not always doin' it right maybe, but he stayed steady with you. I got to give him credit for that, yes I do. He loves you, no doubt of it."

Camellia pulled a pan from a nail on the wall and started spreading lard in it. Stella took cornmeal from a jar and poured it into a bowl.

"What do you think I should do about my folks?" asked Camellia. "They sent me five thousand dollars; want me to come meet them."

Stella poured water into the bowl with the cornmeal. "That be hard to say. Five thousand dollars is a heap of cash."

Camellia recalled the events that had unfolded in the last year and a half.

In mid-November 1859, a stranger named Sharpton Hillard had come from Richmond to tell York that a man who had been carrying five thousand dollars for Hillard's employer was missing. Then in February, Hillard had visited The Oak again—this time to see Josh. Josh had told Hillard about the dead man he'd found at Mossy Bank Creek in November 1858 but, not wanting to get York in any trouble, hadn't mentioned York's presence.

On April 12, just before the duel at dawn, Hillard had come to Josh again, and both had told their stories. Hillard reported that Camellia's folks had sent the man with the five thousand dollars almost three years earlier to find her and her brother, Chester. The money was an offering to them to show they loved them and wanted to see them. But the man bringing the money had been robbed and killed on the way to The Oak. To Camellia's surprise she'd recently found out that York had the money; that he and Josh had found it with the dead man at a creek on the way home from Charleston. With no clue as to the origin or destination of the money, York had kept it in spite of Josh's protests about finding the rightful owner.

"I'm not taking the money," Camellia said to Stella, focused again in the present. "I plan for Pa to keep it."

Stella dropped flour in with the cornmeal. "That money says your ma and pa got serious notions about seein' you."

"That's true," said Camellia, spreading salt and pepper in the bottom of the pan. "But it feels like they're trying to buy me with it. I mean, what kind of mama goes off and leaves an almost four-year-old girl behind and a boy even younger? Chester's dead now—never even got to know she's alive. I got a right to be mad at that, don't you think?"

"'Course you do."

Camellia sighed. "I got another feeling too, though—a part of me that wants to see what Ma and Pa look like, wants to talk to them. I thought

Mama was dead all these years but now . . . now . . ."

"A lot happened in the last few weeks," said Stella.

"Amen to that." Camellia's face suddenly clouded over. "What's the news about the war? I've stayed so busy with Josh I've hardly noticed."

Stella took the pan and poured the cornbread fixings into it. "It beat all I ever saw. Men gettin' horses ready, musterin' up the militia, packin' clothes and food. I hear tell ol' Abe Lincoln called on seventy-five thousand men to join up with the Yankee army."

"You think the war will bother us here?"

"War bothers everythin'. Unless it ends real fast like everybody say it will."

"You think they're right?"

Stella took the cornbread to the fireplace, hooked it over the smoldering ashes, and walked back to Camellia, who now held an unopened jar of peas. "I got no way of knowin' what'll happen in this war. But my years showed me that a body hardly ever gets what she be expectin'."

Camellia opened the jar and poured the peas into a bowl. "Like my pa and Mrs. Tessier."

"That be an example," said Stella, taking some dried ham from a gunnysack by the window. "Who could see that turn in the road? One thing leads to another, but nobody can foretell none of it."

Camellia heard a dog bark. "Must be Beth and Butler."

Footsteps sounded on the stoop, and Camellia wiped her hands on her apron. The door opened, and Mrs. Katherine Tessier stepped inside, her slightly graying hair in ringlets around her ears and her cheeks tinted with a hint of rouge. She wore an ankle-length pale green dress and held a white handkerchief. Camellia glanced at Stella, then back at the Lady of the manse.

"Mrs. Tessier," said Camellia, finding her voice. "Here, sit down. I'll get you a drink of water."

Mrs. Tessier took the chair Camellia offered and perched there, as if hoping to sit without actually touching the chair bottom.

"You sit too," Stella told Camellia. "I gone fetch the water."

"Yes, sit with me," said Mrs. Tessier. "We have things to discuss now that I'm to wed your father."

Camellia started to remind her that York wasn't actually her sire but decided to let it go. If Mrs. Tessier wanted to speak of him that way, she had no objection. Stella brought two glasses of water to them, then slipped into the corner. Mrs. Tessier wiped the edge of the glass with her handkerchief, then sipped lightly from it. Camellia took a long drink, then set the glass on the table.

"How is Mr. Cain?" asked Mrs. Tessier.

Camellia's voice took on an air of refinement she didn't really possess. "He slept well today. I hope he'll soon regain consciousness."

"A real tragedy that he got shot," said Mrs. Tessier.

"I feel the same about Trenton's wound."

Mrs. Tessier's jaw tightened. "Trenton is not a good patient. Losing a leg sits poorly with a man of his spirit."

Camellia hung her head. She and Trenton had grown up together, the only white children of their age on The Oak. They'd frolicked in the sun near the Conwilla River, had picked flowers off its banks, had ridden bareback on horses all over the plantation. Since childhood they'd pledged their love to each other. When he had gone off to Charleston for his schooling, she'd waited for him, refusing the advances of all other suitors because she believed he would one day marry her. What had happened to all that? He hated her now, and how could she blame him? She'd rejected his offer of marriage after he lost his leg, and he'd accused her of turning him down because of his crippled condition. The whole thing broke her heart. Saddened, she decided to change the subject.

"You must be busy with wedding plans."

"We wanted to wait until we knew the fate of Mr. Cain," Mrs. Tessier said. "But with the war, we had to speed things up. It won't be a big ceremony. Again, the war; it made us tone down the affair."

Camellia wondered if her pa had told Mrs. Tessier that his first wife was alive in Richmond. Would that change her plans to marry him? At first she'd figured it would. But her pa had told her he'd talked to a barrister in Charleston, who had informed him that seventeen years of absence between a husband and wife led to a situation called a "common law" divorcement. Apparently that was the case because her pa had said nothing to anyone, so far as she could tell. The nuptials seemed certain to happen.

"I'm sure your wedding will be glorious," Camellia said.

"Enough to maintain appearances," Mrs. Tessier stated stiffly. "People expect certain things. I'm sure you learned that from your days as Trenton's intended."

Camellia looked at her hands. At one time she'd desired all the trappings of the social standing held by the Tessiers. She'd wanted to live in the fine house in Charleston, wanted to wear the large hoop skirts and high-feathered hats, wanted to slip silk gloves on her fingers and shoes with buttons onto her feet. She'd wanted to eat pheasant baked by servants who stood by to handle her every desire, wanted to . . . well, she'd dreamed of becoming a princess like every other girl did. Was that such a sin? To imagine herself pampered and tended to like a woman of high class and fine taste? Of course it was. Now she saw her former notions for what they were—empty dreams as bare of life as the shells that lay on the beach no more than a few minutes' walk from where she sat.

"Will Pa go to war?" she asked, putting her mind off the shallow nature of her former hopes.

Mrs. Tessier waved her handkerchief, as if shooing away a fly. "Let's talk of other matters. Like you and Trenton."

Camellia shrugged. "There's nothing to say. He despises me now."

Mrs. Tessier placed her water on the table and wiped her lips with her handkerchief. "You must marry him," she said, as if announcing she'd baked biscuits for supper.

Camellia gulped. "But you refused to let us marry when we both wanted it," she stammered. "I don't understand."

Mrs. Tessier's smile held no warmth. "I'm a complicated woman. I denied his desire because we needed him to take a woman of means; nothing personal about it. I've always seen you as a strong young woman and certainly a most beautiful one. That marvelous dark hair, wonderful blue eyes, skin like smooth butter; I can understand how Trenton's heart settled on you."

Camellia's face reddened as Mrs. Tessier continued. "He's always wanted you, even when he got engaged to that girl from Columbia. Now I want him to have you."

"You make it sound like I'm a horse."

"Don't take offense, child. We all have our values—you, me, your pa. Let's not pretend anything else. You know I'm marrying Mr. York because he's come up with enough money to save The Oak from its creditors. I don't even care how he got it—maybe by gambling like he insists or perhaps by stealing it from me. But now he's got it, and that's enough. And what's his gain in the bargain? Well, he's marrying me because of The Oak. It's a square deal according to our worth to the other."

Camellia studied Mrs. Tessier. Age lines had begun to creep into her eyes and around her mouth. Although known in the past for her daily use of laudanum—a mixture of whiskey and opium—Ruby had told Camellia that Mrs. Tessier hardly ever did that anymore. Since her husband's death in the fall of 1858, she'd shown herself a most resourceful woman, even if sometimes also a most ruthless one. Like Camellia's pa, she did whatever was necessary to protect herself and her offspring. Was that what had drawn them together?

Yet, still, how could her pa marry Mrs. Tessier? She was harsh and unkind; her face showed not a sign of charm or kindness.

Camellia sipped from her water. She knew why her pa wanted to marry Mrs. Tessier. It came from his biggest fault, the one thing that surely lay behind all of his faults. He wanted to prove to everybody that he had what it took to make something out of nothing. That's what drove Hampton York—the notion that a man had to grab any chance, even a less than honorable one, to become a person of note. Marrying Mrs. Tessier gave him his opportunity, almost certainly the only one he'd ever have. He wanted people to whisper about him as he rode by on a prancing horse, and this is the way he could make that happen.

The union between Hampton York and Katherine Tessier would occur because they both wanted something from the other. Sadly, love had nothing to do with it.

"I love Josh Cain," Camellia finally said, her mind back on the matter at hand. "I can't marry Trenton."

"But you have to," insisted Mrs. Tessier. "It's the only thing that will make him happy."

"Since when do you care about his happiness?"

Mrs. Tessier's eyes hardened. "You forget your station."

"I'm sorry. But you never seemed real concerned for him before."

"You've stated a truth, I admit it. But things have changed."

Camellia tried to figure Mrs. Tessier out. Why the change now? She tried to catch Stella's eye, but the old woman didn't move. Then the reason came to Camellia. "It's the war. You want him to stay here, and you're afraid he won't. You're afraid that he'll want to lead men, to go off to battle."

Mrs. Tessier shrugged. "You read me so easily. If he weds a pretty thing like you, perhaps he'll stay home a few more months to heal . . . maybe even long enough for the war to end."

Camellia stared into her water. Mrs. Tessier didn't usually give up so easily. Something else must be on her mind. Either way, though, it didn't matter. "Your reasons aren't my concern. I won't marry him, simple as that."

Mrs. Tessier sighed. "A pity. It would have pleased him greatly."

"He said he hated me," said Camellia, remembering the last time she'd seen Trenton, the time he'd proposed and she'd turned him down.

"Men," said Mrs. Tessier. "They're so temperamental. He'd marry you tomorrow if you'd say the word."

A new thought came to Camellia. "Did he send you here?"

"That's not your business."

Camellia considered the matter. Unwilling to lose face by coming himself, it wouldn't be unlike Trenton to send his mother to make one more try to win her affections. If she said yes, he had what he wanted. If she said no, he kept his dignity in spite of another refusal. But really, what did it matter either way?

"You're right," Camellia finally said. "It's no concern of mine. But the answer is still no."

Mrs. Tessier wiped her lips. "You give me no choice then. I want you off The Oak, as soon as we can arrange it."

Camellia's face blanched. "You can't do that!"

"Of course I can," said Mrs. Tessier, standing.

"But Pa won't let you run me off!" Camellia shouted, rising too and glaring at the cruel woman.

"So you'd go to him against me?"

Camellia considered the situation. "What if I did?"

"If he stands against me on this, I'll refuse to marry him."

"But you've already said yes. Everyone knows it."

"A woman can change her mind," said Mrs. Tessier slyly. "With the war starting, who could blame me? I don't want to marry a man who's about to leave. Who knows if he'll ever come home?"

"But you need his money."

Mrs. Tessier flipped her handkerchief again. "The war's changed everything. Bankers won't foreclose on a rice plantation, won't take the chance of shutting it down when everybody knows the soldiers will need rice to eat, and lots of it. An army can't fight a war on an empty stomach, you know."

"You'd take that risk?"

"Look at it this way," suggested Mrs. Tessier, as easily as if advising a child how to tie her shoe. "If you don't go to your pa, I'll give you enough money to leave The Oak in comfort. You choose your place, I don't care. But if you do go to him and I break the engagement, you both leave The Oak. You're just as gone as in the first case, but in the second situation, your father goes too. That won't make anybody happy."

"But he's got twenty-seven-thousand dollars," said Camellia. "We'll do fine without you."

"I can tie up your pa's money for a long time . . . let the courts figure out how he came about his dollars."

Camellia rubbed her eyes, unsure what to do. She looked at Stella again, but the old woman kept her head down. Camellia understood. A darky knew her place—stand mute, deaf, and blind when white folks did their business.

"You think you've left me no choice."

"Your choice is to marry Trenton," said Mrs. Tessier. "He truly wants you."

"How long before you want me off The Oak?"

"The week after your pa and I marry, that should suffice."

"Give me time to think about this."

"I'm not certain how long I have." Mrs. Tessier spoke arrogantly, as if dismissing a child, and started moving toward the back door.

"You are as awful as your dead husband," accused Camellia, her anger rising at the woman's tone.

Mrs. Tessier pivoted and grinned wickedly. "I believe you and he spent some time together."

"Did Trenton tell you he tried to take advantage of me?"

"Something like that."

"That he died the day he made his last advance?"

"So I understand. According to Trenton, you believe you might have contributed to his death."

"If I did, he deserved it."

"The law might see it differently if they knew the details," Mrs. Tessier hinted.

"You plan to hold that over me?"

"Who knows? Such knowledge might come in handy someday."

"You're a horrid woman."

"That's not a Christian thing to say, is it?" Mrs. Tessier grinned again.

"Perhaps not, but at least I'm not smiling about all this misfortune," Camellia threw in.

"As you said, I'm as awful as my husband was."

Camellia's eyes watered as she saw what she'd allowed to happen. Mrs. Tessier had tempted her, and she'd started responding in kind. But Camellia hated such unpleasantness and wanted it to end. "I'm sorry about Trenton," she said, softening some in hopes of easing Mrs. Tessier's bitterness. "He's got a lot of good traits, I know that. I never meant to hurt him. But I cannot marry him. I love Josh Cain."

Mrs. Tessier shook her head. "Mr. Cain is ten years older than you. And he won't live too much longer. Even if he does, he'll go off to war as soon as he's better. Who knows what will happen then?"

"He's going to live!" insisted Camellia.

"But if he doesn't, you'll need a husband—and Trenton can be that for you. Yes, he's mean sometimes. All men are. But he does love you. You have to believe that."

"I'd like for you to leave." Camellia's voice cracked. "I don't know what else to say. I need time to think."

"Oh, I'm going," said Mrs. Tessier. "But mark my word, this isn't over. So long as I can draw breath, I'm going to do what I can for my boy."

Camellia wiped her eyes as Mrs. Tessier slipped out of the kitchen and through the back door. When Camellia slumped into a chair, Stella rushed to her.

"I can't leave!" cried Camellia. "Not until Josh is better."

Stella patted her back.

"What if he's not well soon?" continued Camellia.

"I expect we'll know which way the wind gone blow quick enough," said Stella. "He live or die soon, that's for certain."

"But where will I go?"

"Reckon this be just the thing to decide you about goin' to your real folks in Richmond. Reckon this be the Lord's way of pushin' you out of this nest, makin' you do what you might not do on your own."

"But how will I get there?"

"Sharpton Hillard gone take you."

"But I don't want to meet them."

"This be the time if it's ever to happen," argued Stella. "Before this war gets goin' too fast and furious."

Camellia buried her face in her arms. What should she do? Where would she go? How could she leave Josh, not knowing whether he'd live or die? But the war made it impossible to wait long. Stella was right. If she ever wanted to meet her real folks, she had to do it now.

She heard footsteps from the front of the house and wiped her eyes. She didn't want Beth and Butler to see her crying. As she looked up, her heart began to pound. Josh was leaning against the door leading out of the kitchen! She jumped up and ran to him, throwing her arm around his waist to support him. Stella joined her, and the two of them held him up.

"You're awake!" cried Camellia.

"Our prayers be answered," crowed Stella. "Mr. Josh Cain come back from the dead."

"I'd . . . like some water," said Josh, his voice whispery and hoarse.

"Let's get you back to bed first," soothed Camellia. "Then I'll get you all the water you can drink."

When Josh closed his eyes and leaned against her, Camellia knew that no matter what happened next, Josh would live. She'd have the chance to tell him she loved him. Her spirits soaring, she helped Stella gently lead Josh Cain back to his bed.

Chapter Four

Three days later Camellia and Josh sat down with her pa in the front room of Josh's house. A hot sun baked the small room, filling it with heavy air. Stella set a tray with lemonade and glasses on the table in front of the sofa where Camellia rested beside Josh. After pouring the lemonade, Stella eased toward the kitchen.

Camellia glanced at Josh. He'd spent the last forty-eight hours sleeping, eating like a horse, or sitting in the sun on the front porch. As a result his color had started to come back, and his face seemed fuller. Camellia's heart relaxed a little as she realized he no longer stood on the brink of death.

York took a glass of lemonade, sipped from it for a minute, then set it down. "This may be our last chance for a while to speak with each other," he started. "I got my nuptials in four days, then I'll go to Charleston. Plan to join up with a regiment formin' there, probably the Charleston Cavalry."

Camellia nodded sadly. Men from all over were joining up to fight, and her pa, a veteran of the Mexican War, felt honor-bound to do the same.

"I'm fearful for what will happen here when I'm gone," York said. "Somebody will need to oversee The Oak. I hope that will be you, Josh, now that you're regainin' your strength."

"You got any idea what Master Trenton will do?" asked Josh.

"He wants to go fight," York continued. "But his injury might keep him from that, least for a while. His mother hopes that will be the case."

"So long as he's here, *he* will control things—nobody else."

York sipped his lemonade. "You're right. But he don't know this place like you do, don't handle the darkies too well. I need your hand workin' with them, even if it's not direct, you know what I mean?"

"You want me to smooth out Trenton's rough spots?"

York grinned slyly. "Just like you always did with me, that's all."

Camellia smiled at the half brothers, the two most important men in her life. Although sired by the same man, Josh and York had turned out almost opposites in a lot of ways. Josh was naturally kind, given to books and painting, and had no strong desire for a lot of wealth. York, on the other hand, sometimes treated people roughly, cared nothing for any learning that didn't promise him some advantage, and wanted wealth and prestige more than anything else. Plus he had a weakness for money and tended to give wealthy folks more respect than other folks. Camellia wondered what had caused the differences. Was it just the fact that different mamas had birthed and raised them? Or was it deeper than that? Their pa had never married York's mama. Did that bother York more than he'd ever let on? Did people treat him poorly when he was a boy because of it? Did he think he had to make something of himself because others had constantly pointed out to him that he was nothing?

"I had planned to leave here," said Josh, interrupting Camellia's musings. "Before the duel. Had everything ready to go that day."

"Everythin's different now," York put in.

"I know," Josh returned, "but I'm thinking I should leave anyway—soon as I'm stronger."

"I want you to stay," said York. "Need you here."

Josh wiped his face, and Camellia saw worry in his eyes.

"I don't know," said Josh. "I feel like Trenton and I will not see things the same way. We'll clash . . . maybe not at first but sooner or later. He's not happy that . . ."

York finished the sentence that seemed to have stumped Josh. "That you and Camellia care for each other."

Camellia blushed. She and Josh had not yet spoken of their feelings. Although she wanted to tell him she loved him, she didn't feel it proper until he brought up the matter of their relationship. Sadly he'd not yet done so. She figured he needed to recover a little more, get more strength before talking of such important things. Either that or he'd had second thoughts about what he'd said to her right after he got shot.

"Yes," said Josh. "That could surely cause problems. But that's not all. I figure Master Trenton wants a free hand on The Oak. He won't take well to me or anybody else interfering. He'll see me as your man, and that will not please him."

York stood and moved to the fireplace. "You can handle him," he argued. "You'll be stronger in no time. Please, I want you to stay here."

Camellia's eyes widened. Something in her pa's voice sounded desperate. She'd never heard him say "please" to anyone.

"You know I want to help," said Josh. "I've always followed your lead, sometimes unwisely. But I don't know about this. I fear no good can come of it. And I need to figure out what I'm going to do about the war too. When I'm well I ought to go fight, like everybody else."

York turned back to them, his face firm. "You don't want to fight. We both know it. Your injury gives you a good reason to stay out of it, least for a while."

Josh nodded. "Who knows how long, though?"

York grunted, as if giving up on Josh, and focused his attention on Camellia. "You need to leave here," he said simply. "Go meet your real folks."

Camellia almost choked, but she quickly gathered herself. "I see no reason to do that. Josh, Beth, and Butler will need me."

York pulled out a chew of tobacco and bit off a wad. "I been doin' some figurin'. The biggest part of this war will get fought up in Virginia. You best go now, or events up there might prevent your goin'."

"But I've said it already—I see no reason to meet my folks."

"You're mistaken. Every child needs to know their folks. It's the best thing."

Camellia smoothed the wrinkles in her dress. How could she say what she needed to say? Her pa was no expert on matters like this. Although he had a long list of strengths, dealing with people wasn't his strong suit. Most of her life he'd talked to her only enough to make sure the chores got done. He'd spent most of his time with her two brothers and with his labors on The Oak. Stella had pretty much raised her. True, her pa loved her. She knew that, even though he'd never said it. Why else would he have taken care of her, even though she wasn't his real child? But what right did he have now to try to tell her what she should or shouldn't do?

"If it's the best thing, why didn't you tell me about them years ago? I asked about Ma, but you always kept quiet, told me she was dead."

York hung his head. For the first time, Camellia saw some grief in him. "I thought she was dead," he said. "She wrote me the letter I told you about. That was true."

"But you never told me anything else about her—the way she looked, what she liked, why she ran off. Why the silence, Pa?"

York glanced at Josh, but Josh refused to help him. "Josh already told you this. No reason to chew that cabbage twice."

"Josh told me some," she claimed, "but I want to hear it from you."

"Your ma lived a rough life before I met her," York said slowly. "I thought it best to protect you from knowin' that."

"But you loved her?"

"More than any man ever loved a woman. You look so much like her it used to make my heart hurt. Your hair is the same rich brown as hers, your eyes the same blue."

"Josh said she grew up in Columbia."

"In a church orphanage. Her parents burned up in a house fire when she was eight. I met her in June of 1842 in Savannah. I made most of my livin' at the time at a poker table. She'd come to the bar with a card player named Wallace Swanson, a man who had taken up with her after she left the orphanage the year she turned sixteen."

"Swanson is my real pa."

"Yep. He had a good eye for women, but his card playin' didn't amount to much. I won most of his money that night, and your ma shifted her affections to me. We left Swanson when the bar closed."

"You fell in love with her pretty fast."

"Like a rock sinkin' to the bottom of the river. How could I resist? Your mama didn't have fine manners, but she carried herself like a queen, and her face melted a man's knees. When she smiled, and she always smiled when she wanted somethin', the whole room lit up. I couldn't resist that smile."

"You found out later she had a two-year-old daughter."

"Yep, but that didn't matter to me. We got married within a month. A few weeks later, I found out she had another child on the way, already several months down the line. She was still so thin I couldn't believe it. I got mad for a few days, but then got over it. I loved her too much to stay upset with her."

"Chester," Camellia said, thinking of her one full-brother, who had died before either of them learned about their parents. "So why'd she choose you over Swanson?"

"You don't think it was my good looks?"

"I'm sure that was it." Camellia laughed.

York shook his head. "I'd like to think that," he admitted. "But she told me later she needed somebody to take care of her, her babies. She figured I could do it better than Swanson. She didn't even pretend to love me. Guess that explains what happened next."

Camellia saw the hurt in her pa's eyes but knew he wouldn't like it if she gave him any open sympathy. A man like Hampton York didn't like any show of emotion—from him or anybody else.

"I figured I could make her love me," continued York. "Made up my mind to treat her so well she'd come to that."

"But that didn't happen."

"Not that I could tell. My gamblin' luck turned sour within months after we met, and by the time Chester came along, I'd pretty much run out of money. Decided I needed to do somethin' different. With a wife and two children to tend, I wanted steadier work than the fall of a card."

"That's when you moved to The Oak?"

"Yep. I'd gambled some with Marshall Tessier. He'd told me once that he needed a man like me to help him manage things. I figured I could do that, since I'd grown up around rice plantations in Georgetown. Lynette wasn't too sure how she'd do with it, said it wasn't her idea of good livin', but she moved with me anyway. Guess she didn't see a choice at the time. I became overseer within that first year, made a decent livin', figured Lynette had settled down."

"But she ran off a little over a year after you'd moved to The Oak—only a month after she'd birthed Johnny."

"Like a stray dog after you've fed it good. I woke up one clear morning and found Lynette gone without a word or a trace. Just like that. Vanished like a cloud off the ocean. I looked for her awhile, but deep down I knew she'd run off, probably with Swanson. Then the letter came, and I thought she'd died."

Camellia sighed. "Until their hired man, Sharpton Hillard, showed up, and we found out Mama was alive."

"Yep, I reckon she loved Swanson all along." York's face was grim.

"Now you think I should go back with Hillard and meet them?"

York gummed his tobacco. "Yep. It'll do you good—maybe them too."

Camellia looked at Josh. "What do you think?"

He looked startled but spoke anyway. "This is between you, your pa, and your folks in Richmond."

Camellia bit her lip. She loved Josh and didn't want to leave him. Who knew what could happen with a war going on? How long would it take them to get back together if she left now? And what about Trenton? He knew she loved Josh. What if he tried to hurt Josh while he was still weak and she wasn't around? She was the only one who could reason with Trenton. But how could she say that to Josh? Although he wasn't like most men, he'd still take offense if she suggested that he needed her protection. He'd deny any danger and tell her to go.

"I'm not going, Pa," she determined. "No matter what you say."

York eyed Josh. "You best talk to her."

"I have no say in this," said Josh.

"Sure you do. You're her intended."

"Pa!"

Surprise moved across York's face. "You and she have not talked of . . ."

"No," said Josh. "We have not." He glanced at Camellia, but she quickly looked away, her face red.

"She has to leave here," York stated. "Her ma and pa sent her money. She doesn't know what's best for her. Talk her into it."

Josh shook his head. "She and I will talk. Of many matters. But I'll not influence her to do something she has no heart to do."

York's eyes simmered with anger. Camellia couldn't help but wonder what made him so desperate for her to leave The Oak. Was it just that he wanted her to meet her folks? But why should that matter to him? He didn't care anymore for Lynette, who now went by her middle name, Ruth, and Wallace Swanson. So what was it? Was he sending her away in hopes of splitting her and Josh up? But that made no sense. He wanted them together, didn't he? Then, why did he want her to leave?

She thought of Trenton and suddenly knew the answer. Mrs. Tessier had come and asked her to marry Trenton, but she'd refused. Now her pa seemed bent on forcing her away. Did he fear for her if she stayed on The Oak without him there? That had to be it! Her pa feared Trenton, what he might do! With Josh still weak, she had no male protector after her pa went to war. But what did she care? She wasn't a weakling.

Camellia set her jaw, her mind made up. "I'm not leaving. No matter what you say. Beth and Butler need me."

York glared at her, but she stayed steady. Josh and his family needed her, and she wouldn't desert him.

"You're bein' stubborn," York claimed.

"I learned it from you," she fired back.

York focused once more on Josh. "If she won't leave, then you have to stay." His voice suggested he wanted no argument.

Josh raised his eyebrows. "I've told you I'm not sure I can do that."

"Then you're a fool," York growled.

Josh grunted. "Maybe you need to tell me what's on your mind."

York shook his head. "Reckon you need to figure it out for yourself."

Camellia caught Josh's glance but offered no help. What if she was wrong, and Trenton had no intentions of harming either of them? If she told Josh what she feared, he'd certainly go to Trenton, and that might cause even more trouble. But what if Josh left and Trenton did come after her? Well, she could take care of herself, that's what. She'd already done so with Trenton's father; she could do the same with Trenton.

"I'm a grown woman," she told York. "I can watch after myself, no matter what Josh decides."

York rubbed his beard. "You two are makin' this hard."

"That's not my desire," Camellia insisted. "But we both have to do what we think is best."

After York left the room, Josh said quietly, "He's fearful of something."

"What do you think it is?"

"Time will tell."

Camellia nodded. Yes, time would tell.

Chapter Five

The next few days passed in a blur for Camellia. The day of her pa's wedding to Mrs. Tessier arrived. Although she'd already made her decision to stay on The Oak, the matter kept rolling around in her head. What if Mrs. Tessier insisted that she leave? It didn't seem possible that the lady of the manse could make Camellia go, not now, not since Josh was gradually getting stronger. Yet, who knew what that woman could do when she put her mind to it? Had she threatened her pa some way to get him on her side? Had she told him that Trenton might hurt Camellia? Was that why her pa had seemed so insistent that she leave?

The afternoon of the wedding turned out cooler than most May days. A bank of clouds covered the sun, and a steady wind blew in off the ocean, rustling the leaves of the mammoth oak that gave the plantation its name. Close to two hundred people, dressed in their finest, drifted in and out from under the oak. The women wore colorful plumed hats, long silk dresses pinched at the waists, and glistening leather shoes that buttoned up the sides—all bought in Charleston, Savannah, or Columbia. Frock coats, ruffled shirts, and precariously balanced hats gave the men an air of gentility that only the richest could afford.

About a hundred feet beyond the oak, under a stand of smaller, shorter trees, another cluster of people had gathered. Their clothing, although the best they had, in no way matched that of the crowd under the big oak. The women wore handmade cotton dresses, bandannas instead of hats, and their shoes were scuffed on the toes instead of finely shined. The men wore rope belts, and their shirts and pants fit them poorly. These folks were black.

In the center of the black folks, on the back of a backboard wagon above them, stood a light-skinned darky, a fiddle balanced under his chin. His fingers whipped a bow across the strings like he had fire in his fingers, and the crowd around him shimmied and danced. A low cloud of whitish dust hung near the ground, the dirt stirred by the shoes the darkies had put on just for the occasion. The smell of whiskey permeated the air, and the darkies' faces flushed from the ample portions of the brew they'd swallowed—all due to the generosity of Captain Hampton York, their overseer, about to become their master. The aroma of the alcohol combined with the cheap perfumes that most of the women wore and the sweat that poured off the dancing men in spite of the cool weather created a swirl of sour smells.

Camellia and Josh sat in identical rocking chairs on the porch of the cookhouse, a stone's throw from the dancing servants.

"Little Billy can sure play that fiddle," Camellia said quietly. "They brought him all the way from Charleston."

Josh didn't respond.

"You feeling OK?" she asked him.

"I'm doing fine."

Camellia smiled. "Things were nip and tuck there for a time. I didn't know if we'd ever get the chance to—" She paused, not able to go on.

Josh stopped rocking, took her hand, and held it between their two chairs. "Look," he started, his eyes searching hers, "I know we've not talked of serious matters. But I want you to know this . . . I love you."

Camellia found it hard to catch her breath. A long minute passed.

"I've wanted to tell you ever since I regained consciousness," he told her.

"I've wanted to hear it," she said, finally discovering her voice again. "Wanted to make sure you weren't out of your head the first time you said it."

"I already said it?"

She smiled. "Yes, right after Trenton shot you . . . before you passed out."

"Good. I meant it then, and I mean it now. I've loved you for a long time but figured you'd marry Trenton. It took all I could do not to tell you, but you thought I was your uncle, and I didn't know how to explain things. But now I can say it plainly: I love you."

"I've waited for this day," she whispered. "Prayed that you'd live so I could tell you I love you too. That's why I refused Trenton's proposal. You're all I've ever wanted."

"I can't provide you with fine things."

"I don't care about that. I thought I did for a while. But all I really want is a man to love me, sit with me by the fire in the winter, live as a good father to my children, read books with me, to me."

"I can do those things," said Josh. "Though you deserve more."

"That'll be plenty. I'll be happy."

"I know now why I lived." Josh smiled. "To hear you say you loved me."

"I told you I did even when you couldn't hear me."

"I'm glad I got to hear it."

Just then Ruby stepped out of the cookhouse. She held a tub full of white rice in her hands. Camellia dropped Josh's hand and jumped up. "Let me help you, Ruby."

"Me too." Josh started to stand.

Ruby motioned them back to their chairs. "You ain't got the strength of a newborn kitten," she said to Josh. "And you, Miss Camellia, you the daughter of the man who's takin' up with Mrs. Tessier in just a few hours. Not fitting for you to be helpin' a darky no more. Plus you're wearing that pretty blue dress and those fancy black buckled shoes. You can see your face in the shine on those shoes."

Camellia ignored her protests and grabbed one side of the pot. "Nothing's changed with you and me. Let Pa marry whoever he wants. I plan on laboring here like I always did."

When Ruby beamed, Camellia's heart warmed. She, Stella, and Ruby were friends in spite of their differences in age, race, and background. Without further argument from Ruby, they carried the rice pot to a long table covered with food about twenty feet off the porch.

After setting down the big pot, Ruby wiped her brow with the front of her apron. Her eyes sparkled as she studied Camellia. "You marrying soon too. Isn't that right, Mr. Cain?" She glanced toward Josh, resting in his rocker.

Camellia's face grew hot. She and Josh had just said openly for the first time that they loved each other! Although she hoped it would happen soon, she had no clue as to when he'd actually ask for her hand.

Josh smiled teasingly. "I'm a touch older than Miss Camellia. Perhaps she would prefer a much younger man."

"I'd prefer a man who would actually *offer* me a proper proposal of marriage," Camellia said, surprising herself with her boldness. "Of course, some men find themselves too backward to do such a thing." She moved over and took Josh's hands again.

"I'll see if I can find you such a man," he joked.

Ruby chuckled. "You ought to take some lessons from my man, Obadiah. He saw what he liked and came right after me."

Camellia laughed, her spirit light. "Obadiah is a man who knows his mind. A woman likes that."

"Obadiah is a good man," said Josh. "The best woodworker in this area."

Camellia nodded. Obadiah built coffins for the dead and furniture for the living. A free man of color, he lived near Beaufort and had married Ruby a couple of years back. She spent lots of Saturday nights and Sundays at his place and the rest of the week on The Oak, an arrangement the Tessiers had allowed since their wedding.

"You best not fool around long," Ruby told Josh. "Miss Camellia has had plenty of suitors. More will come soon if you don't get your head straight and ask for her hand."

"That'll be enough out of you, Ruby," Camellia teased. "We don't want to force Mr. Cain into anything."

Nodding with laughter, Ruby headed back inside the cookhouse. The fiddle music slowed a notch. Josh's face suddenly turned serious. "You know I want to marry you."

"Yes, even though you haven't said it until now, I have gathered that."

"I'm hesitant because of this war," he said. "Nobody talks of anything else."

"Pa says we'll whip the Yankees fast."

Josh shook his head. "I'm afraid he's forgotten what war is like. He ought to know better. He fought in Mexico with me."

"But that war took barely two years," argued Camellia. "This one can't be any worse."

Josh slowly eased up from his seat. "Walk with me."

Camellia followed him as he moved away from the manse and down the gravel pathway that led to the beach. About half a mile into the woods, they reached the bank of the Conwilla River, and Josh paused to take a breath.

"Why don't we sit?" said Camellia, noting his weariness. "You're still not strong."

Josh shrugged, and they sat down on the riverbank. He picked up a rock and threw it into the slow-moving water. His brow furrowed, and his eyes seemed fearful.

"What is it?" Camellia asked. "You're not at ease."

"We're in for troublesome days. That's why I've not yet asked your pa for your hand. I suspect this war will last far longer than anyone suspects. Wars, even small ones, change things."

Camellia studied the sky. Josh's time in the Mexican War had changed him. She knew this because he'd recently told her of the awful thing that had happened to him while fighting there. For a long time it had tortured him, put a weight of guilt on his back heavier than a wagon. Having gone off to fight at sixteen years of age, he'd never quite gotten past the hard things he'd seen and done there.

"You think the war will touch us here?" she asked.

Josh patted her hands. "You're so innocent. Of course it will touch us. We're one of the largest rice plantations in the state. We're forty miles from Charleston, almost thirty from Beaufort—both towns are important to the North and South because they're shipping centers. Yankee clippers and steamers will come our way pretty fast, that's for certain. If they block passage of goods from those ports—which they'll surely try to do—how will we sell our crop?"

"But we can stop them, can't we?"

"Nobody knows. War takes strange twists, carries things in unexpected directions."

"I haven't put my mind on any of that. I've worried so much about you, I've not thought of much else."

"A woman should not have to think about war. But I fear this one will cause us all to do things we shouldn't have to do."

A bird chirped overhead. The black water of the Conwilla River gently made its way toward the Atlantic Ocean. "I'm glad you won't have to fight," Camellia said softly.

Josh sat up straighter. "What makes you think I won't?"

"You're hurt. Your wound will take months to heal, maybe longer. Surely you won't have to go."

Josh picked up a pebble and threw it into the river. "It will come to me eventually, unless it does end fast."

"We can pray for that."

Silence fell again. A fish flopped in the river.

"You think we ought to own the darkies?" asked Camellia.

Josh sighed. "That has always troubled me. Any man owning another."

"But Jesus didn't say right out we ought to rid ourselves of them. And I've heard preachers say the Bible teaches our way of living . . . that we've cared better for the blacks than they had it when they lived in Africa. At least here they can have the gospel preached to them."

"A man always finds a way to defend the worst of his offenses. Sometimes he even uses the Bible to do it."

"That's what Ruby says," agreed Camellia.

Josh smiled. "Ruby knows the Bible pretty well for somebody who says she's got no regard for the Lord."

"She says the Lord has done nothing for her, why should she hold any care for Him?"

"I'm sure she rejoiced when word of the war came to her."

"Wouldn't you if you were a darky? Especially if you had a boy back in Virginia that your master had sold you off from, a boy you'd pledged to find again someday? She's figuring this war will free her so she can go back to him."

Camellia thought of what Ruby had told her about her boy, Theo, now eight years old. Born with an empty socket where his right eye should have been, Theo's growing had stalled out real fast, like he didn't have enough skin for his bones. Boys his age stood half a head taller than him, and Ruby said she figured he'd never reach too much higher than bosom level with her. At first Ruby had grieved over the boy's smallness—sorry that he'd taken such a strange turn. But then she noticed how he talked, like his lack of growth had left some extra power for his head to use. A short but wise child with a round face and a mouthful of teeth, he sounded grown up almost from the day he started speaking. Ruby's mammy, Nettie, said the Lord had made Theo special; had taken his eye so as to give him a different kind of seeing—visions that most folks never spied, truths about things that were yet to come. He had seemed like he was a grown man in the head from the day of his birth. The day her master's widow had sold her off, Theo had told Ruby that she'd come back to him someday. He could see it in his head.

"Ruby is pulling for the Yankees, no doubt," said Josh.

"All the darkies but Stella are."

"I'm not sure I'm not with them."

Camellia looked around quickly to make sure no one was there to hear Josh say such a thing. Although she didn't know much about war, she knew that Josh's words could be dangerous in the South; could buy him a heap of trouble. Still, she couldn't help but wonder if he was right. Why should a person be treated differently just because of the color of his skin? It wasn't the first time that question had troubled her mind.

"What will happen to The Oak if the Yankees win?" she asked.

"It really doesn't matter if the Yankees win or not. The glory days of The Oak are past either way."

"Why do you say that?"

Josh tossed another pebble into the Conwilla. "Slavery can't last forever. It never has, not in any civilized nation. It eventually falls. This war will just push it quicker, that's all. And, the way I figure it, that's best for everybody. Cleanse the stench of our 'peculiar institution' out of our noses sooner rather than later."

"You sound like you'll be glad when that happens."

"I suppose I will. We've kept people in their places—high or low stations—in the South too long, you know that. A man ought not to be measured by his status at birth but by what he can accomplish with his brain and strong hands. Look at you, the daughter of the overseer, brighter than any woman I know and as pretty as a picture. But even with your pa marrying Mrs. Tessier, your rung on the ladder is still set.

Oh, the rich folks from Charleston will speak nice to you to your face, but when you turn your back, they will light into you like a stray dog on a bone. We've had the darkies on the bottom of the ladder, white trash folks who don't work on the next rung, white working people like you and me and your pa third up, the bankers and merchants in Charleston above us, and the landed folks—the plantation owners—way up past any of us. And all of it set from the day we're born. That needs to stop, and I expect this war will make that happen."

"But you'll fight for the South if the need comes."

Josh dropped his head. "Any fighting I do will not be to keep our hold on the darkies. Or on our old way of life."

"Then why will you fight?"

The sound of hoofbeats approaching prevented him from answering. Camellia turned and saw a roan stallion headed their way, its face white and broad. The sweating animal thundered almost upon them, then reared back and pulled to a stop. Camellia's eyes widened. What was Trenton doing on The Oak today? Hadn't he sworn he'd remain in Beaufort until the marriage was over?

His eyes blazing, Trenton sat astride his horse, the reins in his hand. Camellia glanced at his right leg and saw the neatly pinned riding pants that ended where his knee used to bend. She marveled at his fast recovery and wondered if part of it wasn't fueled by his anger and bitterness.

Josh stepped between her and Trenton, but she stepped up beside him. Trenton had already shot Josh once. She wouldn't allow Josh to be hurt again.

"Leave us!" Trenton snarled at Josh. "I have things to say to Camellia!"

"She is *Miss Camellia* to you," Josh replied, his tone cold and steady, showing more strength than Camellia imagined his body possessed.

"My dealings are not with you," Trenton argued. "Least not this time!"

"If they concern Camellia, they concern me."

Trenton laughed dismissively. "She'll never marry you. You're not worthy of her."

"You believe you are?"

"Yes, and not too long ago she thought so too."

Camellia cringed. Only a few weeks ago she had still hoped to marry Trenton. But those days seemed so long ago, and now she wondered what she had ever seen in the hateful man who now sat astride his horse before her. How could she have loved him? He was so vile, so brutish in spite of all his learning. What had happened to the good she used to see in him? Had all that disappeared? Or had it never been there in the first place?

She glanced back at Trenton, and his face seemed to soften. "Give me five minutes alone with her," he said to Josh, his voice easier. "I promise I won't do anything unseemly."

Josh turned to Camellia. "You want me to leave you with him?"

She started to say "Yes, what could it harm?" but then she saw an arrogant glint in Trenton's eyes, even as he tried to sound gentler. His mouth carried a hint of a leer, too, and she felt a dim tug of a memory, a touch of unpleasantness from her past. She tried to identify it but couldn't for a second. But then Trenton's horse took half a step her way, and the movement triggered a recollection of a moment she'd tried to keep pushed down, the memory of the day Trenton's father had advanced on her, the smell of his awful breath tainted by whiskey and cigar smoke. Marshall Tessier had died that day, cracked his head against a table as she had struggled against his crude efforts to have his way with her. For a long time she'd kept the manner of his death a secret. Now, however, Trenton knew because she'd told him the same day she'd refused his offer of marriage. Right now she saw the same arrogant look in Trenton that had showed up in his father's face as he'd grabbed her in the cookhouse. It was the look of a man who believed he could get whatever he wanted, no matter what he had to do to achieve it.

"I want you to stay," Camellia told Josh. "I don't believe I should be alone with Trenton right now."

Josh faced Trenton. "You should take your leave now," he said, keeping his voice even. "The lady doesn't want to converse with you."

Trenton looked past Josh to Camellia. His voice sounded soft again as he spoke, even kind, like he used to talk to her when they were sweethearts. "You know I still love you. You know we belong together."

Camellia's heart ached for Trenton; she wanted to help him. After all, they had spent so much time together as children at The Oak, swinging in the swing hanging from the branches of the oak in front of the manse, gathering shells on the beach at the ocean. At one time she'd dreamed of marrying him, dreamed of bearing his children, making him proud of her. Now he had lost half a leg in the duel with her pa, and although a doctor in Charleston had fashioned a wooden piece to attach to the stump, he still couldn't walk properly. Anyone with any heart at all would still feel compassion for him. And maybe she hadn't treated him as well as she should and shouldn't blame him for all of his anger. Perhaps she deserved part of it.

She stepped closer to him and looked up. "I'm sorry about all that's happened. I do care for you—always will, please understand that. But I'm not with you now, will never be again. I've already said this to you; don't make me repeat it and hurt you more."

Trenton's eyes hooded over like a snake's. "OK!" he snapped. "You give me no choice!"

Camellia tensed. What did he mean? Trenton Tessier had a violent temper and refused to overlook any slight, real or imagined, to his honor. She glanced at Josh and realized he carried no weapon. What if Trenton had brought a pistol?

Trenton edged his horse nearer, and its massive shoulders brushed against Josh. For a second Camellia thought that Trenton might charge right over Josh and crush him where he stood, but Josh held his ground in spite of his frailty. Camellia marveled at his courage.

"I want you off The Oak!" Trenton commanded Josh. "By the end of tomorrow!" He spat out the words like they were rotten meat.

"But he's still weak!" protested Camellia, stepping closer to Trenton's horse. "In no shape to travel."

Josh held out his arm and blocked her advance.

"His health is no worry of mine," growled Trenton. "He goes by tomorrow night, or I'll have the sheriff in Beaufort come for him."

"But where will he go?"

Trenton laughed. "What do I care?"

"But you can't do this!" Camellia shouted.

"Stand back, Camellia," Josh said. "This is between Trenton and me."

Trenton ignored Josh and faced Camellia again, his face a grim leer. "Why can't I do it?"

Camellia started to threaten him with something, anything, but she had no weapon, nothing to make him change his mind, nothing except . . . but she couldn't do that, couldn't offer the one thing he wanted—her own life and love. She wondered for a second whether that would make any difference. What if she did agree to go back to him, marry him? Did he really want her because he loved her or because he knew he couldn't have her, because another man had claimed her affections? She didn't know. But would he leave Josh alone if she said she'd return to him?

"Tomorrow night!" insisted Trenton, pointing at Josh. "Be gone from here. That's an order." He spurred his horse, turned it, and galloped back toward The Oak.

Camellia grabbed Josh's hand and faced him. "He can't make you leave!" she cried. "The sheriff won't listen to him. He knows what kind of man you are."

"Trenton owns this place. It's his right to put me off if he wants."

"I'll take this to Pa!"

Josh shook his head. "That'll just cause more problems between your pa and Trenton—Mrs. Tessier too. They don't need any more troubles, you know that."

Camellia wiped her eyes. "But what about Beth and Butler? You'll have to move them too, upset their lives. Where will you go?"

He paused for a second. "I'm not sure . . . maybe down to Hilton Head. I know a man there who grows cotton. He's offered me a job in the past. I planned to leave here anyway. You know that, before the duel. Maybe my friend can still use me. With so many men already gone to war, he'll probably snatch me right up, no matter that I'm not much count right now."

Camellia wrung her hands. How could this be happening? It made no sense—the duel, the war, now this. "What will this mean for us?"

"I cannot say right now. But I can assure you of this: no matter what happens, our love will endure. I'm certain of that. You are too."

"I grieve this day."

"Better days will come," he assured her. "I'll take a job, heal some more, then come back and ask your pa for your hand."

"But what if he's at war?"

"It won't matter. I will marry you. I make that pledge to you before God as I stand here right now. Nothing will keep me from it."

"But when will that be?" she asked. "I don't want to wait."

"Soon," said Josh. "Very soon."

Camellia's eyes watered.

"I need to ask you one favor."

"Anything."

"I need you to keep Beth and Butler here until I can get settled. Can you do that for me?"

"Of course I can—whatever you want."

"I'll come for you by the end of the summer, and we'll be wed by winter."

"I pray that's true."

Josh smiled and took her chin gently in his hands. As he kissed her for the first time, a flood of joy greater than any she'd ever known rushed through her.

But then she remembered . . .

Before sunset tomorrow, Josh would leave. A deep grief stained her joy. What cruel act of fate caused such an awful mix of feelings to happen? Joy in one moment—and agonizing hurt in the next?

As Josh wrapped his arms around her back and held her close, she closed her eyes and told herself she could wait until winter, when Josh would return to marry her. He'd just promised it, and everybody knew that Josh Cain kept his promises.

Standing by the Conwilla River, Camellia had no way of knowing that, this time, circumstances would make Josh Cain's promise impossible to keep.

Chapter Six

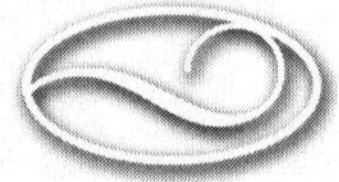

Camellia went to bed late that night but found it hard to go to sleep. Images from the day kept running through her head—Trenton on his horse telling Josh he had to leave; the big crowd gathering around the Episcopal pastor from Beaufort who stood between the columns on the front porch of the manse to say the words that made her pa and Mrs. Tessier husband and wife. The wedding had come off just fine, her pa and Mrs. Tessier wearing the finest clothes Charleston had to offer, their hands clasped in front of the preacher as serene as any two lovers anybody had ever seen. Josh had stood beside Camellia as the vows unfolded.

Now her heart raced as she realized this time tomorrow he'd be gone.

"It's so unfair," Camellia had told Ruby just before the wedding. "Josh and I love each other, but we can't be together. But Mrs. Tessier and Pa—who admit they're doing this for reasons that have little to do with love—get to wed right here and now before God and everybody."

"Don't talk to me about fair," said Ruby. "You think it fair I had to leave a boy back in Virginia, see my man sold off right before my eyes? You see anywhere that 'fair' is the way it's supposed to be, and I'm going to raise a ruckus like nobody ever heard before."

Unable to argue, Camellia let the matter drop, and the wedding went on as scheduled. Trenton never showed back up. His brother, Calvin, stood by his mother to give her away. A few people mumbled about Trenton's absence, but few said much. Best not to talk about a man as rich and mean as Trenton Tessier. Who knew what might get back to him?

After the ceremony the crowd danced some, drank, ate a lot, and generally spent the evening enjoying the lavish party. Although they all knew the war had started and some spoke of the latest news, in between conversation about the handsome Mr. York and beautiful Mrs. Katherine Tessier York, most seemed set on leaving the war out of the things for the present. Time enough for that later. Right now they had a celebration to enjoy—and the fine folks of lower South Carolina *did* know how to celebrate.

Camellia had talked to her pa for a few minutes several hours after the wedding, long after most of the crowd had begun to settle down for the night.

"Other than Josh, you are the most handsome man here," she had said.

He toed the ground with his shiny black boots, his eyes never looking at hers.

She touched his elbow. "Look, Pa, I want happiness for you—"

He held up a hand. "We both know this marriage ain't exactly a fairy tale. No reason to pretend otherwise."

"But you can grow to love each other. I've seen it happen."

He pulled a chew of tobacco from his pocket and stuck a wad into his cheek. "I'll be gone in a few days. Who knows what will occur then?"

She touched his chin, lifted his head so she could see into his eyes. He tried to look away, but she held his face steady. "You did your best with me. Whatever I am, good or bad, you had the biggest hand in shaping that."

"I don't see much bad." He paused, then added softly, "I appreciate the credit."

"What's to happen to all of us?" she asked, a deep sadness seeping into her bones. "The war, the bad blood still between you and Trenton, him and Josh."

York spat to the ground. "I got the same fears. For you, mostly. Me and Josh can fend for ourselves, but who's goin' to watch out for you?"

"I can take care of myself," said Camellia. "You taught me that."

"Still . . ."

Silence came for several seconds. Then Camellia said, "Trenton told Josh to leave The Oak."

"What?"

"Trenton came here today, found me and Josh. Told Josh he had to be gone by tomorrow night."

"Why?"

"I think you know why."

York's fists bunched.

"Josh is going to Hilton Head," Camellia said. "Thinks he can find work there. When he's settled, he's going to send for me, and I'm going to go. Thought you needed to know this before you leave."

York stuck his fists in his pockets. "I feared somethin' like this. But didn't expect it so soon." He faced Camellia, his eyes stern. "You need to leave here. I already told you. If you won't go to your folks in Richmond, go to Beaufort. I'll get you a room at an inn there."

"I can't," she insisted.

"Why not?"

"Josh asked me to watch out for Beth and Butler until he's set. I can't leave them."

"You can take them with you."

"An inn is no place for a couple of kids," she said.

"Just do it," argued York.

"I don't know. I'll need to talk to Josh."

"Make him understand this is the safest thing."

Camellia stared at her pa, wanting to make him feel better. But she didn't know how.

"Trenton might do you harm," he said. "He already tried to hurt Josh."

"What?"

"Several days ago he came after Josh. I stopped him before he could do any harm. He said if he couldn't have you, nobody would. He's just desperate enough to do somethin' real bad."

Camellia waved away her pa's fears. "Trenton would never hurt me. He's mean sometimes, but his heart isn't that far gone. You don't need to worry about that."

York sighed. "Maybe you're right, but I don't know. He seems real dangerous lately."

"He's just mad," said Camellia. "You can understand his feelings, the hand he's been dealt."

It was obvious from York's face that he still wasn't convinced. Camellia touched his arm. "You go on to Charleston with your bride.

Enjoy the days you've got before you go off to war. When you get back, we'll figure out what to do about Beth and Butler. I'll keep my eye on Trenton. If he tries to pull anything, I'll get Obadiah to take care of me."

"I still feel like I need to do somethin' before I go."

"You've done all you can."

York nodded, then walked away. After the rest of the evening passed, Josh walked her back to her house. He kissed her lightly again, then left her. She fell quickly into bed, exhausted and anxious. But she couldn't sleep since so many thoughts were swirling in her head.

When her thoughts finally slowed, Camellia fell asleep. But her slumber wasn't restful. Her body never quite settled, and her dreams weighed heavy with dark images of troubles she couldn't completely see in the shadows. Clouds moved in and out beyond her bedroom window, obscuring the moon one minute and turning it loose in the next. Camellia rolled over in the bed and moaned slightly, her body damp with perspiration from the moist air that drifted in through the open window. As the night passed, her dreams took on more shape, and images that had appeared vague now took form. Josh began to appear over and over in the dreams, his face still thin from his wounds, his body wrapped with a bloody bandage. Trenton stood over him, his black horse appearing larger than a train engine, its wide nostrils blowing steam in and out. A pistol floated in the air before Josh's face. As a bullet fired from it and plunged into the front of his shirt, she jerked in her sleep and awoke, her body trembling.

Taking a deep breath, she pulled up to a sitting position and hugged her knees to her chest. Her nightgown stuck to her back with sweat, and she wiped her hair from her face. Unaccustomed to such vivid dreams, she held her breath for a second, wondering if what she'd seen reflected had already happened or still waited for her and Josh in the days ahead. Shivering, she pulled the covers closer and tried to forget the images she'd seen.

A thump sounded on the back porch and she froze. What in the world? She thought of her little brother, Johnny, and wondered if he'd gotten up and gone outside for some reason. She started to get up and light a lamp, but then everything fell quiet again. After straining her ears for almost a minute, she sighed in relief, lay back down, and closed her eyes. Again she couldn't get settled—too many worries bounced around in her head. Fears about Josh leaving; worries about the war and what it might mean; questions about her ma and pa in Richmond. How could she sleep? Her whole life lay straight ahead—she knew exactly what she wanted but not how to reach it. She and Josh loved each other; they both knew it now. But it seemed that everybody and everything seemed bent on keeping the two of them apart.

Tucking the sheet up under her chin, she tried to push away her nervousness. *Let God take care of it,* she reminded herself. *Nothing to gain by fretting too much.*

Another thump from the back porch broke the quiet, and Camellia sat half up, her ears bent toward her open window trying to hear. The sound of whispers drifted into her room. She stayed still and tried to listen. It sounded like . . . no . . . she couldn't tell. The voices weren't recognizable. Again she waited. Footsteps scraped on the back porch, then she heard the back door open.

Easing quickly off the bed, Camellia grabbed a robe from a chair, slipped it on, and moved toward the door. The door suddenly opened inward, knocking her against the wall in the dark. She pushed the door back, but somebody much stronger than her held it in place. Crying out in the dark, she squinted to see the person behind the door but couldn't. From her left a large hand grabbed her by the elbow and pulled her out of the corner. She scratched at the hand and caught flesh, her nails raking across the top from wrist to fingers. Her attacker grunted in pain but then grabbed her by the shoulders and roughly spun her into the center of the bedroom, her back to him, his wide body holding her close. She kicked backward with her foot and hit the man's shin, but it didn't slow him much. Suddenly she felt somebody else in the room—a smaller presence but one perhaps equally as dangerous, if not more so, than the man.

"Hold her still!" hissed a woman's voice. "You're treating her like she's breakable."

"I won't hurt her!" the man said. "I told you that."

Camellia instantly recognized the voices but had a hard time believing it. Why would they do this?

The woman's hands moved toward Camellia's face as she fought against the man's hold but couldn't break it. In the woman's hands was a cloth that smelled slightly odd. Camellia tried to spin away from the cloth, but the man's strength was too great. His large hands squeezed her upper arms like a vise grip holding a wagon wheel. The cloth covered her nose now, and the strange smell clogged her mouth and face. She fought as hard as she could, but it did no good. Still confused, Camellia's mind drifted away toward the dark, and although she wanted to continue to fight, her body didn't cooperate. The dark reached out to grab her . . . and then took over.

As soon as Camellia sagged into the man's arms, he picked her up, carried her to the bed, and laid her down. Then he bent over her and took a deep breath. "I hope we didn't hurt her."

"She's the one who put up the fight," argued the woman from behind him. "Her choice, not ours."

"She scratched me pretty good," he said, his tone almost admiring. "Kicked me in the shin right hard."

"Nobody ever said she didn't have some spark in her."

The man moved to the table by the bed, put a match to the lamp, and set the wick. A dull yellow glow covered the bedroom. He held up his hand to the lamp and saw a light streak of blood on the back of it. He wiped the blood on his pants, then faced the woman again. "How long will the chloroform keep her out?"

"Not sure," the woman answered. "I'm no expert with matters like these."

"It won't do her any permanent harm, though, right? That's what you said."

"I've seen it used," said the woman. "We didn't give her much."

The man looked back to Camellia. "You sure this is the best thing?"

"You brought the idea to me, remember?"

The man pulled a chew of tobacco from his back pocket and stuck it in his jaw. "We need to get her away from here. For her good and everybody else's."

"That's the way I see it."

"She'll be safer somewhere else."

"Richmond, like we agreed. Sharpton Hillard will take her. He's already told me he would."

"This will protect her from Trenton. He swore he'd not let them marry."

The woman laughed. "You're protecting yourself as much as her. If Trenton hurts her, it would cause us all kinds of problems."

"I would have to kill him this time. If he hurt her or Josh either, you know that. It'd be the only honorable thing."

"I wouldn't think well of you if you killed my son, Mr. York."

"And I see no reason for Camellia to deal with the hardships of the war, Mrs. York. Richmond will be safe, and she can meet her real folks. She deserves that."

"Trenton won't be able to get to her if she's in Richmond," said Mrs. York. "That's best for him too. He's mad right now, but if she's gone, maybe he can put her out of his head."

"We'll send Ruby with her," said York. "She'll need a companion for such a journey. Stella will take care of Josh's kids. I can't leave them here all alone. That wouldn't be right."

"You're a good man," said Mrs. York.

"Camellia can come back later," said York, trying to convince himself he'd done the right thing. "After Trenton heals some more, has time to settle."

Mrs. York stepped to the small chest of drawers across from Camellia's bed. "We need to get moving. Get her packed. Morning will be here in an hour or so."

"I need her gone before Josh finds out. I'll tell him about Trenton's threats and say she decided to go to Richmond but didn't want to see him before she left because she feared she'd change her mind if she did."

"You'd lie to your brother?"

"It's for his good. Camellia's too."

"You're a practical man. I like that," she replied.

"Hillard will meet us by the river," York explained. "He's got a carriage ready. He'll give her chloroform every couple of hours to keep her under until he's far enough away that she can't run."

"I'm a little surprised he agreed to this."

"He said it didn't matter to him how he got her; he got paid to bring her back. Just so we didn't hurt her."

Mrs. York touched the back of his head. "It's the right thing. Send her on this journey and give Trenton time to grow up. When she comes back, who knows? Maybe she won't still hate him so. Maybe she'll see what a good man he is. Maybe . . ."

York turned to her, his face puzzled. "You still hopin' her and Trenton will end up together?"

Mrs. York shrugged. "I don't know what I'm hoping. All I know is that sometimes life takes us on some fateful journeys. Lots of things happen to us on them, things that change us. Who knows what will happen when those journeys end and we come home again?"

"You figure maybe Josh will die in the war," he said matter-of-factly. "And Trenton might not."

"Men do die. War or not."

"Reckon so."

"Not you, though," she stated firmly. "You're the kind of man who always comes home. I expect that, you know. I need you."

He smiled. "You don't need any man. And you don't even love me."

She played her fingers through his hair. "I might not love you. But still . . . you are a handsome man and, well . . . my husband died going on three years ago. That's a long time."

He turned and took her hands in his. "Let's get Camellia ready. Then I'll see to makin' you forget that dead husband of yours."

"Don't you worry any," she said. "I forgot him long before he was even dead."

Chapter Seven

Josh woke before daybreak the next morning, his body a little stronger than the previous day. After washing up at a basin in the kitchen, he woke Beth and Butler. While Beth put on some coffee, Josh hauled out some ham and biscuits. Within minutes they were eating. Josh's eyes glistened as he watched them. In just a few hours, he'd take his leave of his girl and boy—Beth thirteen now and Butler ten. Beth looked like her mama, dead now for two years. She had brown eyes and a thin but attractive face. Although not yet completely rounded out into womanhood, the first signs of it had begun to appear. He glanced at Butler, more like him in appearance, blond and broad. Both kids munched their biscuits, neither of them aware that today their lives would take a turn they had never expected. Josh hated that they lived in such a rough world.

Josh swallowed hard; his appetite had disappeared. Setting his biscuit on his plate, he cleared his throat. Beth and Butler looked up. "I got some news," he said, gazing from one to the other of his children. He wanted to drink in the sight of their faces, while he still could. He would miss them sorely.

"You finally ask Miss Camellia to wed you?" asked Beth, her eyes happy with the idea.

Josh smiled at her. "You think you're so smart, don't you?"

"I know a thing or two. Know how Miss Camellia stayed with you while you were sick, how you've talked to each other a lot in the last few days."

"Well, I do love her, that's true. And we've recently talked of marriage. Will it be OK with you two if I ask Captain York for her hand?"

"That'll be good," said Butler. "She reads to us and cooks better than you or Beth."

"You don't look like you're going hungry," teased Josh.

"When will you wed her?" asked Beth, obviously wanting to keep the talk on track.

Josh propped his elbows on the table. "That's the bad news part. I need some time to settle some things before then."

"What kind of things?"

Josh looked from Beth to Butler, trying to figure how to tell them he was leaving. "You remember back before I got shot—that I planned to move us from here."

"Yep," said Beth.

"Well, I still need to do that. Only you two won't go with me just yet."

"But why, Pa?" asked Beth. "You and Miss Camellia love each other. Why go now?"

"Well . . ." He hesitated, then decided to tell the truth. "You know Master Tessier shot me."

"An accident," said Butler.

"True, but well . . . he's got no care for me. He told me yesterday he wants me off The Oak. Since it's his place, I have to do what he says."

Beth and Butler fell into a stunned silence for several seconds. It was Beth who recovered first. "You figured to take us to Texas before; you going to Texas now?"

"No, not that far this time. Just down to Hilton Head. I can get work there. I'll get settled, then send for you both—Miss Camellia too."

"When?" asked Butler.

"By the end of the summer. Miss Camellia will take care of you until then, and Stella will help."

"We'll do what they tell us," said Butler.

"I know you will."

"You goin' to war?" asked Beth, her eyes suddenly scared.

Josh picked up his coffee and took a sip. He didn't want to lie to his children but didn't want to scare them either. "I don't know. I'm not strong yet. Hope the war ends before I am."

"Who'll take care of us if you go to war?" she asked.

"Still Camellia and Stella."

"Ruby says the Yankees will win the war," said Butler. "You believe she's right?"

"No way to tell. But I don't want you worrying about that. You'll be with me long before the Yankees get here."

A knock sounded at the door, and Beth jumped to get it. A few seconds later, she came back in with York behind her. York's face looked dark. "You got a minute?" he asked Josh.

"We OK with things?" Josh asked Beth and Butler. They nodded, and he left the table and followed York out to the front porch. "What's going on?"

York spat into the yard. "Camellia left this mornin' for Richmond."

Josh felt like somebody had hit him in the stomach with a shovel.

"She wanted to tell you face to face but didn't think she could without changin' her mind, so she decided to just go. Let me break the news."

Josh's eyes narrowed. He knew something didn't add up. Camellia had promised she'd care for Beth and Butler, and it wasn't like her to break a promise. Of course he wanted her to meet her real folks, figured she needed to do that. But this announcement from York smelled peculiar. "She left awfully early," he said, keeping his suspicions quiet.

"She wanted to leave before anybody awoke."

"She with Hillard?"

"Yep, I sent Ruby with her."

"That's generous of you."

York shrugged. "Stella will look after your kids. Camellia asked me to make sure of that."

"I'd like to have seen Camellia before she left," said Josh.

York pulled an envelope from his back pocket. "She left this for you," he said, handing the envelope to Josh.

Josh carefully opened the envelope and pulled out the single sheet of paper in it. A note covered a third of the page.

Dear Josh,

I changed my mind and will go to Richmond. Stella will look after Beth and Butler. Hope you understand why I didn't see you before I left. I'll come back as soon as possible. I'll pray for you every day until I see you again.

Love,
Camellia

"She has neat penmanship," Josh said as he folded the letter and put it back in the envelope. "Much improved since I last saw it."

"You and Ruby taught her," said York. "Not me."

Josh tucked the letter in his pocket, his fears confirmed by the handwriting that he knew wasn't Camellia's. "I guess we're all leaving. Camellia to Richmond, me to Hilton Head, you to Charleston and then to war. It might be a long time before we all return, if ever."

York took off his hat and stared into it, as if looking for the answer to all the riddles of the world. "I'm sorry for what Trenton did to you. You took a bullet meant for me. I never thanked you for that, but I'm doin' it now."

"You're my brother," said Josh. "You'd do the same for me."

"I'd like to think I would, but I'm not so sure. I'm not a good man. You know that."

Josh moved to York and put a hand on his shoulder. York looked up.

"You're a good man some of the time," Josh said. "Just like me, just like all men. Sometimes you're bad; sometimes you're good."

"I reckon my good times come less often than yours, and my bad times last longer. That's the difference in us."

"I've asked the Lord to forgive me my bad times. That's the biggest difference I see."

"You're bein' humble."

Josh sighed. He and York didn't often talk this honestly.

"Why you reckon our pa didn't marry my mama?" asked York, suddenly changing the subject and going in a direction he'd never touched with Josh. "But did marry yours?"

Josh paused, surprised by the question. It wasn't like York to look too much into the past. "I don't know. I never knew him much. He died when I was so young. All I know is he loved your mama, stayed with her until she died. That says something, don't you think?"

"I was the bastard child," said York. "People saw me that way. The other kids said it to my face. I swore way back then that I'd make somethin' of myself, that I'd do whatever it took, good or bad, to improve my station, lift up my name until it became one that mattered. Guess I've lived my whole life with that as my only real strivin'—to become somethin' other than the child of a man that never married my mama and gave me his name."

"That's a heavy burden to carry," Josh put in. "One you ought to put down someday."

"Don't know that I can. It's part of me now, probably the biggest part. Made me who I am. Without that pushin' me, I don't know why I'm even livin'."

Josh took a full breath and stared out into the yard. He wanted to tell York that he ought to live to please the Lord; that a man ought to get up every day with that purpose in his heart. But he knew York had heard all that from him lots of times and had said more than once he should keep his religious talk to himself.

"I wish we were goin' to war together," said York. "Like when we were young and went to Mexico."

"I'd prefer no war at all."

"Yep, well, it seems that wars have a way of springin' up on us pretty often."

"I don't like this one. Not sure I see much reason for it."

"You don't think the South has the right of secession?"

"Not if keeping the servants is the result of it."

"That's not a regular view for a man raised in the South," York stated. "But I figured you for it anyway. You always been soft toward the blacks."

"My mama taught me to treat all folks alike," claimed Josh.

"You reckon the blacks the same as you and me?"

"They're people, aren't they?"

York shrugged.

"I see them that way," continued Josh. "So I got no choice but to think what we do to them is wrong, not the Lord's will. A black man is the same as me, no better or worse either way."

"You'll fight, though, won't you?"

"I'm praying it will end before I'm well enough to face that question."

York spat and put his hat back on. "Well, I reckon it's time to go."

Josh nodded, but his heart felt heavy. He didn't want to leave York with bad feelings hanging between them, and he sensed York's disappointment in his weak support for the Southern cause. Plus York still felt harsh against him for his decision to leave The Oak. Yet, what could he do? Situations didn't always allow people, even brothers, to settle things like they ought. He turned to York. "You take care of yourself."

York faced him, his jaw determined. "You don't have to go to Hilton Head. You can come with me to Charleston. I'll provide for you until you get better, then you can join my unit."

"Thanks for the offer, but I suspect not. I'm a grown man, can't depend on my big brother to care for me all my life. "

"Have it your way, then."

Josh put a hand on York's shoulder. "You're my brother. I'll pray for you."

York grinned. "I'll take all the prayers I can get."

"I love Camellia," said Josh.

"I know you do. And if somethin' happens to me . . . well . . . take care of her."

"If something happens to me, you take care of Beth and Butler."

"I'll leave that to Camellia. She'll do better with them than me."

"That's for sure."

They both laughed, and silence fell for several seconds.

Then York said, "I need to confess somethin' before you go. Camellia didn't leave of her own choice."

"Really?" Josh tried to make it sound like he was surprised.

"It ain't good for me to lie to you, not when we don't know when we'll see each other again. But, well, I took her off this mornin' against her wishes."

"I figured something of the sort," Josh said. "She didn't write that note you gave me."

"You knew already?"

Josh nodded.

"Why didn't you say somethin'?"

"What good would that do? I knew if you wanted to tell me, you would."

"Yep, well, I did her no harm."

"I know you wouldn't."

"But Trenton might, and with you gone, I figured I had to get her away. I hope you understand."

"You did the right thing," said Josh, admitting out loud what he'd already concluded. "Trenton is a dangerous man."

"Hillard gave me an address where she can get letters. You can write her after you get settled." York handed Josh a piece of paper with the name and street of a hotel on it.

"Thanks."

"Watch yourself, little brother," York said.

"Thanks for telling me the truth."

"I got a lot layin' on my conscience. Figured I didn't need no lie against you added to it, especially since I'll have men tryin' to kill me real soon."

"Hard for a man to walk carrying the load you got on your back."

"You said you'd pray for me."

"You don't care much for religion."

"It's true I ain't usually partial to it, but you never know what might help." York grinned.

Josh stepped to York and took his hand, then threw an arm around his shoulder. York patted his brother's back before he pulled away. "Keep your head low."

"You're the one going to war," Josh fired back.

York spat into the yard, then pivoted and walked off the porch, his broad shoulders set squarely as he strode away.

Chapter Eight

Camellia awoke with a start, her head bumping against the back of a leather carriage seat. Her mouth tasted terrible, and a dull ache pounded at the base of her skull. Rubbing her grainy eyes, she sat up straight and licked her dry lips. Ruby sat across from her, Sharpton Hillard beside her. Camellia looked down. She wore a light brown cotton dress with a white collar up to her neck and black buckled shoes. Her hair lay full but combed on her shoulders. A hot sun baked in through the open carriage window to her right, and the angle of the light told her the time was close to midday.

"Where am I?" Camellia asked, her face a mask of confusion spiced with anger.

"You're about half a day's ride from The Oak," said Hillard. "Headed to Richmond."

"You kidnapped me?"

Hillard shook his head. "Captain York and Mrs. York delivered you to me. They figured this was best for you in the long run."

"But they know I didn't want to leave The Oak." Camellia's wrath rose sharply. "I won't abide this. Turn the carriage around!"

Hillard shrugged. "I'm afraid not. Mr. and Mrs. Swanson paid me to find you and bring you back; offered a bonus for the 'bring you back' part. So we're going north."

"But this is a crime!" said Camellia. "I'm a grown woman!"

"Have us all arrested," Sharpton stated calmly.

Camellia bit her lip and for the first time really took a good look at the man who'd first shown up on The Oak back in November of 1859 and shaken things up so much. He wasn't a lot taller than a hoe handle and just about as thin. His nose looked a little off-center from his brown eyes, like somebody had stuck it on without much reference to the rest of his face. His hair, mostly hidden under a black derby hat, matched his eyes. From what she knew about him, he had a lot of snapping turtle in him—once he got his bite into something, he didn't let go too easily.

"What's all this to you?" she asked. "Why so determined?"

"I get paid," he said. "Well, too, I might add."

Her eyes narrowed. Camellia turned to Ruby. "You in on this too?"

"Captain York woke me before first light," Ruby explained. "Told me to pack my things, I had a trip coming. I told him I had no plans to go anywhere, but you know how it is. The captain gives an order, and no darky can say no to it."

"But you know I can't leave Josh, Beth, and Butler."

"I did as I was told," Ruby retorted. "What choice did I have?"

Camellia knew Ruby was right—slaves followed orders. She couldn't blame Ruby for this.

Hillard handed Camellia a canteen, the top already off. "Water. I expect you're thirsty."

Although her throat felt parched, Camellia refused the canteen and glanced out the carriage window, her anger burning. Measuring the distance to the door, she suddenly lurched toward it, her hands grabbing for the handle and pushing it open. Hillard grabbed her from behind, but she kicked him in the stomach. He grunted but lunged at her again, this time clutching her by the waist. She reached for the open door and tried to jump from the carriage, but Hillard had a firm grip on her and hauled her back inside. She turned and bit his hand, her teeth digging into his flesh.

The carriage lurched to the side as their weight shifted, but it kept going.

Hillard grabbed Camellia by the ankles and pulled her hard toward the seat. Camellia fought as hard as she could, every ounce of energy struggling against the notion of leaving Josh, of breaking her promise to care for Beth and Butler. Hillard held on tightly, though, and with her head still hurting from the chloroform, Camellia's strength soon ran out. Grunting, she fought for another minute, but Hillard kept her clamped down. Finally she gave up and lay flat on the seat, her breath coming in gasps.

Hillard slammed the door and took his seat again. Camellia stared at him, her eyes smoldering. He offered her the canteen again, and this time, though still furious, she jerked it from his hands and drank deeply. When finished, she capped it, handed it back to Hillard, and turned toward Ruby.

"I expect you're more than happy to head north," Camellia accused, mad at Ruby for not helping her escape.

"Didn't hurt my heart too much, I'll say that plainly," Ruby said, smoothing down her plain dress.

Camellia steamed for a second at her friend's betrayal. Ruby had come to The Oak from a plantation about a day's ride from Richmond. A plantation owner had died, and his wife had sold some of their Negroes to raise cash to pay off a bank note. Although Camellia didn't know for sure, chances were that Ruby's boy, Theo, still lived on the plantation that had sold her. As Camellia gradually caught her breath, she realized that Ruby might just consider this trip her big chance to go find him.

"You figure you'll run off, don't you?" she asked Ruby. "That's why you didn't fight the idea of taking this trip."

Ruby stared at her shoes, plain brown brogans. "I expect I'll keep any notions like that to myself."

"But you've told me Theo's got the power of vision, and he saw you coming back for him. You'll try to make that vision come true."

"Only time will tell," Ruby replied. "No reason to worry about that right now. We're taking you to your ma and pa, like Captain York told us to. That's what matters right now."

Confusion flickered in Camellia's brain. How much did Ruby know about the situation with Trenton? Did she really care about Camellia's safety? Or was she just a slave who had to follow the captain's orders?

Ruby had fled The Oak once before to find her man, Markus, at another plantation. But she had returned, empty-handed, to The Oak. Fortunately for her, Camellia's father had been away at the time, and Josh Cain—in charge in her father's absence—had forgone the usual severe consequences for slaves who ran. Josh had let her off with a warning but told her he wouldn't be able to protect her from a whipping if she ever ran again.

"What about Obadiah? You just up and leave him without a fight?" Camellia asked, calming some.

"He was there when Captain York woke me this morning. He knows I had to obey the captain." Ruby's tone was flat, but Camellia heard the hidden anger in it.

"Does Obadiah know you're going to run again?"

Camellia thought about Obadiah, a man she'd known as long as she could remember. Over forty years old, Obadiah had gotten his freedom papers the year his pa—a white shipbuilder from Savannah—died. That happened every now and again: a white man who sired children by a slave woman would let his offspring go free once he had passed on. Obadiah's pa had left it in his will that his mixed children would receive twenty acres of land, fifty dollars in cash, and papers of freedom ten days after he died. Nineteen at the time, Obadiah had immediately left Savannah, moved to his property outside of Beaufort, and started building coffins. Working hard, he'd soon become one of the richest black men in the county. He was a caring, loving man too. He'd helped Camellia when her brother, Chester, had died of the fever. He didn't deserve to have Ruby just up and disappear on him, if that's what she was planning.

Ruby paused, her casual demeanor suddenly gone. "Obadiah knows I love him. But he also knows I had a man before him, had me a boy by that man."

"Do you plan to go back to him if you find your boy?" asked Hillard.

"Don't rightly know. Haven't thought that far ahead yet."

Camellia's irritation with Ruby rose again. "Do you think you can just waltz back to your old plantation and take Theo? Even if you can, what happens next? Are you going to Canada with him—and leaving Obadiah forever?"

Ruby rubbed her eyes. "Obadiah's a fine man. Handsome too, big as an ox. And he's treated me well, so it's hard to consider anything that might take me from him."

"You're risking all that if you run," Camellia warned.

"He gave me presents, even before I showed him any favor," Ruby said quietly. "I remember once he rode over to see me seven Sundays in a row and brought me a pretty thing every time—a red ribbon one week, a piece of mint candy another, a small hand mirror on a third. The man's got a good heart, that's for sure."

Camellia nodded and recalled Obadiah and Ruby's courting days . . .

Obadiah had courted Ruby for months before she yielded to his charms. They'd married in August of 1859, their nuptials a simple matter under a canopy of thick oaks behind the servants' houses. Trenton had given permission for it after Camellia convinced him of its merit.

When his work allowed, Obadiah stayed with Ruby in the back room of her house. And when he couldn't, he picked her up in his buggy on Saturday and drove her to his place, a four-room white house with two glass windows on the front, a small spot for a garden out back, and two red rugs that he'd bought from a dead man's widow in the main room. Camellia had visited his house with her pa once when she was a child. Obadiah had cabinets in his kitchen that covered one wall from floor to ceiling. Smooth arches ran across the cabinet tops and finely cut figures of men and women in all manner of dress and doing all sorts of labor decorated the sides and fronts. The figures included white folks and black. Some were chopping wood; some were cooking; some riding horses.

Camellia had carefully studied the wood, then asked her pa, who stood by her in Obadiah's kitchen, who the figures were.

"It's everybody he's ever cut a box for," York explained. "Black and white cut in the same wood."

Camellia had been fascinated.

"Nobody tells Obadiah what to do," said Ruby, pulling Camellia back to the present. "He's a worthy mate. True, like all free people of color, he still can't leave the county without a pass from the sheriff, and he can't buy property without special permission. But he still lives a life a lot better than mine, and marrying him made my station easier. I don't want to lose all that, but I'll give it up if finding Theo calls for it."

Camellia winced. If it were her boy—if she had birthed a son and then been separated from him—would she do things any differently? Camellia turned to Hillard. "Will you stop her if she runs?"

"It's not my place to interfere," said Hillard. "I'm taking you to the Swansons. That's my duty, pure and simple."

"Your speech sounds like a Yankee," said Camellia. "I figured you had Union sympathies. You're from Washington before Richmond."

"I've made that no secret. Once I deliver you to the Swansons, I will resign my position with them and head north."

Camellia faced Ruby again. "You don't belong to me. Once we get to Richmond, you're on your own. Stay or go; it's up to you."

"You better keep quiet," Ruby whispered. "Talking such things as that out loud could cause you lots of troubles."

Camellia cocked her head to listen. But the horses' hooves were so noisy that the driver of the carriage would never be able to overhear their words. "Who's going to hear me? Not the driver. And Mr. Hillard's already made his sympathies known."

Ruby eyed Camellia. "You sure about what you just said?"

"You choose once we get there, that's all I'm saying. But just remember that once you run, there's no turning back."

"You figure you can get by without me?" Ruby asked.

"I don't know what I can do. But I don't plan to stay in Richmond long." Camellia turned to Hillard. "Are we going all the way by carriage?"

"We'll take a train if you'll promise you won't try to run again. That'll make things a lot easier and faster."

Camellia hated the idea of giving up, but she knew she was trapped. Even if she managed to escape, how would she get home without money, a carriage? "I promise," she finally said. "I'll stay put until Richmond."

"Good. We'll go to Columbia and catch a train there. Be in Richmond in a couple of days."

Resigned to her fate for the moment, Camellia relaxed a bit. "Tell me about Wallace and Ruth Swanson."

"They're prominent citizens," Hillard said. "Own a hotel, a general store, several other things. I met them back in Washington a couple of years back, have worked for Mr. Swanson since."

"Why do they want to see me after all these years?"

"You'll need to ask them that."

"They know about Chester's death?"

"I have informed them, most regretfully."

"Why didn't they come south if they wanted to see me and Chester so badly?"

"That's another excellent question to ask when you meet them."

Camellia leaned back. Although she planned to leave as soon as she could, she had to admit to a certain curiosity about the folks who had birthed her. Maybe a short stay wouldn't be too bad. She'd meet them, see what awful people they were, then head back to take care of Beth and Butler. Soon after that Josh would come for her. She'd marry him and put this unfortunate episode out of her mind.

Part Two

So it will be the duty of some to prepare for a separation;

Amicably if they can, violently if they must.

—JOSIAH QUINCY

Chapter Nine

Still slowed by his weakened condition, it took Josh Cain most of two days to make his way on horseback to Hilton Head. He stopped in Beaufort at the end of the first day, and that stop scared him a lot. The whole town was fired to high heat with war preparations. People talked all at once in the square, soldiers came and went in all directions, and the newspaper screamed headlines of Lincoln's terrible doings. Josh had never seen the place so busy or occupied by so many people.

Rumors spread like flies in the summer, this person saying this and another suggesting that. Of all the talk he heard, the story that bothered him the most said that the Yankees planned to send ships to the South as soon as they could to bottle up the trading that passed in and out of the Southern ports, particularly Charleston, Savannah, and Beaufort. Although most folks figured Charleston or Savannah would get attacked first, Josh didn't feel so confident about that. Larger towns than Beaufort, Charleston and Savannah would surely take longer to defeat than a smaller place like Beaufort. But, from what he knew of the harbor area, a Yankee fleet stationed at Beaufort could control the waterways in and out of the whole Southern coast. A smart military leader would surely see that—take the easiest, least defended port first, and control the larger, more fortified ones from there.

After spending a mostly sleepless night in a small inn not far from the Beaufort River, Josh got up early and headed on to Hilton Head, taking a couple of ferries across the Broad River and Skull Creek to finally reach the island. A strong wind blew in off the ocean as he crossed, and a steady sun beat down. Once on the island, he mounted his horse again and arrived at the White Sands Plantation about midafternoon, his body tired from the effort. A flat-faced darky who looked close to fifteen years his senior, with shoulders and a chest like a barrel, met him as he rode up to the front porch of the main house—a two-story with two columns and a wide porch painted a light brown. Thick green hedges grew right up to the edge of the house, and dense moss-covered oak shaded the yard. A hound dog raised his head and yawned at him as he reined his horse to a stop. The black ran down the steps and took his horse.

"I'm looking for Boss Spade," said Josh, wiping sweat off his face.

"He be down yonder," said the darky, pointing to his right. "A little white house by a well. You can't miss it."

"You'll take care of my horse?"

"For sure, he looks like a fine animal."

Josh smiled at the man, noticed his eyes, bright black and clear. "I'm Josh Cain," he said, suddenly extending his hand.

Although obviously surprised at Josh's directness, the darky took the hand. "Lester."

Josh looked Lester over. He stood a little shorter than Josh and had thick hands, a gray scraggly beard, and strong clean teeth. His pants barely reached his calves, and his shirt lay open and had no sleeves. A birthmark sat over his left eye, a milky patch of white shaped like a half moon.

"I'm looking for work," said Josh. "Any to be had here?"

Lester tilted his head. "Best talk to Boss Spade about that. Not a darky's place to say."

Josh nodded, then headed in the direction Lester had sent him. The White Sands looked about half the size of The Oak from what he could tell. The plantation had only one big barn, fewer servants running around, and not nearly as many livestock. He looked for the cotton fields as he walked but couldn't see them for all the trees. He found the well and the white house about a quarter mile from where he'd left his horse. The front door stood open, but not wanting to offend, Josh knocked.

"Come on in," yelled a man from inside.

Taking off his hat, Josh walked through. A short man of slender frame, who looked close to sixty years and wore a floppy straw hat, peered up from a small wood table, then immediately stood and headed his way, throwing out a round hand along with a big grin. "Josh Cain!"

"Good to see you, Mr. Spade," said Josh, taking the hand.

"Come on and have a seat."

Wearier than he'd realized, Josh took the spot Spade offered him, and Spade moved to his seat behind the small table.

"What in the world you doin' here?" asked Spade.

"Looking for a job," Josh explained. "You told me once you thought you could use me if I ever wanted to change from rice to cotton. Well, I'm ready to change."

Spade took off his hat, revealing a head covered only barely with wispy black hair, and dropped it on the table. "You not goin' off to fight?"

"Not just yet," said Josh, not wanting to say what had happened to him. "What about you?"

"I'm too valuable here," said Spade. "Least that's what I'm told. Master Sperry is already gone, a major in the South Carolina Twelfth Regiment. I got a boy that went with him. Sperry left me here to take care of things." He made the statement without bragging.

Josh crossed his legs, picked at the toe of a boot, and decided Spade deserved honest talk from him. "I'm not fit for fighting right now." He tapped his chest. "Took a bullet a little over a month ago."

Spade rocked back in his seat. "You know I got to ask you what happened."

Josh nodded. "Trenton Tessier and my brother, Hampton York—you've heard of them both—got in a duel. I tried to stop it. Trenton hit me instead of York."

"I hear Trenton's a hothead," said Spade, dropping his voice. "But that's between you and me."

"He's volatile, that's for sure. Anyway, he shot me. I'm better now but not recovered enough for a uniform."

"You strong enough to work?"

Josh grinned. "I won't cheat you. You give me a job, I'll get it done one way or the other."

Spade grinned back. "You got a reputation for doin' that."

"You think you can use me? I don't know that much about cotton, but I can learn. And if you don't need me for cotton, I do pretty well with buildings and things—tools too. Can keep the houses, barns, all of that in good order for you."

"Sure, I could use you," said Spade, "but they won't let me."

"What do you mean?" Josh suddenly felt afraid. If he didn't get a job here, where would he go?

"I guess you haven't heard. They're talkin' about buildin' a couple of forts down here—one on Hilton Head, just about a mile from here, and another maybe over on St. Helena's. It's not supposed to be told yet, but Mr. Sperry let me in on the news. In a few weeks I'm supposed to send off as many Negroes as I can spare to help them start up. They need as many hands as they can find, and I don't reckon anybody would appreciate it if I hired a new man when they're tellin' me to send all I can."

"But you'll need replacements," Josh reasoned. "The army will need cotton for clothes, and the Confederacy will need to sell it for money. How do they expect you to grow cotton without enough men to work the fields?"

Spade picked up his hat and put it back on. "Look," he said regretfully, "I've known you for goin' on six years, ever since we met in Beaufort at the general store. But I ain't allowed no new men right now, plain and simple. These forts are more important than my cotton. There's word out that the Yankees might come right at Beaufort, try to use it as a base for their fleet to blockade the Southern coast. Buildin' these forts is first order for these parts—cotton or not."

Josh picked at his boot again and recognized the truth of Spade's words. If the South lost the ability to ship its cotton, it didn't matter how much anybody grew. And if the Yankees took Beaufort and cut off the shipping lanes, the South couldn't get its cotton to market. "Anybody else hiring?" he asked. "There's a big place not far from here—Fish Haul. They need anybody?"

"They're in the same boat as me," said Spade. "You want work? You best go help build the forts. That would probably suit you better anyway. A man with your skills, practically an engineer from what I hear."

Josh waved him off, but Spade wouldn't let him. "No, I'm sayin' it true. You got a reputation as the best in the business. And I know how complicated rice dikes are . . . not just anybody can build them, keep them in order, all the dams and earthworks and such. I bet the army would snatch you up in a second; put you right to work on these forts."

"I don't know that I want to build a fort. I did my part in the army once. Didn't take that well to it."

"You in Mexico?" asked Spade.

"Yes."

"Me too," said Spade. "Ended up in Vera Cruz."

"Mexico City for me."

"War ain't as much fun as the young bucks think it is."

"No fun at all for me. I pray your boy will be all right."

"Least he's stayin' around here right now. Not headed up north yet."

"I hope he won't have to go far."

When Spade adjusted his hat, Josh knew the meeting had ended. He stood to go. "I appreciate seeing you."

"You go find a man named Olan Boggs. He's the engineer hired to head up the fort buildin'. Of course that's on the quiet. Nobody's sayin' anythin' out loud about any forts."

Josh nodded, understanding the need for secrecy. "Boggs on the island?"

"He comes and goes, gettin' things ready. He's got a place not far from Fish Haul. You head that way, you can't miss it. He'll turn up in a while if he ain't there just now."

Josh shook Spade's hand and headed for the door. Before he left he turned back one more time. "I got a couple of kids. A girl thirteen, a boy ten. They can work hard. I thought I'd bring them here after I got settled. You figure this to be a good spot for them if I take a job with Boggs?"

"I'd be glad for them to come here," said Spade. "But I got to say, I don't feel it's too safe. If the Yankees do come after Beaufort, this is the path they'll surely need to take."

"Thanks for your honesty."

"You're welcome."

"You know a place I can stay until I find work?"

"Just stay here. Tell Lester. He'll show you a spot in the barn."

"Much obliged."

"You take care."

Adjusting his hat against the sun, Josh left the house and headed to his horse. Not knowing what else to do, he figured he might as well try to find work with the crew working on the fort. At least that way he wouldn't be fighting. Better to build a fort to protect a man than to take up a gun to shoot one.

Just over a hundred miles up the coast in Charleston, Hampton York, dressed in the finest black suit, round collared shirt, and string tie the city's tailors had to offer, held out a high-backed leather chair for his new bride, then sat down beside her after she was situated. A long cherry-wood table stretched before them, and two men, equally well dressed, stared pleasantly at them across it. The Lady Katherine York, a white silk handkerchief in hand and a touch of rouge on her cheeks, almost looked pretty in the plush office and fine surroundings. Although York wanted a chew of tobacco, he knew not to cut off a wad. In a room as fancy as this, a man probably couldn't find a spittoon. He situated his hat, a new black one, on the table and smiled over at his bride. She covered her mouth with the handkerchief, but York thought he saw a pleased look behind it. At least for the first couple of days, their marriage had gone well. Who knew? Maybe they'd actually end up happy with each other.

He took his eyes from his new wife and focused on the two men across from him—Luther and Gerald, both of them bank officers with the Charleston City Bank and the husbands of Miranda and Martha, Katherine's two daughters. Luther and Gerald weren't the top men in the establishment, but they were high enough and connected enough to get done what he and the Lady York had decided to do—if they wanted to do it.

He studied the blank faces of Luther and Gerald. Thick muttonchops made Luther's jowly face look almost comical, but York knew that a no-nonsense head lay behind his face. Gerald had a chin that pointed sharply toward his neck, almost like a knife's blade. They both wore tan frock coats, black pants, boots, and white ruffled shirts.

"We are here at the request of Mrs. *Tessier*," said Gerald, always the more talkative of the two. "But these are busy times, as you surely know. What is the nature of this meeting?"

York heard the uppity tone in the man's question and noticed that he'd not called Katherine by her married name. If not for the fact that York had to act like a gentleman now that he had married into high society, he would have stood and slapped Gerald. But he stayed calm. He needed something from these two dunces, so who cared if Luther and Gerald looked down on him? A war tended to either make or break a man, York knew. So before this thing ended, highbrows like Gerald and Luther would probably end up with what they deserved.

"We have a business proposition for you," York began, trying to speak with as much refinement as he could muster. "One we believe will be beneficial to us both."

Gerald glanced at Luther and licked his lips. York wanted to wink at Katherine but didn't dare. Last night she'd told him plenty about Gerald and Luther. Although they were her sons-in-law, she described them both as the lazy offspring of two different wealthy banking families. Neither of them had earned his way to their positions. Preferring drinking, gambling, and social pursuits much more than any kind of real labor, they always had their noses in the air, trying to sniff out easy deals. Greed served as their most basic character trait, and anything that promised them a chance of financial reward always got their undivided attention. Although York knew them only by what his wife had told him, he already detested them both. Not for their gambling and drinking—York admired those activities in most men. But their laziness and snooty ways gave him a queasy stomach. Having earned his way to where he sat, York just plain disliked any man who didn't work as hard as he did. If he could use their weak character to his benefit, so be it.

"We're always open to business propositions," said Gerald. "What's the nature of this one?"

York looked at Katherine, who gave him a nod. "We owe your bank money," he started.

"We're aware of that," Gerald added in a bored, condescending tone.

"The war has made it impossible for us to pay at this time."

Gerald sat up straighter. "That's most unfortunate. Although we surely know how difficult things are these days."

"We want to make you a counteroffer," York explained. "Instead of cash, we propose to give you land."

Gerald rubbed his hands together. "What kind of land?"

"Not The Oak," York quickly replied. "Two other places. The house Katherine owns near Columbia. She's rented it the last few years, ever since Mr. Tessier's untimely death."

"I know the house," said Gerald. "What else?"

"A hundred and ninety acres up near Georgetown."

"Why should we take these places instead of money?" Gerald arched his brow at Luther.

"They're quality properties. You know that. The house in the state capital has ten acres. The place at Georgetown grows cotton. With the war, we're goin' to need all the cotton we can find, so prices will surely go up. We owe you just over fifty thousand dollars. These properties, the darkies who keep them, the houses and land should cover most of that."

"How many darkies?" asked Luther, speaking for the first time.

"Forty, I believe," York answered. "They alone are worth almost thirty thousand."

"That's true." Luther's eyes narrowed with obvious suspicion. "So why give us such a good deal?"

York checked Katherine again for a reaction, but she kept her face as blank as a clean piece of paper. "We want The Oak free and clear. We're gettin' rid of all other properties, no matter where they are."

"Even your house here in Charleston?" Luther added.

"Yes," said Katherine. "I'm going to sell the house and purchase a smaller place."

Luther's face clouded. He propped his elbows on the table. "I'm not sure I understand. Why would you do this . . . unless . . . ?" He raised his right eyebrow and leaned backward. "You're covering yourself," he said, almost in awe. "In case the war goes badly. You're getting rid of assets while people still believe the war will end quickly, offering the properties at less than their true values so you'll find buyers, gathering as much cash as you can." He put a hand on his chin and rubbed it slowly.

"Think whatever you want," said York, surprised that Luther had figured it out. "But it's perfectly legal. Anybody else can do the same thing."

"But why?" asked Gerald. "If you believe we'll win this conflict, as we surely will, why throw money away?"

"He doesn't think we'll win." Luther's expression revealed satisfaction in his deductive skills. "It's as plain as the nose on his face."

"But that's treason!" exclaimed Gerald.

"It's got nothin' to do with whether we'll win or not," returned York, his ire up at the idea that he'd do anything but defend his homeland. "And I'll have a uniform on within the week to show my loyalty. I daresay you two won't do the same anytime soon. So don't call me anythin' but a patriot, or you and me will have to step outside and take to pistols."

Gerald held up a hand. "Calm down, Mr. York. I'm only trying to make sense of this."

York eased back into his chair. "All you have to make sense of is whether or not the property we've discussed is worth what we've offered to sell it for. If it is, you take it instead of the cash we owe you. Then we can all leave and get on with other matters."

Luther rubbed his chin again. "We'll need to take this to the bank president. But I believe it makes sense to accept your offer."

"Good." York relaxed again. "We'll be waitin' for your answer." He looked to Katherine, and she smiled lightly. Grabbing his hat, York stood and pulled out Katherine's chair. "Hope you gentlemen have a pleasant day."

"We'll contact you soon," concluded Luther.

York led Katherine out of the room. Once they were in the hallway, he pivoted to face his bride. "I want you headed to England as soon as we sell the house here," he whispered. "You'll take that money and the twenty-seven thousand we already got and deposit it in a bank there. We accept no Confederate money either, strictly United States dollars."

She put a hand on his hip. "You're a smart man."

"I know a few things." He leaned close. "This war could go either way. But no matter what happens in the end, I'm certain the Yankees will come after the coastal area real fast, and we ain't got any navy to speak of. The property in Georgetown is too close to the Santee River. The Yankees will steam up there and take control in a hurry, and that land won't be worth spit. Then they'll come after Charleston . . . might take it or might not, but this way we're covered, win or lose. We'll keep a small house here, but not one that'll claim too much attention if the Yankees come ashore. We'll double insure it and The Oak with an English company. That way if the Yankees do harm to either place, we'll get the money back when the war ends."

"We come out prosperous either way."

"I'm countin' on us winnin'," he said. "I don't want you to doubt that. But . . ."

"We make a good pair." She smiled as he took her arm again.

"A man couldn't trust most women to carry out what you and me cooked up."

"You think you can trust me?" she asked slyly.

His grip tightened. "You want your boys to stay alive, don't you?"

"Of course I do."

"Then I can trust you, can't I?"

"We understand each other," she said. "What a wonderful basis for a successful marriage."

Chapter Ten

Camellia arrived in Richmond about midday of the third day after Sharpton Hillard hauled her away in his carriage. After arriving in Columbia, they had spent the night at a small inn, then caught a train the next morning. Filled with soldiers and all manner of other humanity on the move, that train had broken down twice and seemed to stop at a town every hour or so before reaching Raleigh, North Carolina. In Raleigh they had spent a second night, then caught another train. That one had taken them the rest of the way into Richmond. Crowds of people met the train at every town, the women waving white handkerchiefs at the soldiers and the old men and boys whooping and hollering as if cheering on young gods. As she watched, Camellia couldn't help but wonder at what bloodlust caused such outlandish displays. Did people truly want war this badly? Although she knew nothing of a war's horrors, she saw no way that killing could bring anyone any joy, much less glory.

Staying quiet, Camellia had stared out the train's window and prayed that the hostilities would not last long. Gradually the miles slipped away, and she turned her thoughts to what she'd find in Richmond. Although still furious at her pa for the unkind way he had kidnapped her, Camellia found her curiosity rising higher the farther she got away from The Oak. Other than Charleston and Beaufort, she'd never traveled anywhere; and she'd only visited Charleston every couple of years. The sights and sounds of the trip amazed her; she could hardly believe all she saw. Soldiers by the thousands moved in and around Columbia, then Raleigh. Scores of them rode the train, packed into the cars almost like cattle.

Because of the lack of seats, Ruby sat for most of the trip in the middle of the train's aisle with the two bags Mrs. York had packed for her. The soldiers kept casting brave glances at Camellia. Once, when the train stopped for water, Ruby told her that, if not for Hillard's presence, Camellia would have received more than one proposal of marriage on the journey. Camellia laughed, but the amount of attention the soldiers gave her made her more nervous than flattered. On The Oak she'd hardly seen more than three or four white men at a time. She didn't feel easy with so many now staring so boldly at her.

The train whistled and drew Camellia back to the present, to the depot in Richmond. Gathering her belongings, she followed Hillard off the train. Her eyes adjusted to the bright sun as she stepped down. Unable to do much to maintain her appearance on the trip, she tried to smooth back her hair. She knew she looked unsightly, soaked with grime and sweat, and felt worse. Her mouth tasted like a dirty boot. She studied her wrinkled blue dress and wished for a bath and change of clothes. "I have to prepare myself," she told Hillard. "I refuse to meet anyone looking like this."

"Follow me," Hillard directed. "I'll get a carriage, and we'll go to the hotel. You can freshen up there before we meet Mr. and Mrs. Swanson."

A couple of minutes later they loaded everything into a brown carriage. With a click from the driver, the horses clomped off. In spite of her desire to stay detached from it all, Camellia found herself leaning toward the windows and staring at the city as she passed. People of every stripe and color milled about, their clothing a mixture of the best to the worst. Darkies appeared to be as plentiful as whites, but many appeared to be alone without their masters. Soldiers were as numerous as bees at a hive—their clean uniforms evidence that none of them had yet done any fighting. Voices called out from every direction—officers giving orders to soldiers, men hailing carriages, women bargaining with merchants. The air held an odd smell to it, like a heavy brown smoke.

Overwhelmed by it all, Camellia turned to Hillard, her eyes wide.

"Probably sixty thousand people live in Richmond," he explained. "Forty thousand before the war, lots more now. The whole Confederate government is moving here since they've named it the capital."

"What's that smell?" Camellia wrinkled her nose.

"That's tobacco," Ruby answered. "Richmond sells more than most any city anywhere."

Camellia peered out the window again. After a few minutes, the carriage passed a huge domed white building with a line of columns. She pointed to it.

"The Capitol Building," Hillard told her. "The whole Capitol Square is the government area."

"It's beautiful," she said. "And churches are everywhere."

"At least one per corner it seems," Hillard stated. "Piety is a big thing in Richmond."

"Where's the river?" she asked.

"To your right," he said. "The mighty James."

Camellia stared at the buildings as they passed—scores of fine structures, many as good as the best in Charleston.

"Richmond has textile mills, flour mills, nail factories, the Tredegar ironworks, lumberyards—you name it and somebody in Richmond does it."

"You got auction blocks too." Ruby's dark face scowled. "I've been there."

A flicker of pain registered in Hillard's eyes. "Yes, I'm sorry to say, but it's true."

"A place like Richmond might not be too healthy for a man of your political notions," Ruby threw in.

"I expect not," said Hillard. "So I'll keep my views quiet if you don't mind."

"I don't expect I'll be telling anybody," Ruby concluded.

"Me either," added Camellia. "I'm not going to be here long enough to tell anybody anything."

Several streets off the main square, the carriage turned right, then back left. A couple of blocks later it pulled to a stop in front of a three-story stone building with a wrought-iron black fence around it. Tall maple trees bordered a cobblestone walk that led to the double front doors. Large iron lions guarded the two columns that framed the doors.

"Welcome to the Victoria Hotel," announced Hillard as he opened the carriage door and stepped down. "It's not the Spotswood or the Ballard

House, but it's a fine establishment just below their luxury. Owned by Mr. and Mrs. Wallace Swanson."

Camellia and Ruby joined him on the cobblestones while the carriage driver hauled down their bags. Camellia's mind swirled with all that had happened in such a short time. It seemed like a million years had passed since she'd left The Oak. She felt as though she'd traveled through some kind of time tunnel and ended up on a side of the world that she never knew existed. A touch of fear rolled into her stomach and made it squeamish. Who knew what kinds of things could happen in the midst of a war? What strange twists and turns might life throw at her next?

"This way." Hillard gestured toward the doors. "Ruby, you go with the bags through the entrance over there." He pointed left. "A man will meet you at the desk by the door. Tell him you're with Sharpton Hillard and that your mistress is staying in room 110. He'll take you and the bags there."

Ruby trudged off, the bags in hand. Guilt touched Camellia, but she pushed it off. Everybody knew how things were with the slaves. There was nothing Camellia could do to change it. But more and more, after her talks with Josh, she was bothered by the slaves' fate.

Hillard led Camellia into the hotel. Within five minutes he had gotten her a key to the room, led her down the hallway, and through the door of 110. A thick green rug lay on the hardwood floor; a painting of a ship at sea adorned the wall. A large bed with a canopy occupied the center of the room. The dresser, boasting a tall mirror, stood ready with a wash basin and pitcher. A table held a lamp with a shade. Two chairs—one brown leather, the other a soft tan cloth—and a pair of windows that opened to the alley completed the room's décor. Ruby rose from the cloth chair as they entered.

"The closet is over there." Hillard pointed Ruby to the right of the windows. "The bath is here." He stepped to a door by the closet, opened it, and moved back so Camellia could see inside.

She moved to the door, and her mouth fell open. The ceramic bathtub had four brass feet. Beside the large tub was a stand that held a piece of soap in a dish.

"You can order hot water from downstairs," he explained. "You might want a bath."

Camellia wanted to shout out with pleasure, but not wanting to give Hillard the satisfaction, she held back. Not even The Oak had a bathtub this big! Camellia had grown up taking baths in a large metal tub out behind her house. The notion of actually stretching out in such a thing and letting hot water wash over her seemed the most decadent of luxuries, one she looked forward to enjoying as soon as Mr. Hillard left.

"I believe a bath would do quite well," she said, moving out of the room, her voice as steady as she could keep it.

Back in the bedroom, Hillard moved to the windows and drew down the shades while Camellia stepped to the painting over the bed and scanned it. "Josh Cain paints better than this," she noted, trying to think of something other than the bathtub.

"I never saw any of his drawings," said Hillard, finished with the shades.

Camellia stepped away, glanced into the mirror, then back at Hillard. "I look horrible." She played with her hair. "When do you suppose we'll meet the Swansons?"

"Why don't I let them know we've arrived," Hillard replied. "See what they'd prefer; perhaps dinner, if not earlier."

"I could use a rest after I clean up."

"I'll suggest dinner," said Hillard. "You require anything else?"

Camellia shook her head, eager for him to go.

"Until later, then. And remember—you promised you wouldn't try to flee."

Camellia thought of the bathtub. Until she'd used it, she didn't plan on going anywhere. "I'll keep my promise. You can be assured of that."

Almost three hours later, Camellia woke to a knock on her door. When she sat up, she saw Ruby on the floor by the bed, her eyes also just opening. Another knock on the door fully awakened her. "Mr. Hillard?" she called.

"Yes. Are you prepared?"

"Give me a few minutes."

"I'll meet you in the lobby."

Camellia quickly dressed in a gray skirt, a navy cotton blouse, and a pair of flat black shoes. "You're going with me," she told Ruby as she put her hair up in layers and pinned it with a number of berets and clips. "Can't have you running the first day I get here."

Ruby said nothing as she got dressed. Within minutes they joined Hillard in the hotel lobby. A minute later they climbed into a carriage and headed through Richmond, going east. The afternoon sun had just about disappeared, and Camellia again felt out of place, as though she were in a dream. Yet at the same time, she felt wonderfully refreshed and quite hungry.

"It's about a ten-minute ride," said Hillard. "You enjoy your rest?"

"It was heaven."

They rode on in silence, and Camellia's mind jumped ahead. In just a few minutes she'd meet the woman who'd birthed her, then left her behind. She wanted to stay mad at the Swansons for deserting her, but somehow couldn't muster up the energy. Right now she felt numb, almost as if somebody else sat in her place, freshly bathed and riding in a fine carriage to the home of a wealthy man and woman who had entered her life and flipped it over like a cook throwing a pancake. She didn't know what to feel, say, or do. Everything seemed outside of her, distant and unconnected. She wondered if that was normal. But what was normal in a situation like this?

The carriage turned left and entered an area of residences, most of them fine brick places with cobblestone sidewalks and tree-lined yards dotted with bright spring flowers. As Camellia kept her eyes on the scene past the window, her heart started racing. Though she tried to calm it, she found it impossible. The carriage slowed, then came to a stop. Camellia wanted to jump out and run in the opposite direction—run until she reached Josh in Hilton Head, run until all this disappeared behind her, never to return. Something told her that this wouldn't end with just a short visit. That once she opened the door to the Swanson house—voluntarily or not—she wouldn't find it easy to close. Strange people stood on the other side of this door—people who would shake up her life more than anything she'd ever faced.

Then the carriage door opened, and Sharpton Hillard climbed out. Camellia's heart yearned for Josh, Beth, and Butler; yearned for the hard but simple labor she did at home; yearned for the ocean and the sand, the rush of tides and foam. *I'll go home as soon as I can*, she told herself as she stepped from the carriage.

Breathing heavily with anxiety, she followed Hillard to the front door. Before he could knock, a black man in a formal black coat and white shirt answered the door, bowed, and invited them inside. "Good to see you again, Mr. Hillard," said the black man, his words clear.

"You, too, Mr. Roof."

Mr. Roof took Hillard's hat, bowed again, and eased away.

"Mr. and Mrs. Swanson own no slaves," explained Hillard, leading them through the entryway.

"I'm surprised," said Camellia. "I saw plenty of darkies at the hotel."

"They earn a wage," Hillard continued. "They're free people of color. It's cheaper than keeping them in bondage. Mr. Swanson pays them for their labor, but they provide for their own upkeep—house, clothes, food, everything."

A sense of unease passed through Camellia. She glanced at Ruby. How could people as mean as the Swansons end up with such enlightened notions about the blacks? As Hillard led them through the entry, Camellia refocused her attention. The Swanson house was as beautiful as the hotel—a large glass chandelier glistened overhead, a thick gold rug lay under her feet, and finely cut molding framed the walls at top and bottom. The entry opened to a large parlor, and Hillard pointed toward the mantel of a fireplace half the size of the room.

A woman stood by the fireplace; a man sat by her in a large brown leather chair.

"Mr. and Mrs. Wallace Swanson," Hillard announced, as if introducing royalty, "this is your daughter, Miss Camellia York."

Hillard eased back and Camellia, her legs shaky, stepped forward. Mrs. Swanson curtsied slightly toward Camellia, whose mouth felt glued shut. Mrs. Swanson wore a tight-waisted, ankle-length green dress that puffed out at the hips. Her hair, the same color as Camellia's, only with a touch of gray at each temple, framed her face nicely. Her eyebrows were full and arching, her lips prim and perfectly shaped.

Camellia felt the odd sensation of seeing herself, as if God had opened a window to her appearance in about thirty years. Mrs. Swanson extended a hand as she crossed the room. Although still in a daze, Camellia took it and copied the curtsy Mrs. Swanson had offered her. Mrs. Swanson's eyes glistened with tears, intensifying their rich blue color. For a second Camellia wondered if she should cry too.

"I never believed this day would come," whispered Mrs. Swanson. "But now you're here."

Camellia stayed quiet.

"Can you believe it?" Mrs. Swanson asked, dropping her hand and turning to her husband. "It's our Camellia."

For the first time, Camellia looked closely at her father. His skin, yellowish in color, hung loosely on his chin. His hair, though black, long, and thick, seemed tired and fell to the side in spite of the oil he'd used to comb it down. A thin mustache made him look a little rakish, as if he'd once lived dangerously. Although a tall man, he leaned to the side as he sat, almost as if unable to keep his spine straight. He covered his mouth with a handkerchief, coughed, then used both hands on the arms of his chair to push himself up.

Camellia realized immediately that something was wrong. Swanson's eyes, though dark, were a little unfocused, and his right hand shook as he tried to stand. Instinctively she moved to him. "No need to get up."

He sagged back down. "Forgive me. But I'm quite ill."

Camellia glanced at Hillard, her eyes accusing. He'd said nothing of any sickness.

"He's got the tumors in his stomach," Mrs. Swanson explained. "They first showed up almost four years ago. The doctor says it's a miracle he's hung on this long."

"I've been waiting on Hillard to return with my children," Mr. Swanson said. "Such a heartache about Chester, but at least I can see my little girl." And then he coughed again.

Camellia's emotions tangled. She felt sorry for him but angry too. Did they think she'd forgive what they'd done to her and Chester just because Mr. Swanson was sick; that she'd forget the way they'd deserted her and her brother? Never!

"This is why we sent Hillard to find you," said Mrs. Swanson, who was now standing by her husband with a glass of water in hand. "Your father wanted to see you and Chester before he . . . he . . ." Her voice trailed away.

And then Camellia realized: no matter what offense the Swansons had committed against her, they wanted her with them so her father could get to know her before he died. Camellia stiffened. She knew that grudges ate a person up, but could she let them off so easily? Didn't they need to suffer like she'd suffered? Their selfishness had caused her to grow up without a mama's gentle hand. She'd believed her mama dead all these years and had grieved beyond words!

"Why did you desert me and Chester?" she asked sternly.

Mrs. Swanson's hands went to her throat, as if Camellia had stabbed her with a hot knife. Her eyes turned to her husband.

"Please sit," he said, pointing to a sofa across from the leather chairs. "We'll tell you the story."

Camellia looked to Ruby, as if seeking an escape, but Hillard motioned to Ruby and led her from the room.

"Please sit," urged Mrs. Swanson after Hillard and Ruby left. "We want you to know it wasn't because we didn't love you."

Camellia faced them again, her anger burning hotter than ever. How simple people wanted to make things! Just offer a few consoling words and wipe away years of heartache, years of neglect. Well, she'd listen but she wouldn't believe!

Taking a spot on the sofa, she placed her hands in her lap and sat straight.

Mr. Swanson coughed into his handkerchief, then began. "Your mother left me for Hampton York in 1842. The worst thing I'd ever faced. I loved her, more than I even knew."

"I left him because he didn't provide," she added. "Not because I didn't love him. He saved me, you know, after I got out of the orphanage. I was just sixteen, on the street, about to do some things a girl ought never to do. But he found me outside an inn in Columbia and took me in. Didn't take advantage of me, though. Instead he fed me, gave me a place to stay, clothes to wear. He didn't touch me for over two years, not until we married."

"I was a gambler but was raised right when it came to a woman's virtue," Swanson said softly. "I loved your mama from the first time I saw her—she's got that effect on men. As you can see, though, I'm older than she is and didn't want her if she didn't love me. So I waited until she did."

"But you married my pa," Camellia accused her ma.

Mrs. Swanson shrugged. "I never told him I was married to Wallace. It was a lie to fit the times."

"So your marriage to my pa was never legitimate?"

"I'm not sure it was ever legal."

Camellia thought of Mrs. York and her pa. If her pa's marriage to Mrs. Swanson wasn't legitimate, that meant his marriage to Mrs. York was. She focused again on Mrs. Swanson. "You're not an honest person, are you?"

Her husband quickly came to her defense. "I told her to leave me."

"What?"

"I had no money," Swanson continued. "No way to get any. I'd lost everything at the card tables. Your pa probably told you this. Down on my luck like I was, I knew I couldn't give Lynette what she and her babies needed. We already had you, and Chester was on the way. I didn't want your mother to suffer—you either. So when we met Hampton York, we agreed she should go with him—at least for a while. I thought I could handle it, then found I couldn't."

"You never loved Pa," said Camellia, accepting the awful truth for what it was.

"In a way I did. And it grew in the time I stayed with him. But I never pretended to love him like I did Wallace. I was honest about that."

"So you just ran off when he moved you to The Oak."

Mrs. Swanson lowered her eyes. "It wasn't my plan. I'd gotten comfortable with Hampton. He's got his charms, you know. And I thought Wallace had left for good. But I don't know . . . I was so young, so foolish.

And Wallace had done so much for me. After Johnny was born, I found The Oak stifling—a lonely place and . . . other things too. I just couldn't stay . . . too much . . ." She wiped her eyes.

Camellia thought she saw something else in her mother's face—perhaps the look of fear and fury all mixed together. But what did it mean? Camellia didn't know her mother well enough to ask.

"I lived in Savannah while she was with York," Swanson went on. "Tried to get over your mother but couldn't. Kept thinking of her—of you and Chester too. Wondered what had happened to all of you. I made my way up to Beaufort, asked around about York, and found out he liked to go to Charleston every February for the races. I showed up at The Oak one day when he was gone, talked to your mother, and begged her to come back to me. At first she said no, but I kept coming back every time I knew York was absent. She kept refusing, but then"—Swanson's eyes narrowed, as if in anger—"things happened, and she knew she had no choice. She had to leave with me."

"So you just left us?" Camellia looked accusingly at her mother.

"I had to . . . you . . . you don't understand." The haunted look came back to Mrs. Swanson's eyes.

There had to be something deeper going on, Camellia thought. "What don't I understand?"

Mrs. Swanson's eyes went blank; then a frightening expression passed over them.

"I had changed," interrupted Mr. Swanson before his wife could answer. "I'd come to understand that I had to do better, give up the gambling. I told her I'd do that for her, anything she wanted."

"I gave in," said Mrs. Swanson.

"I took her to Columbia," added Mr. Swanson, "then here. I'd done some card playing here in the past, knew a man in the hotel business. I went to work for him."

"We hoped to send for you and Chester as soon as we got our feet under us," Mrs. Swanson filled in. "But that took a while. Then life got so busy and time rushed by. I knew Hampton would take care of you. I have to give him that. He was a dependable man. After a couple of years had passed, it didn't seem fair to him or you and Chester for us to show up and take you off from the home you knew. So we just stayed here, building our lives."

"Before long I managed a hotel," continued Mr. Swanson. "Then I took part of the money I earned and made one last run at poker. My luck turned good and I won."

"That was the last time he played." Mrs. Swanson smiled. "We parlayed that money into our first hotel, a small place that we fixed up, then sold and bought something bigger."

"We've been doing that ever since," Mr. Swanson went on. "I buy a rundown place, your mother fixes it up, then we sell it for profit. Now we're set—we have more money than we ever dreamed of."

"We can provide for you," said Mrs. Swanson. "You'll never want for anything again."

"I don't want for anything now." Camellia's anger rose again at the thought that they believed they could buy her allegiance with a few nice dresses and a fine bed to sleep in. "I have everything I need."

"We'd like for you to stay," said Mr. Swanson. "At least for a while . . . until . . ."

Camellia knew what he meant. They wanted her to stay until he died. But how could she do that? He'd already lived four years since his sickness started, so who knew how much longer he might linger? They didn't deserve her presence for such an unknown length of time, and nothing they'd said had changed that. What about Josh and his children? They needed her. If she stayed here, she'd break her promise to him to care for them. Josh would expect her to return as quickly as she could. She owed him that.

"I can't stay," she said. "I have obligations."

Mrs. Swanson sighed. "We can't force you. But we did want you to understand. We wanted to come to you years ago but didn't know . . . didn't want to upset your life."

"But it's OK to upset it now?"

"He's dying, can't you see that?" Mrs. Swanson snapped a little. Her eyes pleaded with Camellia to feel some compassion for her father.

Camellia stared at Swanson, but he kept his eyes on his hands. "I'm sorry for your sickness," she told him. "But there's nothing I can do except pray for you. As soon as I can make arrangements, I'm returning to South Carolina."

Mr. Swanson didn't respond except to cough into his handkerchief.

Camellia faced Mrs. Swanson once more. "I'd like Mr. Hillard to take me back to the hotel."

Her eyes moist, Mrs. Swanson moved to Camellia, then whispered so only the two of them could hear. "The doctor says he'll die within the month. Please stay until then. It'd mean so much to him."

Camellia shook her head and once again started to refuse.

"Don't say no," insisted Mrs. Swanson. "Don't let the fact that we did the wrong thing with you make you do the wrong thing for him. You'll regret it if you do. I can tell you that from experience."

Camellia's anger fueled higher. She wanted to scream that she wouldn't be pressed this way. It wasn't fair, wasn't right. Yet she knew Mrs. Swanson had spoken the truth. Just because they had made a bad choice that affected her didn't mean she was fated to do the same thing. She took a breath.

"I know that life sometimes forces us to do things we don't want," she offered.

"Yes, it does," Mrs. Swanson murmured.

"Like my coming here. It wasn't my choice. I had no power over it."

"I felt that way when I left you," explained her mother. "Out of control—life had washed me out to sea, and all I could do was go with the tide."

Camellia tried to get a handle on her feelings. This woman and her husband *had* acted poorly in leaving her and Chester so long ago. But judging them without knowing exactly what had happened didn't seem fair, no matter how hurt and angry she felt. And lingering in the air of their explanation was that hurt, haunted look in Mrs. Swanson's eyes. What did that mean? Perhaps that expression held the key to what was yet unspoken?

Mrs. Swanson interrupted her thoughts. "Think about it over dinner."

Camellia hesitated, then agreed. "Dinner. I'll stay for dinner."

Mrs. Swanson smiled.

Without knowing why, Camellia felt different, as if the world had turned and she had shifted suddenly. Although she'd never expected to do it, she knew now that she'd stay in Richmond until Mr. Swanson died. No matter how badly he'd treated her, she couldn't find it in her heart to do the same to him.

Chapter Eleven

Josh spent the next few days on the island asking around for Boggs and resting up some more from his wounds. With no labor ready at hand for the first time since he'd come home from the Mexican War, he took the time to sleep later than normal. Lester had shown him a small room at the back of the barn, and Josh had put his things there and slept soundly every night. After waking he usually checked with Spade to see if there were any chores to help with; then, after finishing them, Josh headed to the beach. For several days in a row, he had waded into the water, shoes and shirt off, and stayed there for what seemed like hours at a time. The water, although still chilly that time of year, acted as a balm to his wound, the salty liquid healing the spot where the bullet had almost taken his life. When not in the water, he lay on the beach, let the sun bake down on his body, and looked up into the sky with its blue canopy and puffy white clouds. As sea gulls darted here and there, and the waves lulled him in and out, in and out, his mind drifted to the years he'd lived so far.

Sometimes late in the day, Lester, the black man, walked down to the beach too. After a period of companionable silence, Josh started talking to him. Before the week had ended, a friendship had begun. Josh learned that Lester had been born and raised on a cotton plantation near Savannah. He'd taken a woman, but she'd been sold nearly fifteen years ago, and he'd never taken a new wife. His woman had birthed him six children, but three had passed on. The other three had ended up on the auction block at one time or the other, and Lester no longer knew where any of them lived.

After Lester gave his story, Josh told his. How his mama had worked as a schoolteacher all her life, how she never owned much of anything except her dignity, good character, and unfailing faith in the Lord's goodness, no matter how hard the times.

"My pa died before I knew him," Josh confided in Lester, "so my mama taught me everything I know—how to read, how to deal honorably with other folks, how to labor hard."

"She sounds like a fine woman," Lester agreed.

"She was. Sometimes I wonder what she'd think of me if she was still alive," Josh admitted. "Whether she'd be proud of what I've become. It's not much from what I can see."

"A man ain't measured by what he owns," said Lester. "Least that's the way I see it. It's where he gets from where he started."

Josh nodded and continued his story. "When mama died, I went to my half brother, York. He'd left us when he turned seventeen. Soon after I got to him, he and I rode off to war—me just sixteen."

"Mighty young for a boy to go fightin'."

Josh sighed. "That war showed me all I ever want to see of wars. Taught me how to kill or be killed."

"Most wars ain't good for nothin', the way I see it," offered Lester.

"The Mexican War wasn't. I shot more men than I could count."

"You did what you had to do."

"True, but there was this one that I killed . . . a boy even younger than me—a lad not more than ten or eleven. He snuck into our camp one night as we were sleeping. The war was almost over. I guess he was looking to steal food or something. Anyway, I woke up and saw him standing over my brother, a pistol in his hand, a hat low on his face. I shot him on instinct, before I saw his face, knew how young he was. I've carried a lot of guilt around since then. Never said anything about it until recently, right after I got shot and thought I was dying."

"I expect a body does their best confessin' right before they think they're goin' to meet Jesus." Lester grinned.

"I believe that's so. You a believing man?"

"Most of the time."

Josh chuckled, then thought of York and felt sad. York didn't seem regretful over much of anything. How could two sons sired by the same man take such different paths in life? Not that Josh saw himself as a whole lot better than York. He knew that wasn't so. But he'd trusted his life to the Lord, and that meant his sins had received a washing that York's never had.

"Reckon your brother was mighty grateful to you for savin' his skin," suggested Lester.

Josh shrugged. "He's not one to say much about what he feels. His mama didn't teach him the things my mama taught me, so we're different than a lot of brothers."

"He not a Christian man?"

"Nope."

"You reckon the Lord judges him different because his mama didn't give him any religious upbringin'?"

"I don't know. I've told him about the Lord lots of times, but he always puts me off." Josh shook his head. " Now I don't know how to talk to him about matters of faith."

"I expect you won't give up on him, though."

"So long as we both draw breath, I'll keep asking the Lord to show me how to get through to him."

"That's what I figured."

The next afternoon Josh returned, this time with a pencil and pad of paper that Spade had given him. Taking the pencil, he started drawing pictures of what he saw—the horizon stretching out like a sheet in the wind, the waves pounding on the white beach. Anna's image came to mind—the woman who had encouraged him to try his hand with paints and paper, the woman who had birthed Beth and Butler . . . and Lucy too—his child who had died of the malaria in her seventh year. Anna had suffered headaches for years; then one day she had a seizure and never came out of it. For a while Josh hadn't thought he could live without her. He had wanted to die, too, so he could go be with her forever. It had been Camellia who had brought him back, reminded him of his children and their needs. It was then that he had slowly pulled out of his melancholy and started life over again.

Over the next few months, he had come to depend on Camellia in ways he felt guilty for at the time. He had worried that he was taking advantage of her kindness, her gracious spirit. She had cooked for him and the children, talked sweetly to them, treated him with care and tenderness.

Gradually it had begun to dawn on him that he might be feeling love for Camellia. At first he had felt guilty again, as if loving Camellia betrayed his love for Anna. Besides, did one man deserve happiness twice when so many, like York, never seemed to discover it even once? What made him think he should enjoy it again? He surely had not lived good enough to deserve it.

Yet the day had finally come when Camellia had told him she loved him, and he knew without question that he loved her. Then why did this nagging fear still eat at him so hard—that he and Camellia might never end up together, no matter how strong their love for each other?

Unable to answer the question that came to him that day, in spite of his efforts to avoid it, Josh put away his paper and pencil, slipped back into his shirt and shoes, and left the beach. His troubled mind didn't stop working, though. The notion of fighting another war bothered him. He knew he didn't want to, especially not to defend a way of life he knew the Lord couldn't approve. But how could he avoid the conflict if it didn't stop before he finished the fort? A man his age with any kind of health at all would face the worst ridicule, maybe even punishment, if he refused to fight. He thought of going west, yet didn't see how he could do that without his children and Camellia. But was it fair to them to pull up and head out with no assurance of a job—or a place to lay their heads at night?

Gradually the week passed. Josh kept his eyes open for Olan Boggs, a man everyone knew and had described to him. Finally the man showed up, early in the morning on the Saturday of the second week after Josh had arrived. Boggs came to the general store by the ferry that carried folks to the mainland.

While at the store to pick up a few things for Spade, Josh recognized Boggs instantly. A man close to sixty, Boggs walked with a slight limp, sported a face that looked like somebody had baked it in an oven too long, and wore overalls with enough pockets to hide a dozen biscuits.

Heeding Spade's warning about secrecy, Josh watched Boggs for a few minutes to make sure he was alone, then approached the engineer as he loaded a wagon hitched to the general store.

"Morning," said Josh. "You Olan Boggs?"

"Who's askin'?" The voice came out almost a whisper, like a man in church, but Boggs didn't stop working as he asked his question.

Josh grabbed a keg of nails from the store's porch and placed them in the wagon. Boggs arranged them against the side, then looked up.

Josh stuck out his hand. "I'm Josh Cain. Spade from the White Sands told me I should look you up. I asked around. Folks told me what you looked like."

Boggs took the offered hand and shook it. Josh noted the calluses in the man's palms, the plain cotton pants and shirt, the dirty black brogans. Boggs didn't back away from labor. Josh knew that right off and liked him instantly.

"You say Spade sent you?"

Josh's volume notched lower to match Boggs's. "Yes, he said you might know of some work for a man like me."

Boggs raised an eyebrow, then picked up a couple of new axes and laid them in the wagon. Josh grabbed a box of hammers and put them by the axes.

"What kind of man are you?" Boggs asked as he lifted a stack of lumber and set it in the wagon.

"Kept up the dikes on a rice plantation," answered Josh, taking one side of the lumber and helping Boggs arrange it. "At The Oak, thirty miles from Beaufort."

Boggs wiped his hands on his overalls. "I heard of the place. Marshall Tessier owned it, right?"

"Yes."

"Why did you leave there?"

"Seemed like the right time. Been working rice for years, wanted something different. Came here to try Spade, do some cotton. But he said other needs were more pressing."

"Spade name those other needs?"

"Oh, war things, you know."

Boggs rearranged some tools in the wagon bed. Josh helped him move a couple of boxes from front to back.

"Why ain't a fella like you goin' to the fightin'?" Boggs asked.

Josh pointed to his chest. "Got an injury. It'll get better soon, then I expect I will. Until then I want to do something useful with myself."

"I reckon you can build things if you kept up the dikes on a spread as big as The Oak."

"I'm good with my hands."

Boggs looked him over head to toe. "Spade knows not to send me no slackers. He'll vouch for you if I ask him?"

"I believe he will."

"You see to the darkies' labor on The Oak?"

"Everybody who worked the dikes, yes."

"I hear they got over three hundred hands there."

"That's true."

Boggs rubbed his face and then nodded. "Come with me. Let me show you somethin'."

Josh and Boggs climbed into the wagon. After leaving the dock area, they headed southeast. A low cloud cover eased the worst of the sun's heat, and a steady breeze helped some more. Josh kept quiet as the wagon bounced through the sand. Within a few minutes, they'd come to a spot that overlooked Port Royal Sound. Boggs climbed down without a word and moved toward the ocean. Josh followed. The breeze picked up even more, blowing Boggs's unkempt hair in all directions. As he pointed out at the water, his voice rose until Josh could hear it over the wind.

"Over three thousand miles of coast on the Atlantic," Boggs explained. "This is one of the best ports on any of it. The ships of the world can sail through here."

"The Yankees will want it if they can get it," said Josh. "They could go straight to Beaufort from here. Set up operations there, then go right through the middle of the state, cut off the railroad from Savannah to Charleston. That's a prize worth taking, and surely they know that."

Boggs nodded. "They'll want this port as a coalin' station too. Can go north or south from here, control the whole coastline."

"You'll need a fort on both sides," said Josh. "Otherwise, they'll just sail up the sound, out of reach of your guns."

Boggs stared at him with appreciation. "That's the notion. One on St. Helena over there"—he pointed northwest—"and ours right here."

"You have guns that can reach them if they keep their ships in the middle?"

"That's a question the artillery boys will need to answer. We just got to get the forts built. Leastways, this fort here."

Josh scanned the beach. The ground rose slightly from the ocean to the dunes and up past them. "You'll use logs and earth?"

"Yep, that should do fine."

"Slave labor?"

Boggs shrugged. "We use whatever we can find. Gone build the fort in a fanned-out M shape. Point the middle directly ahead and the two sides to the north and the south. Have a clear shot at any ship that heads our way."

"How many soldiers you think will come here to man the place?"

"Hard to say. We're to build for around two thousand. Better hope we get that many."

"When's the date to get it finished?"

"Soon as we can, but no later than the fall. Major Lee figures the Yankees will come after us before the worst of winter comes, probably after the late summer storms pass."

"That's not much time," Josh put in. "And it gets mighty hot here in the summer. The hands might not take to laboring in the worst of the heat."

"They'll work," said Boggs. "Won't have a choice."

"Where you plan to bunk them all?"

"We're bringin' in tents. Bosses will sleep in and around some of the plantations. Most are within a few miles of here—easy to get out and back."

"You going sunup to sundown?"

"Yep, no task system, if that's what you mean."

Josh took off his hat and scratched his head. Except for harvest season, the blacks usually worked task to task, not hour to hour. When they'd finished their main job, they could stop for the day. That meant that if they worked hard and completed their labor quickly, they got to do what they chose—grow their own gardens, make baskets to sell, mend clothes, play a fiddle, talk on their porches. Most of the rice plantations followed the method, even some of the cotton places. It kept the servants in a better mood than slaving them sunup to sundown.

Josh spoke before he could stop himself. "Does it bother you that you'll be making people build a fort to protect a way of life that's held them in bondage all their lives?"

"That's mighty bold talk for a man I don't know who's askin' me for a job," Boggs claimed. "Shouldn't you keep such questions quiet?"

Josh cringed at his mistake, then figured he'd already offended Boggs, so he might as well speak plainly. "I love this land. But I don't cotton to the notion of one man owning another."

"You're honest, I got to say that."

Josh held his breath and waited for Boggs to make up his mind.

Finally Boggs waved a hand and spoke again. "I ain't no politician. So I won't hold your views against you so long as you do your job and keep your opinions quiet."

Josh stared out at the water. Could he in good conscience give direction to the Negroes as they built this fort? Of course, he'd gone against his conscience for years while working on The Oak. He hung his head in shame.

"You positive Spade will vouch for you?" asked Boggs.

Josh looked up. "Sure he will."

"You certain you want a job on this?"

Josh thought of Beth and Butler, then Camellia. No matter how distasteful the work, he had to do something to provide for them. What choice did he have? It was either this or join the army. "Yes," he told Boggs. "I'm sure."

Boggs headed back to his wagon. "Come on, then. We got things to do."

Later that day Josh returned to his place at Spade's. Taking paper and a pencil from his gear, he sat on the room's small bunk and started writing.

First he sent a letter to his children.

Beth and Butler,

I am situated with a job to keep me busy. My wound is much better, and I'm almost back to full strength.

I'm sure Stella is taking good care of the two of you. Do what she tells you.

He wiped his eyes as he wrote the next words.

I'm sorry to say this, but I might not get to move you here with me just yet. Lots of soldiers will come here soon, so it's not much of a place for a couple of youngsters. I'll let you know as soon as that changes.

For now, say your prayers every night and kiss your pillow like it's me.

I love you both and will come see you the first chance that comes.

Love,
Pa

Then Josh took out another piece of paper and started a second letter. The words pulled deep grief from him as he wrote. He had to stop more than once to wipe his eyes.

Dearest Camellia,

I trust this finds you well. I know the manner of your leaving The Oak did not please you or me. But I now believe it's the best thing. Sometimes I believe the Lord works His will for us this way. What we see as ill-timed or even completely wrong turns out to be exactly what we needed.

I'm on Hilton Head, as I'd planned. But I'm not working cotton. I've hired on to help build a fort. It's not my choosing to do this, but I see no way to avoid it. Since there's a war going on, I'd rather fill this duty than shoot a man for a cause I can't support.

One thing, though. This means I cannot be with you by this fall. The island will soon become a beachhead for soldiers—not a fit place for a woman of your delicate temperament, nor Beth's either. So I beg you to stay in Richmond. Do not return to The Oak. I fear it's not safe.

I know Stella will care well for my children. You need not worry about them. I release you from the promise you made me. Sometimes promises are wrongly asked and wrongly given.

Please know of my deepest love. You can write me at the White Sands Plantation on Hilton Head. I'll check often for your letters.

You are daily in my thoughts and prayers. As soon as this fort is finished, I'll try to come for you. Until then, God keep you and protect you.

Love,
Josh Cain

After folding both of the letters carefully, Josh got up and headed for the barn to get his horse. Before the day ended, he wanted to get his letters to the post for the mail. As soon as possible, he wanted Camellia to know she needed to stay in Richmond. If she returned to The Oak now, he'd have no way to protect her.

Chapter Twelve

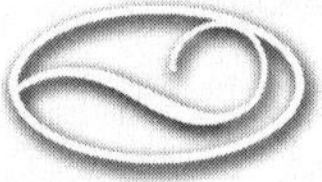

Hampton York strode into an office just off King Street in Charleston on Monday morning the first week of June, his spirits high and his plans set. He wanted to join the Charleston 27th, the most highly respected band of men in uniform in the whole state. Although he didn't have the blue blood or the fine education that every other man in the outfit possessed, that didn't matter to him. So what if he didn't know which fork to use at a fancy dinner, that he couldn't read Latin, that he didn't know about the latest fashions from Paris? He now claimed part of The Oak as his own property, and the Lady Katherine had taken to his bed as his wife. If that didn't raise a man a step or two on the ladder, he didn't know what would.

"Have a seat, Captain York," said the man behind the desk, a gent named Lewis Pringle, a square fellow with glasses perched on his nose, a brown handlebar mustache, and a freshly pressed gray uniform on his back. "We received your servant this morning, and he told us you planned to drop by this afternoon. I'm most pleased to see you."

York took off his hat and eased into the wood chair that fronted the desk. Mr. Pringle played with his spectacles for a second.

"I want to join the cavalry of the Charleston 27th Brigade," York announced. "I applied for a commission some time ago."

Mr. Pringle picked up a stack of papers and flipped through them. "I see you served in Mexico, received promotions to captain before that conflict ended. Quite impressive."

York rubbed his beard. "I did my duty and showed no cowardice. The fact I got promoted came from that, nothin' else."

Pringle peered at him over his glasses. "You've served a long while as the overseer of The Oak, is that right?"

"Me and Marshall Tessier made it the best place in the state. Least we saw it that way."

"How many darkies you run?"

"Over three hundred, give or take a few."

"An extensive operation. I'm certain it takes a particular kind of man to lead that many people, keep up with that much material—make it all happen smoothly like it should."

"We kept it in order."

"I hear you recently married the Widow Tessier."

"That ain't in your paperwork."

Pringle smiled, then stood and opened a tall file drawer behind his desk. A few seconds later, he pulled out a folder and flipped through it.

Although wanting to stay patient, York found Pringle's pace too slow for his liking. "We don't need no federal investigation for this. I had a letter written for me, sent all the way to the governor. Several men here in Charleston made the recommendation. You're supposed to have a signed commission for me. Just make it official and send me on my way. That's all you got to do."

Pringle played with the tips of his mustache but didn't speak, just continued reading his papers. York tried to stay calm but was growing irritated. Something in Pringle's manner seemed too haughty.

"You ever done any fightin', Lieutenant Pringle?"

Pringle cleared his throat. "Well no, but I studied military tactics at a boarding school in Europe close to ten years ago."

"I'm sure that was a fine place. They shoot any bullets at you at that school?"

"Certainly not, but . . . that's not the issue here. We're trying to get you properly situated so you can best use your skills and experience to help the Confederacy in its noble cause."

"I'm joinin' the 27th," York insisted. "The cavalry. Fill out the papers, show me to my commandin' officer, and let me start."

Pringle's smile thinned away to nothing, and he rubbed his forehead. "I'm afraid maybe we have something confused. The commission I have for you says you will become the chief quartermaster officer here in Charleston."

"What?"

"You've been assigned quartermaster, put in charge of material and supplies. Obviously, you've got the know-how to handle people, make things run smoothly. We've got tons of supplies flooding in here."

"I'm joinin' the cavalry."

"I understand your desire," Pringle claimed. "But somebody's got to get things in hand around here. We're getting wagonloads of material every day—shoes, hats, guns, and food. I can show you warehouses and barns filled to the rafters with all manner of things. We're bogged down in organizing it. A man like you—plenty of experience in putting things in their proper place—will be much more valuable than one cavalry officer."

York was stunned. At his wedding he'd talked to a number of officers from the 27th about this, and they'd assured him they'd accept him with open arms. Yes, the men of the 27th primarily came from the sons and fathers of Charleston's most elite families. But now that he'd married Katherine, he belonged with them—all the men at his wedding had said so.

"Look, I expect you're right about needin' somebody to organize all the goods you've got comin' in. But that man ain't me, that's all. I'm a man for a horse, a saber, ridin' and raidin'. I did that in Mexico, and I plan on doin' it in this war too."

Pringle shook his head. "That's not my order. Read this." He pushed a sheet of paper over the desk to York.

Sure enough, York saw that the papers called for him to receive a commission with the South Carolina Militia as a colonel in charge of the Quartermaster Corps.

"There's been a mistake," York said, still upset.

"Maybe so, but I doubt it." Pringle pushed back from the desk. "Look, this obviously comes as a surprise to you. But it's not an insult. Somebody must think pretty highly of you to give you this much responsibility. Just accept it and do your job. You'll be safe and close to your family. Plus a man in charge of supplies won't ever want for anything, I can tell you that. Everything that comes through, you get first pick of it."

York rubbed his beard and weighed Pringle's notions. Although he'd set his heart on cavalry, Pringle did make some sense. As quartermaster he'd stay in the back of the lines; get to travel around to find things the soldiers needed. Plus, he'd live in accommodations as fine as any the war could offer. Not a bad duty, either way he looked at it.

Yet he couldn't help but wonder what had happened with his commission with the cavalry. Had somebody in the 27th seen him as unfit and shut him out? He'd have to check on that and find a way to take his revenge if he discovered it was so. In the meantime he had another idea or two about what he'd do with the assignment the army had given him.

"I guess a man could get worse duty," he told Pringle.

Pringle laughed. "I don't see how he could get much better."

York took out a chew of tobacco and stuck it in his jaw. A thought struck him. If true, it made him feel two ways—real mad on the one hand . . . and slightly pleased on the other.

Pringle pushed the stack of paper toward him. "Sign at the bottom of that top one. You'll be all set."

York leaned toward the paper but didn't sign it. "I need to check a couple of things first. Just hold it for me."

"Whatever you say, Captain York."

York stood then and left the building. If what he suspected was true, he didn't plan on signing anything yet.

York spent the rest of the morning talking about his possibilities with a number of military officers up and down King Street. As a former captain in the United States Cavalry, he had a lot of choices about his service to the cause. More than one outfit offered him rank even higher than captain, and he measured them all carefully. Part of him wanted to go ahead and accept the commission from Pringle, but another part refused to take it. How could he stay so snug and safe while other men stepped right to the front lines and faced bullets as readily as they ate a biscuit every morning?

About noon he stopped by an enlistment office set up by Wade Hampton's officers. Hampton, the richest man in South Carolina, hailed from Columbia and had advertised in the *Charleston Gazette* for troops for a cavalry brigade he planned to form and outfit. The officer there told

York they'd surely like to have a man of his training and experience, but that he'd probably get no promotion from his former rank.

Shaking the man's hand, York left King Street and headed back home, hurriedly climbing the steps to the second floor, where he found Katherine in the bedroom. She wore a pale gold dress that hugged in tightly at her waist, then draped all the way to the floor. Her shoulder-length hair was unbound; she was brushing it in front of the mirror. As she turned and smiled at York, he felt almost pleased. Although Katherine wouldn't cause a man to stop his wagon to look at her as he passed, she wouldn't scare him if he ran up on her on a dark night either. A man didn't need a beautiful woman if she brought other assets, and Katherine certainly did that.

"Your day been busy?" he asked, placing his hat on a table by the bed.

"Some. I met a man this morning about buying the house. He's interested but says we might be too close to the water. If the Federals attack Charleston, he's afraid we'll end up in the line of fire."

"You offer to come down on the price a little?"

"I told him to see our bank. Maybe we could negotiate through them."

"He seem interested when he left?"

"I think so. We'll know in a couple of days."

"That take you the whole day?"

"I ate lunch with a few ladies and talked over plans for funding a new hospital here if we end up needing one. You think it will come to that?"

York moved to her, took the hairbrush, and started stroking her hair. "No man can predict a war. Once the first bullet fires, all his best-laid plans go out the window. War is the art of fightin' what you don't expect."

She closed her eyes, obviously enjoying his attention to her hair. "You're as hard to predict as a war. Who'd expect the rough Captain Hampton York to put his hands to hair brushing?"

"I'll trust you to keep it our secret." He grinned. "Wouldn't do my reputation no good for such a thing to get out."

She turned and kissed his hand. It felt good, in spite of the fact that he held little true affection for her. Maybe that would eventually change.

"You get things in order with your commission?" she asked as he went back to stroking her hair.

"Well, it wasn't what I went in for."

"Oh?"

"No, it ain't the cavalry with the 27th."

"What, then?"

"They gave me a commission as quartermaster," he explained. "Rank of colonel and stationed right here in Charleston. They want me to put some order to a few things. The boys at the front will need food, blankets, medicines, clothes, guns, ammunition, and somebody needs to make sure they get it."

She laid a hand over his, and he stopped his brushing. "Are you pleased with the assignment?"

"Well, it ain't my first choice, but it could be a good place for the right man."

"I'm glad." She turned, a hint of a tease on her face. "I wanted to make you happy."

He tried to stay calm, but she'd just confirmed his suspicions. "You had somethin' to do with this?" he asked, not indicating he'd already figured that out.

Her smile was bright. "I talked to a few people. An aide of the governor's who came to the wedding. I told him you wanted to join the cavalry, but that you had wonderful skills in organization. He said the state could use a man like you in the quartermaster's office; that if we didn't get some things arranged, the fighting soldiers would suffer terribly. I told him you were perfect for that kind of thing."

Although he'd suspected it, York still found her meddling hard to accept. He struggled to keep his rage down. "You got no right puttin' your nose in my business!" he snapped. "It ain't a woman's place!"

Katherine jerked her hand away. "I'm not a typical woman. You ought to know that by now. I do what I think best for me and those around me. I don't want you leaving Charleston right now. We just wed. I've lost one husband already and don't like the idea of losing another, least not if I can do something to prevent it."

"I ain't one of your sons!" York yelled. "A boy you can squeeze in one direction or another as you see fit. I'm a grown man, and I won't have this, you hear me?"

She took his hands again and stood, her body equally as straight as his. "I know what kind of man you are. That's why I married you. And if you'll simmer down for a moment, you'll see how perfect this is for us. Yes, I said 'us.' You play your cards right, and this can end up being the best thing that ever happened to you. Who knows what this war will bring? Maybe it'll end in a few months and nothing much will come of it. But if it goes on for long, if men start dying, if places like Charleston, Savannah, Columbia come under attack, all we've ever known will end. But a smart person—somebody with courage, good sense, and a little twist of good luck here and there—that person can make war come out to his advantage. You know that, I know you do!"

York calmed some as he listened to her logic. No reason to blame her for doing what came so naturally. It's a wonder he hadn't thought of it too. Their minds worked a lot alike that way. Yet she'd interfered with his business, and no woman had the right to do that to a man.

"A war can destroy fortunes or make them," she coaxed.

"You're right about that."

"So you see it my way?"

"Oh, I see it your way, all right. But that don't mean I'm goin' to do it your way."

Her eyes blazed. "What do you mean?"

"I ain't staying in Charleston. I've decided to sign on with Wade Hampton's outfit—the cavalry, like I want. They'll keep me at captain."

"I can't let you do that!"

He chuckled. "You got no choice."

She glared at him and balled her fists. "What about Calvin? I wanted him to serve here with you."

"I don't know about him."

"The governor probably won't put him in Charleston if you turn them down. Every mother in the state is trying to put her boy in the quartermaster's office."

"I'll see if Calvin can ride with me with Hampton if you want."

"But cavalry is as dangerous as war can get."

York shrugged. "I'm offerin'; that's all. Do what you want with Calvin."

"You want to make me a widow again?" she soothed.

York softened a little at her less angry tone, but he knew better than to trust her. "No. But you know I ain't a man to sit around while others go to a fight."

She picked up his hands and kissed them, apparently deciding to try another tactic. "Men are all the same. You, Trenton, Calvin—you can't wait to get shot at."

He relaxed some and wrapped his arms around her waist. "You give me reason to keep my head down."

"Will you protect Calvin if I send him with you?"

"I'll do the best I can. But you never know with a war."

"That's not the answer I want to hear."

"It's the only honest one."

"You're a hard man, Hampton York."

"Don't go forgettin' that if you know what's good for you."

Chapter Thirteen

A heavy rain fell in the early evening of the last Thursday in June. Camellia and Mrs. Swanson sat in cloth chairs by a large bed, their eyes open but not focused. Wind whipped against the windows to the left of the bed. Mr. Swanson lay on the bed beside them, his eyes closed, his breath shallow and unsteady. A light gray beard covered his thin face, and his lips were dry and chapped. Mrs. Swanson held him by his right hand, but he didn't seem to notice. He took a deep breath, his body shook a little, and then he took another. Camellia stared at him, her mind blank.

Mr. Swanson coughed, then breathed again, and his body shook once more. She watched him for his next breath, but this time none came. Camellia glanced at Mrs. Swanson, who leaned forward anxiously and also waited. Nothing happened. Camellia held her breath. Mrs. Swanson froze. At least a minute passed, and then Camellia knew. She'd seen death before, and now it had taken Mr. Swanson by the hand and led him through to the next world.

"I believe he's passed," she whispered.

"The tumors," said Mrs. Swanson, as if announcing the name of a curse. "They ate his body away, chewed him up from the inside."

"You want me to send Mr. Roof for the undertaker?" asked Camellia.

"Let's let the rain settle some," said Mrs. Swanson. "There's no rush now."

Camellia nodded.

Mrs. Swanson looked back at her husband. "His last words were the Twenty-third Psalm. He prayed them early this morning—barely got them out."

Camellia's eyes widened. "Was he a believer?"

"Sure." Mrs. Swanson straightened her shoulders. "Both of us are."

"That surprises me," said Camellia.

"I suppose it does," Mrs. Swanson answered softly.

As the wind whipped something against the window, Camellia sat still and silent. Her father had just died, and she grieved for him, but no tears rose in her eyes. She studied Mrs. Swanson, wanting to comfort her, but didn't know how. Shame rose in Camellia's throat. She knew she ought to go to her mother and console her, but she still carried too much hurt to let herself do so.

"We came to faith about five years ago," Mrs. Swanson explained. "A year before he got the tumors. The Lord gave him time to get his heart ready before the disease took over. I'm grateful for that."

"How did you come to the Lord?" Camellia asked.

Mrs. Swanson smiled lightly. "Nothing dramatic. Your father and I simply came to realize we had everything we'd ever wanted—fancy clothes, a good name in town, a stately house. Somehow, though, all of that failed to bring us the peace of mind we wanted. Both of us felt awful about leaving you and Chester. The guilt from that weighed on us, kept a dark cloud near."

"Regret is a rough thing." Camellia's mind flashed back to the day of Marshall Tessier's death. What she wouldn't give to change the events in the cookhouse.

"I hurt York too," continued Mrs. Swanson. "Lied to him, used him. You do that to another person, and it'll gnaw at you, if you got any conscience at all. We needed forgiveness, and we knew it."

"Everybody's got sins," said Camellia, thinking of her own.

"We seemed to possess more than our share."

"Did you start going to church?"

"Not at first, though there are plenty of them here."

Camellia smiled. "I've heard that no matter where you are in Richmond, you're within the sound of a church bell."

"I knew a few ladies from the Baptist church on the square," added Mrs. Swanson. "I talked to them, and one sent their preacher out to see us. He told us about Jesus, straight and easy. We studied on it awhile, and it just seemed right. We both needed a good washing of our sins and trusted Jesus to do that for us."

"I'm a believer too," Camellia explained.

"I guessed it," said Mrs. Swanson. "You have a way about you, something pure and good."

Camellia blushed, knowing that her actions and words since her arrival at the Swansons had been anything but that. "I'm not too sure about that, but I do trust the Lord. He's seen me through some hard days."

"I'm sorry I contributed to those."

"I hardly ever went to church, though," said Camellia, eager to change the subject. "Nearest one was a long way off."

"Maybe you can go with me sometime," offered Mrs. Swanson.

Camellia fell quiet again.

"I'm glad you stayed," Mrs. Swanson murmured.

"I did what any Christian woman would do," Camellia whispered. "No more or less."

"It meant a lot to your father. He always wanted to know you, take care of you."

Camellia glanced back at Mr. Swanson and realized the truth in her mother's words. Although he'd not said a lot to her since her arrival in Richmond, Mr. Swanson had made clear his regret for leaving her behind. More than once he'd gently said he hoped someday she could find it in her heart to forgive him.

Turning toward the window, she gazed out. "The rain is calming some."

"Guess it's time to fetch the undertaker, then," Mrs. Swanson said softly.

"Suppose so."

Mrs. Swanson stood, leaned over her husband, and kissed his cheek. Camellia rose with her and drew the covers up to Mr. Swanson's neck. Then she looked up into Mrs. Swanson's eyes, saw the sorrow in them, and teared up herself. "I do believe he loved me," she admitted.

Mrs. Swanson smiled in spite of her tears.

Camellia swallowed hard and knew she should forgive Mr. and Mrs. Swanson. But somehow she couldn't yet do it. They had hurt her too deeply.

Mrs. Swanson wiped her eyes, then walked out of the bedroom, with Camellia following, and into the kitchen. They found Ruby there, her hands busy in dishwater.

"Mr. Swanson is dead," Camellia whispered.

Ruby paused. "Sorry to hear that."

"Roof around?" asked Mrs. Swanson. "I need him to go for the undertaker."

"He's already gone for the night," Ruby explained. "But I'll go if you'll set me off on the right path."

Mrs. Swanson gave directions while Ruby listened closely. Camellia pulled a shawl off a hook by the back door and handed it to Ruby. As Ruby put it on, Mrs. Swanson stepped out of the room. Camellia moved to Ruby and touched her shoulder. "This isn't the night to skip away from here."

Ruby appeared surprised. "I've been in a fine hotel or at this house all the month. Why would I want to flee from that?"

"Ruby, I know you're biding your time before you can get back to Theo, and I don't blame you. But tonight's just not the time."

"Why don't you just give me my freedom papers?" Ruby pleaded. "I'll go find Theo, then come right back here and labor for you for a wage like Mrs. Swanson's help does."

Camellia sighed. "You don't belong to me, Ruby. So I don't have the power to do what you suggest."

"I ought not to belong to anybody," Ruby murmured.

"You're probably right," Camellia said weakly.

Ruby hesitated, and tears formed in her eyes.

Concerned, Camellia moved to her and took her hands. "Ruby, what's wrong?"

Mrs. Swanson walked back in.

Ruby dropped her head, but Camellia insisted that she speak. "What is it? Tell me."

Ruby wiped her eyes on the shawl and looked up. "I got a question."

"You know you can always ask me," Camellia said gently.

"Is the baby of a free man and a servant free or slave?"

Camellia's heart jumped. "Are you expecting a child, Ruby? You and Obadiah?"

"I've wanted to tell you since we left The Oak. But the time never seemed right, you being so upset and all. And with Mr. Swanson being so sick. The time is still not good, but I'll start to show soon, so you might as well know the truth."

Camellia tried to clear her head; so much was happening all at once. "How far along are you?"

"Close to four months, I believe."

"You should have told me. Are you feeling OK?"

"I'm a little sour in the stomach in the morning but not too bad."

Mrs. Swanson had been listening quietly. Now she spoke up. "We'll get a doctor to look after you."

"Don't need a doctor," Ruby insisted.

"Does Obadiah know?" asked Camellia.

"No."

"He'd never have let you come here if he did."

"Probably not."

Camellia led Ruby to the table. "Sit down, Ruby," she offered. "This means you can't go for Theo. At least not anytime soon."

"I know," said Ruby. "That's why I'm upset. My boy, Theo, might be only a day away from here, but I can't go for him."

"Maybe you can go after your baby comes," soothed Camellia.

At these words Ruby started crying again. Camellia's heart broke. How she wished she'd known. Maybe she would have been kinder, not wrapped up in her own troubles so much. How blind she'd been—seeing only her troubles and nothing of Ruby's sorrow. What kind of world did they live in anyway? The kind of world where somebody could order a woman to leave her husband right at the time she came up expecting a child? Even worse, that same woman had already been forced to leave behind a baby boy she loved more than her own life.

Mrs. Swanson handed Ruby a handkerchief. The servant wiped away her sniffles, straightened her back, and stood. "I best go on for that undertaker."

"We'll send somebody else," said Mrs. Swanson.

"Don't start treating me like a child," Ruby retorted. "Having a baby doesn't make me a cripple."

"But it's bad weather," Camellia insisted.

Ruby shook her head. "A bit of water never hurt anybody."

Giving up, Camellia stood and gave Ruby a hug. "Go on, then. But hurry back soon as you can."

Ruby broke off the embrace, threw the shawl over her head, and hurried out the back door without another word. Camellia's mind returned to her mother's grief. "What can I do to help you?"

Mrs. Swanson pointed to her chair. "Sit. We need to talk."

Camellia noted Mrs. Swanson's dry eyes, her steady focus on the matters at hand. Is this how a woman handled this kind of loss? Camellia wondered. Could she stay so calm if tumors had just taken Josh away from her? Did the Lord give a woman this kind of strength when she most needed it?

"I know you said you'd leave after Wallace died," Mrs. Swanson began. "And I won't ask you to change your mind. But please know that I'd like for you to stay. I can take care of you and Ruby. Her baby too—at least until this war ends."

Camellia hung her head. Although she'd come to appreciate many qualities of her parents—such as the kindness and generosity she saw in them toward all folks, slave or free—she didn't feel any true connection with them. Yes, they were her flesh and blood, but too many years of absence had passed for her to think of them as family.

What made it even more difficult was that neither of her parents had ever truly explained their past offenses. Other than her initial words on Camellia's arrival, Mrs. Swanson had not said anything else about why she ran from The Oak all those years ago. And that action was one Camellia couldn't find it in her heart to forgive. What kind of mother would run off and leave one of her children, much less two?

"You can move from the hotel to here," continued Mrs. Swanson. "You know how much room we have. You and Ruby both. I'll give her a wage; let you work too if you want, so you won't feel obligated to me."

Camellia's eyes watered, not so much from grief as from anger and frustration. "I don't want to stay here," she insisted. "I need to go back to The Oak."

Mrs. Swanson studied her hands. "I know you're still upset with me. Mad too. But . . . well, you don't know everything. You don't understand."

"What don't I know?" asked Camellia.

Mrs. Swanson opened her mouth, then shook her head. The haunted look Camellia had noticed earlier returned for an instant. "Nothing," the older woman finally said. "Nothing worth saying after so many years."

Camellia wanted to stand up and storm from the room but knew she couldn't. She felt as trapped as a fenced-in deer.

"Then treat me like a hired hand for now," Camellia insisted. "And understand that as soon as I can save enough money to leave, I'm heading back south."

Mrs. Swanson's eyebrows arched. "You mean you're staying?"

"I have nowhere else to go."

"What?"

Camellia wiped her eyes with her apron. "I got a letter from Josh Cain at the hotel about a week ago. He's the man I told you about, the man I hoped to marry before this war came. Josh is at a town called Hilton Head, working . . ." She told Mrs. Swanson of her hopes to go to Josh in the fall, how he'd promised to come and take her there, where they could become husband and wife.

"But he can't come now," Camellia lamented. "And I can't go to him. He's laboring on a fort, so there's no place for me or his children, Beth and Butler. I can't go back to South Carolina right now, no matter how much I want to."

Mrs. Swanson's eyes lit up. "I know this isn't what you hoped. But maybe this is the Lord's will. You're safe here. Richmond has more army around it than any other city in the South."

"But I made Josh a promise," said Camellia sadly.

"What kind of promise?"

"To care for his kids. They're all alone, surely fearful. I've got to find a way to provide for them."

"I wish I could help you," Mrs. Swanson replied.

Camellia's frustration rose again; she wanted to scream. She couldn't just sit here in this fine house while Beth and Butler waited for her back at The Oak! Who knew what Trenton might do to them in revenge against her? But what could she do? How?

Then an idea hit her. "I'll bring Beth and Butler here! Keep my promise to Josh! Can they come here? Stay till the war ends?"

"Sure they can, but how will we get them?"

"I'll go to The Oak and bring them here," exclaimed Camellia, warming to the notion.

"But travel is so hard right now. The trains are filled with soldiers, and people are moving all over the place."

"I don't care. I have to do this."

Mrs. Swanson paused, then spoke sternly, as if she'd take no argument. "I'll pay for whatever you need."

Camellia hesitated. If she took money from Mrs. Swanson, she'd feel obligated for a long time, and she didn't want that hanging over her. But what choice did she have? "I'll keep a record of what you spend. I'll pay back every dime you loan me."

"I'll do it however you want."

Camellia sat back, her mind racing. Why hadn't she already thought of this? Then a wave of guilt washed over her. Worried about her own problems, she'd again forgotten Mrs. Swanson's grief over her dead husband.

"I appreciate your kindness," Camellia said with genuine sorrow. "You don't have to do this."

Mrs. Swanson patted her hand. "You're a precious young woman, and I'm proud to be of assistance."

Camellia began to plot her trip south. She and Ruby would take a train; they'd hire a carriage from Charleston.

Mrs. Swanson retrieved the coffeepot and two cups from the stove, then settled down at the table. She poured the coffee and handed Camellia a cup. "I need to tell you something," she insisted.

Camellia paused. Something in Mrs. Swanson's tone seemed fearful.

"I should have told you sooner, but I didn't know how. But now, well . . . there's no getting around it. He's already on his way home."

"Who?"

Mrs. Swanson stared into her coffee. "Your brother Jackson."

Camellia rocked back. "What?"

"You've got a brother named Jackson."

"Where is he? Why haven't I met him? I don't understand."

"He's in London. Been there for about a year, attending school."

"What about Mr. Swanson's illness? Why didn't this son come home?"

"The illness didn't turn bad until the last few months. Even then your father insisted I not inform Jackson of its seriousness. He didn't want his last living son to see him when he looked so bad."

"You agreed to that?"

"How could I go against my husband? He wanted Jackson to remember him as a strong man, not the shell lying in there on that bed." She sipped her coffee. "Maybe I did the wrong thing by not telling him, who knows? But I didn't write Jackson until a few weeks ago to tell him he needed to come home."

Camellia's mind spun. "Why did you wait until now to tell me about him?"

Mrs. Swanson shrugged. "I didn't want you to know of him. Not until I knew you better . . . until I could decide if I wanted you to stay here, become part of us."

Camellia's anger boiled up, fresh and strong. "You wanted to *test* me?"

"That's not the way I'd put it. You have to understand—I'm so proud of what you've become. You're exactly what I hoped you'd be, but I had no way of knowing that until I met you. What if you'd turned out mean, hateful, out for money and selfish gain? Why would I want Jackson to meet that kind of person?"

"So he doesn't know about me? Or Chester either?"

Mrs. Swanson held on to her coffee cup tightly, with both hands. "No. Why should he until now? That part of our lives was over, and we weren't proud of it. Why should we tell Jackson I'd had a husband other than the man he knew; that I'd lived unchastely, then run off from two of my children? If you'd lived that kind of life, would you want your child to know it if you could protect him from it?"

Camellia put her elbows on the table and tried to get a handle on her feelings. How could this be? How should she respond? All of her emotions switched on her. A minute ago she'd started to feel glad about meeting the Swansons because through them she could help Josh, Beth, and Butler. Now she wasn't glad at all. She felt dirty instead, like an unwelcome stranger showing up at a fancy ball wearing muddy boots and a torn dress.

"When will I meet this brother of mine?" she asked.

"He's making arrangements to leave London."

"So he won't be here for the funeral?"

"No." Mrs. Swanson set her cup on the table.

"He might not be here for a long time," Camellia reasoned.

Mrs. Swanson nodded. "The Yankees have blockaded the coast. Ships to the South are finding it hard to land. Jackson will have to plan carefully for his trip. If the Yankees catch him, they'll put him in prison."

"I've read in the paper that many Southerners abroad have to come home through Canada or Texas—some as far as California."

"Can I ask you to postpone your trip to The Oak until Jackson gets home?" Mrs. Swanson asked. "I'd hate it if he showed up and you weren't here."

Camellia weighed the matter. "It could be months."

"True, but perhaps not."

Camellia considered her options. Without Mrs. Swanson's money, she had no way to go for Beth and Butler. Again she was trapped, unable to refuse the request to wait. "I'll hold off for a few weeks. But I can't promise anything after that."

Mrs. Swanson leaned back. Camellia wondered about her brother, what he looked like. He'd be so much more learned than she, so much more accomplished.

"What will Jackson think of me?" Camellia whispered.

"He'll love you, same as I do."

Camellia shook her head. Jackson Swanson. She had a brother she'd never seen! A brother who didn't know she existed. She thought of Josh and wondered if he'd faced as many twists in the wind as she had in the last few weeks. Perhaps so. Were they good turns? Or ill winds? Gentle breezes or violent storms?

She faced Mrs. Swanson again. "What other secrets are you keeping?"

Mrs. Swanson shrugged but said nothing. Again Camellia sensed the same odd fear she'd witnessed earlier. What was it? What was her mother holding back?

Camellia decided it was best to never let her guard down again. If nothing else, the last few minutes had reminded her of what she never should have forgotten. She couldn't trust Lynette Wheeler Swanson. The woman had let Camellia down once, hard—and she might just do so again.

Chapter Fourteen

The early summer months passed quickly for Josh as he fell into the routine of work on Fort Walker. More Negroes than he could count gradually filtered into the area and went to work in the blazing heat of the lowlands. Most of them lived in small tents pitched in makeshift camps and ate the meager food provided by the military. The blacks trudged to their tasks each morning, their eyes steady, their shoulders bent to the work.

To Josh's surprise Lester had showed up at the fort too—about a month after Josh had begun work there. The two of them often talked near the end of the day, after the work had ended and they'd taken dinner.

One evening in mid-July, Josh asked Lester, "Why don't you boys just rise up and throw off the yoke we've put on you?"

Lester raised an eyebrow. "That's a right risky question," the black man murmured.

"You're my friend," Josh explained. "Sometimes I just have to speak what's on my heart."

Lester chuckled. "It's simple—your boys got all the guns."

"But you outnumber us at least ten to one."

"That be true." Lester shrugged. "But we don't know nothin' about how to go about such a thing."

"I figure that's what happens when one group puts another in irons. A man forgets what it means to live freely. He just bows his head, does what he's told, and gives up the notion of plotting his own destiny."

Lester stuck a piece of beach grass in his teeth and nodded solemnly.

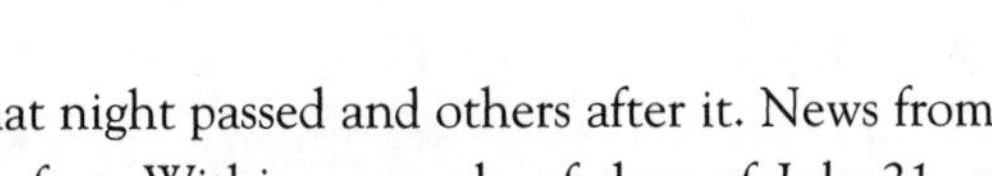

That night passed and others after it. News from the war came quickly to the fort. Within a couple of days of July 21, everybody knew that the Confederates had whipped the Yankees at a place called Bull Run. The talk ran fast through the men that since the Federals had lost so badly, they'd surely give up and leave the South to go its own way.

But the Federals didn't, and both sides continued to be locked in their intense struggle.

Josh tried to keep his mind away from the battles and set on his work. He certainly had plenty enough work to keep him busy. On the days that he showed up to check their progress, Boggs usually talked confidentially to Josh about the project. Before long, Josh had become one of Boggs's most trusted men.

"You got a good eye for the details," Boggs told Josh one day in mid-August as they surveyed a section of the fort that had fallen behind schedule. "And a way with the darkies that gets them to work hard. Those are worthy traits."

Josh shrugged off the compliment, and Boggs said nothing more.

Near the end of August 1861, Union ships and troops took control of Fort Hatteras in North Carolina, and all talk of easily beating the Federals stopped. Everybody knew what the fall of Fort Hatteras meant—the Yankees planned on controlling the coastline, and the fort they were building would eventually end up under the aim of the Yankee guns.

September rolled in. More and more soldiers marched into Fort Walker as the month passed. By the end of September, it seemed that men filled almost every corner of the structure.

"We got close to fifteen hundred men," Boggs told Josh one day when he showed up. "Everybody knows the Yankees will come for Beaufort sooner or later. And they have to come by us to get there."

The soldiers came in all shapes and sizes, most of them rough young men given to foul language and bawdy ways. As they drilled in the hot fall sun, their body odors gave the whole place a foul smell that made Josh's nose wrinkle when the wind hit just right. The only women anybody ever saw were the wives of some of the officers, a nurse or two who cared for the men's ailments, and a group of about ten women of ill-repute who took up housing in Hilton Head and started plying a most unladylike trade. The more he saw and heard, the better Josh felt about leaving Beth and Butler on The Oak. Although he missed them and Camellia so much it felt like he had a hole in his stomach the size of a bucket, he didn't want them in a place like this.

By October 1861 they'd received Fort Walker's armaments. Boggs approached Josh soon after the last of the cannons arrived, and the men started setting them in place.

"It ain't what they promised us," lamented Boggs. "Instead of seven ten-inch Columbiad rifle cannons, we got only one."

"You got nine thirty-two-pounders," said Josh, trying to stay hopeful. "Plus one twenty-four-pounder and one eight-inch Columbiad."

"But they're all older than what we need. And they don't have the range or firepower of the ten-inchers."

"Maybe Fort Beauregard got what they desired." Josh tried again to sound positive.

"We're in real trouble if they didn't and the Federals come hard at us."

"Maybe they'll go for Savannah," said Josh.

Boggs shook his head in disgust. "I'm hearin' otherwise. And we'll have forty to fifty guns at best between both forts. And none of them is the best. Ain't gone be easy."

"We'll do the best we can with what we've got."

Boggs glared at him. "You always so optimistic?"

"Optimism doesn't cost me anything," Josh replied.

Boggs just walked away.

The days moved on. Josh wrote letters to Camellia on a fairly regular basis as the weeks passed. Although the mail seemed to take longer than before to move, she wrote him back. He kept her letters tied up with a cord and wrapped in his bedroll. To his relief the letters confirmed that Camellia had taken his advice and planned to stay in Richmond, at least for the time being. They also told him of Mr. Swanson's illness and death, of his burial in the back courtyard of the city's main Baptist church. In addition, Josh learned that Camellia had a brother named Jackson who wanted to come home from London but couldn't because Yankee blockaders patrolled the shipping route from the James River to Richmond. So Jackson had stayed in London to aid a group of men who had the job of building some Confederate ships they hoped to use to break the Federals' blockade.

Battles popped up all over the country: Wilson Creek, Missouri; Ball's Bluff, Virginia; Paducah, Kentucky; and a whole lot of other places. Sometimes the Rebs won; sometimes they lost. Listening to the news, Josh kept his quiet. But deep inside, he feared the worst. This war would not end quickly, with the blaring of Southern bugles and the boom of cannon fire. From what he could see, this war would go on for years, and many men and women would die. The thought of it made him sad.

By the end of October, they had finished the rest of Fort Walker. In spite of his unease about the war, Josh felt a certain pride in what he and the rest of the men had accomplished. The fort's gunwales faced Port Royal Sound on three different angles—directly east, southeast, and northeast. Ships coming from either direction would find firepower pointed right at them. Josh and everybody else knew by then that Lincoln had set his sight on Southern ports. Federal patrol boats already circled off the waters of Charleston, Savannah, and Wilmington. Worst of all, Southern military leaders knew the Yankees had their eye on Port Royal Sound and that they'd shipped out a huge armada—some said as many as seventy-five ships, including troop transports, warships, and gunboats—bent on invading either Charleston, Savannah, or Beaufort. Although a storm had scattered the armada for a few days and caused a good bit of damage, the news said they had regrouped off North Carolina and now planned to head south for their target.

On November 4 the word came to Fort Walker that Yankee ships had made their way south and had started to gather off the coast of Port Royal Sound. They had Beaufort in their sights, and the only things between them and it were Fort Walker and Fort Beauregard.

Boggs found Josh standing with Lester near the beach late that afternoon. The engineer's face was burned red with sun and excitement. "We done all we could." Boggs stared out in the direction the Yankee ships would have to come. "Now's the time to defend our homes."

"Too bad none of the newer guns ever showed up," said Josh. "When the Yankees come, we'll have inferior weaponry."

"What happened to all your optimism?" Boggs threw in.

Josh smiled. "You saying what we have will be enough?"

Boggs spat on the beach. "It's accordin' to what they bring against us. I got word they're bringin' at least fifteen warships and enough transports to carry ten thousand men."

"What kind of sea force do we have to go meet them?"

"Got a navy man, Commodore Josiah Tattnall, with a steamboat and two or three tugs rigged up—that's about it. Barely enough to annoy the Federals; surely not enough to stop them."

"How do you think they'll attack us?" Josh asked.

Boggs trudged up a sand dune and cupped a hand over his eyes. "You're the military man—you tell me!" he yelled.

Josh and Lester moved up beside him. All three of the men were sweating heavily.

Josh studied the ocean. "They have steamers. That'll change the way they fight. They don't have to worry about wind or ocean currents like the old sailboats did. If I were them, I'd concentrate on us. Fort Beauregard isn't as large and doesn't have the firepower we do. I'd bring my ships in on an elliptical path, staying out of our range, then swing them around and come in from the north. Since we figure they'll set up and fire point-blank from east to west at us, our flank on the north isn't fortified. I'd hit us there, then keep moving and attack us broadside as I passed to the south. There's no reason for them to sit still and fire at us. That would give us the advantage—we have fixed positions. But if they keep moving, we have to shoot at passing targets. That gives them the upper hand."

Boggs nodded. "So they fire at us; move on south; then wheel around and go back north out of range again; then swing around and hit us again as they go."

"That's right. Lester here tells me Fort Beauregard is over two and a half miles away on the other side of the sound. The Federals got plenty of room to go by them, then us, and never get caught in a cross fire. Since we've only got a couple of cannons with enough range to cover that distance—one here and one at Fort Beauregard, I'd keep my ships moving on a swinging path—fire at them, then come by us. It's the smartest thing."

"That's a new way of fightin'," Boggs said. "You figure the Federals gonna figure that out?"

"If I can, they can."

"I hear they got close to a hundred and fifty guns," offered Lester.

"That'll make them hard to beat, no matter what they do," Josh concluded.

Boggs gave another nod, then retreated off the dune. Josh and Lester followed him. When they stood level with the beach again, Boggs stuck out a hand to Josh. "I ain't sure what's gonna happen here. But you made me a good hand, and I'm glad to know you."

Josh shook the engineer's hand, then turned to Lester. "I'm saying the same thing to you. Whatever happens, you worked hard."

Lester took Josh's offered hand and gripped it.

Boggs stared at his shoes.

Lester smiled at Josh. "God's got you in his sights. I know that for sure."

A minute later the three men left the beach. Lester and Boggs headed toward the fort; Josh walked back to his room at Spade's. Before the battle started, he wanted to write one final letter to Camellia. If something happened to him in the next couple of days, he wanted her to hear one last time that he loved her.

As the morning of November 7 unfolded, Josh stood on Fort Walker's ramparts and looked out to sea. The water stood as still and calm as glass—perfect conditions for the Yankee fleet. As Josh scanned the soft blue sky, he saw the outlines of approaching ships. His breath caught. He'd never seen so many ships! And all of them, he knew, were pointed at destroying the fort he'd helped build. Unless some mighty act of God turned up, the Yankees would surely succeed.

Inside the fort soldiers rushed all over the place, stacking ammunition, shouting orders, studying the movement of the Yankee fleet. Josh turned to Lester, who had rushed from his tent to Josh's side as soon as the sun rose.

"It's going to be quite a fight, I'm afraid," Josh murmured.

One of Lester's hands shielded his eyes. His heavily muscled black skin, covered only with a pair of ill-fitting cotton pants, glistened in the morning sun. "What's gone happen if they beat us, Mr. Josh?"

"We'll retreat," said Josh. "We have boats ready at the dock. We'll cross Skull Creek and get back to the mainland."

"Somebody gone take me back home?" asked Lester.

Josh took a breath. "Don't know about that. I expect if we lose today, you might end up on your own for a while."

"I been on a cotton place every day of my forty-nine years. Don't reckon I want to go back there. They leave me on my own, maybe I just wait on the Yankees to come and get me. I hear they'll ship a darky north—maybe even put him in the army someday."

"You'd fight against the South if you got the chance?"

Lester inclined his head toward Josh, as if trying to decide whether he could speak honestly. "You a good man, Mr. Josh. I seen it in you these last months. You give the boys water when we thirsty, don't whip us, give us a touch of respect—all us in the gang say it. You ain't got no heart for this war—that's plain to see for all who want to see it. What you expect me to do? You bet your last dollar I'll fight for the Yankees if the chance comes."

Josh stared at the ground. Lester had him figured. Although he'd help build a fort, he couldn't, with good conscience, fight for the South. Although a lot of folks tried to say that the war was over the matter of states' rights, he knew better. For him it was over the matter of slavery, and he didn't have it in his soul to kill to keep the blacks in bondage. He knew what happened to the blacks on a plantation, and it cut against everything he knew of the Lord. True, Jesus never came right out and said to free the slaves, but anybody who paid any attention at all to what He had preached knew what He meant. So what if nobody had gotten the exact words written down? Deep in his soul, Josh knew that owning another man displeased the Lord. But what could one man do? Should he simply walk away? Head west—away from the fighting—and leave the war behind? Maybe if it was just him, he'd do exactly that. But he had a family; how could he leave them? Besides, he'd bossed slaves for years. Only a hypocrite could wash his hands of the whole matter before it came to a conclusion.

"I pray you'll live to the end of the day," Josh told Lester. "Come victory or defeat."

"You a good man, Mr. Josh."

Boggs suddenly appeared beside them. "Looks like the Federals are doin' what you said," he told Josh. "Comin' at us from the north."

"We're in for it, then," claimed Josh.

"We'll try to keep the guns protected," Boggs promised.

Josh nodded. Although not a fighting man, he still had work to do. With a group of darkies as his troop, Boggs had given him a number of jobs. Keep the fortifications around the guns repaired as the battle progressed. Keep the Negroes busy hauling food and water to the soldiers. Repair the weapons if and when that was needed.

Josh turned to Boggs; the two men locked eyes in the manner of men who know they might never see each other again.

"Stay safe," Boggs said.

"The Lord keep you," offered Josh.

Suddenly there was a shout. Boggs and Josh jerked around as they heard cannons boom from the ships. The soldiers stood ready for a command to open fire. Josh's heart raced.

"Fire!" The order roared through Fort Walker, and cannons boomed. The ground under Josh's feet shook, and smoke suddenly choked the air. Josh looked quickly at the sky, figured the time to be somewhere between nine and ten o'clock. Boggs rushed away and Lester ducked. The Yankee ships fired again and again, their cannons ripping into the log and sand ramparts of the fort. Josh turned to Lester and shouted at him to stand ready with the rest of their group.

The battle raged into the early afternoon. The Yankee salvos blasted away nonstop, spraying sand, logs, and destruction everywhere. The noise never ended—the booming of the cannons from ship and fort, the shouts of men frantically giving orders and cursing the Federals, the groaning of the wounded as they lost life and limb. Sizing up the fray even as he raced about, fulfilling his duties, Josh saw that things were going badly for his companions almost from the first. A dense fog of smoke from the guns quickly settled over the sound, and the artillerymen had trouble even seeing the Union ships. The fact that the enemy ships kept moving made the problem worse. By the time the Confederates managed to find the range on a ship, it had sailed past.

To the north a couple of Union gunboats poured a steady stream of gunfire at the fort's unprotected flanks. Before the morning ended, all the batteries defending that side of the fort were deserted, the men in retreat by orders of General Drayton. By noon conditions inside the fort had become almost unbearable. Many of the cannons were damaged, others destroyed outright in spite of the efforts of numerous crews who fought to keep them operational. Although nearly exhausted and covered with sweat and gritty sand, the inexperienced Southern gunners ran from gun to gun, searching to find or fix enough artillery to keep firing at the enemy. Other men labored in the fort's ovens, trying to heat the cannon-balls they'd fire, hoping they could blast the hot shot into the Federal fleet and set it ablaze.

Josh and Boggs caught up with each other about an hour after midday—both of them grimy from their efforts, Boggs with a bloody left elbow. They sagged against a wall for a short second and fought to catch their breath.

"We're down to three guns!" panted Boggs.

"Our powder supply is almost gone too!" added Josh.

"We got to do something soon, or they'll trap us on the island. Take us all prisoner!"

Josh thought of Beth and Butler and wanted to flee but knew he couldn't. He offered Boggs a drink of water from his canteen, and Boggs drank deeply before handing the canteen back. "See you when it's over!" he yelled.

Boggs ran off, and Josh picked up a bucket of water to carry to the gunners to cool down the cannon. When he reached the front rampart of the fort, Josh spotted Lester on the ground. Blood covered his friend's face, but Lester's eyes were open. Josh dropped to a knee and jerked off his shirt.

"My head," moaned Lester.

Josh dipped his shirt in the water bucket and wiped Lester's head. A gaping wound poured blood. Josh pressed his shirt against it.

A soldier ran to them and tapped Josh on the shoulder. "We got orders to evacuate!" shouted the soldier. "Spike the guns! Fall back to Ferry Point. They got boats there to take us to the mainland!"

Josh nodded and the soldier ran off. All around them men abandoned their positions and headed to the rear. Josh focused on Lester. "Can you walk?"

"You go on!" panted Lester. "I'll wait for the Yankees."

Josh wiped more blood off Lester's wound and saw that the cut gouged deeply into the scalp.

"I said go," Lester urged.

"You'll bleed to death before the Yankees get here," Josh told Lester. "I'll see you to the mainland. We'll fix you up there."

"Leave me," insisted Lester. "I'll just slow you down. You got kids; see to them."

"I'm not leaving you to die. So shut up and hold on," Josh commanded.

He leaned down to Lester and pulled him up. Not arguing anymore, Lester lay against him, his head bleeding on Josh's shoulder. Josh grabbed Lester around the waist and headed to the rear. Something whizzed over his head, then a boom sounded and a spray of sand hit him from behind. A burning stab cut through his right hip and ran down to his foot. Groaning, Josh staggered, then sagged down. Dropping Lester for a second, Josh checked his hip and saw a bloody hole in his tattered pants. Gently he touched the wound and found a jagged piece of wood about the size of a thumb jammed into his flesh. Grimacing with pain, he jerked the wood out, threw it down, and grabbed Lester again.

"Leave me," whispered Lester, his voice weak from blood loss.

"Don't think so."

Josh's vision blurred as he stood, but he pushed up and started moving again, slowly picking his way through the battered fort. Weapons, knapsacks, canteens, equipment of every kind lay around his feet. He saw bodies as well, but not too many, and he breathed a prayer of gratitude that not more had died. Once out of the fort, he staggered down the path, cluttered with dazed soldiers, toward the ferry. His ears roared with the sounds of cannon fire. With each step pain dug into his leg, making the walk sheer agony that seemed to drag on forever.

Lester collapsed completely about halfway there, so Josh threw him on his shoulder and kept walking . . . sliding really . . . one step at a time, dragging his right leg through the sandy soil.

"Hang on!" he coaxed Lester, his voice loud over the booming cannon. "Almost there—we'll get you a doctor!"

Josh's mouth was swelled with thirst, his shoulders ached from the strain, and his leg burned as though it were on fire. Finally he reached Ferry Point, staggered to the dock, and laid Lester down. Looking around for a doctor, he saw Boggs headed his way.

"I been lookin' for you!" shouted Boggs.

"Any doctors around?" asked Josh.

"How bad you hurt?"

"Not me," said Josh. "Him." He pointed to Lester.

"Hang on a second." Boggs ran off.

Josh sat down and checked Lester. The bleeding from the black man's head seemed to have slowed but not completely stopped. A couple of minutes later Boggs reappeared, a doctor in tow. The doctor moved to Josh, who pointed him to Lester.

The doctor shook his head. "Let me check your hip. Get you on a boat."

"I'm OK," Josh insisted. "He's not."

The doctor glanced at Lester but didn't do anything. "I got soldiers to check."

"I said take care of him!" Josh demanded.

The doctor eyed Boggs, but the engineer looked away. "I got more hurt soldiers than you can shake a stick at," the doctor told Josh. "No time for darkies. You want my aid or not?"

Josh grabbed the doctor by the front of his shirt. "That man took that wound defending you!" he shouted. "Now, you tend to him!"

The doctor yanked at Josh's hands and pushed him away. Josh threw a punch, but he lost his balance and fell before the swing could follow through. The doctor kicked him in the side as he lay on the ground. Josh struggled to get up but, exhausted and in pain, couldn't manage it. The doctor held Josh down with a boot on his back.

Boggs took the doctor's elbow. "Move on," he ordered. "You've got other men to tend."

With a look of disgust, he stalked away.

Boggs dropped to Josh. "Let's go. The boats are loadin'. I know some folks north of Beaufort. I'll take you there to stay until you heal."

"Can we take him with us?" Josh nodded toward Lester.

Boggs chuckled. "You beat all. But yes, he can come too."

"OK."

Gathering his strength, Josh pushed up while Boggs grabbed Lester and headed to a boat, Josh right behind him. Settling on the deck of a small fishing trawler, with Lester leaning on his shoulder, Josh tried to catch his breath.

"You still got that canteen?" asked Boggs.

Josh shook his head.

"I'll see if I can find some water," said Boggs.

Josh laid Lester down and checked his wound, which was still bleeding. Josh pressed his shirt against the blood flow. Suddenly, without even considering it carefully, Josh made a startling decision. He didn't want people like that doctor on his side. No way could he fight to defend a man who treated blacks as less than human. Like the sun rising in the morning, Josh's choice just appeared . . . and he wondered how he could ever have considered anything else.

"We're going north," he whispered to Lester. "Just as soon as we're well enough to travel, we're going for my children, then heading out of here."

Unable to answer, Lester remained still, his head bleeding as Josh fought to keep him alive.

Chapter Fifteen

As night fell on Christmas Day, 1861, a cold wind and steady rain whipped across the front porch of the manse on The Oak, and a curl of gray smoke puffed out of the largest chimney. Inside the house Trenton Tessier sat by the fireplace, Calvin in a chair to his right, and his mother to his left. Although they'd just finished an ample supper of fried chicken, mashed potatoes, green beans, and biscuits and jam, Trenton felt no satisfaction. Yes, he'd given the darkies their customary three days off from all but necessary labor, but he'd given them no presents, no jugs of whiskey, no oranges, and no new clothes. As a result nobody had celebrated much.

"The Yankees took Beaufort." Trenton's tone was solemn as he repeated what everyone knew, but nobody could yet believe. "December 11. Walked right in without a fight. The whole place was deserted—not a soldier in sight."

His mother folded her hands in her lap; he felt sick as he watched her. Mrs. York—that was her name now. How disgusting!

"A tactical decision on the part of General Lee," she defended. "He didn't have the men to contest the invasion, so he let the town go."

"The fire in Charleston happened the same night," Calvin added. "Like an act of God. Over five hundred and forty acres burned to a crisp."

"Thank goodness it never got far enough south on King Street to reach our place," said Mrs. York.

"You still trying to sell it?" asked Trenton.

She gave a nod. "Yes, but property isn't selling fast right now. Perhaps we'll find a buyer in the spring."

"Will Charleston fall as easily as Beaufort?" Calvin asked.

"No," explained Mrs. York. "Charleston is more vital to the cause.

The Yankees will try to take it, probably in the summer after the spring rains stop, but it will be defended with much more vigor than Beaufort."

"The Federal blockaders are boxing in a lot of our shipping," said Calvin. "Trying to starve us out."

Trenton stood and moved to the fireplace, his peg leg thumping on the floor. Although the skin on the stump stayed red most of the time and he still got a yellow ooze from it at the end of some days, his leg didn't hurt him too much anymore. "We had a strong rice crop this year."

"Prices in Europe were pretty high," agreed Calvin.

"Too bad nobody wanted to buy it," Trenton fired back.

"The navy has taken most of the ships," Calvin continued. "But even the merchants who still have their boats find it dangerous to run the blockade. Only a few men want to take the chance of buying rice and trying to get it to London."

"Hard times are coming," said Mrs. York.

"Will the Yankees come inland from Beaufort?" Trenton asked.

"Nobody knows," added Mrs. York. "If they do, they'll turn toward Charleston or Savannah as soon as they can. If they go for Charleston, The Oak stands right in their path."

Trenton stared into the fire. The events of the last few months had made his outlook bleak. His mother spent most of her time in Charleston, and Calvin's commission had finally come through, an assignment as a lieutenant with Wade Hampton's cavalry. He planned to ride out soon after the new year started. Although Trenton had also asked for a commission, none had come. The Confederacy wanted him to stay on The Oak and grow rice for the soldiers. Until this morning's arrival of Calvin and his mother, Trenton had spent the last six months pretty much alone, except for the darkies he bossed around every day. With the war, he didn't even have an overseer to help him.

He turned to his mother. "I want to come to Charleston. Talk face to face with the commander of the 27th. I'll show him I'm capable of fighting in spite of my leg. He'll give me a commission."

His mother stiffened. "You know we can't spare you here. If the

Yankees send out patrols from Beaufort, you'll need to do what you can to defend the place."

Trenton stared around the room. They'd moved everything of real value out of the house and up to a place about ten miles out of Columbia. The walls were bare of paintings, the floor cleared of its oriental rugs, the ceiling empty of its chandelier.

"I'm stuck here," he said.

"You're doing your duty. I hope you can come to see that."

Trenton wanted to curse but recognized the truth of her words. Even if he had an overseer, The Oak still needed him to see to things. He stared at his stump, and his anger notched higher. "Have you heard from your dear husband?" he asked his mother.

"He's scratched out a couple of letters but doesn't say much."

"Has he heard anything from Josh Cain?"

"No," answered Mrs. York. "Cain disappeared after the battle at Port Royal Sound."

"You figure he's dead?" Trenton sounded hopeful.

"No way to tell, but they didn't find his body."

Trenton weighed that a second. He liked the idea of Josh Cain dead—and unburied in the sands of Hilton Head.

"Maybe the Yankees took him prisoner," offered Calvin.

Trenton grunted. "I'd prefer him dead."

"His children doing OK?" Mrs. York asked.

Trenton grunted again. "I keep them busy helping Stella."

"The daughter is growing up," Mrs. York commented.

Trenton's eyebrows arched as a wicked thought came to him. "Indeed she is."

Mrs. York narrowed her eyes, as if reading his mind. "Stay away from her. I want no more trouble between you and Hampton."

Trenton waved a hand to dismiss her fears. "I have other matters to attend. No time for such as her."

"Keep it that way."

"What about Camellia?" Trenton asked, his throat suddenly husky. "Any word from her?"

"She's still in Richmond; I believe for a while."

"You took her from me," Trenton accused.

"Of course I did."

Trenton walked to a box on the fireplace mantel, pulled a bourbon bottle from it, and poured himself a drink. "Anybody else want a drink?" he asked, holding out the bottle.

Calvin and his mother shook their heads. Trenton put the bottle away, then gulped the bourbon in one swallow. "Is dear Captain York doing any fighting yet?"

"He's doing his duty," said Mrs. York. "Although he never tells me exactly what that is."

Trenton smiled. "It looks to be a long war. Lots of time for him to get shot."

Mrs. York's eyes flashed. "That's enough! I know you don't approve of him, but he is my husband, and I will not abide your insults!"

Trenton grinned as he poured another drink. "I believe you're smitten . . . by a man lower in station than the bottom of your shoe. Mother, I'm ashamed."

"I'm not smitten," Mrs. York retorted. "But Hampton is a man of strength. You ought to know that by now."

Trenton turned to Calvin. "Are you with her on this?"

"I'm not with either of you."

"But you're going to ride with Hampton York," Trenton hissed.

Calvin didn't answer.

Trenton downed the bourbon. "York's good luck will eventually run out. When it does, I'll be there. You just wait and see."

"You do your job," said Mrs. York. "Let Hampton do his."

Trenton stared at her, his eyes red. "So this is how it's going to be? You in Charleston; me here by myself; you on York's side against me?"

"I'm not against you—you have to believe that."

"I believe nothing of the sort." Trenton glared at his mother. He wanted to strangle her but knew he didn't dare. She'd claw at him like a cat in a corner. Although he knew he could whip her if it came to that, she'd go down fighting hard. It wasn't worth the struggle. There were other ways to see her get what she deserved for her betrayal.

"I'm going to get a chance for my revenge," he promised, staring at her and Calvin. "Before this war ends, that chance will come."

"You best leave that notion behind," Mrs. York warned. "You'll end up dead if you don't."

Trenton took another drink. "Maybe so. But I'll do all I can to make sure that York, maybe Cain too, go with me."

"You're always making threats," she said.

"One day I'll back them up—you'll see."

Mrs. York sighed. "Trenton, you need to remain patient," she pleaded. "Not let what you see right now blur what you've always known."

"What does that mean, Mother dear?"

She moved to him and put a hand on his elbow. "Just trust me. You know I love you more than anything, you and Calvin. And The Oak too—what it means, what it stands for."

Trenton studied his mother's eyes. She hid something there, but he wasn't sure what. "What do you have up your sleeve, Mother?"

She shook her head. "Nothing for you to worry about right now. But you know me well enough to bide your time—and to count on me doing what's best, for all of us."

Trenton smirked. "You do what's best for *you*. That's what I know. Nothing else."

She simply shrugged, so Trenton let the matter drop. His mother was hiding something—of that he was now certain. But he knew her well enough to know that whether or not it would ever benefit him depended on whether or not it would also benefit her.

Almost three hours later, after Trenton fell off to sleep from too much bourbon, and Calvin retired to his room to read, Katherine took a lantern, slipped a heavy cape over her shoulders, and tiptoed out the back door and across the yard to the stables. After checking to make sure no one had followed her, she opened the stable door just enough to let her enter, then rushed inside. Hooking the lantern to a post, she climbed inside her carriage, dragged a square metal box from under the seat, and hopped back onto the ground. A few seconds later, she grabbed a burlap bag from a bin in the corner of the stable and wrapped it three times around the box. Next she took a shovel from a tool area behind the carriage and carried the box and the shovel out of the barn and into the yard, this time without the lantern.

Peering quickly toward the manse, she checked for movement. When she saw none, she decided that no one had missed her. Good.

Her head down, she moved to the base of the huge oak that gave the plantation its name, set the metal box down on the ground, and set to work with the shovel on the side of the oak opposite from the manse. Her excitement made her strong, so she soon dug a hole almost twice as deep as the box. A minute later she dropped the box, still in its burlap wrapping, into the earth and replaced the dirt over it. Once finished she smoothed out the dirt, dropped some loose pieces of straw, gravel, and moss over the scarred ground, and stepped back. Unless she missed her guess, Trenton wouldn't come anywhere near this place until spring, even if then. No way would he ever know that she'd buried twenty-five thousand U.S. dollars there—a significant part of all the cash she possessed.

Pleased, she wiped sweat off her brow and thought of York. Would this please him? she wondered. But why shouldn't it? Although they'd successfully traded the property in Columbia and Santee to the bank in exchange for the money owed from The Oak, the Yankee blockade had prevented her from sailing to London with their money. Afraid to put it in the bank in Charleston, she'd decided to handle it herself; put it somewhere to remain safe until she could determine the outcome of the war.

Glancing again toward the manse, Katherine knew she'd done the right thing for now. As to the future, who knew? She grabbed the shovel and took it back to the stable, then slipped quietly back into the house, her secret hidden in the ground only a short distance from where her older son slept off his most recent drunkenness.

About a quarter of a mile from where Katherine had just buried her money, Lester approached the side of Josh Cain's old house, his tattered shirt and light brown coat not much protection against the swirling rain and whipping wind. Josh followed close behind his friend, his sandy blond hair covered by a soaked floppy hat and a blondish-colored beard covering his face.

Josh touched Lester on the shoulder as they reached the porch and paused in the darkness. "Stay here, Lester. Holler if you hear anything move."

Lester knelt under the porch, and Josh took a long breath to calm his nerves. He and Lester had spent the past few weeks on a small farm about twenty miles north of Beaufort, recovering from their wounds and gathering supplies for their trek north. Two horses, one saddled and one pulling a small wagon, waited for them in the woods out past the rice fields—purchases that had cost Josh almost every dime of the money he'd earned working on Fort Walker. Although he'd had no chance to write Camellia and inform her of his plans, he'd come to a decision about what he needed to do, and he hoped she'd accept it when he got to see her.

Standing, Josh moved past Lester and to the front door of his old home. After a fast look toward the mansion, Josh opened the door and ducked inside. Stella sat in a rocker by the fireplace, Beth in a chair beside her.

"Glory be!" Stella shouted as she spotted him.

"Pa!" Beth jumped up and ran toward him.

"Shush!" ordered Josh, a finger over his mouth.

Beth opened her arms, and he wrapped her up in a big hug. Stella joined them, and Josh opened his arms to her too. But she shook her head and stayed separate. Josh hugged Beth once more, then stepped back.

"Where you been, Pa?" Beth asked. "We heard the fort got taken, but nobody knew what happened to you."

"No time for questions now," Josh explained. "I'll tell you all about it later, on the way."

Beth looked confused. "Where we goin'? Why so secret?"

"I'm taking you and Butler to Miss Camellia," Josh said. "You need to pack—only a few things, though."

"But why are we leavin' in the night? How will we get there? Ain't Richmond a long way?"

"I said no questions!" Josh said sternly. "Just get packed!"

His tone obviously scared her, and she rushed out. Josh faced Stella. "Where's Butler?"

"He sick," moaned Stella, her head down as if she'd done a bad thing. "Real sick."

Josh ran out and into Butler's room. A small kerosene lamp burned in the corner. The air smelled sour. He knelt by the bed and touched Butler's forehead. It almost burned his hand.

"How long has he had fever?" he asked Stella, who had stepped in behind him.

She exhaled heavily. "Off and on for three days."

Josh studied Butler's face. It looked thin; the boy had lost weight.

"You ask for a doctor?"

"Yes, but Master Trenton don't pay me no attention."

Josh's anger boiled, but he pushed it back. "Butler?" he whispered. The boy didn't respond. Josh bit his lower lip. "You think he can travel?"

Stella shook her head. "Mr. Josh, you put him in that rain with the fever he got, and no tellin' what might happen. Young Butler needs rest . . . maybe a lot of it . . . before he good to travel any."

Josh rubbed his beard. "I need to take him," he said, hoping by some stretch of logic that by just saying the words his son's illness might go away.

The old woman's words were stern. "You do that, you takin' a chance on puttin' him in a grave."

Josh groaned. What a choice! Take his boy and kill him—or leave him behind with Trenton Tessier? Which gave Butler the best chance to get better? Making his decision, Josh stood and faced Stella. "We'll leave Butler. Ask Leather Joe to look out for him. Go pack your things."

"What's your rush?" she asked. "Stay here a few days. Let Butler get better, then you can travel."

"I can't do that," Josh said slowly.

"Why not?"

"I got a runaway with me." Josh nodded toward the door. "A man named Lester. We survived the battle at Fort Walker together, and I don't intend on giving him up to the law."

Stella's eyes widened. "What you doin', Mr. Josh? Breakin' the law ain't in your nature."

"I'm going north," Josh explained. "And I'm taking Lester with me, law or no law."

"You gone plumb crazy!"

"Maybe so, but I can't do it anymore. I can't treat people like property. It's not right, not the Lord's way."

"You a brave man, I got to say that."

He shook his head. "It's not bravery when your soul won't let you do anything but what you're doing. Now get packed!"

Stella rolled the snuff in her cheek. "We'll hide this Lester out for a while. Let the weather break. Butler be well by then and you can go."

"I wish I could wait, but I can't," Josh said again. "People saw me leave Fort Walker with Lester. A friend named Boggs—we stayed at his friend's place for a few days—he told me he'd seen a poster. The law's looking for both of us."

"You figure Mr. Trenton knows all this?"

"No way to tell. But you can't hide me and Lester. I won't put you in that kind of danger. If Trenton found out you helped us, he'd kill you . . . and maybe hurt Beth and Butler too."

"I ain't worth enough to kill," Stella threw in.

"Just get packed," he pleaded.

"I don't reckon I'm goin'," she said. "I'm too old and slow. I ain't gone leave Butler to Leather Joe. You need me to look after that boy."

"Trenton will not go easy on you if you stay."

"I ain't scared of him."

"You're not scared of anything, but you need to come with me anyway."

Stella touched his arm. "Look here, Mr. Josh. I'd rather go with you and be with Miss Camellia than most anythin' I can put my head to. But I'd just hold you back. I don't figure we gone go up there on no fancy train, and I ain't fit for walkin'. So I ain't goin. You might as well believe me on that."

Josh rubbed his forehead. Stella was right; he needed her to care for Butler, no matter how much danger that put her in. He patted her arm.

"You're a good woman."

"I do what I can."

"You go back to your house the second we leave," Josh said, focused again on matters at hand. "If Trenton doesn't know you were here when I came, he'll have no excuse to hurt you."

"I ain't goin' nowhere until Butler be feelin' better."

Josh chuckled. "You beat all."

"You say your good-byes to your boy. I'll see to Beth and get you some food for your journey."

As Stella left, Josh moved back to Butler's bedside. "I don't want to leave you," he whispered, his eyes watering. "But I don't see any way around it."

Butler breathed raggedly, and sweat poured off his face.

"Life brings hard choices sometimes." Josh sobbed.

Butler stirred but didn't open his eyes. Josh's heart tore. He wanted to take Butler's place, wanted to let the boy go while he stayed behind. He lifted his eyes toward the ceiling. "I don't understand," he prayed aloud. "Why did You let him take sick now?"

No answer came, so Josh focused again on Butler. "Stella will watch after you. The only thing that's changing is that Beth won't be here. But I'll come back for you soon as I can—I promise you that."

He stared at Butler's face, hoping for some sign of recognition, but none came. He bent to Butler and kissed him on the forehead. "I love you, Son," he whispered. Butler didn't respond. Wiping his eyes, Josh stood and slipped from the room. A minute later Beth and Stella moved back into the front room, Beth bundled in her only coat and holding a burlap bag full of supplies and clothes. Stella carried another sack of food. The fire had burned to a low ember.

Josh faced Beth. "Stella is going to look after Butler. He'll be fine." This time Beth didn't question him. Josh moved to Stella and hugged her.

"You marry Miss Camellia soon as you get the chance," Stella insisted. "After the war ends, you come back and get me, and I'll care for her babies just like I cared for her."

"I'll marry her soon as this war ends," Josh said.

"Who knows when that be?" argued Stella. "You marry her soon as you see her next. Don't wait for nothin'. You promise me that, or I ain't gone let you leave this place."

Josh smiled gravely. "OK, I'll marry Camellia as soon as I see her next."

"That be the right thing, you'll see."

"I'll come back for you and Butler," Josh promised. "Soon as I can."

"We be here," Stella agreed. "Prayin' for you every day, so long as the Lord gives me breath."

Beth moved to Stella and opened her arms. The old Negro, tears in her eyes, snuggled the girl close. "You are a good child. Mostly grown up now. You be fine."

Beth cried loudly.

"You best go on now," Stella urged. "Put some miles behind you before mornin'."

Josh took a letter from his coat pocket. "If anything happens to me . . . you give this to York the next time you see him. It'll explain some things."

"Ain't nothin' gone happen to you. The Lord will see to your protection."

"Just give him the letter."

"OK."

"Tell Butler—"

"I know what to tell that boy, and he'll hear it the second he opens his eyes."

Josh sighed. Beth hugged Stella one more time, then Josh pointed her to the door. On the front porch, Lester appeared out of the dark, and the three of them headed into the rain without a word.

Just past the yard, Josh turned around one more time and saw Stella standing on the front porch, her slender arms hugging her waist, her gray hair whipping out in all directions in the wind. Raising a hand, he bowed slightly and gave her a wave. She raised the bottom of her apron and waved back, a thin figure, frail in the black wet night.

Without knowing why, Josh suddenly knew he'd never see her again. His skin crawled against the thought, and he almost turned back. Was the same thing true for Butler? No clear answer came to that question; no clear answer at all.

Chapter Sixteen

Keeping to the back roads and traveling mostly at night, it took Josh almost a month to steer Lester and Beth the four hundred and fifty miles that lay between them and Richmond. The weather, usually a combination of rain and wind that made the roads muddy and the days short and cold, slowed them down a lot, and Josh's careful avoidance of people did so even more. Patrols of soldiers, gangs of men hunting runaway slaves, and people trying to escape the war made the roads busier than normal. Josh wanted to stay away from them whenever possible. He bedded his group down wherever they could find a secluded spot—sometimes in an empty barn or shed, sometimes in the woods far off the roads, sometimes dug up into the banks of small creeks so they could build a fire. Although he'd brought as much food as he could carry in the single wagon, he still had to stop in towns a few times to buy additional provisions. He always left Lester hidden a few miles out with Beth when he made those trips.

"We know the law is looking for me and Lester," he told Beth the first time he left her behind. "So a man by himself brings less notice than a man with a darky and a pretty girl."

So Beth had let him go without complaint. Gradually they made their way north, up and around Columbia first, then on to Raleigh, again giving the city a wide berth. On the way Josh told Beth what had happened since he'd last seen her—how he'd helped build the fort, how the battle had happened, how he and Lester had stayed on the farm north of Beaufort while they healed. Beth wanted to know everything about the fight at the fort, but Josh kept the details as skimpy as he could. No use filling a young girl's head with the horrible details of war. It was a bloody mess, no matter how glorious some folks tried to make it.

In addition to not telling her much about the war, he said absolutely nothing about what he planned to do after he delivered her to Camellia. With everything else she had to face, why put her through the wringer of wondering if her pa was a traitor? Yet he couldn't help but wonder how she'd take the fact that he'd decided he wouldn't fight for the South.

Slowly but surely the miles melted away—ten one day, twelve the next, fifteen on another. Beth rode the saddle horse some, and Lester and Josh walked beside the wagon. Although Beth never complained of the hard journey, her face grew thinner day by day on the long trek. She seemed to change right before Josh's eyes. Before he knew it, she was no longer a girl but had become a young woman, her weight loss unexplainably offset by a rounding of her body at bodice and hip. As her body changed, so did her demeanor. All of a sudden she seemed less innocent, almost as if someone had come and whispered to her more of the truth of life than Josh had ever dared tell her. He saw it in her eyes and in her walk—the war had already changed them all.

Josh heard bits and pieces of war talk on the occasions he slipped into towns for supplies. The Federals had taken over Beaufort and the Coosaw River, which separated the Yankees from the Rebels just north of there, but they had not gone any farther inland so far. Stonewall Jackson won a big battle up in Bath, Virginia. Charleston and other port cities lay under a stout blockade. A man named Grant had made some headway for the Yankees out west, moving toward Nashville, Tennessee. The reports told Josh what he'd feared ever since Port Royal—this war would not end anytime soon.

It was late on a cold, gray afternoon, the last week of January, 1862, when Josh and his crew reached the outskirts of Richmond. Pulling their wagon from the side road they'd been traveling into a main passage across a bridge into the city, Josh turned to Beth. "Get in the wagon. Pull your coat up tight. And remember—if we get stopped, I do the talking." She obeyed him without complaint. Several minutes later the group entered the stream of humanity crossing the bridge and going into the city.

Josh couldn't believe his eyes. More people than he'd ever seen streamed in and out of the Confederate capital. Wagons full of goods clattered across the bridge and the road beyond it. Soldiers and merchants seemed as plentiful as ants at a picnic. Noise abounded—the creak of wagon wheels, the clomp of horses, the yells and shouts of men and women doing their business.

To Josh's relief, nobody paid them any notice. They were just another family on the move, he realized, like so many others uprooted by the hard times of war. It took him close to an hour to make his way to Capitol Square and find directions to the Victoria Hotel. From there it took another hour to find somebody—a hotel maid at the Victoria in this instance—to take his two dollars in exchange for the address of the man and woman who owned the hotel. By then night had fallen, and the temperature had dropped.

"Mr. Swanson be dead," said the hotel maid as he gave her the two dollars. "But Mrs. Swanson lives on Clairemont—in a fine big house with a black iron gate, a fountain with a bird in it. She took me there once when she had a party. I served the drinks that night."

Keeping his hat low over his eyes, Josh left the hotel, walked back to the street where he'd left Lester and Beth, picked them up, and then headed toward the address the maid had described. Parking the wagon on the corner, Josh told Lester to wait with Beth until he got back. A minute later he walked up the street, found the house, and eased up the walkway, his hands clammy with nerves in spite of the cold. On the porch he peered around once, then rapped on the door. A few seconds later, he heard a man's voice; Josh stepped back as the door opened. A black man in a formal coat and white shirt stood there.

Josh took off his hat. "I'm here to see Mrs. Swanson."

"Who can I say is callin'?" the black man asked.

"Josh Cain."

"I heard tell of you," claimed the black man. "I'm Roof."

Josh stuck out his hand. Roof took it and shook. "Is Mrs. Swanson here?" asked Josh.

"Please come in." Roof stepped back.

Josh glanced over his shoulder. "Is it safe here?"

"What you mean?"

Josh took a breath. "I'm not alone. I've got my child, plus . . . another man, a runaway."

Roof grabbed him by the arm, quickly pulled him inside, and shut the door. "Hold here, Mr. Cain. I get Mrs. Swanson."

Josh looked around as Roof disappeared. High ceilings, nice paintings—mostly landscapes—on the walls, plush rugs on the floors, furniture with multiple inlays and carvings. His heart raced with the hope of seeing Camellia. Footsteps sounded, and a woman rushed his way, her eyes wide, her navy skirt and tan blouse finely tailored, her black shoes well shined.

"Mr. Cain, I'm Ruth Swanson," said the woman, her hand out. "Camellia's told me so much about you. What are you doing here?"

Josh shook her hand, then explained quickly, "I came with my daughter and my man Lester too. I need a place for my Beth to stay. Figured to leave her here—I know that's a lot to ask. But Camellia will provide for her. Is she here?"

Mrs. Swanson glanced at her feet; something in her manner scared Josh. "I'm not staying," he said, wanting to remove any fears she might have. "I just want to rest for a day, then I'm going to get Lester safe in the North and join . . . the Federal army."

When Mrs. Swanson gulped, he saw he'd shocked her. But since he didn't have time to tiptoe around anybody's sensitivities, he pushed ahead, impatient to get Lester and Beth off the street. "Can I bring my daughter in? Lester too?"

Mrs. Swanson looked at Roof, but he didn't speak. "Bring them around back," she suddenly said, obviously deciding to risk it. "There's no light there. I'll open the door."

Josh started to ask again about Camellia, then decided that could wait. Slipping on his hat, he left and rushed to the street. A few seconds later, he led Lester and Beth through the back door and into the kitchen. Beth looked around, her eyes wide in obvious awe of the fine surroundings. Lester kept his eyes on his shoes. Josh took his hat off again. "We're grateful to you, Mrs. Swanson. Lester and I will leave in the morning. We don't want to put you in any danger."

Mrs. Swanson pulled a plate of biscuits from the stove. "Sit. You must be hungry."

All quickly obeyed. Josh examined his hands; he longed to wash them but didn't want to wait for the food. Mrs. Swanson handed him a biscuit; it tasted delicious. Next she poured them water. Josh gulped down a glass and finished the biscuit before he paused enough to take a breath. Beth kept eating, her eyes darting around as if waiting for someone to attack. Josh's heart fell as he watched her. She looked so anxious. Had the war already taught her that anxiety? Put fear in her eyes?

Josh glanced from Beth to Lester and then to Mrs. Swanson, who had taken a seat at the table with them. She handed Josh another biscuit, but this time he didn't eat it right away. His tongue burned with a question that he didn't want to wait any longer to have answered. "Where's Camellia?"

Mrs. Swanson played with the back of her hair. "She's not here."

"Where is she?"

Mrs. Swanson bit a thumbnail. "She left a few days ago to go after Beth and Butler."

Josh laid the biscuit down. "She left?"

"Yes. She's wanted to go since Mr. Swanson died and finally insisted on it. Ruby and I both tried to talk her out of it, but she wouldn't listen. Said she had to get your children safe, that she'd made a promise to you."

Josh put his head in his hands. "I didn't know," he lamented.

"Of course you didn't. She wanted to write you but didn't know where to reach you; didn't know what had happened to you. She feared you were . . ."

Josh nodded his understanding. "Is Ruby with her?"

"Yes. Ruby got as stubborn as Camellia about that."

"Maybe Ruby hopes to see her husband," said Josh.

"She wrote him a letter, asked him to meet her in Charleston. I expect she wants to tell him he's got a new baby girl."

"Ruby had a baby?"

"Yeah, first week of November. Leta—she's asleep upstairs."

Josh tried to settle his thoughts. "I planned to marry Camellia before I headed off."

"You can still do that," Mrs. Swanson said. "If all goes well, she could get home within a few days."

"Or it could take weeks," reasoned Josh. "Travel is difficult. There are not many seats for civilians on trains, and carriages are impossible to find. I can't stay that long."

"Sure you can." Mrs. Swanson nodded at Lester. "I'll let Mr. Lester stay here and work as one of my men. I pay my darkies a wage. You and Mr. Lester can bed down in the little house out back. No one will know the difference."

Josh took a bite of biscuit and considered the matter. It sounded tempting. Yet, no matter how safe it sounded, he knew what happened to folks who harbored runaways, especially with the war going at full throttle. If Mrs. Swanson got caught helping Lester, the law would show her no mercy. A woman who kept no slaves, then harbored one who'd fled a Southern plantation wouldn't get any sympathy from those whose sons were out fighting to preserve the right to do so. The authorities probably already saw her as a Union sympathizer because she paid her darkies a wage. If they found out she had a fugitive at her house, they'd haul her away to jail and look with suspicion at everybody connected to her—and that included Camellia, when she returned.

"It's too dangerous for us to stay," Josh concluded. "We'll leave in the morning."

Mrs. Swanson placed both palms on the table. "Camellia would want me to insist that you remain until she returns," she argued.

"I'd like nothing better," Josh stated. "But it's not possible." He turned to Beth. "You'll stay here with Mrs. Swanson. Miss Camellia will come back soon. You stay with her until . . . well . . . until I come get you again."

"Where you goin', Pa?"

Josh hung his head, but then decided he couldn't hide it from Beth any longer. "I'm going to fight for the Federals."

"I don't understand."

Josh took his daughter's hands in his. "I know, sweetheart," he started. "It's hard to explain. But remember I told you I fought for the United States when I was just a young man?"

Beth nodded and Josh continued. "I swore a loyalty to my country then, and I can't go against it now. And not only that, but . . . well, I can't fight for a cause that wants to keep other folks in slavery. You know how much I love Stella."

"I love her too, Pa."

"I know you do."

"Stella says she doesn't care if she's free or not."

Josh smiled. "But she ought to get that choice, don't you think? It shouldn't be for somebody else to tell her where she lives, what kind of work she does, whether she can stay with her family or not. She's a human being, just like you and me, and I can't shoot another man to keep her as something less than one. Do you understand?"

Beth sighed. "I wish nobody had to fight."

"I agree. But since we do, I have to choose sides—and I'm choosing the United States."

Beth nodded solemnly, and Josh patted her hands. Again Josh thought of Camellia. Hopefully Butler was now well enough to travel. But how would Trenton react when Camellia and Ruby showed up? Would he stand quietly aside and let Camellia take Butler and leave? Maybe not. He'd surely make Ruby stay behind, no doubt of that. Another thought came to Josh. Camellia knew Trenton too well to take Ruby all the way to The Oak, so she'd leave Ruby in Charleston to meet Obadiah and go there alone.

Josh groaned. "Trenton Tessier will be furious, maybe violent when Camellia shows up. We've got to help her."

"But what can we do?" asked Mrs. Swanson.

Josh studied the matter. Could he get a telegram to Mrs. York? But where would he send it? He didn't have her address in Charleston. Besides, it probably wouldn't do any good; she wouldn't go against her son even if she got a telegram in time to go to The Oak before Camellia got there. Josh slammed his hand on the table. "I'll kill Trenton if he hurts her," he growled.

Mrs. Swanson touched his forearm. "Camellia is a strong woman," she soothed. "I've learned that already. She's tough and brave. She'll take care of Trenton Tessier if he tries anything. If any woman can slip your boy out of there and get him back here, she's the one. You can count on that."

Josh studied Mrs. Swanson's eyes and saw truth in them. Camellia had grown up hard. Although she had the grace of a swan, she had iron in her backbone and wouldn't back down from trouble if it came looking for her. She could handle Trenton if his anger got out of control. Besides, Trenton loved her, didn't he? He couldn't hurt her if he loved her, could he?

Calmed some, Josh took another bite of biscuit. "Maybe the Lord planned it this way. Maybe it's not the right time to marry her. What if I get killed? Then Camellia would be a widow."

"She wouldn't let that stop her from marrying you," Mrs. Swanson assured him. "Camellia loves you. She's made that plain to anybody who will listen."

Josh gazed at Mrs. Swanson as if seeing her for the first time. "You're her mother."

"Yes, I am."

"I suppose I ought to ask you for her hand in marriage, since her father is dead."

"I don't think she needs my permission for anything, but from what she's let on to me, you're a good man. I gladly give my blessing."

"I'm not worth much," he said. "But I do love her. Will you let Camellia marry a Yankee?"

She hesitated only briefly. "Camellia is a grown woman. She can marry who she wants."

"You think she'll still take me if I end up wearing Union blue?"

Mrs. Swanson smiled. "I expect a brigade of soldiers with Sharps rifles couldn't keep her from it."

Josh nibbled at his biscuit again but then suddenly felt tired. He'd come so far but had so far yet to go. "You'll keep my children for me?"

"You're to be my son-in-law someday. How could I refuse?"

In spite of his fears for Camellia and Butler, Josh smiled. The Lord had brought Camellia here; he felt sure of it. He could leave her here and trust she'd stay secure. He extracted a letter from his pocket and handed it to Mrs. Swanson. "Will you give this to Camellia when she returns?"

"Of course I will." Mrs. Swanson took the letter.

"Tell her I'll come back when this all ends."

"I pray that day will soon come."

A full six days after Josh arrived at Mrs. Swanson's house, Camellia arrived at The Oak in the back of a one-horse carriage. It was early afternoon, on a clear but cold day. Camellia's bones rattled as she rode up the road toward the manse. She could sleep for a month if anybody would give her a chance. Although she'd spent the first three days of her journey on a crowded, filthy train that seemed to stop or break down on a regular basis, that ride had ended at Charleston. After a night of rest, she and Ruby had looked for another day for a carriage she could hire to bring her the rest of the way. Finally a short man named Ristler, who wore a hat almost taller than his skinny body, had agreed to take her to The Oak for fifty dollars—a price she thought unreasonable, but that she recognized she had to pay.

For safety's sake Camellia had told Ruby to stay behind in Charleston and, due to the fact that she'd previously written Obadiah and asked him to meet her there and he'd agreed, Ruby didn't put up any fuss. Camellia had left with Ristler in the carriage early the next morning. They had spent one night on the road and now had finally reached The Oak.

Gathering her shawl tightly against the chilly air, Camellia glanced out the window and wondered if she should stop and speak to Trenton at the manse. Then she decided against it. In former days such a courtesy would have been expected. But these were not former days. Although she didn't fear Trenton, she knew his temper could get hot, so why agitate him? Beth and Butler were no concern of his. Fact is, he might feel grateful she'd come to get them since their absence would mean two less mouths to feed at a time when hardships were hitting everybody.

"Go past the big house!" she called to Ristler.

The little man clicked at his horse and kept moving. Camellia gazed over The Oak as she rode through it. Things looked a lot quieter; hardly anyone moved around. She stared out toward the rice fields but couldn't see them. Had the war changed things here yet? Would it anytime soon? She leaned back again and told herself it didn't matter. After she got Beth and Butler, she'd never see this place again. She'd made that decision on her trip from Richmond. When the war ended, she didn't know where she'd live, but one thing she knew for sure—she wouldn't return to The Oak. At least not while Trenton Tessier was alive.

The carriage bounced on. Two or three minutes later they pulled up at the small house beside the one where she'd grown up—a square, simple place, livable but not much more. A thin sliver of smoke curled from the chimney.

Camellia jumped from the carriage almost before it stopped. "Come in," she called to Ristler, breathing in short gasps as her excitement rose. "Warm up some. I'll put my hands on some food; then we'll pack and leave before dark."

Ristler hopped down and followed her toward the house. She entered without knocking. "Beth!" she called. "Butler!" Her eyes watered as she moved into the kitchen and saw Butler at the table. He jumped up and ran toward her, his face lit with a mixture of joy and surprise.

"Miss Camellia!" he yelled as he threw his arms around her. Camellia held him for a long time, her cold cheeks against his thin face. Then she stepped back and took a long look at him. Although he appeared taller, he seemed thinner, too, his eyes bigger in his hollow skin, his face looking like somebody had sucked some of the juice from his bones. She noticed a bruise the size of a walnut on his cheek, near his left temple.

"You OK?" she asked, concerned.

He brushed her hand away. "I'm fine—been sick some, but better now. Stella cared for me. I'm glad you've come back."

Camellia smiled, but something about his voice scared her. "I'm not here for long," she announced, her decision to rescue the children seeming more right all the time. "I'm taking you and Beth with me."

"You takin' me to Richmond with Beth?"

"You know about Richmond?"

"Yeah, Stella told me. Said I'd live in a fine house. Pa with you?"

"No, not now," answered Camellia, confused by Butler's words.

"Have you heard from Pa?"

"Not since last fall. But don't worry about that now. Let's pack you up. I want to leave here soon as we can. Beth in her room?"

"Beth's in Richmond," said Butler. "Don't you know that?"

Camellia put a hand on his shoulder. "I don't understand."

"Pa came for her," said Butler. "Stella told me. I was sick and couldn't go with them, but I'm better now."

"Beth's already gone?"

"Yeah, maybe a month ago. Pa took her away, to a fine house in Richmond."

Camellia tried to figure things out. Josh had not written her since the Federals took Port Royal Sound, and she'd feared for his safety. At least this meant he'd lived through all that. But where had he been? Had he been recovering from a wound? And if so, then why didn't the army have some record of that? True, he hadn't enlisted as a soldier, but didn't the army keep up with men who built the forts the soldiers fought in?

"OK," she finally said, deciding it didn't matter so long as it meant Josh was alive and well. "It's me and you—Stella too. Let's get going. I got a carriage outside. We'll all pack in. The sooner we can leave, the sooner we can get to Richmond and see your pa and Beth again."

Butler nodded, and Camellia moved to the shelves by the table and started gathering things. "I need a sack," she told Butler. "We need to pack as much food as we can."

Butler grabbed a couple of burlap bags from the kitchen pantry and tossed them to her.

"Go on now," Camellia urged. "Get your things ready. I'll go get Stella."

"Stella's hurt," Butler stated. "Master Trenton . . . he . . ."

"He what?"

"He beat her after everybody left. Blamed her for your leavin'. Mrs. York has been in Charleston since Christmas. After Master Calvin took off for the fightin', Master Trenton went plumb crazy. He drinks all the time, stays mad. Stella is in bad shape. He won't let her rest. Makes her work even if she is hurt."

Camellia moved toward Butler and touched his bruise, understanding now how he got it. He winced under her fingers. "He's hurt you too," she said softly.

"Not too bad," Butler said bravely. "But I fear for Stella. She's kept him away from me most of the time, takin' my licks. I've tried to stop her from doin' it, but she said that Pa had put her in charge, and I had to obey her or Pa would tan me when he came home."

"You're a brave boy. Now go pack while I see to Stella."

"But what can you do? Master Tessier is mean and hateful."

"I don't know, but I can't just leave her!" She turned to Ristler. "Get his things in the carriage. I'll be back in a few minutes."

"You reckon I ought to come with you?"

"No—it's not your business. See to the boy."

Ristler nodded, and Camellia headed out the back door, her chin set.

Camellia entered the manse through the front door and headed straight toward the small kitchen off from the main dining hall. She could usually find Stella there this time of day, getting things ready to serve for the evening meal. As Camellia entered the house, a host of memories flooded through her—all the times she'd carried food from the main cookhouse into this place, all the times she'd carried steaming dishes into the huge dining room where the Tessier family took their meals. She'd accepted her station through those years, hers and those of the servants, the blacks who'd worked beside her. She'd dreamed of marrying Trenton, and those dreams had seemed so natural, so possible, so real. How strange everything had turned out. Dreams shattered, but new ones built—better ones, dreams with a good man, not a mean one. Dreams with no gold at the edges but love instead, love that would last long after gold tarnished and faded.

Camellia eased into the kitchen and saw Stella standing over a sink. "Stella," she whispered. When the old woman turned, Camellia's breath caught in her throat. Stella's face was bruised and battered.

"What did he do to you?" Camellia cried, rushing to her friend.

Stella smiled her toothless grin, and Camellia wanted to cry even more. Cuts and bruises covered Stella's cheeks, forehead, and chin. Her face, always black, seemed even darker in some spots where the blood pooled just beneath the thin skin. Camellia took the old woman gently into her arms. "You poor soul," she soothed.

"I be all right," said Stella. "You know I's a tough old gal."

Camellia's tears rolled onto Stella's shoulders. For the first time in her life, she felt genuine hatred toward another person—and that person was Trenton Tessier. Her hatred gave her courage, and she made a snap decision. "Come on!" she urged. "We're getting you out of here!"

"What you mean?"

"You're going to Richmond with me, and I'm not going to hear any argument."

Stella's jaw jutted forward; she frowned. "You be breakin' the law. I ain't gone let you do that."

"You don't have a choice. If you don't go, I don't. If I leave you here now, he'll kill you for sure."

"A man can kill the body, but the Lord will raise my soul right back up. Don't you worry none about Miss Stella. I'll do all right."

Camellia shook her head. "No more talk. I'll carry you out if I have to."

Just then footsteps sounded from behind them, and the smell of whiskey walked into the room. Camellia's blood ran cold as she recognized the thump of Trenton's wooden leg on the floor.

"Well, I see we have a houseguest." Trenton's voice was cold. "Stella, why didn't you announce we had a charming lady at the manse?"

Camellia's knees shook, but she braced herself, swung around and stared firmly into Trenton's eyes. He scanned her from head to toes—from her bonnet to dark blue cape, to her ankle-length gray dress and buckled black shoes—and back up again. "You're dressing better than when I saw you last. You find Mr. and Mrs. Swanson to be people of means?"

"I don't have time for polite conversation," growled Camellia. "I'm here to take Butler—Stella too. I'll pay you for her. What's she worth—two, maybe three hundred?"

"How can you measure the worth of an old friend?" he asked mockingly. "Stella helped raise me. No price is high enough for her."

"You've beaten her."

"I've reminded her of her place—an unfortunate but sometimes necessary act with darkies. You know that as well as I."

"Not anymore."

"So you're an abolitionist now? Would Mr. and Mrs. Swanson be surprised to hear that?"

Knowing that direct argument with him would only make things worse, Camellia calmed down her tone. "Just let us go, and I'll not bother you anymore."

Trenton's shoulders sagged slightly, and she saw a touch of weakness, even sadness, seep into his eyes. As she thought of his situation, the intense hatred she'd felt a few moments earlier faded. How terrible things must be for him! He was all alone and a cripple, while his younger brother fought a war Trenton desperately wanted to join. She took a step his way.

"I'm sorry it's come to this," she soothed. "But everything is different. I know that's hard to accept, but it's true, and nobody can change it. So just let me go—Butler and Stella too. There's no reason to make things worse. We were friends once; we cared for each other. Whatever else has happened, can't we remember that?"

When he hung his head, she thought she'd won him over.

"Come back to me," he whispered. "I still love you; we can still marry. I need you more than ever." He opened his arms and reached for her, but she stepped away.

"No," she said softly. "It's over between us. And you have to accept that. The sooner you do, the sooner you can find someone else, someone who'll love you, care for you."

His face bunched, and she saw fury in the look—a fury that scared her worse than anything she'd ever seen. "I'll say when it's over!" he shouted, all signs of tenderness disappearing from his eyes.

Camellia inched back another step, but he grabbed for her as she did, his fingers like extended talons. She pushed him away and turned to run. He growled and jumped at her, hooking her by the hair. She kicked at his bad leg, but he dodged with a quickness she didn't expect. His right hand moved to her throat, wrapped around her flesh, and squeezed, cutting off her breath.

"Leave her be!"

Camellia recognized Stella's scream. She tried to yell at the old woman to stay away, but Trenton was squeezing her so hard she couldn't get out any words. She looked up just as Stella threw an iron skillet at Trenton's head. The skillet hit its mark. Trenton let go of Camellia's throat and hair and staggered backward.

Bent at the waist, Camellia gasped for breath as Trenton recovered, picked up the skillet, and rushed at Stella, his face puffy with hatred. Stella scratched at Trenton, but he ignored her fingers and clutched at her neck.

Able to breathe again, Camellia shrieked and threw herself at Trenton. But he, still grasping Stella with one hand, turned and swung the skillet at Camellia. It caught her in the shoulder and knocked her down. Pain jarred her back as she fell. Trenton threw Stella away and moved to Camellia, the skillet held high.

Roaring like a beast now, he swung the skillet like an ax at her face, but she partially blocked the blow with her arms. He raised the skillet again, and this time it caught her across the side of her upper back as she twisted away. The blow rocked her deeply. She heard a drumming in her ears, like an engine pounding. Her eyes blurred but not enough to keep her from seeing Trenton raise the skillet again, this time so high it almost reached the ceiling.

Camellia struggled to stand and fight against the blow about to crush her. She grabbed his leg and tried to pull herself up, but he pushed her away. She staggered to her knees, but he kicked her down again. Finally her legs gave out, and she slumped back, closed her eyes, and waited for the last blow to fall.

A piercing wail coursed through the room. Camellia opened her eyes to see Stella pounce on Trenton once more, her thin fingers grabbing at his eyes from her perch on his back. He dropped the skillet and punched back with an elbow. Stella bounced off and fell against the wall. For a second everything became quiet. Camellia tried again to rise but couldn't.

Trenton faced Camellia. Blood ran down his face where Stella had scratched him. "You coming back to me?" he asked.

Camellia couldn't believe her ears. How could he even ask such a thing? "No!" she gasped. "Just let us leave!"

A wicked grin came to his face as he turned to Stella. She dragged herself to a kneeling position as he stepped to her. "You wanting to leave me too?" he asked.

Stella shook her head. "I reckon not."

He pivoted back to Camellia. "You sure you won't stay with your friend Stella?"

"You're an animal," Camellia hissed.

Trenton cackled, then twisted and launched a vicious kick at Stella! His boot caught her in the ribs, and Camellia heard a snap. Then Stella crumpled to the floor like a rag doll, all her fight gone. He raised a boot again, and Camellia screamed, grabbed the skillet where he'd dropped it, and rushed at him, skillet held as high as she could raise it. He turned slightly as she reached him. She launched the skillet with all her hatred behind it, and the blow caught Trenton on the side of the head. He fell in a heap by Stella, his eyes glazed but open.

Her breath ragged, Camellia bent to him, the skillet ready if she needed it again. To her relief, she saw from his vacant stare that she didn't have to worry about him again anytime soon. Laying down her weapon, she quickly moved to Stella and took the old woman's head in her lap.

"I'm here, Stella," Camellia whispered. "Open your eyes. You'll be OK."

Stella opened her eyes, but they weren't focused. She worked her lips as if to make them speak, but nothing came out.

"Stella, old friend, you're going to Richmond with me," said Camellia, wanting desperately to convey hope.

Stella's lips moved again, and Camellia bent low.

"Go . . . on, child. He busted up my ribs, I reckon. Can barely get a breath. Maybe a rib stuck somethin' on my insides. I goin' on to . . . the Lord . . . He callin'."

"I need you," cried Camellia. "You can't go yet."

Stella's lips moved again, but Camellia couldn't hear any words. Blood trickled into both corners of Stella's mouth. Tears rolled down Camellia's cheeks. "I love you, Stella," she murmured. "You've been my mama."

A little smile touched Stella's lips. "It . . . pleases me to hear that."

Camellia rocked Stella gently as the old woman closed her eyes. Less than a minute later, her breath stopped, but Camellia kept holding her. Tears ran down Camellia's face as she rocked in her grief. She prayed quietly in her agony, a prayer that seemed to rise up and fill the room with its presence. She wanted to stay right there with Stella; see to a proper burial for her. She wanted to make sure somebody dug her hole deeply and said pretty words over her sweet old bones. She continued to hold Stella until she heard a groan. Then she opened her eyes and remembered Trenton. Peering at him, she saw blood running down his face. A large bruise and a knot had appeared under his eye where she'd pounded him with the skillet. He moaned again, but Camellia felt nothing for his pain, no sympathy at all. Instead she ignored him, wiped her eyes, and faced Stella once more.

"May the Lord bless you and keep you," she whispered. "May the Lord's face shine upon you and give you peace."

Stella didn't answer, but the little smile stayed on her lips. Camellia gently placed the old woman's head on the floor and kissed her on the lips. After fighting off the desire to kick Trenton in the face, Camellia left the room and ran out the back door. Within five minutes she, Ristler, and Butler rode off The Oak without a backward glance.

All things that are made for our general uses are at war,

even we among ourselves.

—JOHN FLETCHER

Chapter Seventeen

Late October, 1864, A battlefield at Burgess Mill, south of Petersburg, Virginia

Hampton York, huddled in a muddy blanket, sat around a smoky fire in a grove of dense pine with his boy, Johnny, and Calvin Tessier. As York blew into his hands to warm them, a chilly drizzle dripped off his slough hat. The plopping of the droplets to the ground marked the time as surely as a clock. Their horses and those of scores of other men who camped in the woods in and around them stood tied and head down about twenty feet away, their bones sticking out of their sides from too much traveling and not enough food. York felt the same way—plumb worn out—but he didn't bother to speak of it. Men who'd fought a war for over three years with almost no break got tired. He'd known that from the beginning, so why make it any big matter?

York picked a dented coffeepot off the fire and tilted it toward a rusty cup.

"I don't see why you bother," said Calvin, pointing to the pot. "That swill holds no resemblance to real coffee."

"It's hot," York stated. "That's good enough for me, I reckon." He offered a cup to Johnny, who gratefully took it. For several minutes the three men sat in silence. York wrapped his hand around his warm cup, remembering how he'd gotten to this place and time. The long line of days since he'd joined up with Wade Hampton, the finest general ever to come out of South Carolina, seemed like one continuous horseback ride through flying bullets, booming cannons, and shouting men.

Along with Johnny and over a thousand other soldiers that had just signed up, York had spent most of June 1861 training outside of Columbia, South Carolina. Back then everything looked all fresh and clean, and the men were full of spit and polish. They marched in a lot of parades and listened to sunny speeches about how they'd whip the Yankees in the summer and return home in time for Christmas. What foolish bravado! Although he knew it as such even then, he'd dared to hope it would be true. Soon enough, though, the hard facts had set in.

On June 28, Hampton's Legion had shipped north to Richmond on a train, and everything got real serious in a hurry. They'd drawn first blood and lost their first man in the war's first battle at Manassas. What a day that had been! All rush and charge, fire and saber, blood and courage. Townsfolk from both sides of the Potomac River had ridden out in their Sunday best to watch the spectacle—their excitement over war an elixir that made them drunk with silly expectations of quick and easy victory.

York grunted quietly. Blood running into the dirt and the stench of dead men sobered everybody real fast that day, and they'd stayed pretty sober ever since. He eyed Johnny and Calvin, and his chest swelled again with pride. Both boys had held up well that day; proven themselves good soldiers. And that had not changed in the time since.

After Manassas, things had gotten pretty quiet for close to nine months. They dug in at Freestone Point to defend the west bank of the Potomac River against Yankee incursions, their artillery exchanging fire whenever a Yankee boat or soldier dared show his head. They just about froze that winter because General Hampton had somehow gotten the notion that his men ought to spend the cold months in tents instead of building any kind of stouter winter buildings. A number of men died from the sickness they took in the cold and snow, and the rest grumbled at the general because he spent most of the winter months in a warm house in Richmond instead of with them.

To York's and everyone else's relief, the end of winter finally came. By April 1862, his duties and those of his comrades took a much warmer, even if riskier turn as the war raged into full swing again. Following their general, the legion had shipped south and engaged in a series of cavalry battles, their quick-strike capability making them a curse to the Federals and a hero to the Rebels.

York's mind whipped through all the towns they'd spilled blood for in the past three or so years—a blur of muddy fields one day, sunny afternoons another, dark nights by campfires with thousands of soldiers all around, early mornings on horseback galloping across flat roads and through tall pine trees, the thundering of the horses' hooves thrumming in his ears, and the screams of wounded and dying men pounding in his head. Sometimes he and his men carried the day; other times they slunk off in hurried retreat. The success or failure of their escapades mirrored that of the whole South. Sometimes it seemed the Yankees must surely surrender and let the Rebels go home in peace, and other times it looked certain they'd end up whipped and humiliated.

Williamsburg . . . Seven Pines . . . White Oak Farm . . . Fredericksburg . . . Antietam . . . Chambersburg . . . Brandy Station . . . Gettysburg . . . Spotsylvania . . . how many there had been! Some large and monumental like Gettysburg; others so small he couldn't even remember their names.

Brandishing saber and pistol he, Johnny, and Calvin had rampaged in on their sturdy, swift horses, galloping around, behind, and through the Yankee lines, breaking Bluebelly charges at their point, stealing supplies when they could find them, disrupting troop movements by spying out and reporting their positions, destroying railroad lines and then rushing away.

York grinned as he recalled their latest escapade. Just about a month earlier, he and the rest of General Hampton's boys had slid around to the rear of Grant's lines, rode a hundred miles in three days, and captured over two thousand head of Yankee cattle and three hundred enemy soldiers—and all at a cost of barely fifty men. Commendations rolled in from General Robert E. Lee, and the boys in the lines had whooped and hollered and tossed their hats in the air when they'd showed back up, all safe and sound and herding all the beeves. For weeks afterward they bellowed out a loud "mooooo" every time they came into contact with the Federal boys to let them know they were dealing with Wade Hampton's Legion.

"I wish I had some juicy steaks to cook up," York suddenly said, remembering the taste of the beef they'd cooked for days after that raid.

Calvin chuckled. "Wish General Hampton had kept all those cattle just for us instead of sharing them with the rest of the army."

"You're a selfish soldier," Johnny threw in, grinning.

"That I am."

York smiled and studied the two boys.

Over the last three years, they'd both fought every battle he'd faced, their lot equally as rough as his, their courage equally as staunch. Although he'd promised Katherine he'd do what he could to protect Calvin and tried to do the same for Johnny, the truth was, he held no power to do much for either boy. When the bullets flew, one man could do little for another but pray. And since York didn't believe in that kind of thing, he held few cards he could deal to aid the two young men. To his relief the two boys had moved through the rifle shot and flashing bayonets that came at them as if wearing uniforms that made them invisible to the enemy. No bullet hit them; no sword bit into their flesh; no disease took root in their bodies. If York had any religious nature at all buried in his bones, he'd have surely come to believe in miracles as a result of their good fortune. But since he didn't, he just passed it off as pure dumb luck.

York chuckled in admiration, wondering how Calvin and Trenton could have turned out so differently. Calvin fought with a steady courage, his temper even, his eye sharp, and his aim true. He took orders without complaint and accepted the rough life as if he'd been raised to it, as if he'd never slept on silk sheets or sipped on French wine. He and Johnny had become constant companions. More than once they'd ridden off into a town when they got some time away from the war, their young voices filled with eager banter in spite of the hardships of war.

York sipped his coffee and wondered about the change in Calvin. Had the boy always possessed the bravery and loyalty, the honesty and good humor that the war had revealed in him? Had he been such a fine man all along, the good character just waiting for the war to bring it out? Or had the war created something in him that he never would have discovered if he'd stayed forever at ease on The Oak? York didn't know the answer to any of the questions, but he did know that the friendship between Calvin and Johnny encouraged his heart. Maybe when this whole fracas ended, Calvin and Johnny could find a way to bring some calm between their two families. Wouldn't it be a strange thing if a war helped cause some peace?

"What do you plan to do when the war ends?" Johnny asked, interrupting York's musings.

"I don't think that far ahead," York explained. "When you're fightin', it's best to keep your whole self set on the battles and let everything else fall from your thoughts."

"You don't ever think of home?"

York spat. His worries about The Oak had become distant memories, his marriage to Katherine York a fading image, his fears about Trenton and his actions a blur.

"Not much if I can help it," he said. "With mine balls flyin' around on a regular basis, I reckon the only way to survive is to keep my head down and my mind straight ahead—no bother about anythin' else. If I live through all this, I'll worry about those things then."

"You ever think about Uncle Josh?" asked Johnny.

York stared into the fire. "I do. But since I don't know what's become of him, there's nothin' to be done—so I best let it go."

Calvin nodded. York shook water off his hat and considered all the death he'd seen; how dying had become a constant companion in the last three years. Rifle shot took down a lot of the boys, their bodies ripped open by the random aim of Yankee soldiers. Many others fell by the aftermath of the rifles and cannons—the infections that set in when the men went to the hospital. York hated to see that: some boy with a wound that looked real fixable left the battlefield for the hospital but never came back. Word in the ranks said, "Just leave me in the field if I take a bullet. Goin' to the hospital spells doom for sure."

Disease killed many of the boys too—fevers swept the camps on a regular basis, and dysentery and scurvy and all manner of other ailments kept the troop ranks thinned out. Add to that the occasional few that just plain froze to death and a handful of others who couldn't get enough to eat to keep them alive, and before you knew it, death stayed real close by as a constant companion.

"How many men you reckon this war has killed?" asked Johnny, obviously thinking along the same lines as York.

"Not much sense in askin' that," York replied. "Thousands—I know that for sure."

"You expect we'll ever get used to it?" Calvin threw in.

"I hope not." York's voice was solemn. "Every time a man falls, another little piece ought to break off your heart. One thing I've always felt, here and in the Mexican War too, is a healthy respect for the life of another man. Seein' a man die, comrade or enemy, ought to make you hurt a little. If it don't . . . well . . . then you got more problems than tryin' to live through a war."

"I don't seem to feel much of anythin' anymore," said Johnny. "Seems like my heart is cut from granite."

"You just doin' your job," York explained. "That's good. Just do what you got to do and don't get sidetracked. That's how you stay alive."

"That why you don't take any furlough?" asked Calvin.

"You gettin' mighty nosy for a young fella."

"But you don't take your time off when they give it to you."

"I know what soldiers do when they get time off from the shootin'," said York. "They go to the nearest town, get liquored up, visit the bawdy houses and gamblin' joints; act like the world has thrown a big party and they're the honored guests."

"What's wrong with that?" laughed Johnny. "You used to enjoy a party more than any man I knew."

"I get through this war, I'll do it again too," York claimed. "But not now. I've seen it happen too many times. A man takes a few days of ease in a town, then returns to the fightin'. But his eyes ain't sharp when he comes back, and his hands aren't quick. The bullets start flyin' again, and the man that just got back goes down first. I don't plan on that happenin' to me."

When the two boys went silent, York knew they'd seen it too. Perhaps that was why, although they went to Richmond every now and again when furlough came, they didn't stay gone too long.

York inspected his uniform, the last of four he'd brought with him from South Carolina back in 1861. They'd all been clean then, gray with gold buttons on the sleeves and front. A tailor in Charleston had made them for him. York had hooked a gold sash around his waist, slung his saber through it, and put on his slough hat and black shiny boots.

He'd looked as grand as any captain in any army in the history of the world. Now three of the uniforms were completely worn out, and this last one was a muddy, dingy color that he couldn't quite identify. Only two buttons remained on the front, and the sleeve cuffs were frayed. Blood soiled the coat all over the front, and two cuts in the cloth showed where saber blades had cut through the material—one under his right shoulder, the other at the bottom left, not far from his hip. Fortunately, neither of the blades had punctured too far into his body, and the wounds they'd left behind had healed in a few days.

"You hear from my mother lately?" asked Calvin.

York shook his head. "It's been a few months. You know how the mail is."

"Less dependable than the food," said Johnny.

"She wrote pretty regular early in the war." Calvin's tone was wistful.

York nodded. For a while Katherine had kept him well informed. She'd never managed to sell their Charleston house, and the Yankee blockade had kept her from sailing to London. Although most of her society friends had fled Charleston, she stayed there, except for an occasional trip to see Trenton or to check their belongings at the place they'd leased outside of Columbia.

"Don't fret, though," she had written when her plans to go to London fell through. "I will take care of things anyway."

Although not sure what that meant, York let it go. What could he do otherwise? Right now she held his money in her care, and he had no power to control it. If she betrayed him, he'd deal with it when he got home. Until then he saw no value in fretting.

"I hope Trenton is doing all right," Calvin added. "He never got that commission he wanted."

York set down his coffee cup, pulled out a deck of cards, and held them out to Johnny.

Johnny flipped a seven of hearts off the deck of cards.

York turned over a ten of spades. "His leg never healed," he said, remembering Katherine's early letters.

"Things are rough on The Oak." Calvin took a four of clubs from the cards.

"Most of the blacks run off after the Federals took over Beaufort," continued York, taking a penny from both Calvin and Johnny.

"What did you expect?" asked Johnny.

York reshuffled the cards.

"No rice crop now," continued Calvin. "Not that it matters since the Yankee blockade is keeping all the ships bottled up."

"Your mama said Trenton is takin' it hard," said York. "More bitter each day."

"At least the Yankees didn't invade any farther after they took Beaufort," Calvin replied.

York nodded; they'd had this conversation many times. "The Oak is safe for now. It's growin' no rice, and we got no darkies to keep up the place, but it's not in Yankee hands either. We can find some cause for pleasure in that."

"Least until General Sherman marches through, it's safe," said Johnny.

"How long you figure before that no-good Union scoundrel marches toward Charleston?" asked Calvin.

"Maybe he won't. Since he's got Atlanta, maybe he'll settle there," suggested Johnny.

York sniffed. "I wouldn't count on it. Sherman's a smart man—ruthless too. He'll shift his sights toward Savannah, I expect. Maybe Columbia."

Silence fell for a few moments, then Calvin changed the subject. "You don't write Mother back much, do you?"

"Nope. I'm not much given to paper and pen."

"It's hard to tell a woman about war."

York nodded.

Calvin stared into the fire. "We ride, we fight," he mused. "We shoot men with pistols, stab them with sabers, trample them with our horses when we can. We hear the screams of the wounded, see the white faces of the dying, and smell the foul odors of the dead."

York held out the deck of cards to Calvin. Calvin turned up a jack of diamonds as he continued to speak. "We eat stale bread, drink poor coffee, and sleep on hard ground. In the winter our bones feel so cold we figure they'll break, and in the summer, our sweat drenches through our clothes until they're heavy. We survive one day, fall asleep, wake up, and hope to make it through another. How do we tell a woman of such things?"

"You don't." York held the cards out to Johnny. "And I'd just as soon you not bring it up to me again either."

Calvin chuckled, Johnny pulled a deuce of hearts off the deck, then silence fell again for a few seconds. A horse neighed and stomped. York flipped up a six of diamonds, and he and Johnny each handed Calvin a penny.

York glanced at his horse, at least the eighth animal he'd ridden since the war started. A mine ball had claimed two of the mounts; a cannon shot got another. The other four had collapsed from plain and simple weariness, their legs tuckered out from too much hard riding and too little rest and sweet grass.

"I wish I could see Camellia," Johnny murmured. "Seems like forever since I saw her back in the summer."

Johnny nodded. "At least she's safe."

"Beth and Butler too," York added.

"I'm glad they're with her mama," said Johnny. "Out of Trenton's clutches—no offense to you, Calvin."

Calvin shook his head. "I know my brother."

"Wonder what happened to Josh?" York asked.

Johnny shrugged.

"His name never showed up in the list of dead and wounded at Port Royal," continued York. "I still figure he joined the army."

"But you checked around, didn't you?" asked Calvin.

York nodded. "Nobody's heard of him." He was as puzzled as always about the whereabouts of his brother.

"You think he's fighting out west? Tennessee or something?" asked Calvin.

"Maybe, but why go way out there?"

"You ought to go see Camellia when we get our next furlough," said Johnny.

"I've studied on it, but I reckon not," York replied.

"Maybe she's heard from Josh."

York wondered again if Johnny knew something he wasn't telling about Josh—but he decided not to ask. If the boy had news, York felt sure he'd offer it. "I said no to goin' to see Camellia."

"It's Ruth Swanson you're afraid of," said Johnny. "That why you won't go see Camellia?"

"It's none of your business."

"Mr. Swanson is dead," continued Johnny. "No bother to you anymore."

York spat. "I don't reckon I need to see her ever again. A woman breaks your heart, you're afraid you'll strangle her the next time you see her. You wait—maybe you'll find out someday."

"You still got feelings for her?" asked Calvin.

"Of course not. I'm married to your mother." York spoke quickly, hoping neither of the boys noticed the quiver in his voice. Although he'd deny it as long as he lived, he knew that deep down he still loved Lynette Wheeler—uh, Ruth Swanson—more than he'd ever loved anyone or anything.

"I've thought about that some," Calvin went on. "If you were still married to Mrs. Swanson when you married my mother, was your marriage to my mother legal?"

"I talked to a barrister before I married your mother," York explained. "He told me that since Lynette was already married when she married me, the marriage to me was illegal. So my nuptials with your mother were on the square."

"It sounds complicated."

"It is, but not too much for a smart fella like you to figure out."

Calvin smiled.

York put away his cards and drew as close to the fire as he could without burning his face. "Time for some rest, boys," he suggested. "Reckon we'll end up fightin' again sometime before daybreak."

"Seems like that's all we do these days. Sleep a little and fight a lot," Calvin put in.

"Petersburg is vital," said Johnny. "If it falls, the railroad falls, and Richmond gets cut off."

"You think the war's about over?" asked Calvin. "A lot of men say it is; say we can't last through next spring."

York spat. "Food, weapons, ammunition, and clothin' are scarce. The horses sent to replace the ones we wear out show up older and sick. Desertions are worse too. More and more men goin' home on their furloughs and never comin' back."

"The men who are still here seem real gloomy too," Johnny added.

"The Rebel yells sound quieter and don't last as long when we attack," agreed Calvin.

"The tides have turned against our cause," York admitted. "Atlanta taken; Richmond and Petersburg under siege; all the men know it."

"Wish somebody would tell us somethin'," said Johnny.

"It don't matter what anybody tells us unless it's to say the war is over," York fired back. "So long as we're soldiers, we'll trudge on."

"Yes," agreed Johnny. "If it's comin' to an end, we'll at least go down fightin'."

"I have a bad feeling about tomorrow," said Calvin.

Johnny laughed. "You say that about every day. You're worse than an old woman."

Calvin grinned slightly, but York noticed it was forced. Calvin reached into his coat, pulled out a paper, and handed it to York. "Take this to Mother if anything happens to me."

"You've given me at least a dozen of those in the last two years," said Johnny. "Why you givin' this one to him?"

Calvin shrugged. "Who knows? Something might happen to you too."

Johnny waved him off. "Somethin' might happen to all of us. But tomorrow ain't no different than no other day. We'll all do fine."

York pocketed Calvin's letter, then tucked his blanket closer around him. He listened to the rain dripping off the trees. Unless he missed his guess, the end of this war would come soon. He just hoped that nothing would happen to either of these two boys before it did.

Barely two miles from where York rested, Josh Cain sat cross-legged by a low fire, his blue coat buttoned tightly around his shoulders, his kepi dripping rain. Lester sat beside him, his floppy hat yanked low over his eyes, his hands busy rubbing the scruffy neck of a yellow cur dog that had taken up with him outside of a farmhouse they'd passed about a year ago. A scab the size of a pecan covered a spot on Josh's cheek under his right eye, and a scraggly beard covered his chin. Scores of other men sat or lay all around Josh and Lester, many of the men already asleep, others talking softly as the night passed.

Josh removed a coffeepot from the fire, poured two cups, and handed one to Lester. Lester took the cup and sipped the hot drink. "That's mighty fine coffee," he said, as he always did when Josh gave him a cup. "Best I ever burned my tongue on."

Josh smiled at the familiar words. "You're easy to please. I used those grounds at least four times."

"I speakin' the truth," Lester claimed. "Everybody knows it."

Josh took a swig of coffee and tried to relax. But he found it hard. Although nobody had said anything officially yet, he knew from rumors that before the day started, he and Lester would be right in the thick of another battle, just as they'd been right in the middle of them for close to three years now.

"How many times you think we've faced off with the Rebels?" he asked Lester.

"Don't reckon I got any answer for that," said Lester.

"Lots of times, that's for sure. Lots of nights staying awake waiting for the sound of the bugle, the cannon fire."

"Lots of mine balls have been shot at us, that's for sure."

Josh sipped his coffee. After leaving Richmond back in 1862, he and Lester had slipped away and headed to Washington. Within two weeks he'd joined the Federal army and soon ended up in the Second Corps under the command of General Winfield Scott Hancock. When the man who'd enlisted him asked of his origins, Josh had told him the truth: The Oak Plantation in South Carolina. The man had made him wait a minute while he talked to a superior officer, then returned.

"How we know you ain't a spy?" asked the officer.

"I fought in Mexico," said Josh. "Check the records if you want. I earned a lieutenant's rank. I'm loyal to the United States."

"You wantin' a commission?"

"No, just a uniform. Don't want an officer's job; just a soldier's."

Shrugging, the man looked him over once more, then signed him up as a lowly private. He was paid thirteen dollars a month and had nothing to do but follow orders—that was just how Josh wanted it.

The Second Corps ended up in some terrible fighting.

Bloody Lane at Antietam.

Marye's Heights at Fredericksburg.

Chancellorsville.

Gettsyburg. Their troop under General Hancock had set up at Cemetery Ridge, the strong upper ground from which the Union soldiers had withstood Pickett's Charge and won that battle.

The Wilderness.

Spotsylvania.

Cold Harbor.

Now south of Petersburg.

Blood, dirt, death, he'd seen it all.

Josh glanced at Lester. Although the Union had started accepting blacks into the army in 1863, Lester had never joined, so he wasn't an official soldier. That meant he didn't stay with Josh during the day. Lester disappeared every morning after they ate, spent the day with the band of folks that traveled in and around the soldiers, then showed back up when night fell or the most recent battle ended. At first it surprised Josh that the Federals let him do that. But then he saw that hundreds of people followed along with the Union army: merchants selling their wares; families—mostly of the officers; women making a living off their bodies; and scores of blacks who'd run off from the South. Every time the soldiers moved, the others shifted too. The army became a moving town of all kinds of people—all of them attached to the war like ants to a picnic basket. The civilians needed the army, and the army needed the civilians.

Occasionally one of the other soldiers gave Josh a hard time about a lowly private like him having his own boy at his beck and call, but he and Lester just laughed it off.

"I be alive 'cause of Mr. Josh," Lester always said when the teasing came. "I stay with him till this old war comes to its end, and I know I've seen him safe through it."

The soldiers always grinned and let it go. A man like Josh made friends easily, and who really cared if a private had his own darky close by? So long as he didn't become a bother to any of them, they let it be.

"What you gone do when this war be done?" asked Lester, bringing Josh back to the present.

"You know the answer to that," said Josh. "I'm going to Camellia and my kids. I'll marry her as fast as I can, then figure out a place to settle and make a life again."

"You figure to go back to the South someday?"

"Don't know about that."

"You think Miss Camellia and your children still in Richmond?"

"Don't see why not."

"We may be in Richmond real soon too," said Lester. "It's no more than twenty or so miles away."

Josh's blood ran cold. The Union army had tried to take Richmond once before, back in the early days of the war, but General McClellan—"Young Napoleon" the newspapers called him—had failed after getting within seven miles of the city. Now, once Petersburg fell, they stood poised to strike at it again. What would happen then? Would the Federals burn Richmond to the ground as he'd heard so many say they would? Would the Union soldiers go in wild and mean, raping and pillaging as he'd seen them do a few other times when their whiskey got the best of them? What would happen to Camellia and Beth? Would Butler fight for them if the Union soldiers threatened them? Would he put himself in danger?

Josh sighed. Cruelty didn't seem to care what uniform a man wore. Blue or gray, war made all men turn out bad if they didn't watch out; caused them to do mean things that they'd regret for the rest of their lives.

Josh shook his head. "We've had to kill a lot of men in these last years."

"I reckon so—kill or be killed."

"We'll have to kill again soon."

"It's a hard thing, that's for sure."

"I grieve this war."

"I glad you fightin' it, though. Fella like me wouldn't ever see no freedom without it."

Josh looked at his friend. "Where are you going when it ends?"

A frown crossed Lester's brow. "Not sure I know. Got no real family."

"You can come with me—how about that? You and that mangy mutt too."

"Me and Sugar would feel right honored to do that."

"Good, that's what we'll do. I'll find my family, then we'll all go somewhere, work hard, and buy some land. That's what I want—a nice quiet place to live in peace and calm, never to have to hear a rifle shot again, except to shoot a deer or something for supper."

"I got no doubt you'll get that. The Lord will see to it."

Josh smiled. He knew from past talk that the war had made Lester's faith stronger. Then Josh's smile faded. "Where's the Lord in all this killing?"

Lester sipped the last of his coffee. "The Lord be in a man like you. I see Him real plain there."

"Not much of the Lord in me."

Lester licked his lips. "A man that can make coffee taste the way you do after it's been used over and over sure is a miracle man to me."

Josh grinned. "Like I said, you're an easy man to please. Now let's get some sleep. Shooting will start soon."

The battle at Burgess Mill, south of Petersburg, Virginia, started about three in the morning. York and the rest of Hampton's Legion were part of a group given the task of protecting the Boydton Plank Road and the South Side Railroad that ran west of it. All through the first morning of fight, the Bluebellies kept throwing men at them, and they kept pushing them back. Hundreds fell dead or injured. The battlefield lay littered with bodies; cursing and crying filled the air.

About an hour after noon, word spread that General Hancock's

Union men had gotten behind their lines and now threatened White Oak Road, which lay too close to the railroad for anyone's comfort. General Hampton ordered his legion to move that way on the double-quick. Calvin rode up on one side of York, Johnny on the other, as York galloped toward the thick of the battle. Rain pelted them, its cold bite turning the fields under their horses' hooves into a muddy pasture.

"Gonna be a hard clash!" shouted Johnny.

"Reckon so!" called York. He glanced at Calvin, but the young man kept his head down.

"Stay close to me!" York yelled.

Calvin didn't reply.

Scores of other riders moved around them, their horses trudging forward, too worn out to run much but still game for what they sensed about to happen. York patted his animal, a large gray with a lump the size of a cantaloupe on his neck from some blow that York never saw hit. He touched Calvin's letter in his pocket and thought of Katherine. Although he didn't love her, he did like the notion of having a woman waiting on him, especially a woman who wanted the same things he wanted. He only hoped she knew what she was talking about when she said she'd taken care of everything. If so, and he lived through this war, he'd return to South Carolina as one of the richest men in the state. If not, well, who knew what would happen then?

The horses quickened their pace, and York gave his attention to matters at hand. He touched his saber scabbard, and the feel of the cool steel comforted him. As cannons boomed in the distance, an odd feeling ran through York. What if something happened to him today? He'd written no note for anyone, no last words of love or counsel. Of course he'd never done such a thing; figured it would bring bad luck—kind of like painting a bull's-eye on his back. York had no desire to draw that kind of attention to himself. Right now, though, the hair on the back of his neck stood up, and his face felt like a bee had stung him on both cheeks. Maybe he was getting the haints—the prickly feeling that made a man think a rifle shot or a bayonet point surely carried his name on it. Lots of men did at one time or another.

Clutching his horse's reins, York gritted his teeth and pushed away his fears. Whether he lived or died today depended on two things—keeping his wits and a whole lot of good fortune smiling on him. One thing he could control—the other he couldn't.

He heard a bugle to his left, and then they made contact with the enemy. The Union troops rushed at them from a low stone wall just past a stand of woods. Within minutes the battle raged hot. A soldier to York's right fell from a bullet and toppled off his horse. Somebody shouted and another man cursed.

York's blood ran to his face as he rushed his horse into the mass of Federals, his sword raking left and right at the men wearing blue. Bodies of dead and wounded men quickly covered the ground at his horse's hooves. Sweat poured down York's face as the minutes passed. A soldier fired a pistol, and a bullet cut into York's left boot. Blood ran between his toes, but he didn't stop fighting. His breath came in gasps, and his arms thrust this way and that at the men trying to kill him. Every now and again, he found a second to scan the battlefield for Johnny and Calvin but never saw them in the tumultuous fray. Rain continued to fall. His horse slipped more than once. Every time, York feared he would fall and end up unhorsed—one more man afoot in the mud with scores of enemies wanting to hack him to death.

Yet somehow he stayed on his mount's back, and the battle raged on and on. For close to three hours, it flowed—the Rebels pushing ahead one minute, then falling back the next. Sometime after four, as the sun started to dip, almost as if by common agreement, the two armies both dropped back for a spell to regroup and reconsider.

York found Calvin and Johnny in a grove of trees, a burned-out wagon beside them as they sat on the ground, their winded horses tied to a bush. York carefully hopped down, hitched his horse, and yanked a canteen off his saddle.

"You two all right?" he asked, taking a swig from the canteen as he walked toward them.

"I got a cut." Calvin held up his right hand to show York a bloody slash on his wrist. "But I believe I will survive."

York turned to Johnny. A blank whiteness covered his son's face, like he'd seen a ghost a thousand times in one day. "You all right?"

"I'm without harm," Johnny said.

"What's wrong then? You look glassy-eyed."

"I'm fine."

York spat, found a spot on the ground, and took off his left boot. Blood caked his thin sock. Pain ran under his toes as he pulled off the sock and poured water over the wound.

"You shot?" asked Johnny.

"Not much. Bullet didn't lodge in the flesh, and it ain't bleedin' no more. It'll do OK." York put the sock back on, then the boot, his face wrinkling in pain as his toes wedged back inside the worn-out leather.

Cannons boomed in the background; the battle had already started again.

"We'll rest a minute," York said. "Then we got to move."

"It's rough out there." Calvin shivered. "You still got my letter?"

"I got it."

"Don't lose it."

"Stop such talk. It'll bring bad fortune."

Johnny stood, moved to a tree, and gazed out on the battlefield a hundred yards away.

York watched him for a few seconds, then stood and hobbled his way. "What is it?" he asked, putting a hand on his son's shoulder. "And don't say nothin', 'cause I know that's a lie."

Johnny faced him, his eyes confused. "I'm not certain. But I thought I saw . . ." He stopped and shook his head.

"Saw what?"

"Not what but who." Johnny turned back to the battlefield.

"You talkin' funny," York said. "Who you think you saw?"

When Johnny spoke, his words came out in a whisper. "Uncle Josh . . . I thought I saw him this mornin'."

"I don't understand."

"With the Federals. I saw Uncle Josh wearing a blue coat."

"You're addled!" York twisted Johnny's body so they could speak face to face. "Josh wouldn't turn traitor on us like that. You know how honorable he is!"

"I'm just tellin' you what I saw—the soldier was on foot, had a beard and all, but it was him. I'm almost sure of it."

York rubbed his chin. "I know Josh didn't take well to slavery. He used to complain some about it. But he never showed any feeling for the Yankees either. What could make a man like him go over to the enemy?"

"If Uncle Josh believes the Yankees hold the high card in the matter of right and wrong, he'd fight for them."

York weighed the notion. He knew Johnny had Josh pegged right, but he refused to admit it. "Your eyes deceived you. Leave it at that."

"I hope you're right. But I don't know. Back when I last visited with Camellia, she—"

"She what?"

Johnny bit his lip.

"What?" insisted York.

Johnny rubbed his mouth. "She said maybe Josh had gone to fight for the Yankees."

"Why'd she say that?"

"He told Mrs. Swanson that's what he was plannin' to do when he brought Beth there."

"I thought Camellia brought Beth there."

Johnny shook his head. "She brought Butler. Beth was already there."

York spat. "Tell me everythin'," he ordered.

"Not the time," Johnny replied.

York fumed but knew Johnny was right. A rider thundered up and told them to mount up; General Hampton was ready to re-engage the enemy.

Within minutes they were in the thick of fighting again, so York had no choice but to put aside his questions about Josh and crash into the fray, his pistol firing, his saber stabbing. He stuck at least three men in the body in the first ten minutes, then lost count as others rushed at him—some on horses but most on foot. Somebody jabbed him in the right calf, but he barely felt the wound; it didn't slow him down. Every now and again, he saw Calvin and Johnny, but since he was surrounded by Federals himself, he couldn't do much to aid them.

The battle moved from one spot to the other; soldiers ran here and there, with bullets whizzing and cannons booming all around them. York thought of Josh from time to time as he fought. He tried to imagine what it would feel like to see his brother on the battlefield; wondered what he'd do if the two of them had to face off. The notion made him sick to his stomach. He wanted to throw up right then and there, but he held back the nausea and kept fighting. Although not given to any religion, York still fired off a prayer that the Lord wouldn't ever pit him against his own brother . . . because who knew what would happen if that ever came to pass?

As the hour passed, the Rebels gradually got the upper hand. Dusk settled, and the Yankees began falling back. A Federal bugle sounded a retreat, and York wheeled his horse to cut off a couple of the enemy as they ran from the field. His saber pointed straight ahead, he kicked his mount and charged as if the outcome of the war depended on the outcome of his efforts. The Yankees rushed toward a shack standing in the field, York hot on their heels. His heart pounded as he rushed them and reared back his saber to cut the first one down. Then a handful of Bluebellies appeared from the shack. York jerked up his horse as they ran at him.

Scanning the battlefield, York spotted Calvin halfway across the pasture, off his horse, with his back to a tree. At least three Union soldiers were rushing at him, their bayonets pointed straight forward. York spurred his horse and plowed through the Yankee soldiers as he rushed to help Calvin.

To his rear he heard a shout and, even in the din of battle, recognized his son's voice. He pivoted in the saddle and saw Johnny on his knees about thirty yards away, blood pouring down his face. A Yankee was standing over him, pistol in hand. York glanced back at Calvin; one of the Yankees threatening him was facedown on the ground, but the two others were at him now, their bayonets thrusting.

Cursing, York wheeled his mount and galloped toward Johnny as he pulled his pistol and fired at the Yankee beside him. The bullet sprayed dirt at the Yankee's feet; he turned toward York and shot at him. York's horse buckled at the knees and fell as the bullet popped into its nose. York rolled over the horse's head but hit the ground on his feet, his saber forward as he ran at the man threatening his son. York's left foot dragged from the bullet he'd taken earlier. The Yankee grabbed a rifle off the ground and aimed.

York threw his body at the man, his sword jabbing at the man's torso. When the sword met flesh, York shoved it as hard as he could into the enemy's stomach. The Yankee fell, his life pouring out almost instantly.

His breath ragged with exertion, York peered across the field at Calvin. Three Yankees lay at his feet as he slumped on the ground at the base of the tree, his boots pointed up and out toward York, his head sagging to one side. York wanted to go to him but couldn't, not until he took care of Johnny.

Grinding his teeth, York focused on his son. Blood rushed from Johnny's scalp, but York couldn't tell how deep the wound was. He yanked a soiled handkerchief out of his pocket, stuffed it into the wound, and pressed as hard as he could. Johnny opened his eyes. The battlefield suddenly became quieter as both armies retreated in the darkness, the battle for the railroad at a stalemate for the moment.

"Pa," Johnny moaned.

"You're OK. I'll get you to a doc."

"Calvin?"

"I'll check on him after I get you safe."

Johnny reached for the handkerchief. "I'm steady. Find Calvin."

York looked through the gloom toward Calvin but couldn't tell if he'd moved or not. He feared the worst but said nothing. He wondered where the rest of the legion was. Would anybody send out a detail to bring back the dead and wounded?

"Go on," whispered Johnny. "Come back after you provide for him."

York checked Johnny's wound once more and saw that the bleeding had slowed. "Back in a minute," York promised.

Johnny nodded, and York moved to Calvin as fast as his wounded foot allowed. He passed through a scattering of men on the ground—some dead, others moaning in pain. A Yankee bayonet lay half-submerged in

Calvin's chest and, even in the dark, York saw that blood soaked the young man's shirt. When York pulled out the bayonet, Calvin stirred and opened his eyes. York picked up a handful of mud and spread it over Calvin's wound to stop the bleeding. Calvin groaned.

"Come on," whispered York, sliding an arm under Calvin's back. "We'll find the surgeon."

Calvin pushed his hand away. "No use. I won't make it."

In no mood to argue, York grabbed Calvin's hands, held them still, then braced his good foot as best he could and jerked the younger man up. Calvin didn't fight him anymore. Staggering with every step, York headed back to Johnny.

"Don't give up," he panted to Calvin. "I'll get you home."

Staying as quiet as he could, he picked his way back across the pasture. About halfway there his strength gave out, and he stumbled and almost fell. Taking a second to regroup, he listened for Calvin's breathing and, to his relief, heard a ragged but steady draw of air. Moving again, he headed toward his son. Although still close to thirty yards away, he saw Johnny clamber to his feet and begin to stumble toward them.

"Stay down!" York whispered loudly.

Johnny didn't seem to hear.

Then, out of the corner of his eye, York saw four Yankees running at them—three from the left and one from the right. Cursing, he dropped Calvin and rushed as best he could at the group of three.

Pulling his pistol, he took the first one down with a quick shot. As the man fell at his feet, York focused on the other two. But the Bluebelly he'd shot jabbed a knife at his bad foot and caught him in the heel. Screaming, York turned and smashed his pistol butt into the man's head; the enemy soldier dropped dead as a stone. York pivoted and started back to Johnny, his left foot in fiery agony. When his left boot sank into a hole, he tripped and fell.

Looking up, his heart shook from what he saw. One Yankee lay facedown not more than twenty feet from Johnny, who squatted on the ground, one leg crooked under him as if trying to get up. The other two Federals were squared off in front of the dead soldier, their bayonets thrusting at each other!

York tried to move but couldn't get up. His mind whirled, not sure what he was seeing. What were the Yankees doing? All of a sudden, it became clear. One of the Yankees stood with his back to Johnny, defending him from the other Federal!

Not believing his eyes, York crawled toward them. The Yankee farthest from Johnny shoved his bayonet into the stomach of the other one, and the stabbed man sagged to his knees. The triumphant soldier raised his rifle and brought the stock down on the fallen Yankee's skull. An awful crack rang in the gloom. The surviving soldier lifted his rifle and aimed at Johnny.

Screaming, York jerked up and staggered toward the man about to kill his son. To York's amazement, the Union soldier on the ground reached out a hand, picked up a rock, and threw it at the other Yankee's back before he could fire his weapon. The rock caught the man in the back of the head; he staggered but didn't fall. His rifle in hand, he turned and faced his former comrade.

"No!" yelled the wounded Federal.

The other Yankee lifted the rifle again and pointed, this time, at his own comrade.

The stabbed soldier jerked out his pistol and fired.

The man with the rifle jerked sideways and fell backward toward Johnny. The other man collapsed too, his pistol dropping from his hand as he fell over.

York reached Johnny an instant later. He checked quickly for new wounds but found none. Satisfied, York hurriedly moved to the two Yankees. One of the men was dead; the other close to it. York studied the face of the second man and noted the scraggly beard and a scab on his right cheek. Not sure of what his eyes told him, he pulled off the man's hat, then almost collapsed to the ground.

"What happened, Pa?" asked Johnny, crawling to him.

York faced his son, his eyes vacant.

"Why was that Yankee—?"

"That's no Yankee," interrupted York. "It's your uncle Josh."

"What?" Johnny moved to where he could see Josh. The bayonet had penetrated his belly just below the ribs.

"It's Josh," York repeated. "He's hurt bad. I got to get you and him to a doc."

"Calvin too."

York peered into the gloom, hoping to find a horse but seeing none. "I can't carry all three of you," York whispered. "Not with my foot all messed up."

"Take Calvin and Josh first," Johnny ordered. "I'll be fine 'til you come back."

York surveyed the area—they were on an open patch of ground between two stands of trees about four hundred yards apart. Other than the shack in the middle of the pasture, he knew of no other buildings anywhere close. He wondered how far the Yankees had retreated and when they'd come back for their wounded. When they did, they'd take prisoners, too, if they found any alive.

"I don't like the notion of leaving you," York said. "The Yankees might come back. And even if they don't, that head wound of yours will surely take an infection if we don't get you some help pretty fast. No tellin' what'll happen if fever sets in."

"Just provide for Calvin."

York grunted, but then agreed. He headed back to Calvin as fast as his injured foot allowed. Although Calvin was still breathing, his eyes were closed, and blood had soaked through the mud York had dropped into his wound.

"Calvin?" York whispered. Calvin stirred but didn't speak. York rubbed his beard, then tried once more to rouse the boy but got the same result. York studied the black sky. His eyes watered at the hard choice he had to make. With a yank and a curse, he grabbed Calvin by the shoulders and half hauled, half dragged him to the shed and laid him inside it.

"I got no choice, Calvin," he said softly. "It's you or my boy and brother. I hope you make it, that's all I can say."

Calvin didn't respond.

York spat and headed back to Johnny and Josh.

"I'm takin' you and Josh," York stated.

"But you promised Calvin's mama you'd care for him."

"I've done all I could. I don't figure Calvin is goin' to make it either way. You're my son, and Josh is my brother, who just saved your hide. It's come to a choice, and I ain't got but one so far as I can see."

"It ain't right, Pa."

"I ain't a religious man," York shot back. "So I got no good clue about what's right or wrong right now. I'm doin' the only thing I can, so I'll take no more argument from you."

Johnny glared at him and tried to struggle when York went to lift him, but he was so weak from loss of blood that York held his arms down without too much trouble. Throwing Johnny over one shoulder and Josh over the other, York braced his legs and started slowly toward the woods.

"I'll come back for Calvin," he promised through labored breathing. "Soon as I get you and Josh safe."

Moving into the woods, York thought of the note in his coat pocket and felt glad he could at least take that to Katherine. No matter what he'd just promised his son, he knew almost for certain that he'd never see Calvin alive again.

Chapter Eighteen

After hauling Johnny and Josh through the woods for close to an hour, York stumbled into a small clearing and sagged down, his shoulders raw and his foot screaming with pain. After stretching Johnny and Josh on the ground, he spat and glanced around. An eyebrow arched as he spotted a beat-up horse standing in the moonlight by a tree, its reins dragging the ground no more than ten feet away.

Moving slowly, York forced his body up, eased to the horse, and grabbed the reins. A huge breath escaped him as he secured the horse to a tree, sagged down, and took off his left boot. His wounded foot burned like it had a live coal under it, and his sock stuck to the skin. Groaning with pain and weariness, York took off the sock, rose, removed the canteen from the supplies on the horse, and again poured water over his wound. After removing as much of the dried blood as he could, York drenched his sock with water and slipped it and the boot back on.

Moving back to Calvin and Josh, he poured water down their throats, then took a drink for himself. Finished, he capped the canteen, set it down, and examined Johnny and Josh. Although both were still unconscious, their wounds had pretty much stopped bleeding. York touched their heads and found their skin hot. They both breathed raggedly, as if trying to get air through a burlap bag. A knot the size of a small apple stuck out on the back of Josh's head.

Fearful that either or both of them might die soon, York tried to figure his next step. Try to find his comrades? But that might take hours. York stared into the woods and wondered where his comrades in gray had gone. Had they retreated farther than he'd expected?

He considered what would happen once he reached Confederate lines. The soldiers would take Johnny to a surgeon and Josh to a prison, and neither of those notions appealed to him. Over half the wounded never survived the hospital; as many men died of gangrene or a disease as they did a bullet. And even if he did hand Johnny over to a surgeon, who knew when a doctor would actually get to him? He'd seen a lot of men left untended for hours, even days, while the sawbones worked on everybody else.

York looked at Josh. As bad as the hospitals were, even fewer men survived a prison camp, especially men with injuries as bad as Josh's. Could he deliver Josh to prison, after the way he'd saved Johnny's life? But what choice did he have?

A dangerous idea suddenly came to York, and he rolled it over in his head several times to see whether he could act on it. Not exactly a soldierly thing, he concluded after a couple of minutes, but maybe it was the only hope if he wanted both Johnny and Josh to survive. Of course, if he got caught, he'd probably face a court-martial. But what other option did he have?

York evaluated his wounded foot and considered his own tiredness. He wondered if he could manage what he'd just decided but then figured he'd never know unless he tried. He had to take Josh and Johnny to the Swanson house in Richmond. With Lynette's money they could find a doctor to give proper care to Josh and Johnny. Without such attention they'd both surely die.

York spat and wished he could do something to help Calvin, but no idea came to his mind. Sometimes war put a man between the ground and a wagon wheel, and he couldn't do a thing about it. He wondered what he'd tell Katherine when she asked what had happened to her son, but he came up with no answer. For the time being, he pushed the matter aside. Right now he had more immediate concerns to handle.

Setting his chin firmly, York grabbed Johnny up and draped him across the horse, then turned back for Josh. Something moved to his left, and York pivoted in that direction, his hand automatically grabbing for his pistol. A man emerged from the dark. York dropped to a knee behind the horse and strained to see what kind of uniform the man wore.

Gray.

York's pistol hand relaxed as he saw the familiar color, but he didn't step out. Horses were rare treasures, and any soldier would want this one for sure if he spotted him.

York wanted to curse as the soldier looked his way and then moved toward them, obviously having seen the horse. Determined to fight for the animal, York reached for his pistol again. He started to stand and order the man to halt but then stopped as four more soldiers emerged from the darkness. York glanced toward Josh and Johnny, wishing he had some help. Even with the element of surprise, York probably couldn't take four men by himself. Not knowing what else to do, he stood away from the horse and waved at the soldiers.

"Ho there, men," he called softly. "Captain Hampton York here; cavalry unit of Wade Hampton's Legion."

The soldiers quickly hoisted their rifles and approached him cautiously. Once they got within clear view, they lowered their weapons, at least a little. York surveyed their ranks and saw none above his. Good—they'd have to take his orders. He checked their insignia, noted the marks of the Tennessee Second, a good unit for the most part.

"What you got here, Captain?" asked the man who'd come from the woods first, a sergeant with a mop of blond hair in his eyes and a face that looked like somebody had pressed his cheeks together with a vise.

"A wounded soldier," York said, indicating Johnny. "And a Yankee prisoner." He pointed to Josh.

"Heck of a fight today, wasn't it?" asked the sergeant.

"Yeah, but we gave as good as we got."

"The rest of our boys are a ways east of here," said the sergeant. "We're headed that way."

York pondered how to tell the sergeant he wasn't going toward the Confederate lines. "I got other orders. I'm goin' north."

"That's toward Richmond." The sergeant's tone was now suspicious.

"I reckon I know that."

The sergeant glared at him.

York's eyes narrowed as he realized the men had come from the woods from the east, the same direction the sergeant had just said they were headed. If the Confederate army lay behind them, why were they going away from it? He studied the five men in the moonlight and noted how tattered they looked. One wore no shoe on his left foot; another had a bandage all around his head. And every one of them looked thin and scraggly.

Deserters—all of a sudden York was sure of it.

"You boys just go on your way," York said softly, not wanting matters to get more serious. "It don't matter to me where that is—toward Tennessee, I expect, from the uniform markins' you're wearin' on your shoulders. But I don't care about that. Just leave me be. I got business to attend in Richmond."

The sergeant raised his rifle to waist level and pointed it at York. "I got no care where you're headed either. But we'll want that horse of yours."

"I need that horse," soothed York.

"Not if I shoot you."

York eyed the other men and tried to figure how tough they were. "You boys got the stomach to shoot an officer?" he asked.

"Ain't nobody ever gone know it if we do," the sergeant boasted. "The war's about finished. We figure it's time to go home, and we'll do what we have to do to get there. We want the horse and the Yankee prisoner."

York's mouth tightened, but he tried to stay calm. One wrong move right now, and he'd end up shot. And then he couldn't do a thing for Josh or Johnny. "Take the horse," he said. "But the prisoner stays with me."

All five men pointed their rifles at him. "The prisoner goes with us," the sergeant demanded. "Whether you're alive or dead, it don't matter."

"What you want him for?"

The sergeant laughed. "Never know who you gone come up on in the dark. We got Yankees all around us; probably more between us and home. We come up on some of them, maybe this prisoner gives us a little bargainin' room. Somethin' to trade when we need it."

York weighed the odds of winning if he fought but quickly saw they were slim and none. If he got shot trying to save Josh, Johnny would die too. Even though he'd willingly give up his life for Josh, he couldn't do it at the expense of his son.

He decided to appeal to these hard men with the truth. "That Yankee is my brother. He got hurt savin' the life of the man on the horse, and that one just happens to be my son. That's why I'm so set on hangin' on to him."

"That's a mighty touchin' story," said the sergeant, eying York coldly. "But I reckon it don't mean a thing to me."

York's hands twitched; he almost fired his rifle. He wanted to shoot the sergeant dead on the spot but knew he didn't dare. So somehow he held his anger in check. Unable to see any way out of the predicament, York stepped toward the sergeant until the bayonet on the man's gun almost touched his belly.

"OK," York growled, "you got me in the cross hairs. But you better hear this. I've killed a lot of men in my day, and not all of them in this war. You best take care of this Yankee prisoner 'cause if he don't survive all this—your fault or not—if he dies before I see him again, I will come to Tennessee or anywhere else you end up, and I'll find you. And when I do, you'll wish that your mama never brought your sorry life to birth."

"You're a brave man, Captain." The sergeant smirked. "But I got five guns, and you just got the one, so I reckon I ain't too scared of you."

"Just mark my words."

"They're marked. Now take your boy and move on."

York started to move but then couldn't do it—couldn't leave Josh with these bad men, couldn't give up without a fight. Without thinking of the consequences, he lunged at the Confederate sergeant, his hand landing on the blade of the bayonet. When the sergeant jerked the bayonet away, the blade ripped through York's hand. Blood instantly flowed. York kicked the sergeant in the knee, and the Rebel cursed; then the other deserters jumped on his back. Something cracked down on his skull, and he staggered and fell. More boots than he could count pounded into his sides and head. York tried to fight again, but they had him pinned on the ground, and he couldn't do anything more.

"Hold it!" shouted the sergeant. His men fell off York and stood over him, panting.

"Let me shoot him!" yelled the man without a shoe.

"No!" ordered the sergeant. "You can't blame a man for fightin' for his brother. If I wasn't such a scoundrel, I'd almost admire it." He bent low over York, then pulled him to his feet. "You done now?"

York pressed his palm against his leg and tried to stop the bleeding. The sergeant kicked him viciously in the ribs, then stepped back a pace. "Say your good-byes," he told York. "We got miles to cover."

Gritting his teeth, York crawled to Josh. "Sorry, brother," he whispered, touching him on the head. "But I'm in a hard spot here."

Josh didn't respond. After another few seconds, York left him, hobbled to Johnny, and hauled his son's limp frame off the horse.

The Rebs took hold of the horse's reins. After wrapping a dirty handkerchief around his bleeding hand, York hoisted Johnny onto his shoulder. Bracing his bad foot, he twisted back to the sergeant. "You care for my brother like I said," he ordered.

The sergeant chuckled as York stumbled out of the clearing without another word, his eyes set toward Richmond, the city he'd avoided with every ounce of his strength since the day he'd stepped foot in Virginia. Now, though, none of that mattered. He had to get Johnny to safety, then turn around and go after the thin-faced sergeant from Tennessee.

Dragging his left leg, it took York the rest of the night and most of the next three days and nights to make his way to the city. He stopped to rest only when he couldn't go on any longer, and he ate nothing more than an apple and a piece of stale bread that he found on a dead soldier about halfway through the second day. Thankfully a full canteen of water lay beside that same soldier, and York kept pouring water through Johnny's parched lips and onto his head wound.

By the time he reached Richmond, York's strength had almost reached its end. When he ran into some Rebel soldiers about two miles out, he had to squeeze up every ounce of strength he possessed to hail them and offer his name and troop division. To his relief they waved, handed him a piece of cornbread, and let him pass through the lines without any questions. With wagons dragging wounded men into the city from all directions, the sight of Johnny on his shoulder and the blood seeping from his shot-up boot seemed to tell them all they needed to know. No reason for any suspicion about one more.

York entered the city just after sunup, his body aching with pain and fatigue, but his mind set on getting Johnny safely to the Swansons' hotel, where he could wash out his wound and lay him in a clean bed. The noise of the place gave him new energy, and his pace picked up a little. People rushed to and fro all about him, and soldiers, in all manner of poor dress, seemed to be everywhere. Horses stomped and voices shouted and train whistles blew in an odd mixture of loud noises. York saw and heard it all but didn't stop to ponder it. Right now he had one thing in mind, and nothing else mattered.

He remembered the name of Lynette's hotel and found it within an hour of entering the city. With Johnny over his shoulder, he gathered up the last of his energy and lugged his son inside. Men lay all over the place—some in rows on low cots, more on thin blankets on the floor. A large chandelier hung overhead, but no light came from it. Several women—about half of them black, the other half old—moved in and among the men. A long table sat in the corner to his right, and cloth lay stacked on the floor by the table. A hospital, York realized; they'd made the hotel into a hospital.

Glancing around, he saw a desk straight ahead and moved toward it. A squatty black woman stepped to him as he neared the desk, her clothes worn and wrinkled.

"I'm lookin' for Mrs. Lynette Swanson," said York, taking no time for small talk.

The darky looked at him blankly.

"Show me to the woman who owns the place," demanded York, his tone impatient.

The woman turned and motioned him to follow. At the hotel desk, she stopped and faced him again. "Wait here."

As the maid disappeared into a room behind the desk, York eased Johnny off his shoulder and onto the stained carpet. At least forty men lay on the floor around him—some of them snoring, others moaning and turning every second or so. Flies buzzed all over the place, and York suddenly noticed the sour, thick aroma in the room. It made his nose burn. His eyes blurred, and his stomach growled with hunger and nausea at the same time. He wondered how much blood he'd lost from his heel and how many miles he'd walked in the last three days. He leaned against the desk, his strength ebbing away.

A few minutes later, the maid stepped back out, with a middle-aged woman behind her. York rubbed his eyes and tried to clear his head. The woman wore a black skirt that reached to the floor and a blue blouse that buttoned at the neck. Her hair was pinned into a neat, wavy dark bun, and a touch of gray gathered at her temples. To look at her, you'd never know that scores of dying men lay at her feet and a desperate war was being fought within twenty-five miles of where she stood.

The woman spoke before York could find his voice. "May I help you?"

York stared at the woman, her face fuller than he'd last seen it but just as beautiful, at least to him. He almost laughed as he realized that she didn't recognize him. But then again, why should she? Over twenty years had passed since he had seen her last, and given the ravages of the war, he knew he looked far different than she'd remember.

"I'm Hampton York," he said, standing to his full height. "And this"—he pointed a boot at Johnny—"is our son, Johnny."

Lynette Swanson almost buckled at the waist. York started to reach for her, but his eyes blurred, and his hand collapsed as he raised it. Before he could do anything to stop himself, he fell to the floor, his head coming to rest right at eye level with Johnny's.

Chapter Nineteen

Camellia kept almost constant vigil over her pa and brother throughout the next three days as she waited to see if they'd recover from their injuries. She sat in a plain wood chair between their two single beds on the top floor of the hotel. As the hours passed, her mind struggled to grasp that they actually lay right in front of her, their thin bodies scarred by the injuries of war. She doubted she would have recognized either of them if she'd passed them on the street . . . and certainly not if she'd seen them lying on a cot or on the floor downstairs, where she had worked every day. Her pa's beard, now peppered with gray, almost reached his chest. His skin was the color of white bread; black circles surrounded his eyes, and a scar the size of a cat's paw marked his left cheek. Thankfully, though, they'd found no ball in his foot. The shot that had hit him had gone right through the heel. With Ruby's help Camellia had cleaned it and wrapped it in fresh bandages.

Unfortunately, Johnny was faring even worse than York. His young body was emaciated, not only from the loss of blood from his recent wound but also from the years of rough living through the war. Large sores covered his lips, and it took almost two days of constant cleaning to clear his body of lice and other bugs. Although Mrs. Swanson and a surgeon had stopped the bleeding from his head and stitched the wound with a fine white thread, nobody knew if he would live. The saber that had gashed his skull had cut a swath close to four inches long, front to back, and at least two inches wide.

Camellia talked continually to Johnny and her pa, her voice as steady and quiet as a sweet flowing brook. Although she didn't know how, she believed her talking might give them a sound to hold to in their sleep; that it kept them somehow tied to the world. Often she just prayed as she talked, her lips busy asking the Lord to give them both enough strength to hold on until their bodies healed.

Mrs. Swanson stayed with her much of the time that Camellia sat by their beds, especially after she finished her work downstairs each day. Camellia accepted her mother's company without complaint. In spite of the fact that she and Mrs. Swanson had never quite come to friendly terms and still didn't talk except for whatever was necessary, Camellia realized she needed the help and privately welcomed it. Sometimes, when the nights grew longest and Camellia became especially weary, she was tempted to give up her hurt and just throw herself into her mama's arms. She longed to rest there, rest like a little girl who'd missed her mama all her life and now wanted to come home for gentle solace. But somehow she just couldn't let herself do it. Not now, not after so many years of distance between them. Although Mrs. Swanson had carried her within her body and given her birth, she still felt like a stranger, and Camellia was convinced that nothing could ever change that.

Camellia's pa came to consciousness first. On the fourth day after his arrival, his bleary eyes opened right before morning. His parched lips croaked something that woke Camellia from her dozing. Moving quickly, she brought him some water and poured it into his mouth. After a couple of minutes, he took the water dipper himself with shaking hands and drank deeply. When he'd finished, Camellia took the dipper away, then asked, "How are you feeling, Pa?"

"Like a horse stomped on me," he whispered. "Twice."

She smiled with relief. "You took a ball in your foot, but it's healing fine now. No gangrene that we can see."

"I thank you," he said. "Johnny OK?"

She pointed to Johnny. "We got a doctor to him pretty fast. One good thing about having a hospital here, I suppose. We got care for his wound, have provided for him since, and he seems a little better every day."

"How long has this been a hospital?"

"As long as I can remember, it seems."

York closed his eyes.

"You hungry?" asked Camellia.

"I could swallow a bite or two."

She stood to go to the kitchen, but York suddenly grasped her wrist and held her still. "Don't go yet," he begged, his eyes open again.

"You need to eat."

"I know, but I just want you to stay for another minute."

She relented and sat down again.

He stared at her a long time. "You look all growed up."

"It's been a while since you saw me," she said. "I'm a lot different now than I was."

"War changes all of us."

"I've worked in the hospital since it opened. Seen men hurting, crying, dying. That ages a person, I guess."

"I'm sorry you've seen such sufferin'."

"I'm sorry anyone has."

"Beth and Butler doin' OK?" he asked.

"Yeah. Talk about growing up; they're so different, you wouldn't recognize them. They both work here—not in the hospital, though. I don't want them seeing the worst of things."

"I'm pleased they're safe. You did good bringin' them here."

Then a grief that made her bones hurt welled back up in Camellia. "Stella's dead. Trenton killed her."

York's eyes flickered, and she saw pain in them too. "Johnny told me. Trenton's a sorry man. I'm glad you didn't marry him."

Camellia thought of Josh and started to tell York about him joining the Federals but then held her tongue. No reason to bother her pa with such sad tidings right now.

"You did a wonderful thing getting here with Johnny," she said. "Saved his life for certain."

He waved her off. "I'll probably get shot for desertion."

"You were about dead yourself."

"I did what any decent pa would do."

"You've always done that."

He shook his head. “I ain’t no hero—you know that as well as I do.”

She smiled. “You do have your rough spots, but nobody can ever say you didn’t provide for your children.”

He closed his eyes.

“Let me get you some food,” Camellia insisted.

“I left Calvin,” he whispered.

“What?” She stopped dead still.

“He rode with us, you know that. He got shot, and I had to choose him or Johnny to haul out.”

She touched his shoulder. “I know you did the best you could.”

“I tried.”

She wanted to cry for him, for the grief and helplessness she saw in his eyes, since she knew he wouldn’t let himself do it.

“One more thing,” York added.

“What?”

He cocked his head toward her. “Your mama. I did see her when I got here, didn’t I? I wasn’t dreamin’ it?”

“No, it was her. I live here at the hotel with Ruby, her baby, Leta, Beth, and Butler. Mrs. Swanson stays at her house some, here some.”

“How’s Ruby’s baby?”

“Growing fast. Children always do.”

“I’m surprised Ruby never run off.”

“The baby’s kept her here, I guess, and the war is so bad around her old homeplace. I don’t raise the subject with her anymore.”

“Where’s Obadiah?”

“Ruby saw him in Charleston a couple of years ago when I went to fetch Butler. He told her he’d wait for her, no matter what.”

“He’s a solid man.”

“Ruby believes so.”

They were silent for a minute, then York asked, “Did you get much time to know your pa?”

“Not really. He passed on back in 1861, right after I got here.”

“That beats all.”

“It came as quite a hurt to Mrs. Swanson. She really loved him, I believe.”

"Better than she loved me, that's for sure."

"I'm sorry she hurt you," Camellia said gently. "Makes me mad every time I ponder on it."

"Don't make me feel any too good either, I can tell you that."

"I know. I've held it against her too—the way she hurt you and all. Least she's been nice to us, though. Pays me an honest wage and lets me live here."

York frowned. "She wouldn't let you stay for free?"

"She offered, but I wouldn't take it."

"Good—don't be beholden to her. She's not trustable."

"I won't. I'm not prone to taking her charity or anybody else's."

York nodded with satisfaction but then scowled. "Did you like your pa before he died?"

"You're my pa."

York's eyes watered. "I need to tell you somethin' else."

"Not now. Rest some; then we can talk more."

"Josh," he said. "I saw him."

Camellia froze. "What?"

"We fought on the same battlefield a few days ago, where Johnny got hurt. I've heard of it happenin'—brothers, even fathers and sons end up on different sides of this thing. Stories tell of kin passin' letters to each other on the night before a battle, hollerin' out to one another during the fightin'. I never knew whether to believe any of it or not; surely didn't ever figure it would happen to me and Josh. I didn't even know he'd taken up with the Yankees. Johnny didn't tell me until right at the end."

Camellia's stomach was knotted with fear. "Do you know what happened to him?"

York wiped his eyes. "He protected Johnny when he went down. Saved his life. I got to both of them, hauled them out of there. But then . . ." He told her the rest of the story—how the deserters had taken Josh and the horse.

"I let them have him," he grieved. "I should have fought harder . . . done somethin' . . . oh, I don't know what. But there must have been some way to keep them from takin' him."

Camellia wanted to scream at her pa for giving Josh up but realized that wasn't fair. He hadn't had a choice. So she held back her anger and soothed him instead. "You did all you could. I believe that. And anybody who knows you knows you'd give your life for Josh, no questions asked."

"I would," he agreed.

"How bad was he hurt?"

"I won't lie. Bad—but I've seen men hurt worse and live through it."

Camellia tried to figure what the deserters would do with Josh. "They'll keep him alive if they can," she said, her hopes rising. "Least as long as they think they need him."

"I agree," York said. "If they don't run into any Yankees, they'll either leave him behind or hand him over to somebody somewhere. I don't think they'll haul him all the way to Tennessee. My guess is he'll end up in a prison between here and there."

"Did he say anything to you?" she asked. "Recognize you or anything?"

"He never gained consciousness."

"You did all you could."

"I wish that made me feel better."

Camellia's mind spun with possibilities, but since she couldn't do anything to make any of them happen, she focused on her pa's needs again. "Let me fetch you that food now."

"That would be good." York closed his eyes again.

Someone rapped on the door, and Camellia rose to open it. Mrs. Swanson stood in the doorway, her hands wrapped in her apron.

"How is he?" Mrs. Swanson queried.

"He just woke. I'm going for some food."

"You want me to get it?"

Camellia started to say yes but then hesitated. Although her pa probably didn't want to see Mrs. Swanson, she figured he might as well get it over with, painful or not. "I can do it," she said.

"There's bread on the kitchen table," Mrs. Swanson offered. "Some fried potatoes from last night. You can warm them."

Camellia nodded.

Mrs. Swanson moved through the door to the bed. "Hampton?"

He opened his eyes, and color flooded his face. He tried to straighten up, but Mrs. Swanson sat down and touched his shoulder. He lay back on the pillow.

"Go easy," she said.

Camellia knew she should leave and give them privacy, but her feet refused to obey. They stayed stuck to the floor.

"It's been a long time," York commented.

"I did wrong by you," said Mrs. Swanson.

"I can't argue with that, but it's water under the bridge."

"But I need to say it anyway."

"OK, it's said. Now leave it be," York ordered.

She sighed. "I need your forgiveness."

"You don't need nothin' from me. You've shown that more than once."

"Yes I do. You deserved better. I've asked God's forgiveness. Now I need yours."

"Then you have it."

She quirked an eyebrow. "I don't believe you. People don't forgive that easily."

"I forgive you," he said.

"How can you say that?"

York turned his head away, and although she couldn't be certain, Camellia thought she saw tears in his eyes.

"Look at me," coaxed Mrs. Swanson.

York faced her again. "I just want you to leave. I'm obliged to you for lettin' me rest up here, but soon as I can, I'll head out. No use in any more conversation between us."

"You don't really forgive me, do you?" Her voice was sad.

"You're askin' too much."

"I know, but it's all I can do."

"So you've done it. Now leave me alone."

"So you're lying about loving me?"

"No, that part is true."

"But you won't forgive me?"

"That's a whole lot harder than lovin' you."

"You can't still love me—not after what I've done to you?"

"I've loved you since the first time I saw you, and that's never changed, no matter what's happened between us."

"You're a sweet man," she said.

"Sweet has nothin' to do with this."

Mrs. Swanson changed the subject. "I hear you're married now."

"I expect you're surprised I could find a woman to have me."

"Not at all. I'm glad you found love."

"I don't know that I'd call it that."

"You don't love your wife?"

"Not so I can tell."

"You're a rough man, Hampton."

"You just said I was sweet."

"I take it back."

"I expect you should."

She pulled away from him and glanced at Camellia, as if searching for help, but Camellia knew nothing to say to make things better. Her pa held grudges, no way around it. For that matter, so did she. And Mrs. Swanson had deeply wronged both of them.

"I'll assist Camellia with that food," said Mrs. Swanson.

"Perhaps you should."

A second later Camellia and Lynette Swanson left her pa's room, their bodies stiff as they both struggled with the distance that lay so far between them.

Chapter Twenty

Crouching behind a thick stand of pine trees, Lester gripped the barrel of the Enfield rifle he'd picked up off a dead soldier a few miles back. He eyed the scruffy band of deserters that lay stretched on the ground beside a low fire, about twenty yards away.

He and Sugar had tracked these deserters ever since they'd taken Mr. Josh from that Rebel captain the night he'd fallen at Burgess Mill. They'd come searching for him right at dark and been told that Josh had fallen in a field near a shed. Not finding him there, they'd started walking carefully through the woods toward the Rebel lines, Sugar sniffing for Josh as they went. They'd come across the track quickly enough and followed the captain until the Tennessee boys had showed up.

Then, once again, Lester and Sugar had followed Josh, picking their way around the lines of both the Rebel and Yankee armies. Up until today the Tennessee boys had traveled at night. But now, obviously believing they'd moved past the worst of the danger, they'd bedded down for the evening. Josh rested to the left of the group, his hands and feet bound, his mouth gagged.

Patting Sugar quietly, Lester watched Mr. Josh for movement for several seconds. If his friend wasn't conscious, this might go poorly. "I hope he be awake," Lester whispered to Sugar. "Hope he gave attention to you early this evenin'."

Sugar stayed quiet as Lester waited under the late-night moon. Trying to let Mr. Josh know he was in the area, an hour earlier he'd sent Sugar into the camp like a stray looking for food. Although the deserters had shooed him away, Lester figured Josh had gotten the message. Lester rubbed the stock of his rifle and wondered if he could out-fight all the deserters. Although not sure, he figured he had no choice but to act now or lose Josh forever. From what he'd seen, Josh's captors hadn't fed or watered him at all. And unless Lester missed his guess, Mr. Josh wouldn't make it much longer unless he got some relief from such bad treatment. In addition to that, Lester wanted to rescue Josh before his captors traveled any farther south because runaway darkies who got caught sometimes ended up on the short end of a rope in Dixie country.

Lester patted Sugar's head. "We goin' for Mr. Josh," he murmured. "You ready?" Sugar licked his hand in agreement.

"Good thing they got liquored up," Lester added. Sugar seemed to grin, almost as if he knew about the deserters finding a couple of bottles of whiskey at a burned-out farmhouse just before nightfall; as if he knew how they'd swilled down the bottles as they'd walked, how they'd finished them before falling down to sleep.

Lester pulled a knife from the waist of his pants and crept, with Sugar close behind, toward the sleeping, loudly snoring men. Lester reached the first man within seconds and took him out without a sound. Moving quickly to the second one, Lester did the same, but this time the man shrieked a little as he died, and the three remaining men woke up. Everything went crazy after that. Men started shouting, jumping, and grabbing for guns and knives.

Sugar pounced on a stumpy man with a red blanket over his shoulders while Lester rushed for the sergeant who gave all the orders. To his left, Lester saw Josh roll over. He shouted at his friend and threw his knife toward Josh. Josh crawled to the knife and grabbed it between his bound hands.

Facing the sergeant, Lester ran at him and pulled the trigger. When the Enfield failed to fire, Lester spun it around, the butt out and ready. The sergeant pulled a pistol and fired, but Lester dodged and cracked the Enfield into the sergeant's face. A knife appeared in the deserter's hand. The blade caught Lester on the top of his right wrist but not enough to slow him down. Lester jabbed the rifle's bayonet at the sergeant, and it caught flesh. A second later the sergeant crumpled and fell, his thin mouth creased with a sad frown.

Panting heavily, Lester pivoted toward Mr. Josh and saw him on the ground, a deserter standing over him, pistol ready. Lester squeezed the trigger of the Enfield again, and this time it worked. The man crumpled to the ground as the bullet took him in the back. Sugar barked, and Lester whirled to see the stumpy man with the red blanket running toward the woods, his head down and legs churning. Lester started to chase after him but then stopped. The man had had enough; that was plain to see. Let the man run—Lester had what he'd come for.

Lester hurried to Josh and knelt down. Mr. Josh's eyes were closed, and dried blood caked the front of his shirt. Although he'd managed to get his feet free, his hands were still tied. A bruise the size of a small apple marked his right cheek, and he had a knot on the back of his head. Lester grabbed a canteen one of the deserters had left and dabbed some of the water on Josh's face.

"Mr. Josh?" he whispered.

Josh didn't respond. Then Sugar licked his face and his eyes opened. Lester grinned and cut Josh's hands loose.

"We come for you, Mr. Josh," said Lester.

Josh stared blankly at Lester, who began giving him sips of water to wet his parched lips. "You gone be fine," the black man murmured.

Josh's eyes looked confused. "Who are you?" he croaked.

Lester tilted his head. "It's me, Mr. Josh. Lester and Sugar."

Josh closed his eyes for a second, then opened them again. "I'm . . . hurt. My head's mixed up."

Lester folded back Josh's shirt, poured some water slowly over his wound, and gently rubbed off some of the dried blood. His heart lifted a little as he examined the wound. Although a saber had cut a three-inch gash in the flesh, mostly on the right side, no entrails poked out. Lester took a handkerchief from his pocket, wet it, and wiped away more blood from the wound.

"Don't worry none," he soothed, laying the shirt back over the wound. "I'm lookin' after you now. Been followin' you since back at Burgess Mill. When the battle ended and you didn't come back, I headed toward the field where you fought. I saw a Rebel captain haul you away. I had to stay hid for a while till I could figure what to do. Then the captain run up on a bunch of deserters, and they took you from him. I bided my time, then had at them. Now you be fine."

Josh tried to sit up but couldn't.

"Stay easy, Mr. Josh." Lester turned Josh's head so he could inspect the swollen skull. "You be mighty weak. Drink some more water."

Josh obeyed, then lay back again. "What . . . who . . . what did you call me?" he panted.

Lester tilted his head again. "What you mean? I called you Mr. Josh, like I always do."

Josh raised a hand and rubbed his scalp. "I can't . . . remember . . ."

Lester smiled. "I get you to some food. Give you a day to rest, you be fine."

Josh took the black man's hand and stared into his eyes. "You don't . . . understand. I can't remember . . . who you are, how I got here . . . who I am."

Lester paused. He'd heard of this happening but had never seen it. Men sometimes took leave of their thinking when a rough battle hit; some said it kept them from remembering the hardest of the things they saw, the worst of the foulness around them.

"Don't you worry none," Lester assured Josh. "I take care of you. Fix you up real fine."

When Josh closed his eyes again, Lester tried to figure what to do. Although he'd thought a lot on how to get Mr. Josh away from the deserters, he'd planned on Josh knowing what to do past that. But with his head all blank, Josh knew even less than Lester about what path to take now.

"What we do next?" Lester asked Sugar. The dog whined. Lester rubbed his beard and considered his options. Take Mr. Josh and try to find the Union lines? But who knew where they were? And what about the Rebels? They might run into them instead of the Federals.

A different notion came to Lester, and he rolled it over a couple of times to see if it made sense.

"What you say, Sugar?" he asked. The dog licked his lips, and Lester decided to go with his new idea.

"I want you to take off your clothes," he told Josh.

Josh opened his eyes but didn't speak.

"I help you do it." Lester reached for Josh's shirt. "I tryin' to keep you safe. You got to trust me on that, whether you know who I am or not."

Josh nodded slightly and tried to help Lester, but his hands were too weak. So Lester removed Josh's shirt for him, then grabbed a blanket and lay it over the injured man's torso.

"I need the britches too," Lester said.

Josh didn't argue. A second later Lester picked Josh's shoes and trousers off the ground, tossed them into the woods, and moved quickly to the Rebel sergeant. After removing the tattered clothes off the sergeant's dead body, Lester hurried back to Josh and started to put the Rebel britches on him.

Josh grabbed Lester's wrists. "What are you doing?"

"I got to do it," Lester insisted.

Josh shook his head.

"I be takin' you to Richmond," Lester explained. "To that house where we left your kids. Somebody there will tend your wounds. But I can't take you there in no Yankee uniform, so I'm switchin' your clothes for that Reb's. You understand, don't you?"

"Can't let you do it."

Lester paused, not liking the notion of disobeying Josh but realizing he had no choice but to do just that. It was this plan or nothing. He'd tell the Rebels guarding Richmond that he was taking Josh to the hospital. Hopefully they'd see him as a loyal darky caring for his fallen Southern master and let him through. Then Lester could carry Mr. Josh to his family. If not, they'd take Josh to the hospital themselves while he went on, found Josh's kids, and told them where they could find their pa. Either way, Josh would get better treatment than Lester could give him.

Pleased that he'd come up with such a smart idea, Lester pried Josh's fingers from his wrist. To his relief, Josh didn't fight him anymore. When Lester had finished dressing Josh, he picked his friend up, threw him over his shoulder, and set his chin toward Richmond, Sugar trailing behind him.

Over four hundred miles from where Lester picked Josh up, Trenton Tessier sat by the fireplace in the front room of the manse, a bottle of whiskey in his hand. His hair was mussed, his ruffled shirt wrinkled, his pants covered with stains where he'd spilled liquor on them, and his boots dirty and thin of bottom. He stared into the fire as if dead, his face a blank. The dark circles under his eyes made him appear at least ten years older than his true age. He glanced out the window to his right. A slow, soaking rain fell from a lead-colored sky.

Trenton lifted his flask, eyed it as if looking for a friend, then took a long swallow. For once, though, the drink offered him no solace. His head hurt, and his mind whirled with fury. The last years had gone hard on him.

Lincoln, the Yankee dictator, had declared the darkies free in January of 1863, so all of his hands, except for the toothless and middle-aged Leather Joe and a couple of the older ones, had run off, heaven only knew where. Since then he'd managed no rice crop at all, and weeds had grown over the fields.

As news of Yankee victories began to mount, things got worse. With no darkies around, Trenton had to take up farming himself, doing the best he could to grow enough corn, potatoes, tomatoes, and such to keep his stomach full enough to survive. He glanced over to a square box sitting on the floor by the fireplace and laughed derisively. Handfuls of practically worthless Confederate money lay in the box. He took a swig of whiskey and studied the room, noting how bare the rough years had made it—almost as if each day demanded another piece of furniture, another picture from the wall, another rug off the floor as a ransom for letting him live in the house.

With no spendable money to speak of, Trenton had ended up having to sell everything of value to buy whiskey and food. Now the manse stood almost bare of furnishings. All the rugs, paintings, silver, and chandeliers had long since gone. Even that, however, hadn't provided enough money to keep things up, and the buildings on The Oak had run down. They stood unpainted, the barn doors hanging open, the wheels of the last carriage rusting where it sat in its shed. The Confederate army had taken all the horses but the one he rode and most of the livestock too. Except for a few chickens, one hog, and a cow—and who knew when the army would show up for those—the barns stood empty.

Trenton finished his whiskey and called for Leather Joe. "I need another," he ordered, holding up the empty bottle when Leather Joe stepped in.

"You runnin' low," Leather Joe warned. "Might ought to go easy on the next few bottles."

Trenton waved Joe away and stared down at his stump. After all this time, and the best efforts of every doctor he could find, it had never completely healed. It stayed red at the tip a lot, and in the summer, an infection always seemed to set in at least once. It still oozed from time to time, almost as if trying to discharge some foul torment from the center of his soul. He cursed under his breath at his fate—a number of men with half a leg had gotten war commissions. But, due to the continual eruptions from his leg, none had ever come through for him. He'd spent the entire war stuck in South Carolina. In the beginning he'd gone to Charleston as often as he could, but after a while that became an embarrassment. How do you tell people in polite company that your leg seeps a vile substance, so you cannot go and fight? Not only had his wound kept him from the glory of the battlefield, it also kept him a virtual prisoner on The Oak. He felt twice cursed because of it.

As Leather Joe left, Trenton stood and hobbled to the fireplace to drop in a fresh piece of wood. Again he thought of Camellia. In his whiskey-soaked mind, he blamed all his troubles on her. How different his life would have been if he'd never met her; if she and her sorry pa had never showed up at The Oak. He'd be on a horse somewhere right now, a saber in hand, his eyes full of fight, his heart in his throat as he led men in the name of the Confederacy's noble cause.

His hand trembling, he licked the neck of the empty whiskey bottle, then lifted it and threw it against the wall. The bottle shattered and fell to the floor, mixing with the glass of three other bottles he'd finished and broken over the last two days. He glared again at his stump. One of these days he'd take his revenge on Camellia . . . and anybody and everybody she loved!

Leather Joe stepped back in with his new bottle. Trenton opened it quickly and took a long swallow, thankful he'd had enough sense to buy cases of the stuff before the war turned so bad and Confederate money became worthless. Without the whiskey, Trenton didn't think he could have survived.

"You need anythin' else, Master Trenton?" asked Leather Joe.

Trenton shook his head. "Not for now."

"All right, then."

Hoofbeats sounded from outside, and Trenton exhaled in surprise as Leather Joe moved to the window.

"Somebody comin'," Leather Joe said.

"Not many travelers headed our way these days," Trenton commented.

"It's a carriage," explained Leather Joe.

Trenton grabbed a crutch and thumped toward the front door. Opening it, he saw a beat-up black carriage pull to a halt. Before he could move down the steps, the door popped open and his mother hopped out. Although surprised, Trenton didn't move. His mother walked quickly toward him. Her hair was tucked under a navy bonnet, her brown dress was slightly aged but still in decent condition, and her hands were covered by tan gloves. When she reached him, he didn't open his arms in greeting.

"What brings *you* here, Mother dear?" he asked sarcastically. "Looking for something else to sell so you can remain in Charleston in the manner to which you've grown accustomed?"

"Come inside," she barked, bustling past him and through the front door. "We need to talk."

His whiskey in hand, Trenton followed her into the parlor, where she pointed him to the last of the room's chairs.

"I prefer to stand," he said, easing over to the fireplace. "You're usually not here long enough for me to take a seat."

His mother shrugged and sat down, her hands in her lap. For the first time, Trenton noticed her thin face, the redness of her eyes. Obviously, the war had not gone too well for her either. A sense of pleasure rippled through his bones; his mother deserved whatever ill winds blew her way.

"I know we have not talked much lately," she started.

"Are you feeling sorry for neglecting me? Staying in Charleston while I suffered in this godforsaken place?"

Her lips tightened, as if she had to fight to hold back her tongue. "This isn't about you."

"Then it must be about you; how surprising."

"It's about your brother.'"

Trenton sobered a little. "What about him?"

"I have bad news."

Trenton straightened, and all his anger ran out. "Where is he?"

"Calvin is dead," she announced.

All of a sudden Trenton felt faint. "It can't be."

"It's true." There was a catch in her voice; her eyes brimmed with tears. "At a place called Burgess Mill, south of Petersburg. The Charleston newspaper prints the names of the dead and wounded, you know that. I saw it yesterday. He's officially listed as missing, but that usually means dead."

Trenton fought back tears. Of all the people in the world, he loved Calvin the most—even though, of course, he'd never told his brother that. In fact, the two brothers had spent a lot of time before the war at odds with each other, sparring verbally and physically, but that didn't change the one thing Trenton knew to be true—that Calvin alone understood him. Although he'd envied Calvin his battlefield commission and had been angered by it, he still loved his little brother. "How?" he asked.

"I don't know."

"He rode with your precious Captain York."

"Yes."

"You told York to look out for him."

"Yes."

"Is York still alive?"

"I don't know. He's missing also."

Trenton almost smiled at the thought of Hampton York lying dead on a battlefield. But he held it back, not for his mother's sake but because of his fears for Calvin. He started to take another drink but, wanting to keep his head clear, hesitated. "Where will they take Calvin's body if they find it?"

"I sent a telegram to find out. They took most of the soldiers killed at Burgess Mill to Richmond and buried them there at a place called Hollywood Cemetery."

"I want him brought here," Trenton demanded.

His mother stood and made her way to the window. "How can we manage that? Train travel is just about impossible. The Federal army is all over the area. Even if we can get up there, we may not be able to find either of them, get them dug up and hauled back here."

"I'll go to Richmond," Trenton offered. "Do whatever it takes to find Calvin, bring him back. He'd want that, I know it. He loved The Oak."

His mother silently faced him, her face void of hope. For the first time he could remember, Trenton saw his mother at a loss. Something about that touched him. Thumping toward her, he put a hand on her shoulder. "Come with me, Mother. We'll bring Calvin home." As he spoke he realized that he still wanted to please her in spite of all that had come between them; that he still wanted her to love him, respect him, approve of him.

Her eyes watered and she nodded. His heart warmed as he saw how much she needed him. No matter how strong she seemed, she still had her weak points, moments only a man like he could handle.

"We'll find Hampton too," she sobbed. "Bring him home with Calvin."

Trenton's fingers knotted into a vise on her shoulder. How dare she mention Hampton York at a time like this?

"I hope York's dead!" he exploded. "But if by some chance he is alive, you best hope I don't find him! Because if I do, I'll do everything in my power to kill him!"

"You're a fool," she spat, jerking away from his grip. "A drunken, weak, one-legged fool."

"Maybe so!" he shouted. "But I still have some pride, something you gave up the moment you agreed to marry York! You've made me ashamed to carry your name, Mother! And no matter what else happens, if

Hampton York *is* alive, I aim to see to it that he never again sets foot on The Oak!"

"What if I told you I loved him?"

He laughed the first good laugh he'd had in a long time. "I'd say you were incapable of loving anybody but yourself."

"You know I love you and Calvin."

"If that's true, you have to forget Hampton York. He's probably dead anyway, so put him out of your head."

She nodded sadly and seemed to calm down. "You're all I have left. My only son."

"That's right," he said, enjoying the power such a predicament gave him. "I'm all you've got."

Feeling strangely pleased, he turned his thoughts to how to reach Richmond. "Train tickets cost a lot these days, and we have no way to pay for them."

Mrs. York raised an eyebrow, and her tears disappeared. "I have money."

"You do?"

She wrung her hands. "Yes, I've . . . well, I held some back from the beginning. U.S. dollars. I thought it wise."

Trenton's mouth fell open, but then he smiled with satisfaction. "I should have known. How much do you have?"

She glanced down. "Enough. Let's leave it at that."

"Where? The Charleston banks hold nothing but Confederate currency."

She shrugged. "In a safe place. I'd rather not say."

Trenton recalled the situation just before the war broke out. Hampton York had come up with twenty-seven thousand dollars—from gambling, York had said. Did his mother have that money stashed away somewhere? But where? Surely not in Charleston; everyone expected Sherman to head that way before winter fell. Trenton walked to the window and scanned The Oak, then faced his mother again. "You've hidden it here, haven't you? Charleston isn't safe. It's got to be here."

"Perhaps it's in Columbia," she said. "Don't waste your time searching."

He chuckled with an odd mixture of pride and joy. His mother walked toward his open arms and fell into them. "We'll find Calvin and bring him home," he soothed. "Then you can tell me where you hid the money."

As she relaxed into his shoulder, Trenton realized she did need him, especially now that Hampton York had disappeared. Hopefully York was dead. But if not, Trenton planned to find the man—and to enjoy the pleasure of putting the finishing touches on his miserable existence.

Chapter Twenty-One

Six days later, about halfway through the night, a sharp rap sounded on the door of the room where Camellia slept. She sat up, rubbed her eyes, and wondered about the noise. Ruby rolled over on her pallet on the floor.

"Camellia!"

Recognizing Mrs. Swanson's voice, Camellia hopped up, gathered her nightdress around her, and opened the door. Mrs. Swanson waited there, holding a burning candle, a black housedress over her nightclothes. A rough-looking black man, beat-up, wide-brimmed hat in hand, stood by her side.

"Let us in!" ordered Mrs. Swanson.

Camellia stepped back, and they pushed past her.

"This is Lester," explained Mrs. Swanson. "He came with Mr. Cain when he brought Beth here."

Camellia stared at Lester, noted his bloodshot eyes, frayed coat, and muddy boots. He looked like he hadn't slept or eaten in a long time. "You worked at Fort Walker with Josh," she said, remembering. "He wrote me about you."

"Yes, ma'am, I did."

"You look hungry."

"I could eat a mite, but I reckon that can wait. I come to tell you about Mr. Josh."

Camellia's knees shook as she heard Josh's name, but she locked them and told herself to hold steady. "See what food you can find in the kitchen," she told Ruby.

Ruby nodded and left the room.

"The Confederate boys took Mr. Josh when we got to the city," Lester began.

Camellia's heart jumped; Josh wasn't dead!

"I carried him for near to a week," continued Lester. "Weaved through all kinds of soldiers. Figured to haul him straight here so you could nurse him healthy, but them Rebel boys didn't seem to like that idea when I run up on them a couple of miles out."

"Is he hurt?" Camellia asked.

Lester's eyes looked pained.

"Tell me!" ordered Camellia.

"He's got a stab in the belly, but it didn't go too deep, far as I could tell. Maybe the worst thing is the crack he took on the head. He's all confused in his thinkin'."

"What do you mean?"

"Mr. Josh don't seem to remember much—who he is or nothin'."

Camellia pondered that a second; she'd heard of men losing their memory after a battle. Thankfully their recall usually returned after a few days' rest. "He's going to live, though?"

"I expect so, if nothin' worse happens to him and he don't get no gangrene from his belly cut."

Camellia pointed Lester to the room's only chair and sat down on her bed, her mind a swirl of questions. "Why did the soldiers let you go when they took Josh?"

"I told them I was just a loyal darky bringin' in a soldier, that's all. They got other worries than botherin' with an old man like me."

Ruby stepped into the room and handed Lester a biscuit and a half-full jar of jelly. Camellia thought of the thousands of Yankee prisoners scattered around the city—in Libby Prison, on Belle Isle, in various warehouses that once held tobacco. From what she'd heard, the places made stables look good by comparison. Poor food, spotty medical care, and foul aromas created awful living conditions. Other than the ones who got exchanged in the prisoner swaps, most of the men who went into one of those places never lived to walk out. "We have to go find Josh," she said sternly.

"How do you propose we do that?" asked Mrs. Swanson.

Camellia decided that not everyone should hear what she had to say. "Rest here a minute," she told Lester. "Eat your biscuit."

Lester nodded, looking grateful.

Camellia pulled Mrs. Swanson into the hall and dropped her voice. "I don't want anyone else involved," she whispered. "It's too dangerous. But Josh is probably at Belle Isle. They put enlisted men there. I'm going to look for him."

"But he's a Yankee soldier!" argued Mrs. Swanson. "The enemy, in case you've forgotten! You go fooling around trying to find a Yankee, and somebody will yell 'spy' for sure. You know how bad things are getting. The provost marshal's office is arresting so-called spies left and right."

"I'll keep your name out of it," Camellia promised. "Tell anybody who asks that you know nothing. But I have to try. You know how bad the prisons are. If Josh is as hurt as Lester says, he'll die without some help."

"You're asking a lot."

"I'll leave here if you want. That way you'll get no blame if anything goes wrong."

Mrs. Swanson considered for a moment, then shook her head. "I don't want you to do that."

"I'll be careful," Camellia said.

"I want to stay in Richmond when this war ends," Mrs. Swanson explained. "What you do or don't do might affect that."

"If anything happens, I'll take the blame. And I'll make sure the authorities know you're not involved in anything I do."

Mrs. Swanson gave a relieved nod, and then the two returned to Lester and Ruby. Lester finished his biscuit and jelly and wiped his mouth as they entered.

"I thank you for caring for Josh," she said, putting a hand on his shoulder.

"I just returnin' the favor he did for me."

Camellia offered her hand.

Lester shook it and grinned widely. "Mr. Josh gone be fine."

"Let's get you some more food," Camellia offered. "Then a place to sleep."

"I be obliged for that," the black man said. "Then I head out in the morning."

"You going back to the Federals?" asked Ruby, standing from the bed where she was sitting.

"Figure that's safest. Don't want nobody to start askin' questions about where I come from."

"You can stay here," said Camellia. "We'll hide you."

Lester shook his head. "This war ain't over yet. Reckon I'll go see what I can do to end it a little sooner."

"Amen to that," said Mrs. Swanson.

"You heading southeast, then," Ruby commented.

"That be where the closest Union boys are, so I reckon so."

Ruby glanced at Camellia, then back at Lester. "You want some company?" she asked him.

His big face scrunched. "I ain't sure I know your meanin'."

Ruby faced Camellia. "It's time I go for Theo," she said strongly. "I've waited too long already. But Leta is old enough for me to leave her with you."

"I've wondered when this day would come." Camellia sighed.

"I couldn't figure how to do it," explained Ruby. "Too many soldiers about, too much confusion, and I had Leta to tend. But now Mr. Lester shows up, a man who seems real capable. Maybe he'll take me to my old place before he joins back up with the Federals."

"It be real dangerous out there," Lester warned. "Soldiers on both sides of the line tendin' to shoot first, ask questions later."

Ruby lifted her chin. "I'm not afraid."

"I'll pay you for your troubles," Mrs. Swanson told Lester, surprising Camellia once again with her generosity.

"I'll pay him myself," argued Ruby. "I've saved the wages you paid me."

Lester grinned. "I don't expect I'll take money from either of you, but it sure is sweet to hear somebody say they'll give me real dollars for a job."

Ruby faced Camellia again. "Will you let me go?"

The day Camellia had long anticipated had now come. "You don't belong to me," she told Ruby. "So it's not for me to say what you do."

Ruby put a hand on Camellia's elbow. "I don't belong to anybody."

Camellia wanted to argue, to remind Ruby that nothing in their world had changed, that the war hadn't ended yet. Who knew what would happen when it did? Ruby's mama had birthed her to serve white people, and Mr. Marshall Tessier had paid eighteen hundred dollars for her. Yes, Camellia and Ruby had grown to trust each other; had become friends since Ruby's arrival at The Oak. But both had known that a white servant, even one as lowly as she, lived in a higher world than a slave. One was free, and the other bound. What would happen if the ways they'd both known all their lives suddenly disappeared? If all slaves became free, how would Ruby survive? How would she get work? How would the plantations make it? How would anybody in the South survive?

Camellia thought of her pa and brother, still recovering from their wounds just a couple of rooms away. They'd fought the Yankees for over three years; had taken bullets more than once to defend the exact institution Ruby now wanted to upend. For that's really what this war was—a fight between those who believed in slavery and those who didn't. Could Camellia go against her kin so easily? Put aside the sacrifices they and so many thousands of other men and women had made?

Camellia walked to the window and stared into the dark. Josh Cain, the man she loved, lay out there in a prison somewhere, shot because he wanted to see folks like Ruby set free. Because he believed in his heart that no human being should own another human being. If she truly loved Josh, how could she refuse Ruby this request? How could she do anything but bless Ruby as she went to find Theo?

Camellia's thoughts spun as she looked toward the heavens and the twinkling stars. Suddenly, she saw the answer as plain as day, from the Scripture she and Josh had read together when they were still at The Oak: "There is neither bond nor free, there is neither male nor female: for ye are all one in Christ Jesus." That's what the Bible said, and how could she argue with the Word of the Lord? To do so marked her as . . . well . . . as an evil woman.

Camellia knew the answer then, as if there had never been any true question. Although she'd lived with slavery all her life and her pa and brother had almost died to protect it, the whole system grieved the heart of God. Josh was right. God did see all people—whether black, white, or any other color—as equal. And she, Camellia York, had been grieving the heart of God to have accepted the evil of slavery for so many years. No wonder Ruby had responded so poorly to Camellia's efforts to tell her about the Lord. So long as she treated Ruby like a piece of property, Camellia had no moral basis to talk to her about Jesus. Why should Ruby listen with her heart when her body was still in the chains of slavery?

Camellia winced as the revelation hit her. Why hadn't she understood before? Josh had tried to explain it to her, but her heart and mind simply hadn't been open. Now she longed to tell him she understood. No matter what happened from this point on, her heart had changed forever.

Camellia pivoted to Ruby, opened her arms, and gathered Ruby into them. "I don't own you. Neither does anyone else, except for the Lord. I want you to hear me on that, Ruby. I believe the Lord made all of us, and His claim comes from that." She sighed. "You're free in Christ, the same as I am or anybody else. There's no other way to be truly free."

Ruby stiffened, then drew back from the embrace, and eyed Camellia, as if trying to see if her words were a trick. Something in Camellia's gaze must have reassured her, for Ruby smiled, obviously relieved.

"I hear your preaching," Ruby said. "But you need to hold it until I get back with Theo."

"I'll look forward to that day," Camellia said. She looked at Lester. "You haven't said if you'd take her."

"I do whatever you want," he replied. "I owe Mr. Josh that much."

Camellia smiled. "I'll keep Leta. You can leave when you want."

"We go at dark tomorrow," said Lester.

"OK. Now let us feed you some more and let you take some rest."

"You reckon you got a biscuit for my dog?" Lester asked. "He's out back."

"Sure." Camellia patted Lester's shoulder. "We'll find a biscuit for your dog."

Wearing the best clothes he had left—a black frock coat and pants, a tan shirt with ruffles on the collar and sleeves, and a black hat with a firm brim—Trenton rode the train with his mother into Richmond the day after Ruby and Lester headed out. Although his eyes were scratchy from a lack of sleep, Trenton's head felt clearer than in a long time because he had refrained from all whiskey drinking on the trip. Yes, it had taken all his will power, but now he felt pleased that he'd managed such soberness. With a dead brother's body to find, he needed to keep his wits about him.

With his mother at his side, Trenton hauled the three bags they'd brought off the train, stepped onto the platform at the depot, and smoothed down the front of his shirt.

"You look prosperous," said his mother admiringly. "A man of means."

"As do you." He noted the blue parasol she carried and the long navy cape and dress she wore with her buckled shoes. "As if the war never happened."

"I kept this outfit back," she said. "For just such a time as this."

Satisfied, Trenton scanned the depot area. Soldiers in all manner of dress milled about—their hats and uniforms tattered and mismatched, their boots muddy and worn. Many of them marched this way or another; others appeared as casual as if out for a Sunday stroll. Carriages of all kinds were pulled by sway-backed horses. The late-afternoon air hung heavy with smoke, and every building he saw needed painting.

"Things look pretty bleak." He picked up their bags and looked for a carriage to hire.

"I hope General Lee's army looks better."

"If not, they won't be able to fight much longer."

"Just think how bad things will get if the Yankees whip us."

"General Lee will never surrender."

A brown carriage pulled up, and Trenton motioned to the driver, helped his mother into the back, loaded their bags, and climbed in.

"Victoria Hotel," he ordered the carriage driver.

The man clicked at the horses, and the carriage clomped slowly down the street.

"You sure you want to start there?" Katherine asked.

"I'd prefer it otherwise," he lied. "But the hotel is the most logical place to begin. Camellia's folks surely know Richmond well and will have many valuable contacts. They can help us reach the right person—somebody who will know the best way to search for Calvin."

"What if Camellia is there?"

Trenton gazed out the carriage window and lied again. "I'm no longer interested in her."

His mother took his hand and squeezed it. "She never deserved you."

Trenton smiled briefly but didn't speak again as the carriage continued to clack through the streets. Within a few minutes, they reached the hotel; Trenton climbed out, helped his mother down, and paid the carriage driver. Now they stood together, facing the cobblestone path that led through a black wrought-iron fence and up to the door. A line of soldiers moved up and down the stone steps of the entrance, several of them carrying wounded men on stretchers into the building. A thick stench of body odor mixed with medicinal spirits saturated the air, and Trenton wrinkled his nose. He gazed with confusion at the markings over the hotel door. Yes, it was the Victoria.

"They've made the place a hospital," he said.

"We should have expected it," his mother commented. "It's happened all over; anything for our boys."

"You think Camellia will be here?"

"We have to go inside to find out."

Straightening to his full height, Trenton took their bags and led his mother past the maple trees that lined the cobblestone walk and up the steps to the double front doors. Scores of wounded men lay inside, and the rank odors grew stronger as he stepped past them. Groaning and talking mixed into a steady stream. For the first time, Trenton felt a little relieved that he'd never put on a uniform. Poor wretches!

"Calvin could be in a place like this," his mother said, a catch in her voice. "Lying in a corner, out of his head."

"We'll find him," Trenton assured her. "Until then, don't think about it."

She nodded as they made their way through the injured soldiers and stepped to the desk. A middle-aged woman with striking cheekbones looked up at them. She wore a plain black dress.

"I'd like to see Mrs. Wallace Swanson," he said stiffly.

The woman looked curiously at him, then his mother, then back at Trenton. "Who are you?"

"Trenton Tessier," he explained. "This is my mother, Mrs. Katherine Tessier." He glanced at his mother to see if she'd correct him, but she stayed quiet.

The woman's eyes widened. "You come from The Oak Plantation."

"Yes," said Trenton, surprised. "You've heard of the place?"

His mother laid a hand on his arm, and he turned to face her. But before she could speak, Camellia walked out from a hallway to their left and headed toward them. Trenton held his breath in awe. Although a bit thinner, Camellia looked lovelier than ever. Her face had matured, and her eyes, always that rich blue, now seemed deeper, richer . . . as if that were possible. She wore a light green blouse that set off her lustrous dark hair and a flowing brown skirt that covered but did not conceal her figure. Although he'd just told his mother that he no longer cared for her and even hoped that maybe it was true, Trenton now knew it for the lie it was. In spite of everything, he still loved Camellia York, still needed her, had to have her!

Camellia stepped to the desk without a word and stood stiffly by the woman questioning him. Trenton kept his eyes fixed on Camellia until the woman spoke again, this time to his mother.

"You're Marshall Tessier's wife?"

"Yes."

Surprised by the woman's question, Trenton tore his gaze away from Camellia and faced the woman again. "Did you know my father?"

The woman's face flushed as her hands formed into fists; Trenton saw fury in her eyes. Why?

"I knew him," she said simply.

Trenton beamed in spite of his confusion. "My father did business in many places. I'm glad to see he's remembered here in Richmond so long after his death." He glanced at Camellia, hoping she'd heard this woman's acknowledgment of his father's reputation. Maybe then Camellia would speak to him, acknowledge his presence, give him the respect he deserved.

The woman stepped from behind the desk. For a moment Trenton thought she wanted to embrace him, and he almost backed up to prevent it. Then she stopped, raised a hand, and slapped him across the mouth.

Trenton reeled back; his right hand grabbed the edge of the counter to keep him from falling. His mother gasped and Trenton cursed, pulled himself back up, and wiped a trickle of blood off his lower lip.

"What are you doing?" he growled.

The woman raised her hand again, but his mother stepped between her and Trenton.

"Who are you?" demanded Trenton.

"My name is Lynette Ruth Swanson!" she snarled. "And I've wanted to do that for a long time!"

Trenton glanced at Camellia and now saw the resemblance. "You're Camellia's mother!"

"That's right."

"What's your complaint with my dead husband?" The question came from Trenton's mother.

"You figure it out!" Mrs. Swanson snapped.

"He was a man of quality," Trenton insisted.

Mrs. Swanson balled her fists again, and Trenton eased back half a pace.

"Hold it!" his mother ordered.

"Don't ever mention Marshall Tessier's name in my presence again," Mrs. Swanson commanded. "Now, what do you want?"

Trenton's face burned with humiliation. "You best be glad I'm a gentleman."

"Or what?"

Trenton licked his lips and wished for a drink. To his relief his mother answered for him.

"We'd like to talk to your husband."

Mrs. Swanson's words were curt. "My husband is dead."

"Then perhaps I could talk privately with Camellia," said Trenton, hoping to escape this crazy woman as soon as possible.

Camellia's eyes narrowed. "I have nothing to say to you."

"I won't bother you. I promise that."

"You killed Stella. Stay away from me!"

Trenton bit his tongue and tried to figure his next step. Even though Mrs. Swanson hated his father, he still had a job to do and needed a place to stay until he could finish it and leave. "Look," he finally said, "we hoped you could help us handle a family matter. But since you obviously won't, we'd like a room for a couple of days. We'll do our business and leave as soon as we can."

Mrs. Swanson waved a hand over the crowded lobby. "Every space I have is filled, mostly with dying men."

"Where do you suggest we go?" he asked.

"I have no idea. All the hotels are full."

For the first time since he'd left home Trenton's spirits fell, and the sense of usefulness he'd felt since his mother had asked for his assistance disappeared. His shoulders sagged, his stump began to ache, and he again wished he had a drink. Frustrated, he glanced at his mother, and she once again took the lead.

"Look," she started. "I'm sorry for whatever offense my late husband might have caused you. But that was a long time ago, and my son and I had nothing to do with it." She addressed Camellia now. "We're here to find Calvin's body, that's all. He disappeared at Burgess Mill."

Mrs. Swanson nodded. "Hampton told us. He did all he could for him."

"We hope to find him and take him home for a proper burial."

"I'm sorry about your son," Mrs. Swanson said, her eyes losing their anger.

Trenton and his mother nodded sadly. "We'll leave as soon as we determine his whereabouts," said Mrs. York. "Not a day later. We'd appreciate any accommodation you have available, no matter how poor."

Mrs. Swanson glanced at Camellia as if to ask her permission for something, but she remained silent. "Perhaps you can stay out back," Mrs. Swanson offered slowly. "I've got a room above the carriage shed. It's barely big enough to stretch out in, but it's yours if you want it."

"I thank you," Mrs. York said graciously.

"You should start your search at the Hollywood Cemetery," added Mrs. Swanson. "They bury a lot of the soldiers there."

"We'll rest for a couple of hours, then go straight there."

"I'll show you to the room."

Trenton picked up their bags and trailed after his mother and Mrs. Swanson as they left the room.

"Is Ruby here with you?" he asked, trying to take his mind off Camellia's standoffish attitude.

"Not at this moment—but yes, she's stayed here the last few years," Mrs. Swanson replied.

"She belongs to The Oak, you know," Trenton commented sternly.

They left the hotel and walked down a tree-lined path to the carriage house.

"I own no slaves," said Mrs. Swanson, lifting her chin.

"Are you an abolitionist, then?"

Mrs. Swanson didn't answer, so they walked on to the carriage house, where she led them up a stairwell to a small space on the second floor and opened the door.

"Here's your room." She pointed to a space just wide enough for the two single beds and wood chairs that sat in it. "It's not much but should do for a short stay."

"It'll be fine," said Trenton.

"I pray you'll find Calvin."

Trenton stepped into the room and set down the bags. Mrs. Swanson started to leave, but Trenton suddenly remembered something. Even though it seemed a little out of place, he decided to bring it up anyway. "You were married to Hampton York a long time ago."

"Yes." Mrs. Swanson stopped and faced him without shame.

Trenton was blunt. "Did you ever get a divorce from him?"

His mother froze.

"You're asking questions you shouldn't ask," said Mrs. Swanson.

"Forgive me, but this is important. I'm just trying to determine if my mother's marriage to York is legal or not."

Mrs. Swanson looked at Mrs. York. "Shouldn't you be the one to ask such things?"

Mrs. York shook her head. "It's not the time to speak of any of this. Perhaps when the war is over."

"I agree," said Mrs. Swanson.

Trenton frowned. "I expect it won't matter. York is listed as missing. I hope he's dead."

Mrs. Swanson looked up. "He's not dead. I can assure you of that."

Mrs. York's hands flew to her mouth. "He's not?"

"Not at all. He's asleep upstairs in the hotel, recovering from wounds taken at Burgess Mill."

Trenton sagged into one of the small chairs and threw back his head. The urge to both laugh and curse overwhelmed him. Although disappointed to hear that York had survived, he also felt a strange sense of joy at the prospect of killing him with his own two hands.

"Do you think I could see him?" asked Mrs. York.

"I'm certain you can," answered Mrs. Swanson.

When Trenton chuckled, his mother looked curiously at him. "Stay away from him," she commanded.

"Of course," he agreed. "What else would I do?"

Chapter Twenty-Two

Following Lester and his dog, Sugar, Ruby cautiously picked her way out beyond Richmond over the next three days. Although they had to go west at least twenty miles before going south and then finally east again and stayed completely off the main travel-ways, they still made steady, even if slow, progress.

"If we traveled straight there, it'd only take a day," Ruby had told Lester as they settled in without a fire on the first night.

"If we traveled straight there, we'd run smack into the fightin'," said Lester. "I reckon I'll walk the extra miles to stay out of that."

Ruby had simply wrapped her blanket tighter against the night cold and not said anything else.

The next day they continued their journey, and even though they did come up on a lot of people, they managed to stay out of the line of real fighting. That didn't mean, though, that they didn't see and hear signs of the war. Cannons often boomed in the distance, and smoke rose in the sky at almost every turn, especially to the east. Everywhere Ruby looked she saw the damage the conflict had put on the land. Trees were blown into charred stumps by cannon shot, and soldiers had cut down almost every fence to satisfy their constant need for firewood. Scores of houses and barns lay charred into ashes, the chimney usually the only thing left standing. Holes dotted the ground in all directions where the soldiers had tried to dig into the earth to hide from the fire of rifle and cannon. In addition to that, soldiers' gear lay all over the ground—rusted rifles and pistols, empty haversacks, canteens, men's hats, sewing kits, bent coffeepots—anything and everything a body could imagine.

"I reckon this ground done seen more death than most anywhere on the earth," said Lester as they moved over the miles.

"I'd hate to see the place that was worse," agreed Ruby.

"Still right beautiful, though," Lester commented. "In spite of the scars man done put on it."

Ruby nodded. All around them, the earth still managed to live. Rolling hills were covered with pine trees. They crossed scores of streams gurgling with white water and crowded with fish that glistened in the fall sun. At night the sky beamed with bright stars.

"No matter how much we seem bent on destroyin' things, the good Lord seems set on goin' on like nothin' ever happened," mused Lester as they lay down to rest the second night after they left.

"You a believing man?" she asked him.

"Since I was a boy," said Lester.

"This war don't put you off from it? All the killing?"

"I see how it might," he said. "But just the opposite happened to me. I see life goin' right on again after the cannon stops shootin'. Bad things don't last forever, and the Lord's got time to be patient. Mr. Josh reminded me of all that."

"What about slaving?"

"That ain't right, I know it. But look what's done happened. It's all comin' to an end. Maybe not so fast as we want it but soon enough. You take your boy, Theo, you wantin' to find. He born slave, but now he can live free. That little girl you got there in Richmond too. Both of them got all kinds of chances now that a new day has come. I give the Lord credit for that."

"But not the blame for the evil that put us in a slave life to begin with?"

"No, I reckon menfolks ought to take the blame for that, not the Lord."

Ruby left the subject then. She stayed quiet for the rest of that night and on through the remainder of the journey, but Lester didn't seem to mind. He said little unless she started the conversation, and she liked that fine. With her mind set on finding Theo, she didn't really care to make much conversation.

Ruby tried to see Theo in her head as she journeyed. He'd be eleven now, almost grown, surely a lot taller and who knew what else. Would he recognize her? Would she recognize him? Did he still talk with such wisdom, so much older than his years? Did he still see visions? Had he seen anything of her future in these last six years?

Early in the morning of their fourth day out from Richmond, they crossed Barley's Creek, a gentle, clear-water crossing near the north border of her former plantation. A thick fog hung over the ground as she topped a slight rise in the ground and stared down toward the place where she'd grown up. She remembered Donetta Rushton, the daughter of the plantation owner, and the way Donetta had taught her to read. Where was Donetta now? What had happened to her family? Were any of them still here, or had they fled to Richmond or somewhere else?

"I can't see nothin' in this fog," said Lester.

"It's down there." Ruby pointed toward the spot where she remembered the plantation standing. "A white brick house, two big columns out front, two barns to the left, a well between the barns. A white fence runs out back of the house, and a stone wall borders it between here and there."

Ruby began to hurry as she talked, her feet sliding over the ground as her excitement rose. The rock wall suddenly appeared in the fog. Ruby noticed gaping holes in it; the rocks were cast out in scattered patterns. Then she realized—cannons had blasted out the holes! Her breath shortened as she tried to see the house through the fog, the wonderful two-story mansion where she'd played by the porch, where she'd served meals once she grew old enough, where she'd listened to the white folks talk, play their piano, and entertain their friends. She tilted her ears toward the house, hoping to hear the sounds of people talking, animals moving . . . something, *anything* to show that life remained in the place. But she heard nothing but the sound of Barley's Creek running behind her.

She moved faster. A few seconds later, she spotted the bones and feathers of a dead chicken on the ground, and she started running. The fog lifted a little, and she peered through it; then she stopped dead in her tracks. The house—or at least what remained of it—stood straight ahead. There was only the one lonely charred wall with the chimney still standing. Everything else, except a small section of the front porch, was burned into ashes, the lovely bricks nothing but black rubble and soot.

Ruby rubbed her eyes as if trying to wipe away what she saw, but when she looked again, nothing had changed. Sugar ran toward the wreckage. Tears welled in Ruby's eyes as she rushed after the dog, Lester trailing her.

"It can't be!" she screamed as she reached the remains of the porch and dropped to her knees.

Lester squatted beside her and took her in his arms. "It happen all over the country. Lots of places are nothin' but soot and chimneys now."

A thousand awful thoughts fought for Ruby's attention. Did this mean everyone was dead? Theo and her mama too? Or had they run somewhere? Escaped the killing and disappeared? Ruby pushed aside her questions and tried to stay hopeful.

Lester stood and hollered, "Anybody to home?"

Nobody answered. The fog lifted more, and Lester turned back to Ruby. "Reckon we ought to go. Seems that everybody done fled."

She shook her head, and Lester touched her shoulder. "It ain't easy. But this is the wages of war. We best leave now."

Wiping her eyes, Ruby stood and tried to regain her composure. Then the fog lifted completely, and a bright sun beamed into her eyes. She looked past the charred house toward what was left of the fence behind it. The ground sloped off from there down a hill. "Stay here," she told Lester. "I need to see one more thing."

He nodded, and she trudged around the ashes and toward the fence. At least twenty servant houses had once sat about a hundred yards down the hill past the fence. She ran to the fence and stared down the slope. One small house remained standing; the rest were burned to the ground. A curl of smoke drifted from the chimney of the last of the servants' quarters. Ruby paused and stared at the smoke. Was somebody still in the house? A chicken suddenly fluttered out of the woods to her right and landed almost at her feet. Ruby jumped back in fear, but the chicken clucked and Ruby almost laughed. As the chicken scratched the ground, somehow the movement prodded Ruby to pick up her feet. She ran down the hill to the smoking chimney. If somebody was there, they could tell her what had happened, where everyone had gone, what had happened to Theo!

Reaching the little house, she banged on the door but rushed in before anyone could answer. The front room was empty. She started to push into the only other room, but Lester hurried through the door behind her and told her to hold up.

"Let me see about this." He indicated the inner door. "Sometimes stray soldiers take up in places like this, or runaway darkies with bad things in their heads."

Ruby halted and took a breath as Lester pushed past her and pounded on the door. A mumbled voice called out from the other side.

"Hold here," Lester ordered Ruby.

She nodded but followed him anyway as he opened the door and stepped inside. Her mouth fell open. An old woman sat in a straight chair by the small fireplace, a threadbare blanket over her legs, her blank eyes staring at the ceiling. The woman wore a burlap bag cut to drape her body and a mismatched pair of boots—one black and one brown—on her large feet. The woman's hair fit under a man's slough hat and partially covered her forehead. For a second, Ruby couldn't tell if the woman was alive or dead, but then she tilted her head.

Ruby rushed to her and bent down. "Mama," she sobbed, still unable to believe it was Nettie. "It's me, Ruby. I've come for you and Theo."

Nettie raised a hand; her fingers searched the air. That's when Ruby realized she couldn't see.

"That really you, child?" whispered Nettie.

Ruby touched Nettie's cheeks. "It is."

"I figured you dead."

"I'm not," Ruby answered, wanting to laugh and cry at the same time. "I'm alive and got a baby girl named Leta and a good man named Obadiah, and I've come to get you and Theo and take you back with me."

"Theo's gone," Nettie said calmly. "He run off close to six months ago, far as I can remember."

"But he's not old enough to be alone; strong enough either!"

"A couple of the boys went with him. Besides, he's a lot older than his years, always was, you know that. He's grown stronger too, still not big but stout in the legs."

Ruby tried to soak it all in. "He shouldn't have left you."

"I made him go. The place was too dangerous. The soldiers come through here over and over—first the Yankees, then the Rebels, then the Yankees again. Burned the place a little at a time—the barns first, the big house next, the darky quarters last. I been goin' blind for a while; got real bad just in the last year. Theo begged me to go with him, but I couldn't, didn't want to hold him back. I doin' all right. Got me the chicken, know where the berry bushes are, a little food left in the cellar up by the house. Nobody bothers me any."

"You know where Theo went?"

"Not sure in a time like this, but I figure he traveled south. Donetta told him you got sold in Charleston, and he's been waitin' all these years for a chance to go find you. If there's a way he can do that, I expect he'll try."

"But I've been in Richmond."

"Then I reckon he ain't gone find you for a while yet."

Ruby wiped her eyes and realized she should have expected something like this. Her hope of finding Theo still here made no sense now that she looked at it, not with the war and all. But what else could she have done?

Sighing, she turned to Lester. "I don't know how to ask you this. But . . . I can't . . ."

"I be glad to help you with her," he said. "Whatever you want, you just ask, and I'll try to do it. Mr. Josh wouldn't want it any other way."

"We have to take her back to Richmond."

"I expect I can take you to the edge of the city," said Lester. "You think you can go on from there?"

"That's more than generous."

Lester nodded, and Ruby turned back to Nettie. "You think you can walk a ways?"

"I blind, child, but I ain't a cripple."

"It's a long way," Ruby warned.

"I's a stubborn woman. You lead, I'll follow."

"OK." Ruby grinned.

Together she and Lester gathered up all the food they could find. A few minutes later, they moved Nettie outside, picked up the chicken, and headed back to Richmond.

Somewhere out there, Ruby thought, Theo was looking for her. Once she got Nettie safely settled with Mrs. Swanson, she'd go once again to try to find him.

Chapter Twenty-Three

Over the next two weeks, Camellia ignored almost everything else except her effort to find Josh. When Ruby returned with her mama, Camellia voiced her sorrow that Ruby hadn't found Theo but paid little attention to either of them after that. When her pa and Johnny finally got well enough to climb out of bed and join everybody as they shared their meager breakfast every morning, she felt grateful they were safe but quickly lost her joy as she remembered how Lester had hauled Josh to Richmond, then handed him over to the Rebels.

Even the arrival of Trenton and Mrs. York hadn't knocked her off her feet too much. What did she care that they'd showed up to locate Calvin? And what did it matter to her that they'd stayed after they didn't find him? How did it change her situation to know that Mrs. York visited some with her pa, but not as often as she would have expected? As long as Trenton and Mrs. York didn't bother her or her loved ones, she'd let them be, no questions asked. True, Trenton did try to talk to her every now and again and had even begged her once to come back to him, but she shrugged him off every time and walked away. She'd heard it all before. True, Trenton seemed to have stopped his drinking and appeared more polite than in a long time, but she knew not to trust such momentary changes in his nature. He'd revert to his real self soon enough, no doubt of that.

By the time November 1864 ended, she'd decided to start her search for Josh at Belle Isle, the largest hospital in the city for Yankee prisoners. Working up her courage, she presented herself to the assistant warden there and told him she wanted to volunteer as a nurse because she felt it her Christian duty to care for the enemy wounded.

The assistant warden, an older man named Trevor Johnson with an ample stomach, white hair, and muttonchop sideburns, sat behind his blocky wood desk in his spare office and eyed her suspiciously. "You're too fine a young woman to take up work in this place," he started.

"I'm already caring for soldiers," Camellia said.

"Where?" asked Johnson.

Camellia hesitated but knew she couldn't lie. "At the Victoria Hotel." She hoped he wouldn't take the questions any further, but he quickly dashed that hope.

"That's Mrs. Wallace Swanson's place, isn't it?"

"Yes."

"I know of her."

"I've worked there since the war started."

"Then why not continue with that? Why would a beautiful Southern woman like yourself care to aid the Yankees?"

"I already told you," she explained. "My Christian upbringing says I should love my enemy. I've cared for Rebel soldiers for years. Now it's time to offer my generosity to the Yankees."

"That's mighty noble," he said. "We got a few other women who serve here who claim the same motive, but they're either much older or much homelier than you."

"You saying only homely women have a heart to serve others?"

Johnson chuckled lightly. "Not exactly that, but I got security concerns here. Lots of spies in the city, and more than one of them a woman."

"I've heard of such women. Elizabeth Van Lew is perhaps the worst of them."

"My point exactly. For all I know, you want to pass on information about our city's defenses to the enemy in this hospital."

"But what good would that do?"

"You play innocent with me, do you?"

"But I am innocent," Camellia maintained. "I have no idea how anything I'd say to the wounded could ever leave the premises."

Johnson fingered one of his thick sideburns. "It's real easy. We do prisoner exchanges every couple of weeks; take the men who've healed enough down the river, meet the Federals under truce, and swap prisoners. Whatever a soldier learns here will end up in Yankee ears pretty fast."

"I didn't know we did that."

"Well, we do. A woman as pretty as you could get a Rebel officer to tell her just about anything; then you could pass it along to a prisoner, who'd carry it out when he goes."

Camellia studied Johnson's face. His eyes looked kind, and she guessed that he had grandchildren, maybe a lot of them. She decided to speak honestly, at least to a point.

"I can assure you I'm not a spy," she began. "You can ask Mrs. Swanson and any others in her circle. But I have a friend, a man I knew back in South Carolina. He didn't take to owning darkies, so he ended up on the wrong side of the war."

Johnson rubbed his sideburns but didn't comment, so Camellia continued. "My friend was injured, then captured at Burgess Mill. I figured he might have ended up here, and I wanted to offer to care for him if I could."

"You'd cease your service to the Rebels to do this?"

"No, I will do both."

"It's a brave thing to tell the truth," Johnson commented. "And a wise thing as well. Your story makes some sense and seems innocent enough. Let me investigate a little; then I'll let you know."

"I'll check with you every few days."

"You do that."

Camellia left the hospital, and the days moved on. The weather turned colder and colder, but she barely noticed. She visited Johnson's office every three days, and on the tenth day, he shrugged and told her that so long as she actually aided the wounded, he didn't care if she came to help. "I knew a few fellows who chose the Yankee side too, and they weren't all long-tailed devils," he explained.

Camellia thanked him by bringing him the last jar of jam from Mrs. Swanson's hotel pantry, with her mother's blessing. She quickly became acquainted with Belle Isle. She woke up every morning before sunup, checked on her pa and Johnny, labored with the sick and wounded at the Victoria until midafternoon, then left and made her way by ferry over the James to Belle Isle.

The conditions there appalled her. Meager food, almost no true medicine, head lice and other bugs, not nearly enough surgeons and nurses for all the men—she wondered how anyone lived through it. Yet she had to keep hoping that Josh had somehow managed to do just that.

Usually she stayed at Belle Isle way past dark, offering whatever assistance she could to the overworked surgeons and nurses who looked after the wounded. On some days no doctor ever showed up, and she and a couple of other women, as poorly trained as she was, gave what little care they could. To make matters worse, Camellia didn't find Josh or anybody who knew of him. Her spirits sank lower and lower. Every night she went home and reported to Beth and Butler.

"No," she always said to their questions, "I didn't find your pa. But I'm not giving up."

Their faces always fell as she spoke. She wanted to say something hopeful but knew of nothing to add. They were growing up right before her eyes—Beth a beautiful young lady of sixteen, and Butler, at thirteen, taller already than she remembered Josh. Both of them labored in the hotel every day, facing the hard matters of war like everyone else.

After a week in which she visited every hospital bed she could find, Camellia wondered if she ought to give up on Belle Isle and go somewhere else to search. The Confederates kept a lot of prisoners in a bunch of warehouses east of the city; maybe they'd taken Josh there, wounded or not. Yet, since the Rebels brought new wounded Yankees into Belle Isle every day, she decided she'd better stay there for a while longer.

Although fearing to even broach the question, she got up the nerve right before Christmas to ask Warden Johnson what they did with the men who died in his hospital. He pointed her to patch of ground out past the tents and outbuildings and told her that a lot of the prisoners were buried there. She walked to the burial ground and stood over the unmarked graves, wondering if Josh had died and been dropped into the dirt as unceremoniously as a stray dog. The notion made her cry. That day she left the graves and decided she'd not go there again.

When she asked Johnson about the dead men's belongings, he directed her to a small weather-beaten building not far from his office.

"What the guards don't take ends up in there until we burn it," he said, his voice gentle. "You can look if you want."

Thankful for his sweet spirit, Camellia checked the building and found all manner of odds and ends—used pipes, broken shaving mugs, frayed belts, hats, mismatched boots, pants and shirts filled with holes, a few battered Bibles, a scattering of letters—the last things of slain men. Her hands trembled as she picked up the letters and read them, but none of them came from Josh's pen. She breathed a sigh of relief as she left the building.

In Johnson's office once more, she sat down and put her head in her hands. He stepped to her and touched her back. "You might not have thought of this, but maybe your friend got better and we shipped him out with the prisoner exchange before you got here."

She raised her eyes. "That's a hopeful notion."

"It's possible if he healed quick enough."

Camellia calculated the days since Lester had brought Josh to Richmond. "You do an exchange every few weeks?"

Johnson nodded.

"I started here about a month after Josh was brought to Richmond," said Camellia.

"I doubt we shipped him out that quick."

Camellia weighed what Lester had told her of Josh's injuries and figured Johnson was right. "He didn't get exchanged. I'm sure of it; not enough time for his injuries to improve."

"Just wanted you to be aware of the possibility."

"You've been patient with me," Camellia said. "I'm grateful for it."

He sighed. "A war shouldn't put an end to kindness. No matter how bad it gets."

"Thank you."

Johnson perched on the edge of his desk. "You love this man, don't you?"

"We planned to marry."

Johnson touched her shoulder. "Listen, child," he soothed. "I've lost two sons to this war, got just one left. And my sweet wife died only a year ago from the consumption. War kills a lot of folks; that's a hard lesson. But we got to learn it if we're going to make it through to the other side."

"You're telling me he's dead," she said, studying Johnson's kind eyes.

He sighed and rubbed down his sideburns. "I wish I could say otherwise, but my experience tells me that's the case."

Camellia's eyes watered, but she quickly wiped them clear. "I can't give up. Not until I know for sure."

"I know that. The heart won't let us give up on those we love."

Camellia smiled in spite of her sadness. "You're a good man."

He smiled back and waved her off. A few minutes later she left his office.

Christmas came and went soon after that, but neither Camellia nor anybody else in the Swanson household made much of it except to spend a few hours in church praying. The grimness of the war made celebration of any kind out of place. Food had become more and more scarce and cost more and more money. The last of Mrs. Swanson's silver and china disappeared out the door as she sold it to pay for the necessities of survival. Bread sold in one, two, and three-dollar sizes, but each size seemed smaller every time they bought one. Their only good news came from the fact that York and Johnny were healing well. Even that was tempered when they both checked in with the army and received orders to go back to the fighting by the first of March.

A cold, gray winter settled over Richmond, and Camellia grew more desperate to find Josh. Knowing that she'd checked every man on Belle Isle, many of them over and over, she stopped going there every day and added other places to her visitation list. Johnson gave her a letter of introduction to the officers in all the other Yankee prisons.

By the middle of January 1865, every man in charge of every place that housed Federal boys, wounded or not, knew her face. Although she usually got refusals for entry to the actual prisons, the men running the other hospitals generally let her in. A couple of officers cursed her for caring about a Yankee, but she barely heard them. She had only one purpose, one goal, one drive, and that was to look for Josh Cain.

February came and left, but she still found no sign of him. Gradually her hopes dropped; her shoulders sagged, and black circles appeared under her eyes. She knew she ought to give up and admit he was dead, but she couldn't let herself do it. Somehow she had to keep believing, had to keep praying, had to keep looking; otherwise, she might as well go on and die too.

Desperate to feel connected to Josh, she started rereading the letters he'd sent her before joining the Yankees, his loving words a balm to her fearful heart. Gradually the edges of the letters became worn from her fingers holding them, and the ink blotted from her tears as she cried herself to sleep with them under her head.

How could God have allowed this? she wept. How could the Lord have brought Josh so close to her, right here to Richmond, only to let him slip through her fingers? Her mind pondered the questions from every angle but received no answers. For the first time in her life, she began to doubt the Lord. Did the Lord cause war? What kind of God did that? But if God didn't cause this awful thing, how did it happen? Couldn't God stop it? If so, why hadn't God already done so?

At the first of March 1865, Johnny and York left the hotel to rejoin the army. Although Wade Hampton had taken the remains of his legion and returned to South Carolina, York and Johnny had received permission to stay behind, and the army had assigned them to duty as couriers between the front lines near Petersburg and the staff in the War Building in Capitol Square.

Camellia watched them off as they rode out to take up their new positions, but her heart felt so numb she hardly responded as they left. Without Josh, what did it matter one way or the other what happened to her or anybody else? What did anything matter?

On the last night of the first week of the month, she sat down at the supper table in the back of the hotel kitchen to eat with Ruby, Beth, Butler, and Mrs. Swanson. Another day of futile searching had ended, and Camellia had just returned home. A plate of fried potatoes and cornbread sat before her, but she did little more than pick at any of it. Nobody said much. Leta, a chubby little thing with dark round eyes, squealed every now and again, but that was the only noise other than the scrape of a fork or knife on a plate. A steady rain fell outside, and the wind whistled under the eaves of the house. A kerosene lamp cast a yellow glow on the quiet room. Camellia's hair lay wet and uncombed, and her blouse stuck to her back from the rain. Although Mrs. Swanson had suggested that she dry herself before she sat down, Camellia had no energy to do so. Her shoulders slumped, and the food tasted flat.

Mrs. Swanson handed Ruby a plate to carry to Nettie, who was in bed upstairs, and Ruby got up to leave. Unable to take it any longer, Camellia suddenly started to cry.

Ruby stopped, set down the plate, and put a gentle hand on Camellia's back. "What's wrong, Miss Camellia?"

"He's dead!" Camellia sobbed. "I can't lie to myself any longer!" She turned to Beth and Butler. "I hate to say it . . . but it's got to be true. I've searched everywhere for him."

"We have to keep hoping," offered Mrs. Swanson. "Can't give up now."

Camellia turned on her, all the frustration of the last weeks boiling over into a blazing anger. "What do you know?" she shouted. "You've not been out there like I have! I've searched every hospital in Richmond and as many prisons as I could get into!"

"Maybe they didn't take him to a hospital," Butler reasoned. "Maybe they put him in a prison where you didn't get to check."

"All the more reason to believe he's dead," argued Camellia. "If he was hurt as bad as Lester said, he'd die for sure without proper care."

Then Beth started to cry too. Camellia's heart broke as she realized what she'd done. Even though she'd lost all hope, she shouldn't have let Josh's children know that. She wanted to scream at herself for her lack of sensitivity but knew that wouldn't help, so she turned to Beth and put a hand on her shoulder. "Forgive me," she said. "I'm just tired. Don't listen to me. I don't know what I'm talking about."

But Beth only sobbed harder.

Camellia put an arm around her. "We'll find him," she said, lying for Beth's sake. "I'll keep trying."

A heavy knock suddenly sounded on the back door. Camellia glanced at Mrs. Swanson, then at Ruby.

"I'll see to it," said Ruby.

Camellia wiped her eyes but kept holding Beth. A few seconds later, she heard loud voices and then Ruby stepped back into the kitchen, a trail of men in tattered uniforms behind her. Camellia's eyes widened when she saw Trenton trailing the soldiers, his mouth curled in a sneer.

Mrs. Swanson stood to meet the men.

A short bald man wearing lieutenant's bars on his shoulders stepped forward. "Are you Mrs. Wallace Swanson?"

"I am. What is the nature of your business here?"

The lieutenant took an envelope from his pocket. "Is there a Miss Camellia York in abode in this place?"

"I'm Camellia York," said Camellia, also standing now.

The lieutenant handed the envelope to Mrs. Swanson. "I'm here on orders of the provost marshal. These are papers of arrest for Miss Camellia York, on the charge of espionage against the Confederate States."

Camellia almost laughed at the silliness of the notion. But then she glanced at Trenton and knew this was serious business.

"I don't understand," said Mrs. Swanson. "What's the basis of this?"

Trenton stepped up beside the lieutenant, but the soldier turned to him and shook his head. With another smirk, Trenton eased back.

"The charges have been made," the lieutenant answered. "It's not my place to specify the causes behind them. Miss York will need to come with me."

"I'll vouch for her," said Mrs. Swanson. "She's not a spy."

"I'm sure the provost marshal will lend strong weight to your word," the lieutenant returned. "But, again, that's his decision, not mine."

"I know Isaac Carrington," Mrs. Swanson told Camellia, speaking of the provost marshal. "He's a coarse man but also a reasonable one. He'll set this right once he hears of it."

"I'll leave that to him," the lieutenant answered.

Camellia glared at Trenton. "You're behind this, aren't you? You pretended to have changed, but you haven't, not one bit. You've wanted revenge for a long time and see this as your chance to get it."

"You did it to yourself," he accused. "You're in love with a Yankee, and you fraternize with the enemy every day; care for their soldiers when we've got need of you to tend ours. No telling what kind of information you're passing along to your Union friends. Plus, you live here with a woman who doesn't own a single darky. And she employed Sharpton Hillard for years. We know he's a Yankee—went off to fight with them soon as the war started."

"None of that proves anything," argued Camellia.

Trenton chuckled and pulled out a handful of papers from his coat. "What about these? Letters from your Union lover!"

Camellia shrieked as she recognized Josh's letters. She rushed at Trenton to take them back, but he held them away and she froze in place. "How did you get those?" she demanded.

"You're so naive," he said. "Never lock your door. It's a simple matter for a patriot like me to examine the room of a suspected Union sympathizer. I found them this morning as you went to aid and abet the enemy."

Camellia turned to the lieutenant. "You're acting on the word of an admitted thief?"

"I'm following orders, ma'am. Let the higher-ups determine the rightness or wrongness of it all."

Camellia looked to Mrs. Swanson, but she held up her palms in a sign of defeat. "You'll have to go with them until I can straighten things out."

"Where are you taking me?" Camellia asked the lieutenant.

"To the jail at Castle Thunder," crowed Trenton. "Where we put all traitors to our cause."

Camellia glared at Trenton but, seeing the fury in his face, suddenly decided to try another tactic. "Why, Trenton?" she pleaded in a soft voice. "How did it come to this? After all we were to each other? Is all of that gone?"

"You ignored me," he seethed. "I tried to be nice to you, just wanted a friend, after Calvin . . . after we couldn't find him. I wanted to talk to you, but you had no time, no kind words for me."

"I'm sorry," she said, her heart sincerely grieving at her lack of sensitivity to his pain at losing Calvin. "About Calvin, about everything that's happened. Can't we forget it, put it behind us, try to be civil to one another?"

"It's too late," he said. "The law's involved now; it's out of my hands."

She faced the lieutenant. "Is it too late?"

"I have my orders," he stated. "I take you in, then somebody else can decide the rest."

Camellia turned to Mrs. Swanson. "Contact my pa. His word will go a long way." She faced Ruby next. "Promise me you'll keep looking for Josh," she pleaded.

"I will."

Camellia moved to Beth and Butler. "Don't give up," she encouraged. "No matter what happens."

They nodded, and Camellia faced the lieutenant once more. "Will you give me a minute to gather a few belongings?" she asked.

"Do it quickly," he said. "I have other matters to attend."

"You best send a guard with her," suggested Trenton.

"Do I look like the kind of woman who will try to escape?" Camellia asked the lieutenant.

"Just hurry," he said.

Camellia left without another word, rushed upstairs to her room, and slammed the door. Her breath ragged, she leaned against the wall for several seconds and tried to clear her head. What would happen if she ended up in jail? She'd heard horror stories of spies that got sent to prison and mysteriously died. Other tales told of women molested by guards. Although she'd never believed such horrid lies, how could she be sure? If Trenton could get her arrested, what else could he manage? Her knees shook with fear; she wanted to sag to the floor and cry but knew she didn't dare. Tears wasted time, and she had none of that to spare.

She glanced around the room, saw the window by her bed, and thought of running. Could she do such a thing? But where would she go? How would she live? No answers came to her. Yet as she considered the alternatives, she realized she had no choice. No matter what happened, she couldn't allow Trenton to put her in jail. Rumors said Grant might take Richmond within weeks. Chaos would erupt if that happened, and suspected spies in prison in the last days of a fallen government weren't popular people. No, she wouldn't go to jail, not if she could do anything to stop it!

Hurrying now that she'd made her decision, Camellia grabbed a brown bag from under the bed, stuffed as many clothes as it would hold into it, slipped a shawl over her shoulders, carefully lifted the window, and climbed out onto the rain-slick roof. A minute later she climbed down a lattice on the side of the hotel and stepped into the muddy street, her head low, her eyes busy to make sure no one saw her as she rushed away. Although she didn't know what would happen next, one thing she knew wouldn't happen—she wouldn't end up a prisoner at the mercy of Trenton Tessier. Anything, even death, was better than that.

Chapter Twenty-Four

Although he didn't know who he was, Josh Cain lay in what remained of his ragged and stolen Rebel uniform on a threadbare blanket on the floor in the corner of a long warehouse that sat on the heights overlooking the James River, less than five miles from where Camellia had just fled. The building, one of over a hundred like it that combined with another hundred conical tents to make up the Chimborazo Hospital, housed close to 150 men. Like the one where Josh lay, all the rest of the buildings were also chock-full of wounded and dying Rebel soldiers. Although their boast got them nothing in terms of more help or medical supplies, the surgeons who labored from sunup to sundown at Chimborazo liked to brag that they served in the largest military hospital in the world.

Scratching the dirty bandage that wrapped his chest wound, Josh pulled up to a sitting position, leaned against the wall, and peered up and down the rows of men lying around him, almost all of them on the floor. He wondered briefly about the absence of cots, but since his head still hurt whenever he thought too long on anything, he quickly dropped the worry and wrinkled his nose. A foul stench constantly hung in the room, especially in wet weather when all the windows stayed closed.

Licking his lips, Josh wished for a drink of water but saw none around. A surgeon walked by, his apron bloody, his shoulders slumped in weariness. Josh glanced to the corner nearest his blanket and breathed a momentary sigh of relief. The surgeons, a hardy crew of men who lived mostly on sorry stew, flatbread, and any kind of mean whiskey they could put their hands on, often stacked the limbs they amputated in that corner until somebody hauled them away. On some days nobody did that duty, and the body parts stayed there overnight.

Josh ran a hand over his stomach and noted the tenderness under his bandages. Although he couldn't remember how, he'd received a serious stab wound in the gut—one that his surgeon, a waif of a man named Clossen—had told him killed most men. Thankfully, Clossen had stitched up his wound, put a salve on his head, and kept him alive, at least to this point.

Josh glanced to the far end of the building and saw Clossen bending over a cot, his bone saw in his hand, his thin body barely visible in the dim lanterns that hung on the walls over the patients. A thin but long mustache covered Clossen's lip and curled down the sides of his mouth. A low and constant groaning rose up from the cots around him, and Josh's ears ached for some quiet. The groaning never stopped, it seemed, not even in the latest hours of the night. In addition to the groaning, the men also moved continuously, turned this way and tossed that way, no matter the time of day or night. For at least the one-hundredth time, Josh wondered how he'd gotten where he was. Even more, he tried to remember his name, his background. Although he wore the ragged uniform of a Tennessee artillery sergeant, he couldn't recall that he'd ever been to Tennessee or handled any cannon. As he'd done at least once a day since the morning he'd awakened and discovered his situation, Josh once more checked his pockets for some identification but found nothing.

Picking up a hand-sized mirror that he'd found in a haversack by his pallet the day he woke up, Josh examined his face. A scraggly beard covered his chin, a thick sheaf of sandy blond hair fell into his eyes, and a scar the size of a walnut marked his right cheek. Thankfully, the knot on his skull had pretty much disappeared, and when he touched it, he felt no more pain.

Josh laid the mirror down, stared at the ceiling, and told himself to relax and not fret about his lack of memory. When pressed about it, Clossen had told him he didn't know if it would come back or not; he'd seen it go both ways. Although that didn't give Josh much comfort, it did offer at least a little hope, and right now that's all Josh could expect.

A man three cots down screamed. Josh scratched his head and inspected the rows of men once more. Occasionally a man did get better and leave the hospital, sometimes to go home and sometimes to return to the fighting. To prevent the latter, a lot of the men seemed to stay sick long past the time their injuries called for, so the doctors spent a lot of time pushing the malingerers back to the front.

Josh scratched at the lice again, wishing for enough water to wash himself. He wondered what kind of soldier he'd been. Clossen had told him he didn't know about his soldiering, but he did figure him as a man with a stiff constitution because wounds as bad as his usually got infected within a few days. The patient without a particularly stout backbone didn't generally make it.

"You came through," Clossen had told him when he'd first come back to consciousness. "Still weak as a kitten, but I expect you're going to live."

Josh had thanked him, but Clossen had waved him off. "I'm just glad one survives every now and again. Gives me cause to come back to work the next day."

Josh had smiled and Clossen had left. But since that day, he'd stopped by Josh's bunk pretty often.

"I ain't here because I'm worried about you," Clossen always said in the couple of minutes he spent with Josh. "I come because it buoys my own spirits."

"Glad I can assist you," Josh replied.

Clossen always tweaked his mustache and walked off.

Other than the occasional word to Clossen, Josh didn't talk much in those early days at Chimborazo, just lay flat on his back and stared at the ceiling. After a few weeks, though, he got enough strength to sit up some. Within a couple of days of that, he found a piece of blank paper lying on the floor. The next time Clossen walked by, Josh asked if he had a pencil.

"Lots of boys ask for one." Clossen produced a chewed pencil from his apron and handed it to Josh. "They want to write a sweetheart or a wife."

"Don't reckon I'd know who to write," said Josh. "Since I'm still missing my memories."

Clossen patted him on the shoulder and moved to the next soldier. Without thinking about it, Josh took the paper and pencil and began to draw. By the time the sun had gone down that day, he'd scratched out the image of a scene he couldn't remember ever seeing—the picture of a wide oak tree with a fine two-story house behind it. When Clossen returned after dark to reclaim his pencil, Josh showed him the drawing.

"Where you reckon this is?" he asked Clossen.

Clossen studied it closely. "It's a plantation house. Not sure where, though; could be Georgia where I come from, South Carolina maybe, even here in Virginia."

"You reckon I could get some more paper?" asked Josh.

"I'll see what I can do," said Clossen. "You got a touch of talent in those fingers of yours."

"I just draw what I see in my head," Josh explained.

"Draw your name then."

"I don't see that, least not yet."

Three days after that, Clossen brought him a handful of paper, most of it unused. Josh thanked him and spent the rest of the day sketching. This time an ocean scene emerged from his mind and appeared on the page, the waves rushing onto the shore, the sun dropping in the distance, a sea gull floating in the air.

Clossen approved it as he stopped by that night. "Keep at it," he coaxed. "Your fingers are trying to tell you what your head can't recall."

Over the next few weeks, Josh drew something almost every day—pictures of horses and soldiers one day, images of moss-covered oaks and stately plantation homes the next, scenes of the ocean and beach after that. Yet, try as he might, none of the drawings brought back his name or anything else about his life.

Now, sighing, Josh lifted the latest picture he'd drawn and held it up to the light. Clossen stepped toward him as he did, his face a bleary mess of weariness and bad nourishment. Josh handed him the sketch.

"Handsome people." Clossen squatted down to him and stared at the boy and girl on the page. "You reckon they're yours?"

Josh frowned. "I don't know. It's confusing, making my head hurt again trying to figure it out."

Clossen handed back the picture. "Your head is better. Your chest too."

"I'm obliged to you for your care," said Josh. "I owe my life to you."

Clossen twirled his mustache, and his face looked sad. "Lee is desperate for soldiers. The army is telling us to clean out the hospitals; to send Lee every man capable of fighting again. They'll put men like you outside of Richmond to defend the city when Grant comes in a few weeks."

Josh scratched his beard. "You're saying I'm well enough to go back, aren't you?"

Clossen hung his head. "If I had my way, you'd stay right here until your mind completely cleared up. I think it's going to happen—soon too, I can see it in your drawings. But I don't know what 'soon' is, so I can't just let you stay here forever."

"Maybe the war will bring my memory back to me."

"Or it could prevent it from happening—perhaps stop it completely."

"You mean forever?"

Clossen sighed. "I don't know. The mind plots its own course. But if something that happened in the war made you lose your memories, it stands to reason that going back won't aid things any . . . and might hurt them a lot."

Josh hesitated to speak his next thought but went on anyway. "Any way to keep me here awhile longer?"

"I expect not. Your body is fine, and I don't think it matters to Lee if you know who you are or not. So long as you're capable of aiming a rifle at the Bluebellies, I think he'll take you."

"How much longer can you give me?"

Clossen tweaked his mustache. "I'll need to dismiss you by the first of next week."

"I must be a coward," said Josh. "I have no heart to go fight anymore."

"You had a heart for it before," Clossen claimed. "A man with your wounds didn't run, I can tell you that."

"The whole thing just feels wrong."

"It's been a long war. No wonder it feels bad."

Josh's head ached. "I feel like it's right here," he said, knocking on his forehead. "My name, my history, everything."

"Maybe a good cannon boom will shake it loose."

"Or bury it forever."

Clossen nodded, and Josh pulled all his drawings from under his blanket. "Will you keep these for me? I don't want to take them to the front; fear something will happen to them—rain, mud, fire. I'll have no way to keep them safe."

Clossen took the drawings. "I'll hold them for you until you return for them."

"Maybe I can tell you my name then."

"I'm hoping you can."

"What name do you think I should take until I remember my real one?"

Clossen twirled his mustache. "How about Leonard Vincent? Like in Leonardo da Vinci?"

Josh laughed, and the two men shook hands. But then Josh stared past Clossen to the rows of wounded. Within days he'd leave here and go back to the lines, carrying a rifle he'd pick up at the armory and the name of "Leonard Vincent," a sergeant from Tennessee with no memory of his past. He'd take a spot behind the bulwarks on the outskirts of Richmond as part of the army waiting on the next attack from Grant and his troops.

"You think we can hold Grant off?" Josh asked Clossen.

Clossen looked around, then bent closer so only Josh could hear. "From what I see and hear, Petersburg will fall within weeks. Then Grant will come for Richmond. I don't see how we can defeat him."

Josh shook his head, hoping with all his heart that Clossen was right. He wanted the war to end, and if that meant the South had to lose, so be it. Perhaps that made him a traitor, but if so, he didn't care. The war needed to cease, one way or the other.

Chapter Twenty-Five

The first night away from Mrs. Swanson's hotel lasted longer than any night Camellia had ever experienced. With no clear thought of where to go, she scurried as fast as she dared through the wet streets, her shawl tight around her head, her eyes down. Without thinking about it, she moved toward the railroad depot, the busiest area of the city, her instincts telling her she could lose herself in the midst of all the people coming and going through the last connecting point between Richmond and all points south.

Exhausted from fear, she reached the depot as the rain fell heavier. Easing into an alley behind a general store, she squatted down under a small wood awning to try to figure out her next step. As the rain dripped off the awning onto her head and shoulders, she wished for a drier spot to think. Who could she go to for help? Her pa? But she didn't know how to find him—and even if she did, he had other duties and surely couldn't get relief from them to aid her. What about one of the ladies she knew from church? No, they weren't prepared for anything like this, and she couldn't put them in the danger it might bring.

She considered the notion of running to Elizabeth Van Lew, the most infamous Union sympathizer in the city. Her house stood on Church Hill overlooking the James, and rumors said she hid Yankees who managed to escape Libby Prison and make their way to her. Only the fact that polite society usually refused to throw a woman in prison, even in wartime, kept her out of jail. Perhaps she'd hide Camellia too. But wait! If she went there, people would see that as proof of Trenton's accusations that she was a spy, and she wouldn't give him that satisfaction.

Camellia snuggled down under the awning and ran through her

choices one more time, but none made any sense. The rain fell harder, and her heart sagged. Where could she go? Who cared enough for her to let her hide out with them?

Assistant Warden Johnson at Belle Isle! He'd had plenty of opportunity to judge her character! Surely he'd give her a place to stay until Mrs. Swanson cleared things up. But could she ask him for such a favor? Was it fair to show up on his doorstep and put him in that kind of predicament?

Not sure what to do, Camellia weighed the idea the rest of that sleepless night, then decided near the morning that she had no choice. If Johnson didn't take her in, she'd have to flee the city and fend for herself in the countryside.

The steady rain continued all morning as she made her way up and down the back streets toward the Yankee hospital where Johnson held sway. As before, she kept her shawl over her head and her eyes low. Fortunately, everyone around her seemed busy with more pressing matters and paid her no attention. With thousands of fearsome Yankee soldiers just a few miles away, who cared about a lone woman trudging through the rain?

Her body weary and starving, Camellia reached Belle Isle by ferry a few minutes after noon and identified herself to the soldiers guarding the entrance.

"Miss Camellia, you're plumb soaked," said one of the men, his concern evident as he recognized her. "You ought not to have come out on such a bad day."

"I want to see Mr. Johnson," she requested.

"Just you follow me," the guard said kindly. "The warden's not in his office, but I'll get you a blanket and tell him you've come."

Seconds later the soldier led her into Johnson's office, brought her a blanket, and disappeared. Camellia pulled off her shawl, dried her wet hair on the blanket, then drew the blanket around her shoulders and sat down. Suddenly weary, her eyes closed involuntarily, and she dropped her head to Johnson's desk. The room felt so warm, so dry . . . if she could only rest here a few minutes, find a bite to eat, and sleep a little, she could figure things out.

Footsteps sounded and she jerked up, rose from her seat, and faced the door.

"Miss York." Johnson smiled as he entered and took off his hat. "So good to see you again. Have you come to offer us your services once more?"

Camellia shivered. "No," she said, fighting to keep her teeth from chattering. "I've come to ask for your aid this time."

Johnson rubbed his sideburns, then turned and shut his door. When he faced her again, his eyes showed concern. "What kind of aid might you be requesting?"

Camellia pulled her blanket closer and hesitated only a moment. "You asked me once if I was a spy, and I assured you I wasn't. Now there are others who believe that of me."

Johnson arched an eyebrow, pointed her to her seat, and took a chair behind his desk. "This is serious?"

"A man named Trenton Tessier accuses me of traitorous acts and brought an officer of the provost marshal to arrest me last night. It's Mr. Tessier's effort to wreak vengeance on me and the man I love."

"Have you found this man you love?"

"No. I've finally concluded he must be dead."

"Why does this Mr. Tessier seek vengeance against you?"

"It's a long tale, but to say it quickly, he courted me years ago. We planned to wed."

"It's jealousy, then?"

"Yes, at least most of it." She hurriedly told Johnson of the duel, how Trenton lost his leg, how he acted like he loved her one moment and hated her the next, how he and his mother had come to Richmond to search for his missing brother, then never left.

"You hold no more affection for Mr. Tessier?"

"None whatsoever."

"But he says he still loves you?"

"Yes, though having me arrested for spying seems an odd way to show it."

Johnson rubbed his sideburns and chuckled lightly. "So you escaped him."

"Yes. I fled the hotel, spent the night in an alley. Didn't know where else to come but here. You know I'm no spy."

Johnson wrinkled his nose. "I'm a patriot. Not prone to go against the law."

"I don't want to cause you any peril. But what else could I do?" she pleaded.

"What is Mr. Tessier claiming as proof of his charges?"

She quickly recounted Trenton's list of evidence.

"Though it seems flimsy to me, I can see how the provost marshal might want to question you."

"Exactly. People are searching for spies behind every bush. They need someone to blame for our recent defeats."

Johnson nodded. "We're in the last days of this Confederacy. People feel angry and scared. They'll strike out at anything they can."

Camellia shivered again, this time more from fear than the cold. "If I am a spy, I can help you when the Yankees come," she reasoned. "If I'm not, you've made a lifelong friend at no cost to yourself."

"Unless I get caught."

"Yes."

Johnson fingered his sideburns, and she waited for him to decide.

"Will Mr. Tessier think to search here for you?" he asked.

"I see no reason why he should. He knows nothing of my friendship with you."

Johnson chuckled. "You're a brave girl to have run."

"I grew up the daughter of a plantation overseer. I'm not a fragile woman."

"Where will you sleep if you stay here?"

"Wherever you want. I'll stay out of sight, eat what the prisoners get."

"What about this office? Will it do for you?"

"You mean it?" she asked.

He shrugged sadly. "I never told you this. But I had a daughter once, years ago. She came into the world frail of body and never got much stronger. She died of a fever right after her fifteenth birthday. I've always had a heart for those who need aid—suppose that's how I ended up caring for Yankee wounded. It's not a popular post, and not a lot feel like I do.

Many say we should let them die where they fall, not even try to care for them. But I can't do that."

Camellia breathed a prayer of thanks that she'd come to Johnson. "I'm grateful."

"You will work as you always did," he suggested. "Just won't go home at night—that's the only difference." He extended a hand, but she rose, walked to him, and hugged his neck.

"I'll bring you some of my wife's clothes. They'll fit a little loose on you but ought to be wearable," he offered.

Camellia stepped back and wiped her eyes.

"I'll ask around some too," Johnson continued. "See what I can find out about your situation."

"You're a saint," she said.

"Until you give me cause to distrust you, you can stay as long as you like."

"Be assured that I'll give you no such cause."

Not more than five miles away, Trenton Tessier stood in the provost marshal's office, his fists balled in anger. The young lieutenant who had come to the hotel to arrest Camellia stood beside him, his head down. Isaac Carrington, a middle-aged man with a wide forehead, bushy beard, and mustache, sat behind a massive desk in a brown vested suit. He peered at his pocket watch and waved Trenton away.

"You can't just dismiss this!" argued Trenton. "Your office provided the order to pick her up in the first place. The woman is a spy!"

"You weary me," Carrington fired back. A nervous tic twitched through his face. "Yes, this office gave the papers to arrest her, but now that she's disappeared, I have far more serious matters to demand my attention."

"But why did she run if she's not a spy?"

Carrington turned to the lieutenant. "What is your assessment of these charges?"

"I'm not a judge," the lieutenant offered. "I have no way to determine the truth in this matter."

Carrington rubbed his eyes and stared down at his desk. "The Yankees will take Petersburg soon," he said without looking up. "I'm not sure it matters whether she's a spy or not."

"That's traitorous talk," hissed Trenton.

Carrington's head snapped up, and his eyes blazed. "Don't you dare speak to *me* of treason! Tell me what *you've* done to fight for the cause!"

Trenton's eyes watered with fury. "I've requested a military commission over and over. But because of this"—he pointed to his stump—"no one will accept me into their ranks. I've been on a plantation the whole time, under orders to grow food for the troops. I'd do anything—any duty, any job—for this cause of ours."

Carrington stood and stepped past his desk. "You want duties, is that it?"

"Yes. That's all I've ever wanted," Trenton claimed. "Some way to offer my services to my country."

Carrington moved to a cabinet behind Trenton, pulled out a stack of papers, then shifted back to his desk. "We need men to keep order in Richmond," he said, picking up a pen. "Deputies to guard things here so we can free more soldiers for the front. Is that acceptable to you?"

Trenton glanced at the lieutenant, but the young man kept his eyes straight ahead. "I'd prefer a military assignment," Trenton stated.

"I have no authority over that," said Carrington. "This is the best I can do. You want it or not?"

"What will be my assignment?"

"You'll serve through the authority of this office as a deputy of the law."

"Can I search for spies?"

Carrington grunted. "You'll follow orders . . . but yes, part of our responsibility is to ferret out the traitors in our midst."

Trenton licked his lips at the prospect of going after Camellia with the power of a badge on his side. If he couldn't actually go fight, this served as a pretty good second best. "I'll do it."

"Wonderful," growled Carrington, obviously eager to be rid of Trenton. "Now take this"—he signed the paper—"and get out of my office."

"Do I get a badge?"

"With this paper you won't need one."

Satisfied, Trenton took the signed order, put on his hat, and clomped out, a smile as wide as the James River stretched over his happy face.

Part Four

The human heart dares not stay away too long
from that which hurt it most.
There is a return journey to anguish
that few of us are released from making.
—Lillian Smith

Chapter Twenty-Six

Over the next couple of weeks, Camellia cut her hair short, started wearing one of the thick scarves Warden Johnson brought her over her head at all times, and never ventured from the hospital. Johnson brought her food and water every morning and kept her up with the news. Grant's army seemed set to capture Petersburg at any moment, the warden said, and Richmond would surely fall next. After that, no one knew what would happen. General Lee continued to hold out hope that even if Richmond fell, he could take the remains of his army, join up with General Johnston's forces in North Carolina, and fight on.

"You believe that will happen?" Camellia asked.

"No," Mr. Johnson admitted, his eyes down. "Though it grieves me to say it, I believe we're coming to our end."

Camellia understood. Just from what she saw and heard at the hospital, matters looked grave for the Confederacy. The number of Yankee wounded had slowed to a trickle, and the ones who did come in spoke confidently of the future.

"We got you Rebs on the run," they boasted. "And this time we won't let Lee out of the noose."

Although she never mentioned it to Johnson, Camellia secretly hoped the Yankees were right. The sooner the war ended, the sooner Trenton's accusations about her would cease and she could return to Beth and Butler. With Josh dead, they'd need her more than ever. She wondered a lot about where she'd take them to live after the hostilities ceased but had no clear answer. Although Mrs. Swanson had treated them kindly, Camellia's feelings of resentment toward her mother for her past betrayal had never changed, and she wanted to leave Richmond as soon as possible. Perhaps she, her pa, and Johnny could take Beth and Butler and go back south. Not to The Oak, of course, but somewhere on the coast, near the ocean that she loved so much.

Her head aching over the questions, Camellia pushed them aside and set her mind back on her work. Two things consumed her hopes—caring for the wounded prisoners and staying hidden from Trenton until the combat ceased. If she could manage those two things, she'd worry about the rest when the time came.

Thankfully, tending to the prisoners usually took her mind off her fears, and she poured her whole heart into that task. With fewer Yankees coming in, she had enough time to give each one some specific attention. They soaked it up, their eyes soft with appreciation for her kindnesses. Knowing that she'd want someone to do the same thing for Josh, she put wet rags on their fevered brows, changed their soiled bandages, read them the Bible when they allowed it, wrote letters to their loved ones, and offered whatever other comforts she could think to extend. A couple of the men teasingly offered her marriage proposals, and she tried to imagine the possibility of marrying anyone but Josh and found it difficult. How could she ever love anyone like she'd loved him? But then again, how could she go through her whole life and never take a husband? A dull grief crawled through her bones when she pondered such matters, so she pushed them away and focused again on the troops under her care.

Every now and again, she asked one what unit he served in and whether or not he'd ever met a man named Josh Cain. But since none of them ever responded as she wished, she dropped it after a while.

"A needle in a haystack," one of the Yankees told her one day. "You're hoping to find one man out of the thousands that fought in this war."

Camellia nodded and decided she would never again ask about Josh, because to do so just raised her hopes. And right now she couldn't afford to let that happen.

The last week of March drew to a close. As the boom of cannons rocked through the city on a regular basis, Johnson told her to just hold on. The end might come within days. People in Richmond were beginning to sell their property at cut-rate prices, he informed her—all in an effort to raise enough cash to flee the city. Others were leaving their houses and belongings without looking back, their wagons loaded with all they could carry as they trekked west, out of the firing line of Grant's amassing troops.

Although her hopes rose with each report, Camellia closed her eyes to everything but the men she tended and the necessity to live one day at a time. Such thoughts were the only thing getting her through. One spring storm after another pushed through the city. Everyone suspected that as soon as the weather changed and the roads dried enough for Grant's wagons and cannons to move, he'd strike.

Not even feeling guilty for it anymore, Camellia secretly prayed for the sun to break out, and on April 1, it did. All day long the warm light baked down, pulling moisture from the earth like a thirsty dog lapping water from a pail. Mayo's Bridge, the main route over the James River out of Richmond, stayed clogged all day with people fleeing the expected onslaught of the Yankees.

Near the end of the day, Johnson told her they'd start work before daybreak the next morning because he'd received orders to clean up all the prisoners and put every last one of them on a boat to send down the river for exchange. After that, he said, he didn't know what to expect. If she wanted, he said, he'd bring her as much food as he could gather, and she could flee before the Yankees arrived.

"No telling what the Bluebellies will do when they come in," he warned. "Might burn the whole place down and kill everybody in the city."

Not sure whether to go or stay, Camellia hardly slept at all that night. Where would she go if she ran? Should she try to go back for Beth and Butler? But Trenton almost certainly had somebody watching the hotel. Would she put everybody there in peril if she showed back up? But what would happen to Beth and Butler if she didn't rescue them?

Unable to do anything else, she prayed most of the night, asking the Lord to protect Beth and Butler, Johnny and her pa, Ruby and her mama and baby Leta. She mentioned Mrs. Swanson too, in spite of her continued hard feelings against the woman. After all, she had given Camellia a place to stay—and Beth and Butler too, as well as everyone else.

Before dawn on Sunday, April 2, 1865, Camellia climbed out of her blankets, stuffed her few clothes in her bag, left Johnson's office, and made her way to the main hospital building where she labored every day. If the Yankees showed up and things got bad, she planned to grab the bag and run. Until then she might as well do what she could to help somebody.

An intense blue sky hung overhead, and the sun warmed her back. A bird chirped in the distance. Something about the cheery lilt lifted her heart a little. Even in war, some beauty still remained. She heard church bells ringing, and her spirits rose even higher. Listening to the bells, she pondered the irony of preachers on both sides of the war telling their people that God favored their side. How odd!

At the door of the hospital building, a guard told her a handful of new wounded had come in overnight. "It's surely the last ones. Everybody knows we're just barely hangin' on here."

Camellia nodded but didn't speak. Once inside the building, she moved to a surgeon, and he pointed her to a row of men stretched out on blankets in the far corner. "A couple of them died earlier. But the other ten seem OK. They should survive until we take them for exchange or their boys reach them here."

"You really think it's about over?" she asked.

"I'm not coming back tomorrow," he whispered. "That tell you anything?"

Camellia's heart raced as she left the surgeon and headed to the Yankee prisoners. Within days, maybe hours, Grant would come and she'd be free! Even though she'd never see Josh again, she could at least start her life over; she could take her family and move forward. Picking up a water bucket from the corner, she walked toward the soldiers. An older woman who worked with her smiled as she passed. Camellia reached the Yankees and knelt down to a couple of them. A knot the size of an orange marked one man's skull, while the other had a slash covered with dried blood across his left cheek, from beneath his eye to his chin. The two men looked at her as if seeing an angel.

"My name is Camellia," she explained.

"I'm Bolt," said the one with the slash. "This is Edwards."

Camellia took a wet rag from the water bucket. "This might burn a little," she told Bolt. "But we need to clean that cut." Bolt nodded, and she touched the cloth to his flesh. "You boys don't look too bad. We'll have you fixed up in no time."

"You're mighty kind to hang around," said Bolt. "This town won't be friendly to rebels too much longer."

Camellia smiled lightly but didn't speak anymore as she finished cleaning Bolt's wound and turned to Edwards.

"You married?" Bolt asked.

"That's a mighty personal question," Camellia replied. "Seeing as how I don't really know you."

"I bet you got a Johnny Reb for a husband," Bolt mused. "Or he's already been shot."

"I'm not married," said Camellia, trying to stay kind but not reveal too much.

"We can fix that real fast," Bolt offered. "I'm a handsome man. Just get us a preacher. Now that the war's soon to end, I don't aim to hold grudges against a Southern girl like you."

Camellia touched the knot on Edwards's head. "You're a flirty man," she told Bolt.

"'Cause you're a pretty woman."

"I'm not married, but I am in love," she added, hoping to cool Bolt's ardor.

"No Johnny Reb is good enough for you," Bolt retorted.

"I'm not in love with a Johnny Reb," she said as calmly as she could muster. "I'm in love with a Yankee."

Bolt eyed her suspiciously. "That's a mite of a surprise."

"That's why I'm here." She applied the wet cloth to Edwards. "I've been looking for my man here at the hospital. Figured he might show up one day."

"No luck with that?"

"No."

"You ever think maybe he's dead?" Bolt asked bluntly.

Camellia faced the obnoxious Yankee, her chin set. "Of course I've thought of that."

"I didn't mean no offense," he said quickly.

Camellia relaxed again. "None taken."

"Then let's find us that preacher." When Bolt grinned again, she couldn't help but like him in spite of her grief over Josh.

"I'm still hopeful my fellow is alive," she answered.

"What's his name?" The question came from Edwards.

"Josh," she said. "Josh Cain."

A man two pallets away groaned as she said Josh's name. When she glanced that way, she saw a large blanket-covered man with his back to her. The man moaned again.

"Sounds like somebody else needs me," she told Bolt and Edwards. "Hold on a second."

"Don't leave us," pleaded Bolt.

"You're doing fine," she said.

"You'll come back?" asked Bolt.

"Soon." Camellia stood and approached the groaning soldier. Kneeling, she slowly turned him over. A bearded black face greeted her—eyes open, forehead covered with blood. She dipped the rag into the water, shook it out, and applied it to the man's wound. He stared at her as she wiped the cut. His lips moved, but he managed nothing but a moan. She finished cleaning the cut, examined the rest of the man's body for wounds, and saw a bloody hole in the lower right side of his worn blue shirt.

Standing, she searched for a surgeon but saw none. Although not generally given to taking off a strange man's shirt, particularly a darky's, she wanted to make sure he didn't have a bullet in his side, so she knelt again, unbuttoned his shirt, and carefully pushed it back. To her relief she saw another cut, but no bullet hole. Grabbing a fresh rag, she wet it and applied it to the wound. When finished, she leaned close to the man and studied his face. He looked vaguely familiar.

"I'm Camellia," she said softly. "Can you talk?"

The man lifted an arm and she waited. "Les . . . Lester," he managed.

Camellia's breath stopped. Lester? She bent closer and studied the soldier's face. Was this the black man who'd come to the Swanson house to tell them about what had happened to Josh Cain? She'd seen him for such a short time, and that, late at night. But what was he doing in the Union army? Yes, she knew the Federals had started taking blacks into the military, had done that since 1863. But this man looked different than Lester had, older and thinner.

"I'm Camellia York," she explained. "Do you know a Mr. Josh Cain?"

"I be his . . . his friend."

The blood rushed to Camellia's face. "You're the one who brought him to Richmond!"

"Uh-huh."

"I've searched all over for Josh," she stammered. "Every hospital where we keep Yankees."

Lester's eyes widened. "He . . . not with the Yankees," he whispered hoarsely. "I changed . . . his clothes. He . . . wore gray. The Rebs took him . . . a Rebel hospital."

"What?"

Lester tried to sit up, but Camellia urged him to lie back down. She grabbed a dipper of water and poured it slowly into his lips. The water seemed to give him strength.

He focused on her face, and his voice sounded stronger as he explained. "I figured if the Rebels took him, they'd treat him better if he was one of them. So I switched his clothes."

Camellia wanted to scream; wanted to curse and cry and shout all at the same time. She'd wasted weeks looking for Josh in the wrong places! But wait! This meant he might be alive! Although she had no proof of that, the odds had just greatly improved.

"I don't want to leave you," she told Lester, wishing she had time to care for him, to explain what had happened. "But I have to go."

"I'm all right," said Lester. "You go find Mr. Josh. Take care of him for me."

"I think you're OK," she agreed. "They're going to exchange you later today."

"Go on—I be fine."

After handing Lester the water dipper, Camellia found another nurse, told her to provide for Lester, then rushed out without another word. Running by Johnson's office, she looked for him for a couple of minutes, then wrote him a hurried note. After fleeing from Belle Isle, she headed toward Chimborazo. If Josh had ended up in any Rebel hospital in Richmond, it surely had to be there.

About eight miles from Camellia, Josh Cain—who now went by the name of Leonard Vincent—sat in a trench behind a wall of earth and wood breastwork. The wall stretched some thirty miles around the southern boundaries of Richmond; it was a long series of barricades set up to slow down the Yankees when they came. Since leaving Chimborazo he'd stayed here the whole time, the next to last line of defense between Grant's forces, which now besieged Petersburg, and the Confederate capital. So far all the fighting had stayed south of him, and he'd seen no action of any kind, not a single skirmish.

A slouch hat sat over his long hair, and an itchy beard still covered his face. His boots stood beside him, drying in the early morning sun. A dry handkerchief in hand, he wiped off his Sharps rifle and scanned the line, toward the southeast. Word in the line said that Petersburg couldn't hold out much longer; perhaps not even through the day. He looked up and down the row, where he and hundreds of other men waited. A lot of the soldiers were either old men or young boys. Most everybody Leonard's age was either long since an officer, dead, too maimed to fight anymore, or had deserted for safer places.

Leonard sat down on a wood box, slipped on his boots, and gazed up into the warming sun. The sight of the sun after so much rain lifted his spirits. One way or the other, a battle would come soon and, like most soldiers, Leonard preferred fighting to waiting. He stretched, liking the strength he felt slowly returning in his body. Although leaving the hospital had not pleased him, it seemed to have helped his chest and head wounds; now they were pretty much healed. If he could only get some hearty food for a steady stretch of time, he would probably gain some weight and return to his old self, whatever that was.

"What do you guess we'll eat tonight?" he asked the boy to his left, a kid named Billy who couldn't have been more than sixteen.

"Hard to say," Billy offered as he stared out across the lines. "Ham maybe, with sweet potatoes and biscuits."

"I like chicken better," said Leonard. "Corn pudding with it."

Billy turned to him and smiled; Leonard returned the smile. Like most soldiers, the two of them talked a lot about food. "Apple pie would taste good," Leonard suggested.

"Peach cobbler is best, though," Billy added.

"Either would go fine with me."

Billy scanned the horizon again, and Leonard settled back to study the boy who had become his closest companion since he'd returned to the front. At least six feet four inches tall and all bone, beak, and black hair, Billy had shown up in the lines only a few days ago and seemed lonely and eager to talk. In spite of his height, he seemed frail, like a skinny bird out of its nest. He hailed from Lynchburg and had a brother who'd died at Gettysburg. Only in the last month had he convinced his ma that he was old enough to go off and fight, to try to make some amends for the death of his brother.

To the best of his ability, Leonard had tried to make Billy feel safe. Every now and again, Leonard saw the boy reading from a small Bible he carried in his haversack, and he envied him having something to read. Although he didn't have any memory of how he'd learned, Leonard knew he did know his letters.

"When you reckon Grant will attack?" asked Billy, his voice fearful as he faced Leonard again.

"Within hours, I expect. The roads dried all day yesterday. Should be fine now."

"You reckon we can hold him off?"

"You want the truth?" Leonard asked.

"Not really." Billy gazed front again.

Leonard smiled and took out of his haversack the last piece of paper Clossen had brought him. After unfolding it he gazed at his drawing of a woman—her hair dark, her cheeks high, her lips full, her eyes wide and honest. He knew she belonged to his past but couldn't remember how.

He'd drawn her image a couple of days ago, her beauty showing up in his head and hand as clearly as the moon on a cloudless night.

Leonard tried to squeeze his memory back into his head. Where had he known this woman? What was her name? Was she his wife? But she looked younger than he. Was she his sister then? The answers seemed so close to coming back, like a branch of apples about to fall from a tree. Why couldn't he recall? What did he need to do to shake the apples off?

When Billy slid down next to him, Leonard started to put the picture away.

"What you got there?" asked Billy.

"Nothing."

"You got a picture?"

Leonard shrugged and held out the paper.

"You draw real good," Billy said, awe in his voice.

"Well," Leonard corrected. "I draw real well."

"I noticed that too—you got good grammar when you talk. Real educated like. You a teacher before the war or somethin'?"

"Something," said Leonard.

"No . . . really, what'd you do?"

Leonard grunted but didn't speak. Although he'd tried to get to know Billy, he hadn't said much about himself, and Billy hadn't asked until now.

"You ashamed of what you done?" asked Billy.

Leonard folded the picture and faced the boy. "I don't know what I did. Can't recall it."

Billy tilted his head. "That's peculiar."

"Tell me about it. I got cracked in the head at Burgess Mill—least that's what they told me when I woke up. My mind's empty of anything that happened before that. I went to Chimborazo, healed up there, then they sent me here. That's the story so far as I know it."

Billy chuckled. "Never heard such a thing."

"Me either."

Silence fell between them. In the distance cannons boomed.

"So you don't know nothin'?" asked Billy. "About wife, kids, home?"

"Nothing."

Billy chewed his lip, looking puzzled and troubled.

Leonard decided to change the subject. "I see you reading your Bible every now and again. Are you a religious man?"

Billy reached into his haversack and took out the small black volume. "Ma sent it with me. I don't read too good, but I do study it—least what I can."

"You believe in the Lord?" Leonard asked.

"Yeah, don't you?"

Leonard frowned. "I don't know."

Billy weighed the matter for a moment. "What if you believed before you got hurt but don't now? If you get killed tomorrow, is the Lord goin' to take you to heaven?"

"That's a deep question. And I don't know that I've got any answer for it. What you think?"

"I think that the book of John, chapter ten and verse twenty-nine, says it pretty plain. 'My Father, which gave them me, is greater than all; and no man is able to pluck them out of my Father's hand.' Once the Lord's got us in His hands, nothin' can take us out."

"You sound like you got the makings of a preacher."

Billy smiled. "People back home say that's what they expect from me, if I live through all this."

"I'll pray that you do if you think my prayers will matter."

"I appreciate that. And if I don't make it, you keep this Bible."

"I couldn't take that. Your ma will want it back, don't you think?"

"No, you keep it. My gift for your friendship."

Leonard leaned back and stared into the blue sky. All around him, life seemed ready to burst out of the earth. How dare men cause so much hurt to the world, so much grief? "You think we got God on our side in this war?" he asked Billy.

Billy sighed. "Hard to say."

"I don't know why, but I don't like the notion of fighting to keep the blacks in our service," Leonard reasoned.

"This war is about more than that," offered Billy. "The right of states to set their own course, make their own choices. We got to stop the Federals, or they'll run everything."

"Seems to me I'm not a good Rebel," said Leonard. "I figure I must not have owned any darkies, must not have been rich enough."

"But you fought for the cause," Billy insisted. "You must have believed in it to do that."

Leonard scratched his beard. "I don't think the Lord wants us to keep slaves."

Billy grunted. "Best keep that talk quiet."

"I know."

Billy put the Bible away. Leonard took off his hat and let the sun warm his head. The air smelled pure and clean. A cloud drifted across the blue sky. As Leonard took a deep breath, a slew of Scripture verses flooded his head, words that seemed as natural there as a fish in a stream.

"For by grace are ye saved through faith; and that not of yourselves; it is the gift of God."

"For God so loved the world, that he gave his only begotten Son, that whosoever believeth in him should not perish, but have everlasting life."

"Blessed are the peacemakers: for they shall be called the children of God."

"And we know that all things work together for good to them that love God, to them who are the called according to his purpose."

He knew them all and more . . . words from the Bible that he'd memorized a long time ago!

As the Scriptures rolled through his head, an image came to him, and he recognized the face of his mama, who had taught him the Bible from the day he first drew breath. He recalled his childhood in South Carolina . . . the day his mama died. Another image came to him . . . a man . . . his brother, Hampton . . . that was his name. They'd fought in Mexico . . . he'd shot a boy there.

The memories flooded Leonard's head, flash after flash. After the Mexican War, he'd married a woman named Anna, but she wasn't the woman in the picture he'd drawn. Anna had birthed three children to him . . . a boy and two girls!

Leonard's eyes watered as he remembered that Anna had died and one of the girls as well. He closed his eyes against the hurt, and the memories ceased. He pressed his head with both hands and squeezed as hard as he could. He couldn't stop now. Who was the woman in the picture? What was his real name? Who was he?

But nothing more came to him.

He stared back up into the sky, lifted his hands toward the heavens, and asked God to make it plain, to show him the truth, to reveal it all. Suddenly, like a jolt of lightning from heaven, everything returned.

The Oak Plantation . . . rice fields . . . he labored there with his brother, Hampton. He tended the dikes.

Beth and Butler! They were in Richmond, safe and alive!

The woman in the picture!

His mind slowed, and he held his breath.

Camellia—that was her name! He had loved her, hoped to marry her. Then the war started, and he'd had to leave her behind and go to fight; he'd had to postpone his promise to marry her the next time he saw her.

Leonard took a breath and examined his clothes.

He'd fought for the Federals! But now he wore Rebel clothes and served in their army!

His breath came in great gulps now as he tried to come to grips with his situation. Within a few days at the most, General Grant would attack, and here he waited, behind Southern defenses, to kill Yankees to protect something he didn't believe in at all! How could he do that? He couldn't . . . he knew it as well as he now knew his name was Josh Cain.

Josh Cain. That's who he was. Josh Cain, a thirty-five-year-old man with a boy named Butler and a daughter named Beth and a woman named Camellia he loved—and all of them only a few miles away in a city almost certain to fall to the Union in a matter of days, if not hours.

Josh glanced at Billy, but the boy had his eyes on his Bible and didn't look up. As Josh steadied his breathing, he stared into the sky once more, wanting to shout for joy. But, confused about how to escape the mess he was in, Josh could do nothing but gaze at the white clouds drifting overhead. He could do nothing but pray to God that somehow, some way, he could slip away from this trench before he had to shoot another man, no matter what color uniform that man wore.

Chapter Twenty-Seven

Although the authorities probably had more on their hands to worry about than finding her, Camellia decided to remain careful as she left Belle Isle. It took her most of the morning to figure out how to ask about Josh and make her way to Chimborazo. There was no reason to make it easy on Trenton if he was still looking for her and, knowing him as she did, she figured he probably was. Wearing one of Mrs. Johnson's bonnets, an old brown one, Camellia kept the bow tied under her chin and the cap fluffed wide over her ears and cheeks.

The clamor on the streets surprised her. People moved in long lines out of the city, their belongings hanging off wagons, horses, and carriages at all angles. The more poorly dressed folks, those unable to afford horses or wagons—and lots of people fit that category—walked. Loaded down with all manner of bags, suitcases, sacks and satchels, countless men, women, and children shouted and shuffled by as Camellia dodged and weaved her way to the hospital. Soldiers scurried around as if they expected cannon fire to land on them any second. If she'd had any doubts about Richmond falling, the turmoil she now saw settled them. From her observations it seemed the city would surely empty before nightfall.

Camellia entered Chimborazo Hospital from a side door just after midday and made her way down the corridor toward a central room, where she hoped to find someone who could show her a list of their patients. People filled the hallways, all of them apparently busy with pressing matters. To her relief nobody paid any attention to her, so she easily stepped into the big room in the middle of the hallway. Passing several people, she made her way to where a middle-aged, broad-faced woman with a large black mole on her left cheek sat at a small desk. The woman glanced up from a stack of papers as Camellia spoke.

"I hate to bother you right now since I know you're busy, but my name is Camellia York. I wonder if I could ask you a question about a man who might be a patient here."

"You got a name for this man?" asked the woman, amazingly calm for such a tense time.

"Josh Cain," said Camellia.

The woman stood, moved to a box of papers sitting on a cabinet behind her, pulled it down, and placed in on her desk. "When you figure this Mr. Cain came in here?"

"Back toward the first of November of last year."

"What was his unit?"

Camellia shook her head. "I don't know."

"It would help if we knew his unit," the woman said, reading through the papers she'd taken from the box.

Camellia inwardly chastised herself for not asking Lester about the uniform he'd put on Josh.

"What was his rank?" asked the woman.

"I don't know that either."

"You're not a big help," the woman stated flatly.

Camellia balled her fists in frustration as the woman leafed through another stack of papers. "I know he had a belly wound and a head injury."

The woman finished with the papers and threw them back in the box. "Don't see a Josh Cain here," she said, facing Camellia again. "Sorry."

The door opened. Two people left and three more entered. Camellia started to tell the woman to check again but managed to refrain since she'd already gotten more of the lady's time than she deserved. She almost turned to leave, but then an idea hit her. "You got any men here that you can't identify?"

"What do you mean?" The woman's mole twitched as her face wrinkled.

"You know, sometimes a man comes in and he's blank in the head. He's got no memory, no papers, nobody to tell you who he is."

The woman stuck a finger in her mouth. "I'm pretty new here. Filling in for a soldier they pulled out to put in the lines. I never saw such a thing as that."

"You've been so helpful," pleaded Camellia. "But could you do this one more thing and check that for me?"

The woman glanced past Camellia as another group of people stepped into the office. A second lady stepped to the desk and offered her services to the people behind Camellia.

"It's the last thing I'll ask," Camellia offered.

The woman moved to a cabinet in the corner and pulled out a drawer. "You not leaving the city?" the woman asked as she stepped back to Camellia and unfolded a file.

"I don't know what I'm doing," Camellia answered.

"I'm going tonight," said the woman, leafing through the file. "Me and my husband. He's a surgeon here."

Camellia wanted to tell the woman to hurry up; she didn't have time for such useless chatter. But she didn't dare. So long as the woman stayed helpful, she could talk all she wanted. Behind her the room suddenly emptied, and the woman helping the other people disappeared with them. Camellia wrung her hands and tried to stay patient as the woman with the mole continued reading. Footsteps sounded and Camellia turned. A slip of a man with a long handlebar mustache entered the office. The man wore a bloody apron, and his face was ashen, as though he hadn't slept in a long time. He brushed past Camellia without speaking and addressed the woman searching the files.

"You have to go, dear," he ordered her. "The word just reached me that Grant has taken Petersburg. He'll come here next, within hours no doubt." The woman dropped the papers, and her mouth fell open in shock.

Camellia's eyes widened as she heard the news, but she didn't let it knock her off stride. She took a pace closer to the desk and pointed to the file the woman had dropped. "Can I finish going through those?"

The surgeon noticed her for the first time. "Who are you?"

"Camellia York," she replied. "I've worked as an aid to Mr. Trevor Johnson at Belle Isle. Do you know him?"

"Yes, but what are you doing here?"

"She's looking for a man named Josh Cain," explained his wife.

"Don't know anybody by that name," returned the surgeon.

"He may not know his name," said Camellia. "He's lost his memory."

The surgeon stopped dead still and intently studied her. Then, before she could say anything else, he moved to the cabinet behind his wife's desk, slid out a drawer and some papers, then faced Camellia again. "There was a man," he said. "He drew these."

The surgeon tossed the sketches on the desk, and Camellia's heart jumped. Her face tingled like somebody had set it on fire as she stared down at Josh's drawings.

"Josh painted those!" she shouted. "Is he here?"

"No," said the doctor. "He's in the trenches guarding the city."

Camellia stepped back a pace. "I don't understand."

"I'm his doctor, Jim Clossen. Josh got well enough to fight again, so I had to send him back to the front."

"Did he regain his memory?"

"No. We gave him a new name, Leonard Vincent—you know, from Leonardo da Vinci. He thought it was clever. He's a smart man."

Camellia's head swirled. "It's not possible. He's . . ."

"He's what?"

Camellia sagged against the desk, her hands grabbing for a hold to stay upright as she guessed what had happened. "He's a Yankee soldier," she whispered.

"What?"

"He fought for the Yankees."

"How'd he get in my hospital?"

Camellia told the story as quickly as she could, then paused as the shock of it all brought the other two listeners to silence.

"He's out there," Clossen finally said.

"I've got to find him," Camellia pleaded.

"No way to do that," said Clossen.

Camellia closed her eyes and tried to hang on. Somewhere, not far away, Josh was preparing to fight against his former companions for a cause he'd never believed in, not even for a moment.

The order to pull out of the trenches after dark came to Josh and the rest of the men in his unit late that afternoon. According to their sergeant, they were to destroy any equipment they couldn't carry, leave the breastworks as quietly as they could, and join up with the remains of Lee's army somewhere to the southwest of Richmond. From there they'd try to go south, merge with General Johnston's men somewhere in North Carolina, and fight on from there.

If he'd been a Rebel soldier, Josh would certainly have seen the logic of the plan. If they stayed put, Grant's forces would almost certainly crush them. But if they escaped south and connected with Johnston's forces, they might survive long enough to recover, turn on General Sherman, and make a battle of it again. But since he wasn't a Rebel soldier, Josh didn't want any part of that scheme or any other one.

As the men around him gathered their meager belongings in anticipation of leaving, Josh tried to figure what to do. About the only thing he knew for sure was that he didn't plan on staying with the Rebels as they fled southwest to meet Lee's army. After that, though, he wasn't sure. Should he sneak off and try to join the Yankees again? But he had on a Rebel uniform; the Yankees would probably shoot him before he could explain, or they might not believe him after he did. He'd probably end up in prison until they could figure things out, and who knew how long that would take?

Deciding against that option, he considered going back to the Swanson house—but that, too, held certain dangers. What if he arrived there and found everybody gone? Then he'd again have the problem of explaining himself to the invading Yankees. But what other choice did he have? Should he sneak away after dark and try to make his way south, like a deserter? Should he head back to The Oak? But what would he do there? And how could he leave Richmond without knowing that Camellia, Beth, and Butler were safe? He couldn't do it—it was as plain and simple as that.

As night fell Josh made his final decision. He turned to Billy as they sat on their boxes and gripped his shoulder. "I'm going now," he told the boy softly.

"What you mean?"

"It's too hard to explain, but I can't go with you when we head south."

"You desertin' us, Leonard?" whispered Billy.

"My name isn't Leonard."

"I don't understand."

Josh smiled at the boy's confused face. "It is a mystery. But now I know my name is Josh Cain, and I can't fight anymore. That's all I can say."

Billy shook his head in obvious confusion but didn't ask any more questions. "I'll be missin' you," he said simply.

"I'll miss you too."

Billy took out his Bible and handed it toward Josh, but Josh turned it down. "I own one already," said Josh. "Back at home in South Carolina."

"I thought you was from Tennessee."

"Another mystery."

"OK."

Josh shook the boy's hand. "I'll keep saying those prayers for you," he offered. "I believe in them."

"See you when all this ends," said Billy.

"Maybe I can come hear you preach someday."

"I'd like that."

Josh stood then, took his rifle in his hands, and stepped calmly and quietly away from his friend. A few men nodded to him as he left the trench, but other than that, they paid him no mind. Several minutes later he stepped into a patch of woods as if to take care of his natural functions, but then he bent low at the waist and slipped away into the dark, his chin set toward Richmond.

Sitting by a small fire in the little room above the Victoria Hotel carriage house, Trenton Tessier stared at his mother as she gathered up the belongings she'd brought from The Oak and put them in a black bag.

"I'm leaving before it's too late," she reasoned. "I hired a man to go with me for safety. I'd advise you to come with me."

"I have things to do," he insisted. "The provost marshal depends on me."

"It will surprise me if he's still here. But even if he is, he could care less whether you go or stay. Now pack your things."

"But where is there to go? The Yankees have taken Charleston . . . Columbia too."

"I don't know, but anywhere but here. I'll figure the rest out once I'm safe."

Trenton shook his head. "You go on, then. I'll get you a spot on the train."

"I doubt you can. They're packing it with President Jeff Davis and other politicians and their families, papers from the government, all the bank funds."

"Trust me," said Trenton. "I've made some valuable contacts in my time here."

"I'm sure you have. Hand me that bag."

Trenton picked up a cloth bag by his chair and tossed it to his mother.

"You're not going to find her," she said, still packing. "She's long gone if she's smart, and we both know she is. Least smart enough to stay out of your grasp."

Trenton stood and moved to the fireplace. "She's more stubborn than smart. She won't leave here without Josh Cain's children."

"That's why you're staying, isn't it?" His mother paused for a second. "To catch her when she comes back for them?"

"Yes."

"You still think she'll marry you?"

Trenton snickered. "Not at all. It's my honor now, simple as that."

"And how has she offended your honor?"

Trenton waved off the question as if it was unworthy of an answer.

"What will you do with her if you do catch her?"

"I'm not sure." He thought through the possibilities. "Perhaps I'll put her in jail."

"What good will that do?" His mother went back to packing.

"It'll take her off her high horse for one thing. Consider it, Mother!" His voice rose with excitement. "Who knows how long it'll take the Bluebellies to deal with prisoners? They won't know why they're there, won't know who to let out, who to keep in. Perhaps Camellia will remain in jail for months, long enough to learn some lessons she needed to heed a long time ago."

"You'd leave her in a jail with murderers, rapists, thieves?"

He shrugged. "I haven't decided."

His mother dropped her loaded bag and moved to him. "Look," she urged. "You've got to give up this quest for revenge on Camellia York, her family. It's an old grudge no longer worth holding. Understand the danger it's putting you in. The Yankees will march into this city in less than a day. If they catch you, they'll either shoot you or throw you in prison. You want that?"

"I'll leave before the Yankees arrive," he said. "Camellia has to come tonight; I know she will. Where else can she go?"

"York will kill you if you harm her."

"Let him try."

His mother shook her head, pulled another bag from under the bed, and threw a couple more pieces of clothing into it. "You're as stubborn as your father," she mumbled.

"I'll get you to a train," Trenton promised.

"I told you, it's full. I tried to buy a spot, but none was available at any price in Confederate script. But I did manage to purchase an old carriage and horse. It's outside."

"But you have lots of U.S. dollars. Why don't you use them?"

"Try to explain how we've got those dollars," she said. "They'll throw you in jail for it."

Trenton started to protest, then decided against it. Once his mother made up her mind about something, she didn't change it.

"Help me with my bags," she ordered.

Trenton obeyed, picked up her bags, and headed out the door and down the steps. A black man he'd never seen sat on the driver's side, and his mother climbed up beside him as Trenton threw her bags into the back. His mother turned to him. "It's not too late."

"I'm not ready yet."

"OK, but stay alive. Come home to me."

"I promise I will," he said. "As soon as I find Camellia York."

"She's going to be the death of you if you're not careful."

"Then I'll be careful."

His mother lifted a bag from the seat beside her, opened it, and took out a small black purse. Opening the purse, she handed him a clip full of U.S. dollars.

"There's close to fifteen hundred dollars there," she said. "Don't use it unless absolutely necessary."

Trenton's mouth fell open, but he quickly stuck the money in a pocket inside his coat. "You're too generous."

She grinned. "You'll pay it back, one way or the other."

He chuckled as the driver clicked at the horse and they rode off. After watching her go, Trenton walked back inside, picked up his pistol, and headed back out to make things ready. Sometime before morning he knew Camellia York would show up at the Victoria Hotel for the Cain brood. And when she did, he'd be waiting for her. He smiled wickedly, eager for the moment when he'd see her again.

Chapter Twenty-Eight

With Dr. Clossen's permission, Camellia stayed out of sight at Chimborazo until darkness fell. Then she left him and his wife and slipped quietly out the door. Although not sure what she expected him to do, she'd decided she could no longer avoid trying to find her pa and ask for his help. With everything in the city falling apart, she had no choice.

Her bonnet and shawl pulled close against the chilly spring night, she eased through the din of the chaotic city and cautiously approached the War Building in Capitol Square. A steady stream of soldiers, most of them officers with expressions of shock on their faces, rushed in and out of the main door. Although everyone had realized that this day might come, nobody had really believed it would.

Watching the soldiers, Camellia wondered if she dared bother her pa at such a terrible time; then she recognized again that she had no option. Not giving herself a chance to change her mind, she sucked in a big breath and rushed up the steps.

Two soldiers—one tall, one short, but both with bushy beards and ill-fitting gray coats—stopped her at the door.

"I'm looking for Captain Hampton York," she said. "I'm his daughter."

The soldiers eyed her carefully. "He stationed here?" asked the short one.

"Don't know. I'm trying to find out where he is."

"You got a weapon on you?"

"No, but you can search me if you'd like."

The short soldier grinned and moved toward her, but the tall one grabbed his elbow to stop him. "Go on," commanded the tall one. "But don't expect much luck findin' anybody with all that's goin' on."

Nodding her appreciation, Camellia passed the two men and hurried inside. A young man, wearing a kepi with a hole in the front and a waist-length jacket with a private's stripe, sat at a desk inside the door. The boy looked no more than fifteen. Camellia straightened and approached him confidently, as if she belonged there.

"I'm looking for Captain Hampton York," she announced. "He's a courier—he and his son, Johnny."

The boy looked her up and down. "I know of the captain, but he ain't here. You give me your name, and I'll tell him you're askin' after him."

She ignored his request. "You got any idea where he might be?"

"It ain't my part to go blabbin' somethin' like that," retorted the boy. "I just check folks in and out and take messages . . . things of that nature."

A group of soldiers burst through from behind her, but they brushed past her without notice. "Look," she told the boy. "I know you're doing your duty, and that's a good thing. But you and I both know that by this time tomorrow, you won't be here and neither will I. I'm Captain York's daughter, and I need to see him as soon as I can."

The boy hesitated and Camellia waited. Another crowd of soldiers rushed by, this bunch headed into the streets, their arms full of papers, satchels, and guns. "They're leaving you," she said to the boy. "Everybody is running. I'm trying to find my father. Won't you help me do that?"

The boy pulled off his hat and stared into it, as if searching for answers. As his blond hair fell into his eyes, Camellia's heart broke. So many young men wasted in this war!

"You have family?" she asked.

"I got a ma," he said, slipping his hat back on. "She's in Winchester."

"You wish you could see her tonight?"

"Sure, that'd be good."

"That's all I'm trying to do. See my father before . . ."

The boy shrugged. "He's probably at the bank," he said calmly. "Helpin' oversee the transfer of the bank's valuables to the train."

"But he was a courier," she said, confused.

"It's odd times; a soldier's duties take unusual turns."

Camellia nodded, then quickly decided she couldn't interrupt her pa in the middle of something so important. Then how could she contact him? "Is he going with the train when it leaves?"

"Don't know."

Camellia tried to put herself in her pa's boots. What would he do once he finished this latest duty? Would he leave Richmond without going back to the Swanson place for Beth and Butler? No. Although her pa sometimes did rough things, he had a fierce loyalty to Josh. No matter whether he believed Josh alive or dead, Hampton York would make sure Josh's children got safely out of the city. Unless she missed her guess, Captain Hampton York would finish up this last task, then find a way to take care of his own. He loved the cause of the South dearly, but he loved his brother even more. To find her pa, Camellia needed to go back to the Victoria Hotel.

"I thank you for your help," Camellia told the boy.

"I hope you find your pa."

Camellia turned and hurried out. Standing on the steps, she stared down at the rushing mob and wondered if Trenton was among them. Had he already left the city? Could she safely go back to the hotel? Or was he waiting on her there, his hatred driving him to stay when he should have long since fled? Was she putting herself in danger going back to Mrs. Swanson's? But so what if she was? Somehow she had to tell her pa about Josh, had to ask him to find a way to locate Josh and pull him out. In her heart she knew Josh wouldn't fight for the Confederates. No matter that he'd lost his memory; something in him would rise up and say no. Then he'd lay down his gun, and the Yankees would shoot first and ask questions later. Josh Cain would end up dead for certain.

Her heart racing with fear, Camellia rushed down to the street, her face set toward the Victoria Hotel. Whether Trenton waited for her or not no longer mattered. If she had to die to save Josh, she'd gladly pay that price.

At the foot of Fourteenth Street, near the north end of Mayo's Bridge, a long line of train cars stood waiting to leave Richmond. Most of the cars were already loaded to the brim with people and their belongings, the human mob fleeing the conquerors soon to arrive. Two of the cars, however, waited not for people but for bags, barrels, and wooden boxes—each of them loaded either with papers from the archives of the Confederate government offices or with coins, dollars, or bullion taken from the half-dozen safes located in the Treasury Department.

A row of oil lanterns threw a yellowish glow onto the rail platform, and a group of about sixty young men stood guard with fixed bayonets around the last two cars. Hundreds of people rushed past the guards, each of them so intent on their own survival that they paid little or no attention to the loading of the valuables. A troop of soldiers marched toward the cars, a line of wagons behind them. Each wagon was loaded with at least eighty boxes and barrels. When the soldiers reached the platform, they halted, and Captain Hampton York slid off his horse and approached the man leading the guards.

"I got everythin', Superintendent Parker," York said. "We been workin' for hours loadin' the wagons from the bank."

Parker nodded. "Treasurer Hale will be pleased. Got to get it all out of here."

York surveyed the guards around the train cars; they were little more than boys and dressed in uniforms from the navy. Youngsters from the naval academy, they'd gotten the assignment to protect the Confederate treasury because the navy they'd served no longer existed.

That's when York realized all hope for victory was gone. "We best get everythin' on the train. Another few hours and somebody might want to shoot us for it."

Parker saluted, and York turned back to his men. Over the last few hours, they had loaded up more money than he'd ever dreamed of seeing from the Treasury Department. Although not certain exactly how much they'd brought out, he'd heard his superiors whispering the figure of a half million dollars. Everything—from gold bullion, Mexican silver dollars, double eagle gold pieces, ingots in square, squat boxes, and bags and small kegs of assorted coins—lay in the boxes, satchels, and barrels he and his men had hauled into the wagons.

"Unload the wagons," yelled York. "Pack it tight. We're short on room."

Moving fast, his men went to work. York faced Parker again. "I hear they will burn the Mayo's Bridge before daylight."

"Word is they're goin' to pour the liquor into the streets tonight," Parker confided.

"They better get shed of it before anybody drinks it," said York. "Add liquor to panic, and there's no tellin' what people will do."

"It's a hard time," said Parker in a resigned tone.

"When you lose, it always is."

"What you plan to do now?" asked Parker.

York chuckled. "What does any good soldier do?"

"Follow orders?"

"Exactly. I've been told to evacuate after I finish this."

"You'll hook up with Lee again?"

"If I can."

"I don't expect it will matter, do you?"

York chewed the tasteless tobacco in his cheek and pondered the question. From what he could see and hear, even if Lee managed to escape, he didn't have much of an army left. Within weeks, if not sooner, Grant would surely catch him and the war would end. What would happen then? Would the Bluebellies put every Rebel they caught in prison? Would they shoot them? Nobody knew.

York spat. Maybe Parker had it right; his presence wouldn't make one bit of difference in what happened to Lee, so maybe he shouldn't bother to catch up with the general. Perhaps he should do what he could to take care of his own family. Although he'd risked life and limb over and over again for the cause, maybe the time for that had ended.

"Best I help my boys," he told Parker.

"Godspeed to you," said Parker.

York nodded, stepped off the platform, and walked up a wood ramp into one of the rail cars, where his men continued to load the barrels and boxes. Both sides of the cars were opened. The chilly night air rolled in, and York spat the last of his tobacco out the side of the car. The smell of smoke curled in through the car, and York wrinkled his nose. He peered out the side of the car away from the main depot. Although darker than on the other side, he saw a light glow burning in the distance. Fire.

It's already starting, he thought. Before morning all of Richmond might lie in ashes. Maybe from the Federals; maybe from the people of Richmond as they burned everything they thought useful to the Yankees.

Two soldiers—one of them York's son, Johnny—entered the car. York nodded to them as they set a box the size of a piece of luggage near his feet and shoved it into the corner. Johnny wiped his hands, then followed the other soldier out to get another box.

York again stood alone in the train car. He wondered what he'd do after the war. Go back to The Oak with Katherine? But was The Oak still standing? And what about Katherine? Although she'd come to Richmond, he'd not seen much of her since his reassignment to the military. Was she still in the city? Did she still have his money? What had she meant when she'd told him years ago that she'd taken care of things after she didn't go to London? Could he trust her?

York stared at the box Johnny and his companion had just placed in the corner and tried to imagine its contents—gold, silver, Confederate script? What if he ended up back on The Oak without money? What if Katherine had wasted his dollars—everything he'd earned, gambled for, fought for? Lynette's face entered his mind. He hoped she'd taken Camellia and everybody else and fled. But what if she hadn't? Since he'd stayed away from her even more deliberately than he had Katherine, he had no way to know about anybody, anything.

York stepped to the box, studied it for another moment, and without further ado, lifted a boot, pushed the box over to the backside opening in the train car, and kicked it onto the ground. It hit the dirt with a soft thud, and York stood dead still for several seconds to see if anyone had noticed what he'd done. When nobody did, he waited until the next box arrived, then stepped past Johnny and the other man and back onto the platform.

About an hour later, just as his men were about to finish loading the cars, York eased around to the box he'd kicked out, shoved it closer to the railroad track, where the shadows from the boxcar completely covered it, then walked back around to his men. After ordering the lieutenant to lead the men back to the War Building, he told Johnny to wait with him. When the men had left, he commanded Johnny to ride straight to the Victoria Hotel and wait for further instructions there. As Johnny rode off,

York stepped around to the hidden box, lifted it quickly onto his shoulder, and carried it to an alley several yards away.

Dropping the box to the ground, York checked around, saw no one watching, and shoved the box into a corner. After kicking a pile of dirt over it, he wiped his hands, and pulled out the last good chew of tobacco he owned, one he'd saved for the day the war ended. For him the war had just ended.

Savoring the chew, York left the alley and climbed on his horse, urging it toward the Victoria Hotel. Although he didn't know exactly what he had in the bank box, he did know he'd come back for it just as soon as he got everything else ready to leave.

His black hat pulled low over his eyes, Trenton perched on a chair in the shadows in the far corner of the Victoria Hotel lobby. He was well hidden behind a stack of soiled clothes near the stairwell, and his pistol was cocked under the blanket he held in his lap. Scores of people, both soldiers and civilians, hustled all around him, mostly hauling out any wounded they thought well enough to survive a flight from the city. The men too far gone for travel would have to wait for the Yankees or for death.

Trenton glanced at his peg leg and for the first time felt some gratitude for it. Although it still hurt occasionally and the yellow ooze flowed from it if he stayed on it too long without rest, he'd become accustomed to the thump it made on the floor and the way he swayed slightly when he walked. One thing about a war too—men with stumps got far less attention than before the conflict. In most cases people assumed he'd earned his wooden leg on a battlefield, and he almost never bothered to tell them any different.

At ease in spite of the chaos around him, Trenton pulled a bottle from his coat and sipped from it. After going for months without a drink, the whiskey slid down like a warm tickle, and he chided himself for ever giving it up, even for a minute. Chuckling, he took another drink, leaned back, and smiled. Outside, at the back of the hotel, Beth and Butler Cain lay tied up, covered by blankets, and stretched out in the back of a buckboard wagon. Upstairs, the uppity Ruby, her frail old mama, and a little girl endured a similar condition in the former room of the Cain kids. Their mouths were gagged, and their hands and feet were bound by taut cords.

Sipping more liquor, Trenton savored the quick action he'd taken with Beth and Butler Cain. With the help of a man named Boomer that he'd met in a saloon and hired with twenty dollars U.S. cash, he'd climbed the back steps of the Victoria, pulled out his pistol, and knocked on the closest door of Ruby's and the Cain kids' two adjoining rooms. He'd thrust his pistol in Ruby's face when she opened the door, knocked her over when she jumped at him, and grabbed her by the hair. It hadn't taken long to tie and gag her, and to do the same thing with her mama and child. Beth and Butler had fallen into his hands equally as easily, except he wrapped them in a couple of thick blankets and carried them to the wagon instead of leaving them in their room. After that, he yanked Ruby into Beth and Butler's room and left her on the floor in the dark.

Promising Boomer another twenty if the man stayed with him until he finished his job, Trenton had left him on guard at the wagon with Beth and Butler. Boomer was also to keep an eye on the back entrance while Trenton eased back into the hotel to wait for Camellia. Now Trenton took another drink, figured the time at close to nine, and pondered when the Yankees would make their final push. Probably just after daybreak, after they'd had a chance to probe the battle lines and see if the Rebels had pulled out in the dark.

Figuring he had plenty of time, Trenton relaxed even more. Acrid smoke drifted to his nostrils, so he knew something else was on fire. Before the night ended, a whole lot of things would probably end up on fire. Isaac Carrington had told him two or three days earlier that he'd gotten orders to burn anything he considered valuable to the Yankees—tobacco, liquor, ammunition, food, clothing. Although he didn't like it, Trenton accepted the fact that the war was lost. Even if General Lee did escape to fight a few more months, the fall of Richmond spelled the eventual doom of the South.

For some reason that realization calmed Trenton. With the war over, he could once again focus on his own concerns, his family, The Oak.

Although everything he'd ever known had changed, he had no doubt of his ability to thrive in the new world the war had created. With his mother's aid and the money she'd hidden, he could still hold sway, no matter the situation. He grinned at the notion. How would the blacks live? Where would they reside? So what if he didn't exactly own them anymore? They'd still need a job, and he could pay them a wage, then charge them rent for their houses and a price for their food, clothes, and doctor's care. Done right, everything could end up just about where it was before the war started. The only thing that would change would be what they called the arrangement.

He tried to figure how much money his mother possessed—five thousand, ten thousand? Who knew? One thing he had to admit about his mother—she watched out for herself, no two ways about it. Maybe that's where he'd inherited the art; and it was an art, he felt convinced, a gift that only a few received.

The front door of the hotel swung open, and several soldiers pushed through, their voices loud. Behind them a slip of a woman entered the lobby, and although she kept her head down and wore an old brown bonnet and a thick shawl, Trenton recognized Camellia instantly. For a second he held his breath as she paused and let her eyes slide over the room. Her cheekbones were thin and her face washed out, but her beauty still overwhelmed him. His heart raced, and memories of better times rushed into his head. He wanted to run to her and fall on his knees, asking her to forgive him for all his meanness. She'd always brought out the good in him . . . maybe she still could! Maybe she could rescue him from what he'd become!

Camellia eased toward the stairs, her steps direct but unhurried. Trenton marveled at her courage. Although she almost certainly expected him to be here waiting for her, she dared to return to the hotel anyway. Again Trenton considered going to her, making his apologies and proclaiming once more his love for her. She'd hear him out, wouldn't she? He almost stood, but then she glanced his way, and he saw fear in her eyes. With a jolt he realized he'd put that fear there, and he knew that no matter what he said, she'd never forgive him for that. He ducked his eyes away before she recognized him and remembered their last meeting, the way she'd shown her disdain for him. That scene was burned into his soul as if branded with a hot iron—Camellia York hated him and always would.

His face curled into a snarl as he watched her climb the stairs. His harsh resolve returned. Tonight he'd finish his business with Camellia York. Finish it for good and forever.

Her body tense, Camellia moved quickly up the stairs and down the hallway to the room where Beth and Butler stayed. She found the hallway empty of people but littered with bits and pieces of their leftovers—a broken chair here, a stack of old clothes there, a dropped hairbrush in one corner, three belts looped together in another. A number of room doors sagged open, a lonely sign of tenants who had taken their belongings and deserted the premises.

Although hopeful that Trenton had already fled the city, Camellia kept her ears poised for the sound of footsteps but heard none. She glanced inside a couple of the empty rooms as she passed and noted the missing beds, the floors bare of rugs, the tables stripped of lamps. Obviously, some of the people had trashed or stolen the hotel's furnishings, solid evidence of a breakdown in law and order.

Camellia shivered. With chaos the order of the night, who knew what Trenton would do if he caught her? With the law on his side, he could do just about anything, and nobody would pause to ask him why. She thought of the wagon she'd seen at the back of the hotel as she had approached from the shadows, the man with horse reins in his hands. Who was he . . . and what was he doing there? She'd wanted to sneak in through the hotel's back door, but the man in the wagon made her realize that if Trenton was still around, he'd almost certainly have left someone to watch the back for her arrival. Was the man in the wagon one of Trenton's hands—or somebody waiting on a hotel occupant to load up and leave?

Standing before the door to Beth and Butler's room, Camellia halted and took a breath. She'd not seen Mrs. Swanson downstairs; did that mean she'd already left with the children and Ruby's family? There was no way to tell, so she had to make sure. But what if Trenton waited for her in the dark inside? Either way, she had to know.

Camellia shoved the door open without knocking. Darkness greeted her, and she stopped a second to let her eyes adjust. A groan rose from the corner, and Camellia rushed toward it, bumping her knee on a chair as she hurried. A sliver of moon cut through the window. She saw Ruby's face in the light and halted in shock. Kneeling at once, Camellia quickly started working on the knots around Ruby's hands.

Without warning, a thump sounded behind Camellia. She twirled as a large body pushed through the door, crossed the room, and stood over her, a pistol pointed at her face in the moonlight.

"Trenton," she whispered.

"Who else did you expect?" He sounded pleased.

"I hoped you had left."

"You hoped wrong."

Camellia tried to stay calm, but her hands shook and her mouth felt dry. "What . . . do you want from . . . from me?" she stammered.

"What I've always wanted."

"I can't give that to you."

"Then I'll take something else." He grabbed her shoulder and jerked her up. She raised her hand to slap him, but he caught it and held her steady. "I've got Beth and Butler," he growled. "Do what I say, and I'll let them go."

Camellia dropped her hand, but she was even more furious. "You wouldn't dare hurt them!"

"You don't know what I'd do."

She wanted to believe otherwise but knew he was right. "OK," she agreed. "Let them go and take me."

"I'm keeping all of you, at least for now."

"Where are you taking us?"

"Wherever I want."

Camellia scanned the room and looked for an escape but knew none existed. She bit her lip to keep from lunging at Trenton, from fighting him with every bit of bone and gristle in her body. But he had the kids. What could she do? For now she'd have to obey him, no matter where that led.

"You'll pay for this!" she seethed.

"I already have; now let's go."

Unable to do anything else, Camellia stalked out of the room with Trenton behind her, his pistol planted squarely in the small of her back. A couple of minutes later, she stepped out the hotel's back door, and Trenton pointed her to the wagon. She climbed onto the front seat beside a man whose face looked like somebody had cut it out of extra-soft, extra-white dough. Trenton took a spot beside her. She turned to the back and saw a couple of thick forms stretched out in the shadows.

"Let's go, Boomer," Trenton ordered.

Boomer clicked at the horses. The wagon lurched once, then rolled forward. "Beth?" Camellia called. "Butler?"

A couple of groans told her the children were still alive.

The wagon slipped from the alley and into a stream of noise and clatter from all the people in the street.

Camellia faced Trenton. "You hurt either one of them, and Josh Cain will kill you," she said as calmly as she could muster.

"A dead man can't kill anybody."

"You figure Josh dead?"

"Of course."

Camellia almost smiled as she spoke her next words. "You're wrong about that. I know for a fact he's still alive."

Trenton tensed. "You're lying."

"You know I don't lie."

Trenton stared angrily at her. "Where is he if he's alive?"

She averted her eyes, her bluff blunted. "I don't know."

Trenton shrugged. "Then it doesn't matter. I'll be long gone before he can find me."

"You harm me or his kids, it won't matter where you go. You'll never be safe."

Trenton grabbed her forearm and squeezed hard. "Just shut up. I've heard enough blabber."

Camellia said a silent prayer that somehow, someway she could escape Trenton. If not, who knew what would happen before either Josh or her pa could find her.

Chapter Twenty-Nine

Josh arrived in Richmond at close to ten o'clock and carefully made his way to the Victoria Hotel. Although untold numbers of soldiers had deserted the lines exactly as he had, he didn't want to attract any undue attention, so he stayed in the shadows as much as possible. Scores of bonfires burned in the streets, casting an eerie glow over the city. Some houses and hotels passed out food to the hundreds of people passing by—hams, hoecakes, jars of jam, biscuits—whatever the people had and couldn't carry away or hide from the approaching enemy. A long line of mule-drawn supply wagons rumbled through the cobbled streets, all of them headed south toward Mayo's Bridge. Everybody seemed bent on escaping the coming Yankees—and the rape, plunder, and pillage they feared the Bluebellies would bring with them.

Watching the frenzy, Josh considered what would happen if he got caught in the city as the Yankees arrived. Would they shoot him before he got a chance to tell them his story? If not, would they believe him and let him go or put him in prison until they sorted it out, a task that might take a long time? Fear gripped him as he considered the possibilities, but he pushed it away and kept moving. He had a job to do, and until he finished it, he didn't care what danger it put him in.

By eleven he'd reached the hotel and slipped inside. At least twenty men lay to his left, most of them still but a few writhing and moaning in pain. A couple of elderly women in long dresses, white bonnets, and soiled aprons moved in and out among the men, tending to them as best they could. The place smelled like old blood . . . and men who hadn't bathed in a long time.

Rushing past the wounded, Josh raised his eyes to the desk across the lobby and looked for Camellia's mother. He was relieved to see her there, her hair parted in the middle and pinned in a tight bun. She wore a flowered green blouse and gray skirt, and though her body appeared thinner than the last time he'd seen her, she still carried herself with a grace and dignity that seemed to deny the horrid circumstances around her. A tall man with dark hair under a slough hat stood before Mrs. Swanson, his back to Josh. The man wore a tattered uniform with a captain's bars on his shoulders. A younger man stood by the older one, his back also to Josh. Mrs. Swanson's mouth looked firm as she talked to the two men standing before her.

Other than the wounded, the nurses, and the three people at the desk, the hotel looked empty, with everybody else having left the place before the sinking ship known as Richmond went completely down. Josh hurriedly crossed the room, touched the captain on the shoulder, and waited as he turned around. The man pivoted, and Josh almost collapsed in surprise.

The captain's eyes watered as he saw Josh. "Josh Cain. As I live and breathe."

"Hampton York," replied Josh. "A sight for sore eyes if I ever saw one."

"I figured you for dead," said York.

"You never were too good at figuring."

For a second the two men stood in silence, frozen by the unexpected joy of seeing each other after so many years of separation. Tears dripped down Josh's cheeks. York extended a hand. Josh ignored it and stepped closer instead, his arms open. York stepped to him and the two brothers embraced.

For a long minute, the two men held each other, their eyes moist. Finally York broke the hug. "That ain't the uniform you were wearin' the last time I saw you."

"I'm sorry," Josh offered. "But I couldn't fight for . . ."

"You did what you saw as right," York soothed. "I ain't holdin' that against you. Besides, you saved Johnny's life in that other uniform. I'm beholden to you for that."

"Me too," piped up the young man beside York.

Josh turned to Johnny, and the two also hugged each other. Then Josh faced Mrs. Swanson and wiped his eyes. "Where are my children?"

"Upstairs," she said.

"I'm grateful for your care for them."

Mrs. Swanson nodded.

"We need to move," Josh urged. "Gather everybody up and clear out of here."

"I agree," said York.

"Camellia's not here," Mrs. Swanson answered. "I was just explaining to Hampton. Trenton Tessier received a position with the provost marshal and tried to arrest Camellia as a spy close to a month ago. But she ran, and I haven't seen her since."

"Trenton is in Richmond?" asked Josh.

"His mother too."

"But Camellia got away from him?"

"Yes, but I don't know where."

"We have to find her," pleaded Josh.

"She's still looking for you, I'm sure of it," Mrs. Swanson insisted. "That's all she's done since Lester told us he brought you here."

"She's been searching the Yankee hospitals and prisons," York continued. "Where we thought you were."

"I was at Chimborazo."

York sighed. "The city's loco. Not safe for anybody, much less a young woman on her own."

Josh faced Mrs. Swanson again. "You take Beth and Butler and get out of here. Ruby, too, and anybody else you want to go. York and I will look for Camellia."

"Johnny will go with you," York told Mrs. Swanson.

"Maybe Camellia's already out of the city," offered Johnny

"No," Josh claimed. "She wouldn't leave without everybody else."

Just then they heard a muffled shout. Josh looked toward the stairs in time to see Ruby rolling down the steps, her mouth gagged, her hands and feet tied. They ran toward her, and Josh jerked the gag away.

"Trenton!" she gasped. "He took the children—Camellia too!"

"Camellia?"

"Yes, she came back."

"When?" shouted Josh.

"Thirty minutes maybe, an hour at the most. Trenton tied me up. I crawled out of the room, down the hall."

"Where was he taking them?"

"He didn't tell."

Josh undid her hands and feet and faced York. "Where would he go?"

"He'll want to flee as quick as he can, like everybody else," York replied.

"But won't the children slow him down?" asked Mrs. Swanson.

Josh thought a second. "He took the children to make Camellia go with him. Now that he's got her, he'll get rid of Beth and Butler as soon as he can."

"Makes sense," agreed York. "He'll want to move fast."

"You think he'd hurt them?" asked Johnny, voicing a scary thought Josh had already considered.

"I don't think so," Josh reasoned. "The law would come after him if he did, no matter how bad things are right now, and he knows it. He's mean but not stupid."

"He put a lot of store in his position with Carrington," offered Mrs. Swanson. "Seemed real pleased by it."

Josh studied that for a few seconds.

"The jail," York suggested. "He'll take them to the jail!"

"My guess too," agreed Josh. "Trenton isn't responsible for them once they're there. If they get hurt by the inmates or the Yankees, Trenton's hands are clean!"

"That's awful," fumed Mrs. Swanson, her hands clenched. "A girl like Beth . . . thrown in with a bunch of rough men."

Josh touched her elbow. "We'll fret about that later. Right now we need to make preparations to leave."

York nodded.

"Ruby and I will do what's necessary here," said Mrs. Swanson. "You two find Camellia and the children, then come back here."

"Hope they don't burn Mayo's Bridge before we reach it," said York.

"Then we better hurry."

York paused.

"What?" Josh asked.

"Katherine," York said, turning to Mrs. Swanson. "Is she still here?"

"I don't know, but I'll check."

"If she is, tell her to make preparations to leave. I'll come back for her."

Mrs. Swanson nodded, and Josh ran out of the hotel with York right behind him. As he rushed down the steps, Josh glanced quickly south toward Mayo's Bridge. If they couldn't find Camellia and the children and flee the city within a few hours, they'd end up trapped by a Yankee army fueled with the flush of victory and the desire for revenge. He'd seen it more than once. Even reasonable men turned vicious in the midst of a war, and no general, no matter how gentlemanly, could completely shut off the pillage that always followed. By first daylight Richmond's streets might well be aflame with fire, lust, and whiskey. If they didn't escape by then, only the good Lord knew what might happen to them all.

Chapter Thirty

The wagon in which Camellia sat stopped in front of the city jail less than an hour later. Boomer hopped down and moved to the back.

"Untie them," Trenton ordered Boomer. "We'll take them inside."

"You best not hurt them," Camellia warned Boomer.

Ignoring her, Boomer yanked the blankets off Beth and Butler, grabbed them by the ankles, slid them to the back, and jerked off their blindfolds. Butler jumped at him, but Boomer laughed and slugged him in the stomach. Butler doubled over to catch his breath.

Trenton eyed Camellia. "I'm taking them inside, on charges of sympathizing with the Union. I'll put them in a cell separate from the other prisoners and leave orders that they stay that way. The Yankees will let them out pretty fast once they come, I'm sure of it."

"Why are you doing this to them?" Camellia asked.

"It's the only way to make you come with me."

"Why should I go with you once you leave them here?"

"Because if you don't, I'll return immediately and throw them in with the worst bunch in the jail."

Camellia clenched her fists but saw no way to fight him. Leaving Beth and Butler made sense; it was safer for them and easier for Trenton. "Where are you taking me?"

"I haven't decided. Away from here—that's as far as I've figured it."

She narrowed her eyes. "You can't keep me forever."

"I can keep you long enough."

She started to ask, "Long enough for what?" but the possibilities scared her into silence.

Boomer hauled Beth and Butler to the ground and steered them to Trenton, who hopped out of the wagon and stood by them. "Stay here while I take these brats inside," he ordered Boomer.

Boomer nodded.

"Don't try to run," Trenton ordered Camellia. "Not if you care about these two."

Without waiting on her response, he waved his pistol and led the children up the steps toward the jail.

Ignoring the city collapsing around them, Josh and York arrived by foot at the state penitentiary about an hour after leaving the hotel. The prison sat on a hill west of the city square and overlooking the river. Below, the fires in the city burned higher and higher. Scores of looters prowled about smashing windows, screaming at the top of their lungs, and stealing whatever they could haul away.

As he and York reached the main prison building, Josh saw instantly that something was wrong. No guards met them outside, and a thick smoke rose from the top of the center of the facility. A sweating guard, wearing sergeant's stripes and holding a rifle, halted them as they entered the front door.

"They're loose in the courtyard!" panted the sergeant, his eyes wide with fright.

"Who?" asked York, stepping by Josh.

"Over 350 prisoners. The governor took most of the guards for other duties, left just a few of us behind. The prisoners heard the Yankees were coming and broke out, killed a couple of guards already. We're trying to keep them at bay, but I don't know how long we can manage. Some of the guards already ran off."

"Anybody bring two women here?" asked Josh. "With a boy?"

"I ain't seen anybody like that," the guard replied. "'Course I been too busy to notice much."

York faced Josh. "We're at the wrong jail."

"Or Trenton isn't taking them to a jail."

York turned back to the guard. "Let the prisoners loose. They're not worth dyin' over. Leave them for the Yankees to handle."

The guard wiped his face. "Sounds like a fine idea to me."

York pivoted back to Josh. The two of them left the state prison and headed toward the city jail.

After leaving Beth and Butler at the city jail, Trenton paid Boomer his second twenty dollars and dismissed him. Then Trenton steered his wagon toward the Richmond and Petersburg railroad depot. Looters yelled at him and Camellia as they passed. One man even grabbed for the horses' reins, but cursed and dropped away when Trenton pointed a pistol at him. Trenton kept the horses at a steady pace, plodded around and through the mob. Although he'd operated with little but a basic plan to this point, a vague outline of what he wanted to do now began to emerge in Trenton's head. For one thing, now that he had Camellia in his grasp, he realized he didn't really want to hurt her. That meant he couldn't force his affections because he knew she'd die trying to prevent it.

Another truth also hit him: he hated Cain and York, not Camellia. If he wanted true vengeance, he had to take it out on *them*, not her. In a sense he'd ended up right where he'd started back on the morning when he hobbled to Cain's house to kill him. If he had any chance of winning Camellia's love back, he had to remove Cain from her life, not push his physical needs on her against her will.

"We're going south on the train," he said, trying to sound sweet as he turned to Camellia. "But you will need to stay calm about everything, bring no attention to yourself."

"The train's surely packed," she reasoned. "Government officers, soldiers, their families. You think you can get us seats?"

Trenton laughed. "I have Federal dollars, and that guarantees us a place."

"Won't somebody take offense that you have dollars?"

"Not if I keep it quiet that I got them."

"I'll run the first chance I get."

"You've got nowhere to go. The Yankees will be in Richmond by daylight, and the folks you care about are probably already gone."

When Camellia slumped, Trenton knew she saw the truth in his words. "You'll come back to The Oak with me," he continued, pleased with her distress. "York and the others will figure it out and come there to rescue you."

"What will happen then?"

"That's up to them."

She shivered.

Seeing her response, he wanted to put his arm around her and offer her comfort. But he didn't dare, at least not yet, so he put on his softest voice and hoped to woo her with it.

"I want you safe," he said. "I knew you'd risk yourself trying to care for everyone else. That's why I came for you. I'm taking you away, so you can't go back for them; making sure you escape the Yankees."

Camellia stared at him as if watching a lunatic. "I'm bait. That's it, isn't it? If Josh survives and comes for me at The Oak, you'll try to kill him, won't you?"

Trenton stayed quiet as he steered the wagon around a curve. When an explosion rocked the street behind them, he checked the sky. Fire glowed red in at least three directions. "We need to hurry," he said. "No more time for questions."

"What about Beth and Butler? You'll just leave them?"

"I don't love them."

"You don't love me either."

"Of course I do."

Another explosion ripped the sky. As Trenton urged the horse to roll the wagon faster, he marveled at Camellia's wisdom. Now that he had her, Cain and York would, indeed, have to come after him. And, as Camellia had suggested, when they did, he'd be ready.

Josh and York burst into the city jail just before midnight, their faces wet with sweat in spite of the spring's chilly night air. To their surprise they found only one man on post there, an older fellow with a stomach as round as a beer barrel. He was sitting behind a table wide enough to rest a wagon on. A clamor of voices bellowed out from a hallway that led from the room behind the table. The heavy man stayed seated as they rushed toward him.

"I'm looking for two women and a boy," Josh panted. "Brought here by a fellow named Trenton Tessier."

The big man grunted and stood up. A set of keys jangled at the bottom of his belly. "Why should I tell you who I got here?"

York snapped a pistol from his waist. "We got no time for frivolities," he stated firmly. "You got a couple of women here with a boy or not?"

The man jangled his keys and eyed the pistol. "Hold your water, Captain. I reckon I got a girl back there, plus one boy. They're buttoned down in a cell just like all the others."

Josh glanced at York. "Trenton kept Camellia."

"You by yourself?" York asked the key man.

"Yep. Everybody else ran off, scared of the noise." The man pointed at the hallway where all the noise originated. "Over a hundred desperados in here. They've been yellin' for me to set them free for hours, sometimes even worse than now."

"The boy and girl shouldn't be here." York waved the pistol. "We'll take them off your hands."

The guard inspected York from head to toe. "I don't take well to givin' up prisoners. Even to a captain. The boy and girl come in on spy charges."

"They look like spies to you?" asked Josh, his face red with anger at Trenton.

"Who's to say what a spy looks like?"

Josh edged a half step closer to the jailer as York steadied his pistol.

"Look," York said. "You're doing your duty, we appreciate that.

But you know what's going on out there. We've got to clear out of here—you too, if you know what's good for you."

The man rubbed his keys, and Josh took up the argument. "That boy and girl you're holding don't belong here. You can see that if you'll open your eyes."

The man still didn't seem convinced.

York spoke again. "You're a good patriot. I am too. I fought with Jeb Stuart all over Virginia. But this war is over or soon will be. Those kids belong to the sergeant here." He pointed to Josh. "We want them out, and we want them out *now*!"

The man eyed York's pistol once more. "Ain't nobody else goin'."

"We don't want anybody else," retorted York.

The jailer yanked a key from his waist, told them to hold on, and then disappeared down the hallway.

"You'll need to take them," Josh told York. "Go back to the hotel, then haul everybody to the south side of Mayo's Bridge. I'll go after Trenton, find Camellia, then meet you there at first light."

"I'm the one to go after Trenton," York argued.

"No," insisted Josh.

"Camellia's my daughter."

"She's to be my wife."

The two men faced off until Josh knew that York saw the resolve in his eyes. With a grunt York gave up. When the key man stepped back into the room with Beth and Butler right behind him, Josh rushed to them and hugged them tightly; they held him like they'd never let go. He wished the moment could last forever.

Then a big explosion rumbled the floor under his feet, reminding him they had to hurry.

"Go with Captain York!" he ordered, stepping back.

"Where are you going, Pa?" asked Butler.

"To find Miss Camellia."

Butler and Beth nodded their heads with understanding.

Josh turned to York. "Any idea where Trenton might go?"

"He's got Federal money," Butler threw in. "I heard him tell that

Boomer man that he'd pay him twenty dollars Union."

Josh smiled at Butler.

"A train," said York. "It's the fastest, safest way out for those who can afford it."

"They'll burn the trestle soon," Josh reasoned.

"Then you better hurry."

Josh hugged Beth and Butler one more time, then fled toward the train depot, his heart in his throat as he prayed for Camellia.

Chapter Thirty-One

With Beth and Butler in tow, York hurried to the hotel and found Ruby in the lobby.

"You two all right?" She embraced Beth and Butler. They nodded and Ruby faced York. "People going loco out there. Tearing things up, stealing anything they can put their hands on."

"Where's Lynette?" asked York.

"In the back room."

"Katherine here?"

"No sign of her; looks like she left already."

York nodded. Trenton probably took care of her before he snatched Camellia. "We've got to leave here."

"I don't think that's in Mrs. Swanson's head to do."

York paused. "Why not?"

Ruby's jaw tightened. "You best ask her."

"Get your things ready," he ordered Beth and Butler. "Be back here in fifteen minutes." Then he addressed Ruby again. "Any kind of carriage left around here—a wagon maybe?"

"There's an old carriage out back. I think it rolls OK. And Mrs. Swanson still keeps a couple of horses."

"Hitch the horses, and load as much as you can into the wagon. Time is short."

"Mr. Josh gone for Miss Camellia?"

"Yes."

"Hope he finds her."

"He will."

York left without another word and found Lynette in a pantry near the hotel's back door, her arms laden with blankets, her hair messy and in her eyes, her face soaked with sweat. He touched her shoulder, and she pivoted toward him. He caught his breath at her beauty. In spite of everything that had happened between them, he knew he still loved her. "You can't stay here," he said softly.

"Where's Camellia?" she asked, ignoring his statement.

"Josh is findin' her," York replied.

She lifted her chin stubbornly. "I'm not leaving."

"I understand you want to protect the hotel and your house," he reasoned. "But if the Yankees want your property, they'll take it whether you're here or not. And if the fires spread, you can't do a thing to fight them."

She sighed. He wanted to step closer and offer her a shoulder for support but didn't let himself do it. She'd just reject him, and he couldn't take that. Besides, he was a married man.

"It's not just my property," she finally said.

"What then?"

She shook her head. "I can't say."

"I'm takin' you with me," he growled. "We can do it easy or hard—you get to choose."

For several seconds she searched his eyes, as if trying to see what lay inside his soul. Then she broke the look and patted her blankets. "I've got work to do."

"I'll get Ruby to pack for you. You're goin' whether you like it or not."

"You're wrong," she asserted.

He moved to her and took her by the forearms. "Look, I got no clue what's botherin' you. But it's dangerous out there and will turn worse before it turns better. A woman by herself could get hurt. I'm tryin' to protect you, that's all."

She smiled wearily. "I see that. But . . . it's not your place to provide for me."

"It's what any man would do."

"But you're not just any man."

He hesitated, not sure what to do next. When tears welled into her eyes, he knew that something else lay behind her desire to stay . . . something more important than a hope to protect her property.

"What is it?" he coaxed. "I want to understand."

She leaned into him, the warmth of her body making his knees weak.

"I'm waiting on somebody," she sobbed.

"Who?" he asked, struggling to hold back his feelings.

"It doesn't matter. But I can't leave until I know that person is safe."

He tried to figure things out, but he couldn't. His frustration grew until he couldn't hold it back. Finally, not knowing what else to do, he patted her on the back and then stepped away. "Just get ready," he urged. "I'll come back for you soon."

She wiped her eyes and looked at him with a sad expression.

Unsure of anything else to say, he left her and headed out the back door. Before he left Richmond, he had one more chore to do. A certain box sat in an alley at the train depot, and he had to go fetch it. Certainly by the time he returned from that, Lynette's mystery person would have come, and they could flee the falling city.

The train depot rattled with movement. People shouted; soldiers clamored aboard crowded boxcars. The soldier's eyes were vacant—the stares of men who'd fought valiantly for a cause they believed in but lost. Horses snorted and neighed; the train's whistle sounded; panicked officials yelled orders that nobody seemed to obey.

With Trenton gripping her elbow, Camellia stood silently on a side street with him as he bargained with a government official for seats on this next train to leave. Two other trains had already left since they arrived, and Trenton, careful not to approach the wrong person, had refrained from making anyone an offer for their seats. Now, however, with the night growing deeper, he'd finally thrown caution to the wind, found a man who looked safe, invited him to the alley off the main street, and made him a proposition.

"Seven hundred dollars," suggested Trenton.

"But it's one of the last trains going out," bargained the politician, a tall man with a cigar in his hand.

"That's why I'm offering you Yankee dollars for the seats," coaxed Trenton. "You keep your head down for the night; you'll be safe and a whole lot richer when the Yankees come to town."

The man puffed his cigar but didn't seem inclined to agree.

"Eight hundred," snapped Trenton.

"But what about my family?" The politician swished his black cape impatiently, nervously. "A wife, three children."

"Nine hundred!"

"I could report you with that money if I wanted," the man warned.

"One thousand, and that's my last offer!" growled Trenton.

The politician threw down his cigar and snubbed it into the ground. "Done."

Trenton quickly pulled his money out and handed the thousand to the politican. The man slipped the dollars under his cape, handed Trenton a piece of paper with the government seal on it, and hurried away.

Trenton turned to Camellia. "Time to go."

"What if I refuse?"

"We'll go back to the jail."

"You don't have time," she retorted.

"Don't try me," he fired back.

Camellia considered her options and knew they were limited. For now she had to obey Trenton. So she stepped into the last passenger car of the train, and Trenton followed. After climbing aboard they made their way to the back. People loaded with every type of luggage covered every inch of the car; seats made for one held three or four. The car smelled of old sweat, cigars, and engine steam, and a baby cried loudly. Voices were a steady din. Camellia wanted to scream for everybody to shut up, but she stayed quiet. When they reached the back of the car, she stopped. All the seats were filled.

"Guess we'll stand!" shouted Trenton.

Camellia looked down. A spot on the floor about the size of a barrel lid provided the only space for anyone to sit. She glanced around. A small window to her right looked out over the depot, and she stared out through it, a million fears running through her head. She feared for Beth and Butler, Ruby and her family, her pa, even Mrs. Swanson. Most of all, however, she feared for Josh. In one way, knowing he was alive made things worse than when she knew nothing. How terrible if he ended up dying now! She'd feel like she'd lost him twice.

Tears seeped into her eyes. What if something happened to all of them? Had her actions created even more danger for the people she loved? What if she hadn't run? What if she'd stood up to Trenton when he first tried to arrest her? Perhaps she could have proven her innocence and shown his dishonesty at the same time. She clenched her fists, angry at herself, angry at Trenton, angry at everything that had happened. "You're the worst thing that ever happened to me," she sobbed to Trenton. "You, your family . . . ever since that day your father tried to have his way with me. It's all been a nightmare since then!"

Trenton grinned wickedly and bent so only she could hear. "Father did have a way with women, didn't he?"

Camellia raised her fists before she could stop herself and pounded Trenton's chest. His eyes blazed; he grabbed her arms and squeezed hard.

"I should have taken you like my father wanted to do," he snarled. "But I remained a gentlemen; my mistake, I see that now. Tessier men take what they want; always have, always will. I'll not forget that again."

"You're a beast!" she stammered.

A couple of people looked curiously at her as if they'd heard her, but then they went back to their conversations. The noise level rose in the train, so much so that she could have shrieked at the top of her lungs and hardly anyone would have noticed.

When the train's whistle sounded again, Trenton threw back his head and laughed. All of a sudden he looked so much like his father that Camellia felt sick to her stomach. She wanted to jump off the train—even under it, if that's what she needed to do to escape his foul clutches. She jerked her hands away from him and started to slap him, but he snagged her wrists in an iron grip.

"No woman will ever slap me again!" he hissed. "Not even you."

Camellia remembered how Mrs. Swanson had smacked him back at the hotel when he had first arrived. Then she had been surprised; now her heart warmed with admiration for her mother. No matter how much Camellia resented her, Mrs. Swanson had gotten in a good lick at Trenton Tessier, and Camellia liked her for it.

A man wearing a white shirt and a string tie, a vest and kepi, stuck his head into the door at the back of the car. Everybody instantly hushed as they recognized him as a train official.

"Almost ready to leave!" he yelled.

Trenton let go of Camellia, and she dropped her hands. "Why does Mrs. Swanson hate your father so much?" she asked, her curiosity suddenly high.

"How should I know?"

Camellia stared at him, seeing that, as Trenton had aged, his face had shifted so it now looked more like his father than she'd ever noticed. Then the train lurched, and the noise picked up again. Camellia forgot Trenton for just a moment and cast a longing glance back toward the city, back toward the hotel, toward the people she loved, toward Lynette Swanson . . . and suddenly she knew. It all made sense!

She pivoted to Trenton. "It's the same reason she ran away!"

Trenton furrowed his brow, obviously confused. "What are you talking about?"

"I know why she hit you! Why she ran from The Oak!"

"You think you're so smart."

"Your father tried to do to her what he wanted to do to me. Like you said, Tessier men take what they want. He must have pressed himself on her—successfully or not, I don't know. But I saw the way she looked at you. I saw her hatred as she hit you. That's why she left my pa, why she left me, Chester, and Johnny!"

Trenton chuckled, but Camellia kept talking. "She couldn't stay on The Oak. She knew that Pa would have killed your father for what he did, no questions asked."

"You're dreaming," said Trenton. "Making up things so you can feel better about a mother who ran out on you."

Camellia considered Trenton's suggestion but knew in her bones he was wrong. The train lurched again, a final whistle sounded, and Camellia looked out the window toward Mrs. Swanson's hotel. If she lived through this, she'd come back to Richmond someday and have a long talk with her mother. If what she'd finally figured out was true, she had a lot of apologizing to do.

Josh ran through the streets as fast as he could. His legs ached, and his lungs seemed ready to burst from lack of air. It was past midnight now, he judged, and maybe too late. He pushed his body faster in spite of the pain. The air was scented with whiskey, and he figured the city officials had started destroying all the drink they could find. Nothing set an invading army off into craziness any quicker than a lot of free liquor, so pouring out the stuff made good sense.

The smell of smoke mixed with the whiskey as fires burned all over. Glass crackled under his boots, and many buildings already had shattered windows. Looters—many of them blacks—ran in and out of the stores, their hands filled with blankets, bags of food, clothes, anything they could find. With the army fleeing and the law officers outnumbered by those bent on mischief, danger stalked the streets. Yet Josh couldn't blame anybody for what they did, especially the blacks. After years of harsh treatment, years of living as the property of others, they finally had freedom. No wonder they'd gone crazy for a while.

It felt like it took him forever to reach the train station. When he arrived and pushed his way through the crowd, he saw a double set of steam engines in front of a long line of cargo cars, then three passenger cars behind those. A whistle piped as he ran past the depot, and the train lurched forward once, twice, and then settled for another second. Steam blasted from the engines. People hung on to the sides of the train. Several tried to force their way up the steps and into the cars, but a line of soldiers pulled them off. A woman with a baby jumped onto the steps of the last passenger car, and a fat man fell off.

Josh rushed to the passenger cars and peered frantically through the windows, hoping, praying, wishing to see Camellia inside in the melee. Some of the people in the cars stared out at him, and he noticed their eyes—some curious, some afraid, some blank. He ran past one car, then another, but saw nothing of Camellia. He reached the third car, his breath coming in panicked gasps. The train whistle shrieked, and his heart bumped in his throat. His eyes skipped over the people's faces. Was Camellia in there? *Please, God, let her be on the train . . . let her see me . . . let her be . . . there—at the back. Is it . . . ? Yes!*

Josh sprinted to the steps that led into the car, but a man in a black coat and gray vest stopped him, his thick face stern.

Without thinking, Josh pulled his pistol and shoved it into the man's belly. "I'm getting on!" he shouted. "Now move or get shot!"

The man backed up, and Josh ran up the steps and through the back door of the passenger car. Camellia and Trenton stood with their backs to him. Josh pushed his way to Trenton, his gun ready. A woman pointed at him and screamed. Trenton turned and pulled his pistol in the same instant.

Now Josh and Trenton stood face to face, each of them with a pistol ready.

The other passengers instantly fell silent.

"Let her go!" Josh shouted to Trenton.

"You're too late!"

"I don't want to kill you!"

Trenton glanced around. "I'm a deputy," he yelled, pulling a paper from his coat pocket so everyone could see it even as he kept his gun on Josh. "I serve with the provost marshal, and this woman is my prisoner. She's a spy."

"Then why are you taking her from Richmond?" shouted Josh.

"She may have information about the Yankees' future schemes. General Lee will want to hear what she knows."

Josh quickly surveyed the passengers. They seemed uncertain who to believe. "I'm not letting you leave with her!"

"You have no choice."

"Oh yes he does!"

The voice came from the front of the car. The train lurched again, then began to inch down the tracks. Josh raised his eyes as a man pushed toward them through the crowd.

"I'm Trevor Johnson!" declared the man. "Some of you folks recognize me from Libby Prison. I know this woman, and I'm telling you she's no spy!"

Josh's breath stopped. The train slowly edged away. He grabbed for Camellia's hand, and she latched on to his wrist.

"No!" yelled Trenton.

"I don't want gunplay on this train!" Josh insisted. "Too many innocent people!"

"You move again and I'll shoot!" warned Trenton.

Johnson reached them, and Josh caught his eye. In one quick movement, Josh let go of Camellia and threw a shoulder into Trenton's wooden leg. Johnson jerked Camellia to the floor as Josh knocked Trenton over. A gunshot rang out and a woman screamed, but Josh never let go of Trenton.

Scrambling to his knees, Josh grabbed Trenton's gun hand and bent it backward, throwing the gun to the floor. "Go!" he shouted to Camellia.

Trenton grabbed Josh's throat; his fingers latched on like hawk's talons. Josh bashed him in the face with a fist. Blood ran from Trenton's lip, but he still held Josh's throat, cutting off his breath.

From the corner of his eye, Josh saw Johnson pull Camellia toward the door; he smacked Trenton again. His throat burned from lack of breath, and his eyes blurred as he fought to pull Trenton's hands away.

"She's out!" yelled Johnson.

With one last lunge, Josh lifted both hands, clasped them together, then brought them down as a club into Trenton's skull. Trenton's fingers dropped off Josh's throat.

Josh pulled up and rushed to the back door. Trenton moved behind him and grabbed his legs, but Josh kicked him off and kept moving. A second later he reached the door. Another shot rang out, and the bullet smacked into the wall by Josh's head.

Ducking, Josh ran through the back door and onto the stoop at the back of the train. The tracks rushed past, the speed of the train increasing with each second. Another gunshot rang out, and the window to the back door shattered. Josh glanced back and saw Trenton running toward him, his face bleeding, pistol in hand.

Taking a deep breath, Josh turned away from Trenton, poised on the stoop for half a second, then threw himself off the train. His right ankle twisted as he hit the ground, and he heard something snap. A sharp pain ran up his leg as he hit and rolled in the dirt. Grabbing his ankle, he tried to stand but couldn't. He looked at the train as it sped away and saw Johnson staring out the window at him, a big smile on his whiskered face, obviously pleased that he had helped rescue Camellia from Trenton's clutches. Trenton stood beside the warden, his eyes blazing as he became smaller in the distance. Josh almost offered a little wave but then held back. No use rubbing salt in a bad wound.

His ankle burning with agony, Josh looked around for Camellia but didn't see her. He tried to stand again but fell once more. An explosion shook the ground.

"Camellia!" he called into the dark.

Nothing.

"Camellia!"

No answer.

York returned to the Victoria at just past 2:00 a.m., his body soaked with sweat and his heart pounding with nerves. After recovering the box in the alley, he'd found it slow going, fighting his way through the crowds that had gathered in the streets. Because officials had dumped the city's whiskey, looters now bent to the cobblestones and licked the drink out of the gutters. Explosions rumbled every few minutes as ammunition blew up. Half the people in the streets seemed bent on fleeing; the other half seemed determined to steal and loot anything left unguarded. A couple of times a group of drunken men had stepped in front of him as if to take the box he carried on his shoulder. But when he pulled his pistol and told them to back away or suffer the consequences, they quickly obeyed.

Although real curious about the box's contents, York didn't dare take the time to stop and open it. Determining whether he'd taken anything of value would have to wait until a more convenient moment.

Now back at the hotel, York carried the box to the back entrance, loaded it into the carriage, and tromped inside. Ruby, Beth, and Butler met him in the hallway.

"We're ready," said Butler.

"Where's Mrs. Swanson?"

"In her room," Beth answered.

"Get Leta and your mama to the carriage," he ordered Ruby. "I'm going to see if I can find some civilian clothes upstairs, then I'll come right behind you. Beth and Butler, you help her."

"A man named Rutter lived in the third room up from Mrs. Swanson's. He looked about your size," Ruby suggested.

"I'll see what I can find."

York bounded away then, his chin set. Lynette Swanson would now leave of her own accord, or he'd carry her out on his back. One way or the other, he wasn't deserting her.

Less than a minute later, he pounded on her door, then burst into her room before she could answer. To his astonishment, he saw a young man standing beside her bed, the uniform of a Confederate navy officer draping his broad shoulders. A black mustache covered the man's lip, and he looked barely twenty, even, if that. Lynette stood beside him, a suitcase in her hands, a shawl over her shoulders, a bonnet on her head.

"You're set to leave," said York, trying to sound calm.

"I am," Lynette agreed.

York faced the young man. "I'm Captain Hampton York."

The man held out his hand.

"Let me introduce him," Lynette offered. "This is Jackson, my son."

York shook Jackson's hand and stared into the black eyes that boldly held his gaze. "You been fightin' with the navy?"

"Yes."

York continued to stare at the young man. Something about him seemed familiar, but York knew it wasn't the time to deal with it. He looked at Lynette.

"Jackson just got home," she said.

"Where's he been?"

"In England," replied Jackson. "Building ships; then on the *Alabama* for a while."

"I've heard of the *Alabama.* Did some real sea fightin' against the Union ironclads."

"She sank in June," Jackson explained. "Near Cherbourg, France. I sailed here soon as I could, took duty on the *Virginia II.* It's set to blow up before sunup. The commander set the crew free to go if we wanted."

"He came back to Virginia less than a month ago," said Lynette. "I hadn't seen him since the war started."

York's knees felt weak as he continued to study Jackson. A terrible suspicion rose in his head, but again he held back his questions. "It's time to leave," he said.

"I know," said Lynette. "But we're fine on our own."

"No!" York snapped. "I won't leave you."

"But you owe me nothing," said Lynette.

"I know, and once this is over, I'll bring you back if you want. But I'm not goin' without you, both of you."

Lynette glanced quickly at Jackson, then back to York. "I need to tell you something," she said.

York waved her off. "No time."

Her lips trembled, but she said nothing further.

York turned to Jackson. "It's time to go."

"Her bags are ready," said Jackson, obviously agreeing with York.

"Be downstairs in five minutes."

Jackson nodded, and York spun around without another word. He left the room to find some clothes. Less than five minutes later, dressed now in a light black coat, a pair of gray wool pants that barely covered his ankles, and a brown shirt missing all but one button, York led the whole crew as it clattered out of the hotel. Within seconds they'd tossed everything they could carry onto the back of the carriage and headed out toward Mayo's Bridge.

Dragging his busted ankle, Josh staggered toward the lights of the train depot. The ground rumbled every few seconds as another explosion rocked Richmond, but Josh kept his eyes straight ahead. Where was Camellia? Had she run away in fear that Trenton would jump the train and again come searching for her? Was she hurt when she jumped from the train?

Josh searched the shadows of the scattered woods and buildings that surrounded the tracks but saw no signs of her.

"Camellia!" he called. "Camellia!"

Nothing. He moved as fast as he could. Fires burned down a street to his right. The air smelled heavier; more and more smoke drifted in the night.

"Camellia."

The ground shook with another explosion. Over it, Josh thought he heard a voice calling. He peered into the dark and saw someone running toward him.

"Camellia?"

"Josh!"

His heart soaring, Josh dragged toward her. When he reached her side, he threw his arms around her.

"You're hurt!" she soothed.

"You're not?"

"No."

Smiling in spite of his pain, Josh stepped back and faced Camellia. She stood there, bonnet hanging by its strings off her shoulders, her hair a mess, her eyes bright in the moonlight. Although a city burned and trembled around them, Josh felt like the whole world had suddenly stopped to watch what would happen next.

"I never thought I'd see you again," he whispered.

"You took your sweet time finding me."

"I know it's not much of an excuse, but I didn't know who I was for a long time there."

"I can see how that would slow you down some."

He fingered her mussed hair and smiled ear to ear. "You could have fixed up a little better for me."

"You're not exactly dressed for a gala ball yourself."

"Well, there's been a war going on. I'm sure you've heard of it."

She tilted her head. "Are you going to talk all night or give me a kiss?"

He put a hand on her waist. "You're a bolder woman than I remember you being."

She touched his chin. "Do you like it?"

"I figure I can live with it."

"You won't live long if you don't soon give me that kiss."

Josh kissed her.

She quivered in his arms as he tasted her lips and felt the warmth and softness of her body. In that instant Josh Cain knew that no matter what else good ever happened to him in the future, he'd already experienced the first touch of heaven.

They held the kiss for a long time. As soon as he broke that one off, he started another. "I'm never again letting you out of my sight," he whispered.

"You best not." She smiled. "You're not the only man who'd have me, you know."

He smiled back and started to kiss her again. Then another huge explosion ripped through the sky. "I hate to say this, but we need to go," he urged.

"I know."

"I'm marrying you soon as we can find a preacher."

"You better."

"You ready?"

"Yes."

"I can't walk too well."

"Lean on me."

He took her hand and lifted his ankle to keep the weight off, and together they hobbled back to the train depot. Another explosion, the largest they'd yet heard, shook the ground. A large red fire split the sky.

"They're blowing up the ammunition dumps," he guessed. "Maybe the armory too."

"It's almost over, isn't it?"

"Yes."

"What will happen to us then?"

He stopped, took both her hands, and faced her. "I don't know what's going to happen. We'll go back to South Carolina—not The Oak, but somewhere close maybe . . . at least for a little while. One thing I do know. You and I, Beth and Butler, will be together. The rest I'll leave to the Lord."

Tears watered Camellia's eyes. "After all these years, we're finally beginning our lives together."

"The future won't be easy."

"Like you said, we'll leave that to the Lord."

"I love you, Camellia York."

"I'm trusting in that."

Holding tightly to Camellia's hand, Josh hobbled past the train depot. Then the two of them slipped south through the streets of Richmond as the once proud city rumbled and burned and the last days of the Confederacy staggered toward its fall.

Epilogue

As the sun began to break over the James River, a smoky fire appeared on the north end of Mayo's Bridge. Within minutes the fire erupted into a steep, flaming barrier, and no one else dared attempt to cross it. Thousands of people stood, lay, or sat in wagons on the south side of the bridge and looked back at their former city as the night's fires pushed thick black smoke into the air. Suddenly someone shouted, and even at this distance, the crowd saw a handful of Yankee horsemen approach the bridge from the north end. At the bridge's edge, the Federals stopped, stared over toward the escaped Rebels, and raised their guns in a high salute. Safely out of range of any rifle shot, the Rebels hooted and hollered at the Yankees for a couple of minutes, then turned away, quickly bored by the sport. Now they were faced with more pressing matters—things like where to go and what they'd eat in the next few days.

A short stone's throw away from the biggest part of the crowd, Hampton York wiped his face and pulled out a chew of tobacco. Ruby stood behind him, Leta in her arms, her mama sitting in the carriage a few feet away. Lynette and Jackson stood talking in low tones a couple of steps from the carriage.

"You reckon Josh and Miss Camellia got out?" Ruby asked York.

York stuck the tobacco in his cheek. "No way to tell. Don't even know if he found her."

"You think she's still with Trenton?"

"Like I said, there's no way to tell!" he growled.

"Don't go biting my head off."

York rubbed his beard. "Sorry, but you're askin' more than I can know."

Ruby nodded with understanding. "Where we headed from here?"

York worked the tobacco a few seconds. "I'm going south like everybody else. You can choose where you want to go. You're free now, remember?"

Ruby raised an eyebrow. "You finished with the fighting?"

"You don't see a uniform anymore, do you?"

"Guess not."

They watched in silence for several minutes and saw more Yankees across the river in Richmond. "Trenton will go back to The Oak, won't he?" asked Ruby.

"Yes. If he's got Camellia, that's where she'll be."

"Your Mrs. York will be there too."

York glanced at Lynette and sighed. So much had gone wrong; so many bad choices had been made. He wished he could fix it all, change the past, alter what he'd become but knew he couldn't. He looked back at Ruby. "You goin' with me or not?"

"Obadiah is waiting in Charleston for me," she returned. "Maybe Theo too. Mama said Donetta told him I got sold in Charleston."

"Hard to believe we're goin' home," he said. "No tellin' what we'll find when we get there."

"It'll be different than when we left it."

"You think The Oak is still standin'?"

"Not but one way to find out," the practical Ruby added.

York nodded and adjusted his hat. "Time to go, then." He turned toward Lynette and Jackson, but then spotted another man hobbling his way and his eyes lit up. He jerked off his hat, threw it into the air, and started to run, pushing his way through the crowd.

When Camellia saw her pa rushing toward her and Josh, a wide smile broke out on her face. She grabbed Josh and dragged him along as fast as she could. Within seconds she reached her pa and threw herself into his arms. He squeezed her so hard she thought he'd crush off her breath.

Finally, still smiling, she pushed away and looked up at him. Ruby ran up behind him, Leta in her arms, and Camellia left her pa and grabbed the two of them and held on for dear life. Josh moved to her pa, and the two brothers threw back their heads and laughed together. In spite of everything—the death, the destruction, the smoke, the fire, and the defeat of the city she'd just left—Camellia's heart soared. Somehow, some way, she and those she loved had survived and would go on surviving; she knew that now. No matter what life threw in their path, they could face it and overcome.

Tears of joy pushed to her eyes as she pulled away from Ruby and kissed Leta's chin. "We made it," she sobbed. "We made it."

Ruby laughed, and both women wiped tears away.

Mrs. Swanson moved to Camellia, and Camellia started crying again. As her mother stood by her, a young man joined them, his face as strong as her pa's.

"This is Jackson," her mother said simply. "He's your brother."

Camellia held out a hand, and Jackson took it, bowed, and kissed it. "Glad to meet you, Sister."

"And you as well," agreed Camellia. "I hope to know you better in days to come."

Jackson dropped her hand and stood, straight and tall, again. Camellia glanced at her pa, but he and Josh were staring back toward Richmond. Facing her mother again, she took a step closer. As if reading her mind, Jackson eased away a few steps and turned his back to them.

Camellia studied her mother's face, lovely in spite of the ashy soot that covered her forehead, the dirt on her skirt and shoes. Without a word Camellia opened her arms. Her mother didn't respond at first; just stood there as if worried that any twitch, any flinch, might scare Camellia away.

"I know what happened," Camellia said softly, battling to keep her emotions in check.

Her mother tilted her head, and Camellia stepped closer. "Marshall Tessier," Camellia offered. "He . . . I know what he did."

Her mother shook her head, but tears welled up, and Camellia knew that she had guessed right.

"I'll never tell anybody," Camellia whispered. "He tried the same thing with me. That's what happened the day he died. I fought him, he fell, hit his head on a table; it killed him."

As Mrs. Swanson buried her face in her hands, Camellia took the woman in her arms and held her as if *she* was the mother comforting a daughter.

"I shouldn't have left you," sobbed her mother. "No matter what he did. But . . . I didn't know what to do. I feared him . . . feared what your pa would do . . . feared Marshall would kill your pa or your pa would kill him."

"It wasn't your fault."

Mrs. Swanson burrowed her face into Camellia's shoulder. "I failed you," she sobbed again. "All those years."

"It's over," said Camellia, feeling her sleeve growing wet from her mama's tears. "Let it go."

Mrs. Swanson looked up at her through red eyes. "I want to make it up to you," she offered.

"You've already done more than enough."

Her mother shook her head. "I need to make amends."

"I'm the one who should make amends," said Camellia with regret. "I've treated you so poorly, resented you . . . hurt you."

"We both have some mending to do."

"I'll forgive you, if you'll forgive me."

Mrs. Swanson smiled and swiped at her tears. "I'll do that. We'll forgive each other."

Camellia smiled, too, and stepped back half a pace. "You're my mother," she said, as if agreeing to it for the first time. "And I'm your daughter."

The two women laughed. As Camellia hugged her mother once more, the last ounce of the bitterness she'd held finally washed away. She felt purer than she could remember, like somebody had just cleansed her soul with water from a fresh spring.

Her eyes glistening, Camellia turned to Josh. She touched him on the back. "Maybe we should go."

He took her hands. "Perhaps we should."

York pivoted, and they all returned to the carriage, where Nettie sat patiently waiting.

"We best stay close together as we travel," York insisted. "Still got some dangers ahead."

"Seems like we always got dangers ahead," Ruby threw in.

Camellia smiled at the truth in the statement.

"You mind if I say a word to the Lord?" Josh asked York.

York spat tobacco juice on the ground. "I don't reckon a word could hurt anythin'."

Josh chuckled. He took Camellia's hand; she reached for Mrs. Swanson's, who then took Jackson's. Within seconds everybody, even York, had joined hands and formed a tight circle around the carriage. Josh took off his hat.

"Say a word for Lester too," Camellia asked.

Josh nodded. She'd told him how Lester had ended up on Belle Isle.

"He'll be free soon now that the Yankees have come," said Josh.

"Speak a word for Calvin too," Johnny added. "Nobody ever found his body."

Josh lifted his face to the sky, and Camellia shut her eyes.

Then Josh started to pray.

North across the river from Camellia, the Yankee army prowled the streets of Richmond, preparing to pursue her and all those she loved. Southward the sandy beaches and crashing ocean of her homeland called her to return. But right then and there, Camellia thought of nothing but Josh's strong hand holding hers. Although dangers surely lay ahead, she experienced no fear. So long as she and Josh were together, she felt warm and safe and glad.

READ THE HEART-POUNDING FIRST PAGES
OF BOOK THREE OF THE

SOUTHERN TIDES TRILOGY

The Oak Plantation, early May 1865

Dark clouds covered the moon over the South Carolina coastland in the wee hours of the night when Theo saw a vision that showed him he would die soon . . . and that his death would change everything for most everybody he had known. Instead of scaring him, though, the vision comforted Theo somehow. It reminded him of something he had believed since he first got old enough to believe anything: sometimes one body needed to suffer, even die, so others might find a straight path to their true living.

The vision hit the twelve-year-old like most of his "seein's" came to him—within a few minutes after a squeezing headache started. The pain began just behind the ear on the same side as his empty eye socket—the socket that his grandmammy, Nettie, had often told him gave him his peculiar ability to see what nobody else could spy out.

"You got the vision," Nettie always explained it. "Like a piercin' stick that jabs through a fog and tears a hole in it so you can see through to the other side."

Theo, who had known for as long as he could remember that he was different from other darky boys, never argued with his grandmammy.

"That missin' eye's the Lord's special gift to you, boy," Nettie had said. "Make up some for all you didn't get."

"It make up for this squatty body that keeps me a hand shorter than other boys my age?" Theo had asked once.

"That's right."

"And hair that's already started to gray?"

"That's for certain. The Lord made you peculiar, child, but peculiar ain't always bad."

Theo had nodded as he usually did when Nettie talked like that. She meant no offense, he knew. She just faced things like they were, without any fakery in her bones. His growing had stalled out real fast before he ever turned ten, and he had never caught up with the other boys on the Rushton Plantation—a fine tobacco-growing place a day's ride from Richmond up in Virginia.

"The only thing large about you is yo' head," Nettie had added. "Round as a cantaloupe and big as a bucket."

"Mama used to say my big head held a lot of smarts," Theo had reminded Nettie. He had thought of the mama he had not seen since the year he turned five and the Lady Rushton sold her off to make some money when her plantation got in some trouble with the bankers.

Nettie had chuckled. "You got that right. That head of yours is plumb full of wise things—you talked like a grownup almost from the day you was born."

Theo always stood taller after his grandmammy said such things. Grandmammy Nettie said it right—the Lord had plucked out his eye before he ever took birth so as to give him a different kind of seeing . . .

Now, as another headache started, Theo crouched behind a massive oak tree—a tree so wide it would surely take at least four boys his size to put their arms all the way around it. The oak tree's limbs swayed in the breeze that slipped in off the Atlantic Ocean, not more than three miles away. Theo put a hand on the oak, fingered its bark, and wondered at its age—at least a hundred years, he figured. Long enough to have seen a whole lot of changes come and go . . . and long enough to be tired by all those changes.

Theo took a long breath and peered around the oak. A stone's throw away sat a badly charred two-story house. Its whole left side, black with soot, sagged in on itself from some past fire. The chimney on that side lay in broken and smoky heaps.

Theo's headache arched from behind his ear and up into his skull. He shoved a finger into his ear and pushed. Sometimes that helped with the pain.

Overhead the clouds slipped away for a moment, and the moon peeked out.

Theo took his finger out of his ear and again studied the house, wondering if he had found the right place. Although he couldn't see it real plainly in the dark, the paint on the house's right side looked like it had pretty much peeled off. The wraparound porch, a big old thing wide enough to hold a hundred people, fell forward like it was plain worn out. Weeds grew up and around the house steps, reaching all the way to Theo's bare feet. One tiny light glowed from the right side of the house.

Theo stared at the house's front door and dared himself to go knock on it. But what if his mama wasn't there? What if he had walked barefoot over six hundred miles and searched the last eleven months in vain? What if he had journeyed these last forty miles from Charleston without stopping but found no trace of her? What if somebody in that house told him he had come to the wrong place or that they had sold off his mama a long time ago? What if . . . ? His headache got worse.

Theo tried to figure who might be burning the light in the house. Had the owners come home from the war? Or did a vagrant, maybe a darky, sit inside the deserted place? Some bad person who would just as soon shoot as spit if he found Theo sneaking around in the front yard? Maybe he ought to hide in the woods the rest of the night and come back in the morning.

Theo's mind drifted back to what he could remember of the day his mama, Ruby, and pappy, Markus, had disappeared. Since he was only five at the time, the Lady Rushton had figured him too young to fetch much at auction, so she had sold his mama and pappy off without him . . .

"I will take care of this baby," Nettie had said as Ruby made ready to leave the Rushton house. "I will keep him till the day you come back and claim him again."

Theo hugged his mama, then took a spot in his grandmammy's lap.

"Don't reckon that day will ever come," said Ruby, her brown eyes wet with tears. "Reckon I won't see my baby again in this old world."

"Don't be grievin', Mama," said Theo. "I'll set eyes on you again. I seen it."

Ruby knelt and took his tiny hands in hers. He believed what Grandmammy Nettie had told him—that the Lord had gifted him with the power to see what others couldn't. How could his mama argue against that notion?

"You watch out for your grandmammy," his mama said. "Do what she tells you."

Theo touched her cheek, as if he were the adult comforting her. "You and me be together again someday," he insisted. "I done seen it."

"I hope you seen it right," Ruby said.

"I did," he insisted. "Sho as a dog likes a bone, I seen you comin' for me."

After hugging him one more time, Ruby had turned and left . . .

Now, with his headache pounding worse than any he could remember, Theo wondered if his mama had ever come for him. He had waited a long time at the Rushton place—right up until the Yankees came through one more time and burned 'most everything to the ground. Something told him then that he couldn't wait no more. If he wanted to find his mama, he had to go after her.

Theo's belly growled, and his hunger almost made him forget his headache. He looked down at his stomach; his ribs poked out of his belly. He remembered that he had not eaten in close to four days. He sighed wearily. His journey to The Oak Plantation had about done him in. His bare feet, covered with calluses, ached, and a sore the size of a pecan oozed on his right big toe.

When Theo's eye watered with pain, he knew he had to act quickly before the ache knocked him completely out like it sometimes did. He looked back at the house. Was his mama there? Only one way to find out.

He stood and started limping toward the front porch. Something moved to his right and Theo dropped to the ground. Dry dirt sprayed into his face. He raised his head and eased slightly to his left. The moon peeked out, and Theo saw a skinny chicken standing dead still, its eyes huge in the moonlight. Theo's headache eased for a moment.

"What you doin' out here in the dark?" whispered Theo.

The chicken blinked.

"You come to answer my prayer?" asked Theo.

The chicken didn't answer.

Theo smiled slightly, and his teeth—the only perfect part of his oddly shaped body—gleamed. "You just stay real still," he cooed, crawling toward the chicken. When he got within an arm's reach, he paused as a touch of conscience hit him. "You a stray?" he whispered. "Or property of whoever be burnin' the light in that house?"

The chicken puffed its feathers for a second, then relaxed again.

"Seems to me the Lord done sent you," mused Theo as his mouth watered. "Providin' for my hunger. I'd be plumb wrong to let go what the Lord's set before me."

The bird didn't argue.

With a quick pounce, Theo grabbed the chicken and shoved it into the knapsack on his shoulder. The chicken uttered a squawk, but Theo quickly shut the knapsack and muffled the sound. Then he crept behind the oak again and stared around the dark yard. "You reckon we ought to wait here til daylight?" he asked the chicken. "See if it's friend or foe in that house? Or move on and come back another time?"

The chicken didn't answer, but Theo already knew what he needed to do. If he went to the house, he would have to leave the chicken; otherwise the person in the house might accuse him of stealing it. But laying down the chicken—a feast he needed to keep up his strength—even if only for a few minutes, made no sense to him. None at all.

"I come back in the mornin'," he whispered to the night. "After I eat me a fine meal. Maybe that put my headache away."

He turned and took a step away from the oak.

Suddenly the front door of the house swung open. A man stood on the porch. He held a lantern aloft in his left hand and a pistol in his right.

"Who's there?" bellowed the man.

Theo started running, but the sore on his big toe slowed him.

A gunshot rang out.

The dirt at Theo's feet kicked up. He jerked to the side to evade the shot but stepped in a hole and fell on his face. His toe hurt like crazy.

Another shot banged over his head.

Theo heard the man moving toward him.

"I'll kill you with the next bullet!" yelled the man, his voice thick as if from too much whiskey. "Hold where you are!"

Theo raised up to run again, but it was too late. The man was rushing straight at him!

Theo pivoted toward the man and noticed an odd gait to his hurried step. He started to stand to flee again.

Another shot rang out.

Theo froze in place. He sensed that if he ran now, he would never see his mama again. Theo felt certain that this man knew something about Ruby. So no matter what happened, Theo had to stay and find out what the man knew.

"I bein' real still," called Theo. "No reason to go shootin' anymore."

When the man emerged out of the dark, Theo saw why he ran funny. The man had a peg leg from his knee down on the right side. He stood medium high, and his clothes, though faded and frayed at the edges, gave evidence of having once been fine apparel—the clothing of a gentleman before hard times set in. He wore tan riding pants and a white shirt with lace at the collar over his thin shoulders. Brown hair, a touch too long and unkempt, lay on his shirt collar. His face looked rough, like he drank a lot maybe or didn't sleep enough. Theo guessed him maybe twenty-five years old or a touch more.

Theo stared into the man's eyes and shivered. The eyes, hard and red, fixed him in a mean glare. In that instant Theo knew something in this man's past had shriveled up his heart like a grape dried in the sun. The man kept the gun trained on Theo, and Theo knew the man would shoot without regret if given any cause. When Theo smelled the man's sour breath, he knew he'd guessed right. The peg-leg man had done a lot of drinking.

"What are you doing on my property?" asked the man, his words slurred.

"Lookin' for somebody."

"That my chicken in your bag?"

Guilt flooded Theo. "I don't usually do no thievin'," he explained. "But I been starved a few days."

"I ought to shoot you; got plenty of cause."

A pain sharper than any Theo had felt cut through his head, and then the vision hit. His eye watered again, then blurred. Streaks of silver light darted before his face. His knapsack slipped out of his hands and dropped to the ground. His knees shook and he almost fell. A chill ran through his bones like a blast of snow and he shivered. What he saw then almost made him collapse . . .

Licking fire . . .

Angry, evil shouts . . .

Ugly masks of awful things . . .

Theo saw how he would die.

And he saw who would kill him.

About the Author

As a boy growing up in the red clay country of northwest South Carolina, Gary E. Parker quickly came to enjoy the folklore and history of his native state. One of his earliest memories is going to Charleston with his dad on a business trip and standing by the ocean, watching the ships come into the harbor. From that day Gary loved the smell of the salt air, the sound of the ocean's waves, and the stories of the men and women who lived and died in the coastal area.

Carrying that interest in Southern history with him to college, Gary majored in history at Furman University. Feeling called to ministry, he prepared at Southeastern Seminary, earning a masters degree, and at Baylor University, where he completed a doctorate of Philosophy of Religion, with an emphasis in historical theology.

After finishing his formal education, Gary began pastoral ministry, serving as senior pastor at the Warrenton Baptist Church in Warrenton, North Carolina; Grace Baptist in Sumter, South Carolina; First Baptist of Jefferson City, Missouri; and the First Baptist Church of Decatur, Georgia (where he currently serves).

In addition to pastoring a church, Gary obviously loves writing. His previous titles include four nonfiction works and thirteen works of fiction. In addition to books, Gary has written extensively for Sunday school Bible study materials and national magazines.

When Gary isn't serving his church, writing, or spending time with his family—wife, Melody, and two teenage daughters, Ashley and Andrea (plenty to fill his plate most days)—he also enjoys a little golf or long-distance bicycling. After that he mostly likes to eat, sleep, and read.

Enjoyment Guarantee

If you are not totally satisfied with this book, simply return it to us along with your receipt, a statement of what you didn't like about the book, and your name and address within 60 days of purchase to Howard Publishing, 3117 North 7th Street, West Monroe, LA 71291-2227, and we will gladly reimburse you for the cost of the book.

Book One of the

Southern Tides Trilogy

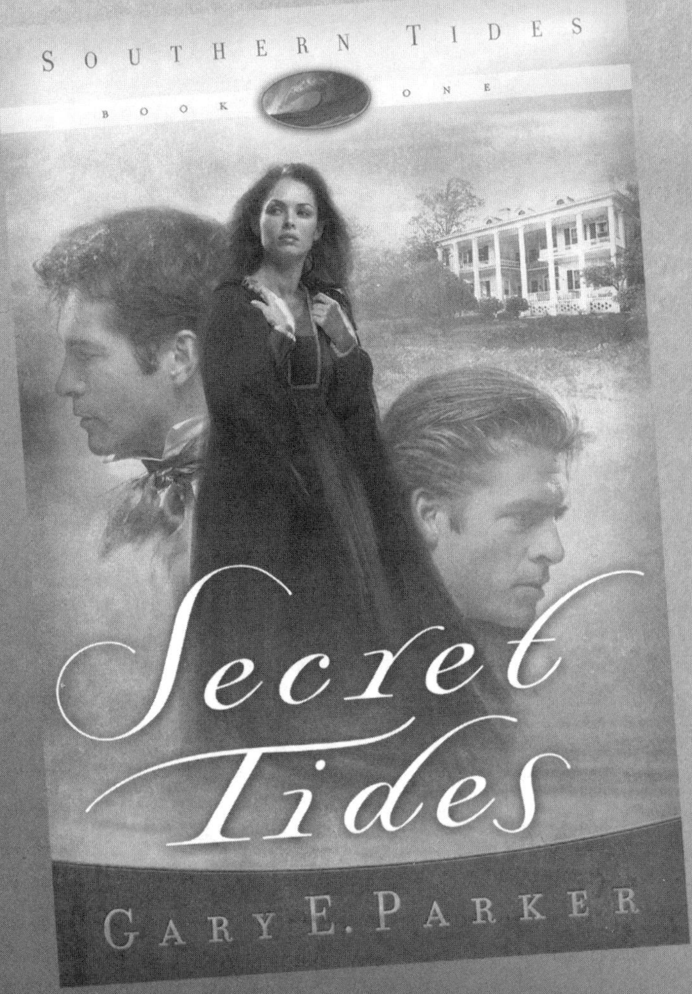

Welcome to The Oak Plantation, an expansive rice plantation in the Old South. When the overseer's daughter, Camellia York, accidentally causes the death of the plantation owner, she is haunted by guilt. But when she finally tells the truth about what really happened in the cookhouse, she discovers a startling truth about her family's past.

ISBN: 1-58229-359-7

Available where good books are sold.